THE WHITE CROSS

THE
WHITE
CROSS

Richard Masefield

RedDoor

Published by
RedDoor
www.reddoorpublishing.co.uk

ISBN 978-0-9928520-7-8

Literary quotations in the novel are taken from a nineteenth century translation
from the Latin of *The Itinerary of Richard I and Others to the Holy Land*, and
Clennell Wilkinson's 1933 biography of King Richard, *Coeur de Lion*

A CIP catalogue record for this book is available from the British Library

Cover design: Brown Media

Typesetting: typesetter.org.uk

Printed in the UK by CPI Group (UK), Croydon CR0 4YY

For all the young people of Chailey Heritage School, their families and teachers, who have taught me so much during the years it's taken to write this novel

PROLOGUS

Fontevraud, Anjou: July 1189

ATONEMENT

'Christ's Holy Shit!'

Six startled nuns, their Abbess and the Primate of all England cast up their eyes to cross themselves as the obscenity rings through the Abbey Church.

'God's bollocks!' Duke Richard adds profanely, as stooping to enter the low crypt he clamps his mouth to breathe as little as he can of its polluted air.

Tall candles cast giant shadows across the walls and ceiling of the chamber; five candles to represent the wounds of Christ, with between them on a pinewood trestle his father's naked corpse. Henry, the second king of England of that name, has always seemed the kind of man who never would grow old and die. But having done so anyway is not a pretty sight. From its breastbone to its genitals the old king's body has been opened like an oyster. Where a proud paunch once rose, a stinking cavity now gapes; and from the buckets on the floor containing his internal organs the stench of putrefaction rises.

For a long moment Duke Richard stares down on his father's ruin.

Henry gutted on a slab, he thinks disgustedly, then turns on the three men whose task he's interrupted. 'Cover it,' he barks at the lay brothers who've been charged to purify the royal remains for burial. 'Cover it and then get out!' And fumbling with the foetid buckets, hurrying to drape the corpse in the plain cloak it's worn

1

for its last journey down from Chinon, the embalmers tread on each other's heels to scramble up the narrow stairs.

To leave the live king with the dead one.

'Stinking vultures! Cringing, shitting little jackals!' Duke Richard saves the main force of his anger for the old man waiting for him in the abbey nave; a thin, round-shouldered figure in the black and white pied robe of a Cistercian abbot. 'God's teeth, those creatures stink of Henrys entrails!' The Duke's metalled boots ring on the flags as he strides forward. 'They claim the Body Royal is indestructible, yet stink to heaven of his guts!'

'The bodies of all men from the lowest peasant to the greatest emperor are subject to corruption of the flesh, my son; death comes to all of us in time.' Archbishop Baldwin of Canterbury turns back his cowl to show the kindly, undernourished face of a committed Christian, its tonsured cranium already freckled with the spots of age. 'I'm sure the Abbess would have spared you this, if you'd but thought to...'

'I tried to fold his arms onto his chest, what's left of it,' the Duke interrupts him. 'But they were set. Dear God, I had to break them, man; and when I looked into his face, his eyeballs moved! I tell you that my father's eyes moved in his skull and black blood trickled from his nose!'

'You broke his joints?' A second shock. But Baldwin hurries on to tell the Duke that, distressing as they are, such things have no significance. 'No, none at all.' He pats the royal sleeve placatingly. 'Involuntary emissions are by no means unusual I believe in the embalming process.'

'My father cursed me on his deathbed. You heard him, Baldwin; the old fox blames me for his fall.' The Duke spits violently and with a hand that trembles, wipes the spittle from his tawny beard. 'God's teeth, if I know aught of Henry he's cursing me from the road down to hell!'

Which maybe isn't so far from the mark, the old archbishop thinks, remembering how desperately the son and father fought

2

each other for control of Aquitaine; how Richard leagued with France and his own brother, John to wrestle from King Henry an empire great as Charlemagne's – to leave the poor man in the end with only England and six foot soil at Fontevraud in which to lay his bones.

No, when it comes to treachery there isn't anyone more dangerous to kings than their own relatives, Baldwin tells himself; and how could anyone, and least of all the man before him, forget King Henry's frightful deathbed malediction:

'I curse the day that I was born! I curse my devil's brood of sons! I call on Heaven to curse Richard's soul! May God and all His saints deny it its eternal rest until I am avenged!'

'My son, it is from recognition of our sins and our imperfect nature that we achieve enlightenment,' he says aloud with a deliberately disarming smile.

Which rather brings us to the point, he dares to think; *a princely penitent, a priest and a religious house – the three conspire. Now is the time and place for Richard to repent his sins, recant his shocking oaths on God's private anatomies, and kneel before me in a state of true contrition.*

The old archbishop tucks his hands into his sleeves, considers the stone pavement, and waits. But when it comes, Duke Richard's next assault upon the silence of the abbey is scarcely in the form of a confession.

'If I've deserved my father's curse, then I'll atone for it in battle,' he states baldly. 'Correct me if I'm wrong, Archbishop; but are we not promised a remission of all penances for riding on croisade? And haven't I agreed to undertake the quest myself when you have crowned me at Westminster – and won't God's blessing follow, as night follows day when we have freed the Holy City from the Turk?'

A full head shorter, more than twice his age, and of less than half Duke Richard's splendid bulk, Baldwin acknowledges his duty, nonetheless. As Primate of England, he is the Church personified for Richard as Thomas Becket was for Henry; and even if the Duke should work himself into a purple fit and pull the abbey down about their ears, he will stand firm – he's almost sure he will.

'No please...' Archbishop Baldwin has a habit of apologising for authority before asserting it. 'No please.' He holds up a deprecating hand. 'Please understand that God's forgiveness must depend on whether you undertake the task for His greater glory, or for your own, my son.' He pauses for effect. 'Can you be sure that coin and territory, that your own reputation, are to play no part in this great undertaking? Can you say honestly that temporal gain...'

'Is not my business as the King? By heaven, that is something you will never hear from *this* king, Baldwin,' Richard bellows inches from his face. 'Fine words from a Church that seeks to govern every step we take, with a snub-devil of a Pope set over it who's living like an Emperor in Rome! It seems to me Pope Clement needs reminding who *I AM* before his bishops dare to tell me what I can and cannot gain from a croisade.'

Not yet thirty-two, the Duke has reached the very peak of manly strength and vigour. His hair is damp with sweat and sticks to the muscles of his neck in auburn spikes. Sandy lashes intensify the greenish colour of his eyes. There is a moment's silence while he fills his lungs.

'I am by right of birth Duke of Aquitaine, of Normandy and the Guienne, Count of Anjou, Poitou, Maine, Touraine, La Marche and the Auvergne,' Richard declaims as if the Pontiff and all his cardinals are in attendance, rather than an audience of one 'I am the Lord of Brittany, of Gascony and of the Vexin, heir to Toulouse, Abbé of Saint Hilaire – and in case Clement has forgotten, very soon to be crowned King of England by yourself, Archbishop, and overlord of Wales and Scotland in the bargain.'

'Which proves exactly what, my son?'

'Which proves I'M NOT *EXACTLY UNIMPORTANT!* Wouldn't you agree?'

'Undoubtedly it does.'

4

Baldwin, who cares nothing for appearance, makes a pretence of smoothing down the loose folds of his robe. 'But where is God in all this worldliness, my son? Where is true repentance?'

'Christ's blood and wounds, is not Jerusalem God's city? Was not my own great-grandfather crowned king there? If I owe Henry anything I'll settle it in Outremer,' Duke Richard shouts, 'and lift his curse by winning back the Kingdom of Jerusalem for Christendom!'

'The Good Lord grant it so.'

But Richard hasn't finished. 'You'll see, I'll get a son there on the Latin princess, fuck her senseless...'

Baldwin winces.

'Fuck her senseless in the Holy City to spawn a prince there who'll be holier by birth than Clement and his cardinals and all the Church's bishops set together! Then by the Virgin's tits, I'll make a better and more valiant Christian king than Henry is or was or ever could be!'

The Duke's eyes glitter in the torchlight. A rampant lion on his red tunic claws the air. Archbishop Baldwin sighs. He knows the man before him can read Latin and compose a ballad in Occitan or French, has had the benefit of learned tutors in his mother's courts, is well grounded in the scriptures on the one hand and in the strategies of warfare on the other. His valour renders him a hero in the eyes of every man alive; and yet like every other pampered prince he has been spoiled. Accustomed all his life to praise for anything he turns a hand to, Duke Richard's used to grabbing all he wants, in bedchambers and at the chase and on the battlefield.

Just like his father after all, thinks Baldwin glumly. *And God help us if like Henry he's defeated.*

But Richard can't envisage anything but total victory. His arrogance is unassailable. 'I'll make my mother Regent while I'm away abroad. I'll mount the noblest croisade that the world has seen, sell homages and land, whole towns to finance it. I've sworn to take Jerusalem, and by heaven that is what I will do! I'll found an eastern empire great as Alexander's. I'll slay with my own hand the devil Saladin; and you'll be there Archbishop to bless me in the undertaking!'

'My Liege I will. No please, decrepit as I am you know that I've already sworn to share with you the perils of croisade.'

'So you have, man. So you have!' The Duke claps a hand on his archbishop's shoulder with so hearty a benevolence he all but brings the old man to his knees.

'By heaven though we'll make a thing of it! Your Church may judge that I'm in need of spiritual improvement. But have you heard the character the people give me in the common taverns from Winchester to Rouen?'

Embarked now on his favourite topic, which is to say *himself*, Duke Richard laughs exposing large horse teeth. 'They claim that I've the muscles of an ox, the balls of a ram and the courage of a Barbary lion!'

Ignoring Baldwin's pained expression he gives his narrow shoulder-blade a bracing little shake. 'So what d'ye think, Your Grace? Am I more likely to sung of in their ballads at the end of the croisade as *Dickard Ramsbollocks*, or *Richard the Confessor?*

Or will it be *King Richard Lionhearted?*' he offers as an afterthought.

BOOK ONE

CHAPTER ONE

'Elise, you're slumping, dear. Do try to sit up properly.' Maman's voice, as ever at my elbow with some fresh idea of how I might improve.

And do they all, all mothers, have to go on treating daughters as incapable until their teeth rot and their hair turns grey? As if we could forget the proper way to dress or talk, or walk or sit or ride or stand, or when to raise our eyes or lower them – as if they'd ever let us!

'But if you must ride out without a veil you might at least set your cap straight, my love?' Her fourth appeal on that worn topic from where she sits behind me pulling down her own straw hat to shade her eyes. 'It's, well it's slovenly, Elise, as if you doubt your own importance.' Beneath the brim her own pink face looks worried and exhausted.

'My sister Garda says it's quite the thing these days to wear the fillet tilted, Maman.' (She doesn't actually. But I'm sure the Blessed Virgin will forgive the little fib. I mean she'd have to be a little lively, wouldn't she, to cope first with the Angel Gabriel then with a jealous Joseph?) I'm smiling helpfully at Maman on her palfrey, with one hand on the reins and the other feeling for my little pie-dish cap to make sure of its jaunty angle.

Behind the anxious parent, Hodierne on her mule has disapproval writ all over her grim face.

'Making an object of yesself as usual.' That's how she'll put it afterwards, I'd stake an oath. She can be very tiresome when she puts her mind to it, can Hod – although I'm glad that the old fusspot is to stay with me when I am married, because I've never known a time without my nurse in train, and wouldn't want to try it.

But best for now to leave the crabstick to her scowls and keep my eyes on Countess Isabel's closed litter five horses and two bearers up the line. Movement. Clomping hooves and tramping feet, the chinking sound of metal harness, wheels turning, timber creaking, hunched shoulders (and not just

9

mine by any means); the sights and sounds of a great household on the move – ahead of us the winding road which in the end will bring us into Lewes. And Jésu, what a journey!

Did I say that out aloud?

We've been eleven hours now on the road from Reigate Castle, if you include the halts. Nesta, my little jennet mare, is pretty near as weary as I am myself, and is it any wonder if we slump? They say that life's a journey of a kind, and if it is I'd say I am a fair bit down that road as well. Because at nineteen, as Maman never ceases to remind me, I'm older by five summers than she was when she married Father. (Not that even she could claim the thing to be my fault, with two sisters to be settled first.)

Oh God, I'm SO uncomfortable! My back aches like the plague. The insides of both my legs are raw, and if we don't arrive at Lewes or some other stopping place in the next quarter-hour, there'll be no help for it whatever Hoddie has to say. I'll simply have to leave the line and hoist my skirts, up there somewhere behind the elder bushes.

Mon Dieu, just think of Maman's face!

Below the track we have to follow, the River Ouse keeps company with us on our left hand – a breeze, the smell of mud, the sharp cry of a seagull. The moon looks like a threadbare linen patch on the pale fabric of the sky. Across the valley a huddle of daub cottages – stone church, a herringbone of fields, cattle in the meadows, geese on the shore... Are they a sign we're nearly there? Will there be feather beds in Lewes, and hot bricks for our feet? Heavens, even thinking of them is a comfort!

Of all the castles in the barony, they say that Lewes is the one most favoured by the Earl and Countess de Warenne.

'The place is on a hill with sewers which remarkably perform the function they're designed for,' the Countess Isabel is meant to have said of Lewes castle after she'd named the drains of Reigate the most abominably foul in England. Which I suppose means that we have to thank My Lady's faith in sanitation for bringing us a full week earlier than planned to Sussex – and to my wedding vows.

We have the gift of a fine saddle in the cart that holds my wardrobe, to be given to my bridegroom when we meet. Blood marries land they say. I have the blood, he has the land – although in truth we haven't all that much of either. On Maman's side I am related to the Countess as a minor cousin several times removed. And if through Father I can claim descent from Aquitaine, it has to be confessed that he first came to England in the Old Queen's train – not as her kinsman but her page!

As for Sir Garon de Stanville of Haddertun, the young man they are to glue me to, we're told his property includes two Sussex manors held in his mother's right, a stretch of marsh, some managed assarts, upland grazing for five hundred sheep and hunting rights in woodlands bordering the Wealden Forest. He has two small estates in other words. I have my blood-tie to the Warennes, and that's all there is to it!

Matrimony is contractual, Maman says, a trade like any other. The base love of the flesh disorders sense, she says, and has no part in marriage. Women as a rule should save affection for their children, Maman says, and treat their husbands with respect. 'We wives just have to make the best of what we find, or else we're bound to be unhappy.'

Which might be good enough for Maman. But not for me, because I plan to be as fond a wife as any man has yet to wed – and make Sir Garon love me whether he intends to or no!

Holy Saint Mary, can you see how earnestly I mean that?

But are we here at last, and is this Lewes Fortress, looming like a crag above the trees? Thanks be to God, I think it is! Yes, there's the blue and yellow chequer of Warenne flying bravely from the keep. I feel as if I'm flying with it, I am so excited!

The watch has spotted us and sounds his horn – a stir, a movement rippling along the line, a horseman stooping to My Lady's litter... The curtains part – a gold-embroidered sleeve, and now the head of an indignant lapdog, yapping fit to shatter steel.

That was all four days ago, and I have to say I've never understood why people who're incapable of affection even for their children can lavish it on frightful little dogs. The Countess sits at ease in her solarium, surrounded by her women and her pages. (I say at ease. But she's bolt upright in her chair dressed gorgeously in gold brocade, with on her lap in pride of place a Maltese cur that looks like a dishevelled rat!)

Whenever people speak of Countess Isabel they mostly use respectful words like 'dignified' or 'illustrious', but never call her handsome. Her mouth is like a trap – pouched yellow eyes as hard as pebbles, big chin protruding from her wimple, big nose stuck in the air. That's how she normally appears, yet here's my plain and haughty lady playing with her lapdog, feeding the pampered creature sugar from a bowl, crooning at it in the way that mothers croon at babies – and looking, well very nearly human!

A woman with, as Hod would say less teeth than summers in her past, with royal blood in her veins from both sides of the Narrow Sea, My Lady Isabel was a princess by the age of twelve as wife to the son of King Stephen. Then married after he was dead to King Henry's natural brother, Hamelin, she's now the new King Richard's aunt. As grand a dame as it is possible to be without a gold crown on your head!

When we reached Lewes Fortress My Lady barely had to nod to have her Flemish tapestries hung on the walls, her coffers and her presses stored, her costume changed, her every wish obeyed – whilst we poor lesser mortals stood for hours to wait for stabling, for porters and for quarters to be found; travel-stained and travel-weary, longing for our beds.

Now four days on, I'm washed and brushed and combed and drenched in rosewater, laced breathlessly into my best blue gown. And waiting still.

I wonder if I'm brave enough to catch My Lady's eye and step out from the window? Ten measured steps, soft-footed with the maidenly decorum I've rehearsed – a flutter of surprise amongst the demoiselles, Maman's bleat of protest. But I'm unannounced, the courtesies are unobserved. My Lady's hand's stops in mid-fondle, distainful eyes consider me from crown to toe, the rat-dog on her lap begins to tremble, crouches, springs dementedly to her defence!

Oh I don't know, on second thoughts I'm probably best where I am.

I dreamt last night that I was still a child, curled up cosily between my sisters, Cecily and Garda. I even snuggled into Maman's back, thinking it was Cessie's – until I felt how soft and fat she'd suddenly become. And that was when I woke to voices in the castle ward, and rubbed my eyes and saw the lime-washed ceiling of the women's dormitory – and then, mon Dieu, I knew the County Palatine of Lancaster, my father and my sisters were behind me never to be seen again this side of Paradise!

'Be good, mon enfant. Be a credit to your line.' That's all my father had to say when I was parted from him.

That's when my childhood ended.

My Lady's solar is a pleasant sort of chamber with a good view of the inner ward. From where I'm sitting in the window I can watch them getting ready for the tournament tomorrow; a thing that no one's seen in England since I was in my cradle. Smiths, fletchers, armourers spill from their workshops on the cobbles to watch the knights at exercise. (I'm sure their language must be shocking. But the wind's against me, I can't hear a word.) A ginger cat up on the roof above the forge is stalking a fat pigeon it's no holy hope of catching…

'My Lady Blanchefleur.'

Holy Saint Mary, no one's called Maman anything but 'Lady Blanche' for years! The bird bobs twice – explosions of grey feathers as it flies. The cat's pretending that it never wanted pigeon dinner in the first place, stays on the roof to wash its bottom, one leg in the air. But inside, Maman is already halfway to My Lady's chair – dumpy, pink about the gills despite the powder, rustling and bustling in her stiff bokeram, collecting rushes in the hem of her long skirts. So eager to oblige she practically scuttles to the curtsey and wobbles coming up.

'I take it that your daughter is prepared and ripe for marriage, Lady Blanchefleur?' the Countess wants to know. She doesn't mention age and nor will Maman. But 'ripe' she says, as if I were some kind of fruit!

'Indeed she is, My Lady, as she'll be pleased to tell you for herself.' It sounds like something she's rehearsed.

An inclination of the noble chin and Maman dimples, looks straight at me; my signal to approach. The walk as I imagined it was quicker and more graceful. It seems to take an age! The Maltese dog's asleep. My Lady waits with one hand on its neck, her gaze as yellow as a hawk's. (You feel its power and her awareness of it, both.) I'll swear she misses nothing as I curtsey, including what's inside my head!

13

'Yes, charming' ('passable' is how she makes it sound), 'and not too narrow in the girth for one of her low stature.'

The corners of My Lady's mouth lift visibly within the white frame of her wimple – a measure of the smile she saves for dogs. 'She should fare well in Sussex, with our favour and a groom who knows what he's about.'

It's true that I am far from tall, and Garda claims that no one could be beautiful with a short neck like mine (hers naturally is like a swan's!). But what's beauty when it comes to it? Pale skin, good eyes, fair hair, straight teeth and plenty of soft curves? Maman says men like as much soft flesh as they can get, in sucking pigs, in poultry and in wives. And although I've often asked the Everlasting God to make me better looking, it's surprising what you can achieve with beanflour and boiled chamomile and veiling from the sun. And clothes of course. The dress I've chosen for today is pale sky-blue, the colour they call celestyne, twist-wrung to fall in fluted pleats from hip to toe; too elegant for words!

I wonder what the Countess meant by calling him a groom who knows what he's about?

'I mention him because Sir Garon is expected.' My Lady's eyes are on my face. 'I'm told he's on his way up from the camp to be presented.'

Which leaves me where? To thank her dutifully for her attention? To go? Or stand and wait? I'm opening my mouth – have been called a chatterbox for years, but just now can't think what to say...

Thank heavens! Maman's hand is on my arm to pull me down into a second curtsey. 'My Lady, we are grateful for your favour.' (Maman's voice, not mine) 'And with your leave will watch for the young man's arrival from the window.'

And what a perfect prune I feel to be led there in silence like a filly on a halter!

The stone mullion of the window's cold against my cheek. The ward below is crowded with horseflesh and men; the best they say, bred on the Earl's estates in Normandie and Conisborough or else shipped in from Friesland (the horses, not the men) – great slug-haunched destriers without an ounce of grace between them.

14

A hit! The quintain must be made of iron from the loud noise it made. But see how quick the fellow was to duck the sandbag on its pole. And here's another lancing for the painted Saracen – just like a boys' game, taking turns.

But when will HE ride in? Oh WHEN?

I must have sat here for two third parts of an hour with my thoughts upon a treadmill turning round and round inside my head. Why when you want a thing to happen does it have to take so LONG?!

COME ON! COME ON!

Please Lord, I know I don't pray near as often as I should. But if you can't make him come soon, could you do something with my patience?

But wait! More riders; someone trotting through the inner gateway, now in shadow, now in light...

It might be. Could it?

Wait, oh wait, I think it must be – two, three, four horsemen in the group. No, more than four, and only one of them impeccably well dressed.

It HAS to be him, HAS TO!

He rides so well, as upright in the saddle as even Mother would advise; a slim young man and dark – I hardly guessed he would be dark – hair black without a trace of curl and a black beard to match the ravens on the keep. Dark men have so much more to them I've always thought, and this one's all in red, a gallant hue; frieze tunic, cloak, gloves, beret – all in Irish red. He surely must know that it suits him?

But now closer, close enough to see his face...

Heaven-sent, he has to be! Oh thank you Lord!

His face is long and narrow – straight Norman nose, the nostrils sharply angled – and singular, no other word for it, as handsome as a herring.

(I wonder what it would feel like to be kissed by someone with a beard?)

But sweet Jésu, he is looking up to see me looking down!

Now just take care, Elise... Hold still, you're not at fault. It's good that he should see you're not afraid. (Eyes dark as well and narrowed in the sunlight.)

'Lady, I am here, the man you've dreamt of all your life' (my words, not his). But on my soul it is the first, the very time I have felt like this. That glance when he looked up stabbed into me, RIGHT INTO ME!

And I thought all that talk of Cupid's arrows was a nonsense. Or am I being silly? (The things that flash into your mind. How can you tell what's false or real?)

But God, oh God – a gift from heaven! I am in love, I know I am. I feel it in my bones!

Which only goes to show how wrong one's bones can be. It's too absurd, no other way to see it! The man's not nearly young enough. Surely I could tell that even from a distance? (And a good thing anyway he isn't my intended. Because a man like that is bound to be unfaithful.)

That's what I thought when they announced him to My Lady, blushing madly as I realised my ridiculous mistake.

'My son-in-law, Sir Garon, has ridden in but recently from Haddertun and is employed in raising tents and paying fees. He begs you will accept me as his envoy,' was how this fellow, Hugh de Bernay, put it to the Countess. 'But if the ladies will entrust themselves to my protection, I'll gladly be their escort to the camp.'

His voice was light and self-assured, and when he smiled he smiled not at My Lady, whose expression gave back nothing, but at me! Which made me wonder how he could have picked me out from all the other damsels in the window.

His hair was oiled and silky, combed behind his ears and parted at the crown, his dark brows constantly in movement like birds in flight – mouth dark inside the neat-trimmed beard – unsettling red lips. And even when he smiled his eyes were restless.

DANGEROUS? Is that too strong a word?

In any case the black beard and dangerous smile are all just now invisible as we clop out across the wooden bridge that spans the castle ditch. All I can see just now of Sir Hugh de Bernay are his cloak and cap above the swaying rump of his bay horse. He rides ahead like Orpheus in the legend, leading me and Maman with Hoddie on her mule, two mounted men-at-arms before us and another two behind. Down from the outer gate, across the moat and into Lewes Borough.

It rained last night and everything in sight is sparkling clean. Every stone *and cobble, every sprouting weed stand out with perfect clarity as if someone has drawn around them with a quill. It's cool enough to ride unveiled. The air smells wonderfully fresh with puddles in the roadway, sky shingled with a mass of little clouds like dapples on a pony – a splendid, helpful kind of day for our first meeting.*

The cottages which crowd about the castle ditch are like a group of gossips leaning in at confidential angles. A woman in the roadway has baskets swinging from a yolk; a bundle on her head and half a dozen sharp-faced children turning back to stare – a donkey cart, a boy with a hand-barrow, two ragged beggars both with sticks, a young man and a girl caressing one another in a doorway. So much to life on every side you can't feel anything but hopeful!

Today and very soon I am to see Sir Garon, and from the moment that we meet my life will change completely! However fair or ill he looks, he is to be my husband and the first man out of water I'm to see entirely naked.

Is it wicked to look forward to a thing like that and still feel hopeful?

'Be sure, chérie, to keep your feet well covered.' (I wondered how long it would take Maman to notice how I'm riding.)

ELISE AND GARON, GARON AND ELISE sound like the names of lovers in a chanson. Like Abelard and Héloïse. 'Brave Sir Garon, storming Lewes Fortress to rescue fair Elise!'

Maman says that marriage is the only means outside a cloister by which a breeding female can avoid a mortal sin. She says that women have to take men in and push their babies out to win respect, and thinks we have to show our worth the hard way with our legs apart and on our backs. But Mother doesn't know it all. Because if knights and ladies can be courteous and loving to one another in ballads and in chansons, why not in life? Why not, if they're well-matched? Why not see marriage to a man as something positive and thrilling?

The way is steeply downhill to the Saxon Gate. My little mare needs a firm hand to keep her footing on the cobbles – as much attention as I have to spare. Which isn't much at all with all there is to see. Beyond the Priory towers the meads are blossoming; a field of moving colour! I've never seen so many tents and banners in so many hues – white, hempen, scarlet, saffron-yellow, emerald and blue, parti-coloured, striped and quartered. Aquitaine, the fairest land in Christendom, has come to England with Duke Richard who was raised there. They say that men in Aquitaine are valued quite as much for penning ballads as for wielding swords, and I can well believe it. Pastimes in Aquitaine include great tournaments like this, and banquets, courts of love and gardens of delight. With Richard come to rule in England, everything will change!

But now we're down the hill and through the gateway to the river wharf – a powerful smell of fish and tar, the masts of ships above the roofs. And what a beastly clamour – all gabbling in Engleis (ugly, guttural language I'll never understand it). A man in leather breeches, hairy top-half bare, is calling out some impudence. I have my nose stuck in the air in the best manner of the Countess, but inside have to smile at Hoddie's answer in the same coarse tongue, and at the laugh that follows.

We've so much more of everything than they have, that it's mean to envy common folk their laughter. But I do.

'Well really!' Maman's observation to no one in particular, but doubtless aimed at me. 'It's well I had the forethought to leave our purses with My Lady's steward. For I swear I've never seen so many rogues and vagabonds at liberty together.'

'Nor I, Maman.' (Which isn't strictly true because they're worse in London.) In fact this crowd at Lewes Port seems wonderfully lively – fishwives in clogs with herring baskets, naughty women with their hair all anyhow and breasts exposed. Hucksters selling everything from tripe to Holy Virgins carved in chalk... and see over there a mummers' show with a fantastically plumed Saint George and baggy-trousered Turk, whacking at each other with their wooden swords. The Christian and the Moslem.

'And I wonder, can we guess which one of them will win?' Sir Hugh says drily as we pass.

The tents look older from this distance, patched and seamed from years of lying folded I suppose, the ways between them mired and stinking of horse piss...

But we've arrived and I am unprepared!

A freckled boy with a snub nose and bright red hair has Nesta's head. Sir

Hugh's already off his horse and at my stirrup offering to lift me down. (Don't look at him, Elise!)

'May I assist you to descend, My Lady, as Hades asked Persephone before he ravished her?'

The red smile in the hairy beard so horridly suggestive. The very devil in that smile! It makes you want to slap him (and I hope to heaven Maman didn't hear). I can't respond in any case without seeming ill-bred.

And thank you very much, I think I can vacate a saddle without your sort of help, Sir!

But his hands are there already, gripping me too hard, too close – a strong man's hands with heavy veins and black hair on their knuckles, and taking much too long to set me on my feet. Oh God, aren't men impossible! But there it's done, and I am free to turn my back upon the wrong man and step forward to the right one.

I'm chewing at my lips to make them red (and calm, Elise – keep calm and do this properly).

'Take heed, my love. A graceful sway, a lifted hip and slightly outthrust belly to suggest fecundity and other qualities I need not name,' hissed in a whisper that Sir Hugh can hardly fail to hear. Maman's convinced that my appearance at first sight will make a difference through the years ahead. 'For recollect, my dear, we're dealing with a young man who very likely hasn't the first notion of what a wife brings to marriage.'

I am presentable, I checked in my steel mirror at the fortress. Attractive modesty is what we're aiming for, but without seeming aloof – and silence, because I'm apt to speak before I think, as Mother's all too fond of pointing out.

The tent flap's up and the sergeant is announcing our arrival, speaking loudly (something pompous. I can't listen while I'm concentrating on the graceful sway.) Now then – a quick glance underneath the lashes...

His mother, Lady Constance, is tall and angular in a sage gown (and looking rather stern). A little whey-faced girl of six or seven summers presses to her skirts. Another vacant-looking woman in the shadows, probably a nurse. He's tall as well, I saw that instantly, and something in his favour, taller than Sir Hugh by half a head – straight-limbed, rawboned and standing stiffly like a soldier – long legs, a horseman's breadth of shoulder

19

underneath the shabby jerkin, large hands (although in keeping with the rest of him, which is more than can be said of his enormous feet!).

He does look strong, and healthy absolutely. But unfinished somehow, not so much more than a boy – short hair, unwashed and a coarse tanner's brown cut level with his ears... Look, someone's darned a moth hole in his sleeve.

I feel... I don't know what I feel, or what I'd hoped for in the first place. (Well yes I do, and it was stupid!)

I am not disappointed in the slightest, not at all. He's as God made him; not uncomely not at all – face shaven, taut and tanned, one ear that's lost its lobe – a neck that's long and muscular (Garda would approve). You really couldn't call him second best. Looks aren't the only measure of a man.

As for him, he's looking at his mother. At the tent pole. Anywhere but at his bride – and you can tell he's nervous by the way he's shuffling his feet. But you'd think he would be pleased at least to see that I am not ill favoured. Not a gorgon or a whale?

'Ladies, your presence honours us. I bid you welcome.' His French is mannerly, voice deep and hoarse – but fumbling the words. And there it is, the smile, at last! Too quick to fade but still quite nice. I think his eyes are quite expressive when he isn't frowning. His teeth are large, but not particularly clean...

Good Lord, I feel as if I'm valuing a horse!

My own smile's small and closed, the one I've practiced to make dimples. He's obviously embarrassed – ducks his ill-trimmed head at me and swallows; looking like a horse and smelling like a stable!

Let's not be silly, he was never going to be a Galahad.
But young, I'm spared a man who's old and rank.

He will look better when his hair is razor-cut.
As in the fable he'll improve when kissed
and is persuaded to grow facial hair.

A neat brown beard for Garon,
not a silky black one.

20

CHAPTER TWO

Some things stand out as clear as day. Others fade completely, or possibly were never very vivid in the first place? I wish I could remember everything about my first meeting with Elise. But oddly it's the hardest thing to call to mind when I look back. Since then I've taxed my brain until it aches to find a memory that I can trust, and failed completely. The more I try the more it seems to slip away. Which isn't a good start for all of this.

As I look down from heaven on the story of my life and try to work out where it all went wrong, I think perhaps that I should start with what my father said when I was seven. Or come to it as quickly as I can.

Or should I start with guilt? Because when I look down upon the world I used to share with her, to see myself as I was when I first met Elise – I am ashamed, no other word for it. I was so set on doing what I thought right. But where was judgement? Was it my fault I was such a self-regarding fool? Or is it another kind of folly to judge what I was then from where I've come to now. I mean, can any addle-pated youth of three-and-twenty expect to understand what drives him?

It takes an effort to remember what was in your mind when you have changed it since. But when I try to make some sense of what I was and how I acted, I see that I was fated from the cradle to become a soldier.

'You have to be the strongest man. D'ye hear me, Garon? The bravest and the best. It is expected of you even by the peasants.'

'But how?' my childish treble, 'How must I do it, Father?'

'We'll send you to the sergeantry at Lewes to be trained, my boy, that's how. A knight who isn't skilled in arms can count for nothing in this world, remember that. It is your destiny to fight.'

I think he only told me once, but I believe I have it word for word.

My father died soon afterwards, before he'd time to teach me any of

21

his skills, before I'd time to know him. I have so little of him even now. His voice in memory seems very loud, and the picture that I have of a red face behind a big moustache might be the real Sir Gervase or merely something from a child's imagination. Because the truth is that I barely knew him. I only know that from that day his words rang in my memory like verses in a chanson: 'A knight who isn't skilled in arms can count for nothing in this world, remember that. It is your destiny to fight.'

Looking back, I see there was no other path to follow. If I'd ever wanted more, or less, I can't recall it. I needed life to mean something and found the meaning in my father's words. To say mine was a simple mind would be to state the obvious.

But boyhood? How should I recall it? At Lewes Fortress in a world removed from all the easy freedoms of the Haddertun domain I was set to cleaning harness, trotting at the heels of any squire who'd take the time to show me what to do. Everything around me was so large and strange that I felt crushed. I learned about the casual cruelties men practice on each other, and on boys. Obedience was beaten into me by squires and sergeants who managed to find fault with almost everything I did. I learned to cope with the pain and take the blows without complaint.

But if I felt small and powerless, I knew that some day I would grow, and when I most missed my nurse, Grazilda, and wept into my pallet, I made sure that I did it in the dark and silently so no one else could hear. Soft living was for women not for boys. If ever I felt weakness through those early days in Lewes, I knew that from hard exercise I'd find the strength to make the most of the peak years of manhood when they came. That was the shield I carried to protect me. I ran headlong and fought and played at war with other boys in service to the Earl to gain the skills I needed. My small body was seldom free of half-healed cuts and bruises. But I took pride them and in the scars they left, as I sought ever to be stronger.

Was I more real then in the body of that child than I am here and now? It hardly seems so from this distance and this height above the world, and yet I have to try to understand the difference.

I hung around the castle armourers to watch them work, collecting notched blades, blunted daggers, shattered spears, learning everything there was to know about the management of weapons, my mind set on a narrow path. And when people talked of life beyond the world of arms and warfare, I closed my ears. I couldn't read or write. But I saw beauty in the sinews of an arm, the true flight of a javelin, the perfect execution of a sword-cut, and if I feared that I would never have the force or courage to become a knight, I hid the fear away. Yes, even from myself.

In due course as a spotty squire I learned to care for what the best knights care for most, their mounts, their arms and armour, and their own oiled bodies. I discovered how to sharpen weapons to so fine an edge they cut a human hair, and all the while I studied to be rigorous and brave, to be the son my father wanted.

'The four best weapons in a soldier's armoury are bone an' sinew, strength of grip, sharpness of eye,' the fortress arms-master, Guillaume, impressed on all of us who trained for knighthood. 'Look after them boys, an' they'll look after you.'

By then we drilled on horseback with cut-down lances and light shields, to stretch the sinews of our arms and shoulders at the pell. We fed our bones and muscles with red meat and gallons of fresh milk, rode at the ring and quintain, fought hand-to-hand with daggers, quarterstaves, with broad and short swords, with bucklers and with clenched fists until we scarce could stand. I learned a number of sure ways to stop a man, by winding, groining, hamstringing, disabling his sword-arm, and other ways to kill him outright. My every thought and action was of arms or warfare, and when I prayed to God I always prayed for more strength, greater valour, prowess in the field, which I believed was where true honour lay.

In time the other fortress boys came to respect me for achievement, although in truth I wasn't so much better than the rest. We sparred and wrestled in the outer ward. We played at quoits and football and at horseplay of all kinds, and talked of girls and cunts and viewed each other's male developments. It was a happy time for me in many ways, all action and bravado. And yes, I see it now, the things that came to count with me when I'd put Haddertun behind me were the approval of my peers and my dead father.

I never learned my letters and had little skill with speech. But one day when I was twelve or thereabouts, I made bid to impress Guillaume. I can't remember rightly how I put it. But I boasted to him in so many words that more than anything I loved to fight. At which he frowned and taught me something else I kept in mind for years: 'You eat for pleasure, sing for pleasure, fuck for pleasure,' he allowed. 'But ye don't fight for love of it, you fight to win.'

Adult life began when as a lanky lad of fourteen I took the Sacrament for the first time, and brought my own colt from the Haddertun domain to train. I lost part of an ear that year and bled a pond of blood. But it had healed by the spring following, when I was dubbed a knight. They shut me in the castle chapel for a night of vigil, bathed me, dressed me in my father's hauberk, buckled on his German broadsword and pushed me forward to assume my right to fight for Church and King. I felt My Lord of Warenne's blade rest on my shoulder for the accolade. I placed my hands between his palms to swear my solemn oaths of fealty, and took for my knight-motto the single word, 'Victoire'.

And yet in spite of all, my title of Sir Garon felt like my father's linkmail hauberk, something I must grow to fit.

At twenty-one I came of age, and through my service to the Earl was granted profits from my mother's manor. She kissed me formally and handed me the key of Haddertun as its Seigneur, a thing which I confess I valued more for its displacement of her second husband than for the income it would bring me. By then my skill at arms had earned me a reputation with the soldiery, and I enjoyed the fellowship of men whose thoughts and actions were as simple as my own. That's one side of the story. The other was that I had grown into an oaf to whom the exercise of violence was a natural as the movement of his bowels.

And something else. Soon after my majority the Old King died, and that same year his heir, Duke Richard of Anjou, licensed a trépignée, a tournament of mounted knights, to meet at Lewes on Saint Augustine's Day to raise funds for his enterprise to save Jerusalem. For me it had to be the perfect chance to show my prowess as a knight.

And something else again. Because if this is Judgement Day, I have to make confession that of all the things that were to change my life that year, my marriage seemed the least important. I didn't choose the girl. She had been chosen for me, and looking down it isn't hard to see that at the time my thoughts were elsewhere, with weaponry and preparations for the fray. I had no time to think about the marriage and was content to leave arrangements to my mother. Sir Hugh, she said, would fetch the damsel from the fortress for inspection. All I need do was bid her welcome.

'And try to look a little pleased while you're about it,' she advised.

I see myself inside that tent when I look back. But I don't see Elise, at least not clearly. What was it that she wore? Something rosy-coloured? I know she had a pink gown for the wedding, that may have been the one. It is so difficult when you look back to separate the things you've seen at different times. I'm sure I must have seen that she was small, because she always made me feel a giant beside her. Her hair? I couldn't say for sure, but seem to think that it was gathered up into some kind of veil arrangement? I would have noticed she was fair, that she was small and fair with ripe breasts and a dairymaid's complexion. But none of it quite adds up to a picture of her in the tent. 'Though now I come to think, there was something a little odd about the way she stood, a pose, the kind of thing that damsels practice for effect?

No one had taught me how to greet a lady. So maybe it's as well that I've forgotten what I said. Some kind of clumsy welcome prompted by my mother? Or something even more block-headed of my own? I'm not sure that I even smiled when she presented me with that ridiculous and useless saddle.

Can I remember how we parted? Or her return to Lewes? Or whether Hugh escorted them back to the fortress. I fear I can't. Because the next thing I

25

recall is seeing her up in the Earl of Warenne's stand when we rode out to take our places on the field of tournament.

Now that I do remember…

Pennons of all colours – sunlight glinting on armour, freshly painted shields, moving figures, horses, bustle. Marvellous!

But here he comes, straight as a candle in the saddle with my green favour on his arm. The black horse is enormous (and we know what's said of men who ride big horses!). And just look at him – so fierce and proud! So thrilled to play the warrior he's positively trembling with excitement!

In just a moment, any moment he'll look up to see if I am watching – the thought I've carried with me since I dressed.

'Lady, I'll strive for you alone.' That's what I'd like him to be thinking – and the thing about a good imagination is that you can take it anywhere you like. (When I was little I pretended sometimes to be Princess Sabra, defended from the dragon by Saint George.) But here's Sir Hugh again on his big dappled grey, helm off for homage to the Earl.

You'd have to be entirely blind to miss the grace of that man's figure on a horse.

And now they're looking up, both looking up at once
to see me leaning forward. Both men smiling.

Would it seem ill-bred if I waved?

She was seated in the west stand at the very front, leaning out with one hand on the rail. At least I have that picture clear in mind. On either side of her were our two mothers, a place or two from where the Earl and Countess sat beneath the blazon of Warenne. It was her green scarf around my arm which prompted me to seek her out, and smirk to think where other knights tied married ladies' favours for good fortune.

She raised a hand and smiled. I thought at me until I heard de Bernay laugh. That's when I really saw her first, and how I see her now. Her gown was blue.

But I'm already out of order, because the tournament began for me much earlier that day.

By dawn my father's old campaign tent was wet with condensation. I'd barely slept, but watched the canvas turn from black to grey before I rose and dragged a cloak about my shoulders.

Outside, a track wound through the camp to the defendants' wooden bar-gate, padlocked to horsemen at this hour but not to barefoot youths. The field of combat lay six hundred paces long and near half as wide, enclosed on all sides by the old town walls, the river and the Priory. In winter-time the place was waterlogged, so damp the Priory monks were said to have webbed feet and sooty balls from hoisting skirts to smoking fires. But by the early dawn of Saint Augustine's Day the field was fit for action.

White mist blanketed the river and my feet left footprints in the dew. Watching jackdaws flutter like black rags above the Priory roofs, I thought of Raoul in his canvas stall and reached in my imagination to stroke his silky neck. Staring at an empty field I heard the blare of clarions and felt the quake of the first charge, thirty against thirty, war-hardened veterans and untried knights like me, thundering full tilt from North to South and South to North to crash together in sight of those to whom they owed allegiance – defendants for the Earl and throne of England, appellants for Archbishop Baldwin and the Church.

For weeks I'd trained for this one day. You could say all my life. 'Oh Lord God for whom all things are possible,' I prayed, 'help me succeed, to suffer wounds without complaint and be deserving of the victor's crown. Help me to win more ransoms in the cause of the croisade, than any other knight!'

I didn't mention Hugh by name, although of course if I'd been God I would have known that's who I meant. But then again, if I'd been God and heard a young fool praying in a misty field to be the first knight of the tournament, I'd probably have laughed at his effrontery and made a note to teach the fool a lesson.

The Priory bell tolling for prime office roused the camp, and others were abroad when I returned, reviving fires and coaxing horses out into the thoroughfares between the tents. Men strolled about half-naked, making breakfast, shouting through the woodsmoke. Inside my father's tent Sir Hugh lay face-down on his pallet with the firm hands of his squire, Fremund, working on the muscles of his back and shoulders. He opened one eye as I entered, then the other.

'Well now, you've been to pace the field then have you, boy, to see the way it lies?' he said. 'Don't tell me that you've planned the trépignée on our behalf whilst we poor dormice slept?'

'No point in asking if you know the answer,' I said rudely, and went on to tell him I had studied where the pitfalls were most like to be, and prayed for victory in the coming fray. Although whatever confidence and depth I tried to put into my voice when I addressed that man, it somehow always managed to sound false, and looking back I see just what a walking invitation I was to de Bernay.

'Ah prayers!' He stetched and yawned, and as he settled back more comfortably I caught the rank scent of his sweat. They say that all of us are woven on the same loom. But that's not true for Hugh smelled differently to me or any of my flesh and blood, and in the difference lay a challenge. Something animal and violent.

'So useful prayers, I always think, against a mounted force of desperate men.' Closing his eyes again he turned his head into his arms. 'I take it then that you've rehearsed the moves you practice in the tilt yard, down to the final flourish?'

I told him sullenly that it was we trained for, and it struck me as I did so that his strong black hair was thinning at the crown. With any luck, I thought, in ten years he'll be bald!

Six years had passed already since he'd made his choice between continued service to the Earl of Warenne or marriage to a widow at his lord's disposal, my mother Lady Constance – and although she's half as old again as him, de Bernay saw his way ahead. His own forbears held Haddertun before they backed the wrong side in the Empress Mathilde's War and lost the manor to my father, Sir Gervase. So by marrying my mother he not only gained life-tenure of the Manor of Meresfeld, which she'd inherited in her own right, but if I died, a claim on Haddertun as well though any children he could get on her. For Hugh the match made perfect sense. But not for me, with his existence robbing me of tithes and any son that either of us sired a threat in some way to the other.

His marriage and the way he smelled gave me two reasons to dislike the man. The third was something meaner. Come Garon and confess it, you were jealous. There's no earthly point in trying to remember, if you can't face the fact that you were jealous of Hugh's confidence and handsome face, the ease with which he took your father's place at bed and board. All right, you felt wrong-footed by him. You thought he talked too much and laughed too readily. But if he'd been less skilful with a sword and lance, less comfortable in his own skin – be honest, wouldn't you have liked him more?

'So are we to infer that lances are the only weapons you know how to use?'

De Bernay chose the very moment that I dropped my cloak and beckoned Jos for my massage, to raise his head and eye my naked body. 'You'll pardon me for wondering. But will that eager bride of yours approve so short a spear do we suppose?'

It was one of those times that stay with you, that you can't forget, another link in the long chain that's drawn me to this place. He mocked me openly before our squires, and like a dog that can't stand being laughed at my first thought was to turn and hide. My second was to use my fists to smash Hugh's handsome face in. But all I did when it came down to it was scowl and flop onto my pallet, scarlet to the hairline, knowing I was outmanoeuvered.

'And do try not to grind your teeth, boy,' I heard him murmur from the hairy cradle of his arms. 'It sounds so unattractive.'

We dipped our lances side by side before the Earl and Countess, Hugh and I, as the appellants dipped theirs on the far side of the field for Archbishop Baldwin – a small man in black and white who sat with his secretaries and chaplains in a stand garlanded with bright red poppies to represent the blood of Thomas Becket.

Returned to England for the trépignée and coronation, the Earl had come by road from Dover to join his lady at the fortress on the west bank of the River Ouse, Baldwin came up-river from Newhaven to his manor of South Malling on the further bank. Word of the tournament they were to hold between the two had spread like wildfire through the County. Spectators thronged the wooden barriers, burgesses rubbing shoulders with the peasants. Sunhats sprouted everywhere like mushrooms, some on children perched up on their fathers' shoulders; and on a scaffold a small group of umpires sat apart, two knights from either camp to see fair play with scribes to keep a tally of the scores.

'Knights of Sussex, hear the laws by which you may compete!' A clarion fanfare announced a mounted herald in the Warenne livery of blue and gold, a man as slight as the archbishop chosen for his mighty lungpower.

'By order of Prince Richard, by grace of God the rightful Lord of England,' he bellowed with his hands cupped round his mouth. 'No combatant on pain of death may bring onto the field of tournament a boar-spear, bow or arbalest, a dagger or a slash-hook. Knights may only fight with lances, swords and axes, flails and bludgeons. Squires must go unarmed. Those taken at a disadvantage must be dragged by main force to the stakes erected and there remain until their ransoms are agreed, with one half of all payments, or half the value of their confiscated steeds and armour to be rendered to the Honour of Warenne for contribution at Exchequer to the Kings' Croisade.

'Knights of Sussex, know that you are subject to your Sovereign Lord to do his bidding, and swear this day in presence of this great assembly to bear fealty to Lord Richard, King Elect.' The herald's face was flushed, eyes like a throttled cat's. But none of us were free to arm until the words he'd memorised had been repeated.

'I do so swear in life and limb and earthy honour,' I recited with the others. 'I swear against all men and women who might live and die, to be answerable to Richard Lord of England, to keep his peace and justice in all things.'

And the girl up in the west stand with the Earl and Countess? The girl I was to marry? She was no more to me just then than a figure on the far side of a hill I'd yet to climb. Just then all I could think of was my own tense body, feeling as I'd only felt before at point of climax with a whore. Panting for achievement!

I know that I was panting, for I'm panting now as I re-live it. 'VICTOIRE!' I couldn't write the word. But it unfolded like a banner in my brain!

Our squires were waiting at the barriers to arm us, my raddle-pated Joscelin and Hugh's Fremund.

'Well don't just stand there, witless,' I called to Jos as we rode up. 'I'll have the short arms and the gauntlets first, and then the shield.'

There's something comforting about the bulk, the sheer weight of armour once you have it on. All I could see of Master Jos as he reached up to tie the flail and bludgeon to the saddle rings and then to lace the gauntlets, was a freckled forehead and a nest of bright red curls.

'Shield and helm, all here My Lord,' he said.

I looped the shield guige round my neck, then asked once more if he would check Raoul's girths.

'Are both bands...?'

'Tight enough and sound?' said Jos, who had a knack of knowing what I was about to say before I said it. He skipped back nimbly in the nick of time from Raoul's savage teeth, to offer me the helm with a broad grin. 'Tight as a nun's cunt as a fact.'

'As soon as I'm accoutred then, you'd best trot up the rail to where the first brunt's like to be,' I told him, busy with my straps. 'If I should fall to an attaint, you know what you must do, Jos? You'll not...?'

'Fail you, Sir Garry? Never!'

I blinked. 'Am I so...?'

'Obvious? No Sir, not by any means.' My squire's eyes, as round as shillings blue as periwinkles, considered me with helm and shield in place and chain-link aventail pulled up to guard my chin. A natural child of Father's brother Anfrid, he'd known me since we both were boys and followed me with cheerful constancy through every stage of training – known me and supported me with cheerful constancy through every step of my career.

31

'Sharp's the word an' quick's the motion, Sir.' He handed up the lance, much heavier than those we'd used for practice and painted in a spiral, red and green.

Another beaming smile. A friendly pat for Raoul's twitching flank, and off Jos ran to do my bidding.

Anyone on Raoul's back must look the part provided he could hold him. I shortened reins and wheeled to join the line of our defendants ready for the charge. Five lances to each line. Six lines deployed across the field to face the same formation at the other end. Two horses in our team were close to shying.

I yawned as I'd been taught to do, to ease the tension in my lungs. *No man is worth his salt,* I told myself, *until he's given and received a blow.*

'Defendants show your mettle!' our leader, Rob de Pierpoint, shouted over the heads of the excited horses. 'Remember men, we fight in company, each one of us accountable for four confrères. We win by looking to each other's interests. A man who fights alone may fall to rear attack, and we've no use for fallen heroes.'

I saw the other knights stare sightlessly as I did, saving energy for all that lay ahead. Even now and at this distance, even here where all about me is serene, I can still feel the pulse, forge-hammer heartbeat, burning breath, sinew, muscle, blood and brain – the trembling muscles of my thighs? Or Raoul's, gloved in satin, shivering beneath me? It scarce mattered which. I was as one with the great destrier whose pedigree I could recite back to Seville, and in another line to Duke William's battle stallion, Mauger. We were as one, Raoul and I, sharing the need to use our fear to spur us into action.

If I fear pain I'll never show it. I fear no man and nothing save dishonour.

The trumpeters put up their clarions to catch the morning sun. A sound like rising wind passed through the stands.

Big breath and steady, Garon. VICTOIRE for the taking!

And am I there? Or simply watching and recalling? Is there still something in me of the foolhardy youth I was that day, taut as a bowstring, knowing the defeat of fear was what made men, trembling on the brink of violence?

WIN GARON! WIN THE CONTEST! I'd willingly have given the fingers of my left hand to achieve it!

The ear-splitting trumpet blast struck like a bolt from heaven, resounding and rebounding from the hills and down the valley to the sea. The crowd's roar reached a bestial pitch, as first the Earl, then the archbishop signalled for the action to begin.

The strain of waiting over. A wall of sound. My sharp-spurred heels and Raoul's response a single impulse, springing forward to a canter which in five paces had become a full-stretch gallop, grinding his great frame up to the speed that he was bred for.

The earth beneath us shuddered. Six muscled legs, two thumping hearts, four bouncing balls and any number of bared teeth. We were unstoppable!

HAVOC! HAVOC! HAVOC!

My own voice yelling with my friends. I felt invincible – like William Conqueror, the Cid of Vivar, Richard of Anjou and Sir Gervase my father all rolled into one. Charging with the heroes of my dreams!

CHAPTER THREE

The lance points ahead of us were glinting in the sun. Against the thunder of a hundred hoofbeats I sought the knight in the archbishop's line who must by rights be mine, and held him him in sight – all else a frame for the marked man who was my target. From a distance of two hundred paces I could see his horse's shoulders milling him to fighting speed. Then as I watched, his lance dropped to the couched position behind his yellow-painted shield. A second lance came down and then another. A rake of lances dropped together.

The gap between us closed as sixty lethal weapons offered to collide at twice the speed of every charging horse. *Not yet!* I told myself. *Wait! Wait, just wait...*

NOW, COUCH! For me the field had narrowed to a corridor of sunlit grass down which two riders hurtled on collision course. The sense of savage joy I felt pumped through my heart to fill my lungs. The only man I saw between Raoul's flattened ears was covered by my lance point.

Nothing now but fifty paces lay between us. His mouth beneath his nasal-guard was open wide

With feet thrown forward in the stirrups, back hard against the cantle of my saddle, I braced myself for the terrific shock of impact.

Now twenty paces and twelve foot of quivering ashwood from the brunt... *NOW TEN!*.

The other's face beneath his nasal guard was near as fearsome as the horse's with it's rolling, white-walled eyes. His lance swung in from nowhere. Struck hard. Deflected from the horn plates of the shield I flung to meet it...

...as my own point jarred – slid- jarred again and reflexed, to lift me bodily and hurl me from the saddle!

The sound of mass collision echoed from the hills, followed by a great roar from the crowd.

Jagged splinters cartwheeled twenty foot into the air. Horses, pierced, uprearing, forced back onto their haunches, screamed in pain and terror. Riders bellowed for their squires against the thunder of the stands.

Stunned. Winded. Sprawling on the turf, the first thing I saw was my opponent's yellow shield, and the pain I felt became a small thing beside the large, surprising thing that was his corpse. It sat and stared at me, surprised itself by the ash shaft thrust through its teeth and sticking out a foot behind its shattered skull.

'Dear Lord, it seems the only thing men love as much as killing one other and pestering us women, is making a loud noise while they're about it.' The voice of Countess Isabel across the bellowing of all those men.

I can't look up, can't tear my eyes away from that poor wretch's head with Sir Garon's lance stuck through it like a skewer. Ugh!

I've seen folk die before, of course I have, both my little brothers. And I won't be sick, I can't be, Maman would disown me.

But see, the red-haired squire has caught Sir Garon's horse. He's on his feet again and mounting – God, he's brave! He has his sword, but not the...

His squire is tugging at the lance with one foot on the dead man's face. At every jerk the dead eyes bulge grotesquely – a rim of tattered lips dragged forward like a pouting lamprey's. Beastly!

'How many more must die, do you think, before we know if we have won or lost and can ourselves retreat?' the Countess is saying to the Earl. I can just see his profile shouting with the rest, but doubt he's heard a word she said.

Her face is in the shadow... But, mon Dieu, she's looking at me!

'I need hardly tell you that My Lord and Lady are your most powerful allies and protectors.' (Maman's latest words of wisdom, just this morning while Hod dressed me.)

'I know you to be contrary, Elise. But if you're sensible you'll take care to oblige them.'

That's why I'm smiling greenly at My Lady
like a perfect gooseberry!

I stared a long time at the other's body. At least that's how it felt, while something vicious in me thrilled to see what I had done. I'd taken a man's life and kept my own, the thing I'd trained for and far easier than I expected. I wished my father could have seen it.

And yet because of you a Christian knight lies dead and excommunicate. His death is on your soul.

A small voice like an argument inside my head, which I ignored. It was my first kill but it wouldn't be my last.

'Steel, Defendants! Steel!' The moment, and that's all it could have been, was interrupted by Sir Rob de Pierpoint. Thanks to my Jos I was back in the saddle straightway and surrounded by the hiss and clatter of drawn swords, of steel on steel, while riders all across the field vied for honours in the mêlée.

'Haddertun, á moi!' Another too-familar voice cut through the clangour, pulling me about to where Sir Hugh leant on the lance he'd used to pierce the hauberk of a squirming combatant and pin him to the turf.

'I need help here if you're still with us, boy?' he shouted, and however much I may have cursed them for it, the rules of tournament obliged me to obey. To leave my bloodstained lance with Jos, to drag my horse around to cover Hugh's retreat. To wheel about and challenge all who blocked our path. To hew and hack, and turn and turn about in practice of the art of *tourney*.

My memory of the mêlée is confused. The action spread back from the centre as more captives, one by one, were dragged towards the barriers and lost their status as competitors the moment that they passed the stakes. Squires running for loose mounts danced in and out and round the fringes of affray with the agility of acrobats. Except one boy who misjudged a horse's stride, to die in anguish, hours later we were told, within the surgeon's tent.

From my view only two things mattered, scoring and surviving. The sun's glare was relentless. Light-headed with excitement I fought unthinking through the heat, trusting to an instinct forged from years of schooling in the castle wards. I sweltered in my padded felt and link-mail, basted in my own salt sweat. It filled my gloves, coursed down my face.Once I looked up to see a loose horse leap the double rails and plunge into the crowd. Twice I made the journey past the stakes with captives for the chequer of Warenne. Figures loomed and vanished. Horses farted. Dung was everywhere. The sound of blades and polearms pounded us like waves on shingle.

We laboured to endure until the Priory bell rang Sext and summoned all remaining on the field to take refreshment, free ourselves of helms and mortar caps, gulp lungfuls of fresh air – to part our hauberk flaps to piss while squires fetched bandaging and ran for washing bowls.

'The odds are with us, men. If we've the bowels for it the day is ours,' Sir Robert told us as we lay on the turf exhausted, too tired even to think.

Our way back to the arena led through the trampled area behind the stakes where captives slumped, attended by bone-setters and nursing brothers from the Priory. Our winded horses no longer pranced with arching necks, but sidled to the line with bleeding mouths and flaring nostrils – all but three who by the Rules of Poitou must be excluded to keep the numbers even for the second charge.

I need one more, must bring another down, was what I thought. But when it came, the gallop and the brunt, my fresh lance shattered on the cantle of the man I'd chosen. Both horses swerved too sharply for attaint. Striking wide, the other's lance-point scored a bloody groove down Raoul's flank, and by the time I brought the screaming animal to trust his feet to solid earth, I'd lost my challenger to...

...well naturally it *had* to be of all men on the field, my wretched stepfather, Sir Hugh de Bernay!

It was a crucial moment for a novice, and having lost my man I made things worse by losing my own head. The guilt, the pain I felt for Raoul, my rage at Hugh, all came together in a red, unthinking fury. I needed urgently to feel my sword-blade biting flesh. To see the blood. To kill!

So when the captain of appellants, Wolstan de Bolbec, came in view, a brute as wide as he was high and solid as an ox, I kicked in spurs and charged him blindly. 'Son of a whore!' I shouted in the grip of battle madness.

He heard me, waited calmly, chose his time and swung his sword with his weight behind it, catching me off-balance and unshielded. The first blow struck my blade in a bright shower of sparks. I took the second on my helm. Its force through layers of steel, a mortar cap and leather coif was stunning, *truly!* With sun and moon and all the stars exploding in my brain, I clutched my head and would have fallen. But my saddle bow upheld me for the fatal blow, the *coup de grâce*.

It would have been, if Hugh de Bernay hadn't intervened to catch Sir Wolstan in mid-stroke. To save me and to and shame me by unhorsing him with a swift lance-thrust to the temple.

It was to be the last fall of the tourney. Leaderless and heavily outnumbered, the appellants had no option but to concede. Nor was the umpires' choice of a Champion for our defendants in any kind of doubt from the time the giant Sir Wolstan hit the turf.

Wrong man again. It would be, wouldn't it!

But no one could deny he looks the part without his helm, now that My Lady's granted him the accolade and laurel crown – rowelling his spurs to make his stallion paw the air, smiling broadly, and directly at me!

If only my Sir Garon wouldn't look so... he hardly seems to know which way to turn, poor thing, to hide his disappointment.

'By my faith, your lord has style as well as courage, Lady Constance,' the Countess Isabel is saying to the woman at my side. 'You must be gratified, for it isn't every knight who'd save the life of one whose sons by right of birth must disinherit his.'

'My husband and my son are bound by ties of kinship, Madam,' Lady Constance tells her stiffly.

'In which case you might do well to give our Champion a son of his own making,' the Countess remarks, 'to square the perfect circle of devotion.'

It was not until the fighting stopped that I was able to take stock of all my hurts. My cheek was cut and one eye blacked. A purple bruise spread half across my chest, with others on my arms and legs. The fingers of both hands were swollen. My head would scarcely turn upon my neck, and when it did, I felt as if a red-hot band was clamped around my temples. In short I was a wreck. But that was only part of it. A well fed cur defending a full manger against a herd of starving cattle could scarce have acted worse than I did at the tourney feast next day.

To be the second knight in tournament was something for a youngster, Rob de Pierpoint assured me with a friendly cuff. The thing was bravely done, he said. My Lord of Warenne, all my confrères said the same. I hadn't failed. My problem was that Hugh de Bernay had succeeded. It was next thing to torture for me to witness his triumph at the feast, and I took refuge in self-pity, drinking steadily to drown my misery in quantities of ale.

The banquet was postponed from midday to mid-afternoon, by which time the great hall of the fortress had been cleansed of old floor-strewings and carpeted with rush. High on its walls hung rows of antlers, old charms to lure the spirits of the deer into the hunters' paths. The light was poor. Strong-smelling tallow candles lit rows of chattering faces down the tables – except at the Warennes' high board on the dais, where my Elise and Lady Blanche were placed and where all the candles were of red beeswax set in silver holders. Sewers bearing laden platters scurried from behind the draught-screens. Ewerers brought finger bowls and jugs of wine.

We knights and squires sat down the hall, so tightly jammed together that we knocked each other's elbows as we ate. On either hand of me were men I'd known for years, Sir Dickon and Sir Mark le Jeune, along with Jos and Fremund and the tourney captives who were bound to us until their ransoms had been paid.

'See Haddertun, your favourite relative is summoned to receive his trophy from the Bishop. You have to hand it to the man, he's earned his prize however you mislike him.' Sir Dickon's idea of good sport was pouring salt into my wounds.

I wished Hugh joy of it.

'I'm sure a coloured stone in a brass basket dressed with feathers from a blighted peacock is just exactly what he needs,' I said bitterly, as through the din of upward of two hundred mouths, through barking dogs and mewing hawks I heard the Earl of Warenne's laughter at some remark de Bernay made as he took up the bauble – and glumly supposing the joke to be at my expense, reached out to fill my beaker from the nearest jack.

I see him at a crowded table in the lower hall, flushed and dishevelled, positively guzzling beer! He's proved his courage and I'm proud of it. So why can't he be too? How silly to feel disappointed when he's done so well. Why can't men lose with a good grace, as women have to nine times out of every ten?

I'd like to go to sit beside him, offer him some comfort, but dare say that would only make things worse. Besides, it isn't often that you have the chance to hear the conversation at high table. Back home in Lancaster we ate in silence, talking only in the gaps between the courses. The silence, Maman said, respected those at lower tables who, unsure of where their next meat might be found, saw eating as an earnest business. Here nothing is in short supply. I've loosed my girdle and am already round as a blown sheep!

The Archbishop's just set down a brimming mazer of red wine to address My Lord the Earl on his left hand.

'The wine is excellent, My Lord. But now perhaps if you have no objection, I should like to give your doughty champion his award while he's still moderately sober.'

The old man's slight with an untidy fringe of grey hair round his tonsure, dressed simply in a woollen cassock none too clean. He speaks French with a gentle drawling accent. (Maman says he comes from Devon.)

'The Knight of Bernay? You seek to honour him yourself, Your Grace?'

My Lord of Warenne looks surprised. But then he always does, because his right eye's clouded from some injury whose scar contorts the brow above into a quizzical expression. The other eye's blood-red from working for the twain. 'Ah yes, I see the smoke of what you're at. You mean to catch him off his guard and pin a cross on the poor fellow while he's kneeling for his prize? Is that the way of it? To sign him up for this croisade you're all hell bent on, hunting Saracens in Palestine?'

'No please, "hell bent" is hardly how I would have chosen to express it.'

The old Archbishop's passing the gold mazer to his host, most carefully to save it dripping on the cloth. 'But in essentials you are right, My Lord, and surely must agree with the necessity for this croisade.'

'Necessity?' Earl Hamelin's banged down the mazer. (The red wine's bound to stain.) 'The only necessity I recognise is loyalty to the Crown. As far as I'm concerned croisades are fools' errands and ever have been – although I'm not so much a fool myself as to stand in Richard's way to free the Sepulchre, if that is what he's set his heart on.'

'Your Grace, I'm grateful for the honour.'

Sir Hugh de Bernay looks amused, as well he might with a green garland on his head and that preposterous prize! But neatly clad, and lighter on his feet than he has any right to be, considering the way he fought.

He surely must have noticed where I'm sitting?

'And with My Lord of Warenne's leave, I'd honour you still further.' The Archbishop speaks for all to hear, his smile exhibiting as many blackened stumps as teeth. 'I'd offer you the cross, my son, and God's own blessing of Salvation, if you will march with us to free Jerusalem and slay its infidel invaders.'

'Forgive me, Your Grace, but I cannot recall Our Lord instructing us to slay our enemies. I thought He held another view entirely?'

Sir Hugh's smile whiter, much!

'Christ's words were not intended for the enemies of God, my son,' the Archbishop assures him. 'The heathen of this world can never be deserving of forgiveness. So tell me, will you ride with us to do His work in Outremer – in Christendom-beyond-the-sea?'

'To leave my wife and daughter unprotected?'

'The property and families of those embarking on croisade will be vouchsafed the protection of the Church. The late Pope Gregory's encyclical confirms it.'

'Your Grace, I have already said I'm grateful for the honour.'

With his free hand Sir Hugh is stroking his long nose. 'And by the faith I'd go and gladly, if the Church could find a substitute to supervise my wife's estates and guard My Lord of Warenne's interest here in Sussex.'

'Hah!' snorts the Earl nudging the old archbishop's elbow. 'Damn me, he's scored a point there, Baldwin! Funds are very well, and I for one will pledge my nephew all he needs. I'll even help him sell off land and titles in the cause if he's a mind to do it. But England isn't going to run itself while he's away.'

My Lord of Warenne winks his one good eye at Hugh de Bernay. 'Not if we send our best knights off on some wild gander's chase across the sea, and keep none back to hold his lands for him while Richard's busy lopping heathen heads in Outremer!'

CHAPTER FOUR

It was not the first feast I'd attended in the fortress but certainly the best. The Earl's cooks had excelled themselves to honour the archbishop. There were so many succulent roast meats brought steaming from the kitchens we hardly knew what we were eating. God only knows how many different dishes were carried down the boards – the carcases of oxen and wild boar, poultry on their spits and small birds seethed in milk, herons, plovers, gulls and even starlings. A swan in all its feathers in a pond of bright green pastry was borne through the hall to loud applause. A goose with the head of a sucking pig sewn onto it was set before the Countess as a jest. And later there were mounds of oysters, pears in honey, brightly coloured jellies moulded in the shapes of animals and castles, each course announced with a great trumpet fanfare.

Not that I was in any kind of frame to do them justice. For if I ate enough to sink a barge, I'd drunk enough to float a merchantman. And as I drank my separate aches became a single pain.

With my chin propped on my fist I watched the candle flames dance in the ale. In my unfocussed eyes the banqueters about me, shovelling the food and soaking in the drink as fast as they could go, appeared as figures in a dream, as noble as the knights of Camelot – the very cream, the very peak of civilized existence. And yet to me unreal. The banquet and the tourney, even the poor fellow I had killed, seemed none of them quite real.

As for my honour... 'De Bernay saved my life and wears the crown, but what of that?' I asked my friend Sir Mark for whom I felt a sudden warm affection.

'The crown's a ring of laurel leaves, that's all, and by tomorrow will be wilted. And what's so special I should like to know about a prize that's no more than a useless bunch of feathers and a lump of rock? Jesus Mary, that's what I call special over there.'

I belched and patted Mark's hard thigh, pointing tipsily at the high table. 'That little maid in blue, d'ye see, the damsel with the face of a church Madonna sitting up as grand as any? She's to be my wife, d'ye hear – MY wife, that's the best of it. *My wife and never Bernay's!*'

I think that's what I said, but can't be sure because it was the last thing I recall before the laughing faces at the tables began to blur and merge into long banners of pink flesh – before the clamour of the lower hall receded into silence, and in a shower of oyster shells I toppled backwards off the bench.

The thing is that he's not about to dance or even stand unaided, propped up against against the serving screen with all the other drunkards. One of them has vomited disgustingly all down his tunic – not a pleasant sight! – the rest oblivious, including my Sir Garon.

Now that they've cleared the bourds My Lady Isabel's retired. So has Maman, and they've had the trestles set against the wall for dancing. The hall's suffocating, reeks of smoke and sweat and onion farts – and God, I'm feeling...

Well, ready for some exercise, that's certain!

The figured dance is boisterous as ever. Twelve couples, with as ever far more girls than men – red-faced and laughing – weaving patterns, swirling fabric, changing partners with each stanza. The minstrel plays to banish melancholy. So he says – an unattractive little man with lantern jaw and large misshapen joints. Yet no one can deny his talent on the lute or think his clear voice aught but beautiful.

> *At the coming of spring season*
> *Trees to leaf require no reason.*
> *Fowls of the air in company*
> *Their different songs then sweetly sing,*
> *And that which lords most long to see*
> *'Tis only ladies who can bring!*

As often as they sing of war men sing of love; of one thing or the other in a chanson (well, usually it's love).

Another circle round again, still clapping hands – and cooler with the neck of my blue gown unfastened. Swoop and sway and circle round. My girdle-tassel's jumping like a live thing.

I noticed him again while they were lighting the fresh candles, no longer crowned with laurels as he moved out onto the floor – noticed him and knew we must touch hands...

> *A prickly branch on a may tree*
> *Is how my love doth seem to me...*

In spite of his exertions, despite the fact that like the rest he's had a deal too much to drink, you'd have to say he's agile – sleek as a wet weasel.

'So here we have the lady who's so unimpressed by champions that she refuses to regard them.'

'You flatter yourself Sir as worthy of regard.'

'When all I meant to do was flatter your attractions. But tell me, are you still resolved to be so cruel?'

His eyes are bloodshot and his voice is dolorous. But naturally he's teasing, these older men say anything they like...

I wish he wouldn't smirk like that. It makes it hard to be severe.

> *In the night-time stiff and frozen,*
> *In the wild wind tossed and blowing,*

'I wouldn't call it cruelty Sir, but preference for another.'

> *Until in sun her blossoms open;*
> *Beneath her petals something showing!*

We finish on the final turn, but 'though we stand apart our shadows go on dancing in the torchlight, vis-a-vis.

He is so close that I can smell his sweat, look straight into the forest of black hair between the neck bands of his tunic. It's strange, but when you've had a little wine yourself you seem to see things differently...

Look down – black hair. Look up – exciting eyes as dark and deep as lakewater (and why is it that dark men, dark unpleasant men, are so often and so much more interesting than fair and pleasant ones?)

A moth with yellow underwings has settled on his shoulder.

'What, preference for the fledgeling youth? But isn't it enough that you have vowed to marry him?' he's asking. 'Don't tell me the young beanstick's to your taste as well? You haven't heard perhaps that he's a small, a very small...'

'Small what?'

'A small to near invisible appreciation of the female sex.'

He's smiling at me, laughing in my face.

But now I'm telling him my duty's to Sir Garon, as his should be to Lady Constance.

'You devastate me. But if you will recall it's taste we're talking of. Not poxy duty, ma petite.'

The moth has risen from his shoulder, is fluttering above our heads. His voice is slurred. He's taking pains to form his words (but curious to hear him call me by the name that Maman uses).

'And when it comes to taste, I should point out that there are few things more exciting in a woman than a pair of soft pink lips.' *(Laughing again quite horridly.)* 'We men see paradise between them, did you know?' *(And bulging where men bulge when they are stirred; a gross thing that he makes no effort to conceal.)*

'Bend over then and show me.'

Detestable! Atrocious! Simply hateful! (His mouth so close it's tickling my ear.)

'You are unseemly Sir, disgusting!'

'Absolutely.' *He agrees.*

> *Oh God it is so hot in here! I'm boiling,*
> *scarlet from my throat to hairline!*
> *But look outraged (I hope I do)*
> *and turn your back on him.*

> *Now, lift your chin*
> *and walk away.*

I see a man reflected in the water. I almost can now that I've found the way to do it.

At low tide the River Ouse lay deep between its banks, escorted to the sea by ducks and dragonflies and swallows catching gnats. I saw him mirrored in it, first upside-down against a scape of hills and roofs and coloured banners, then right-side-up above his own reflection. It's how I see him now.

'Brothers in Christ, the Kingdom of Jerusalem is on her knees!' I see the old archbishop standing in a herring boat moored to the further bank, the violet stole that's meant to be Christ's yoke around his scrawny neck.

Some minor jousts, with wrestling and falconry, cock fights and shooting at the butts had been planned for the day. But Raoul needed time to heal and so did I. My mouth was foul, my head ached like the devil, and the soft turds I'd woken to expel at cockcrow smelled obnoxious. Three of Hugh's and one of my own captives from the tourney had already paid their ransoms and departed. But four were left for us to entertain, and by the time Archbishop Baldwin left his Manor for the river, we'd had enough of trying to amuse them.

'Come lads, let's see him cast his net across the Ouse,' Hugh said when the archbishop's criers reached the camp. 'Let's watch him work a miracle and land men in place of salmon.'

So down we went, all eight of us, Sir Hugh and I with both our squires and four remaining captives including giant Sir Wolstan.

I went in hope of clearing my thick head and forcing my stiff muscles into action.

'For near a century our Christian kings have ruled in Palestine. But now they battle for their very lives,' the old man shouted from the far side of the river. 'At Hattin near the Sea of Galilee His armies have been cruelly slaughtered. The bodies of our warrior monks, our Templars and Hospitallers, are strewn across the land where Christ's feet trod. The holy relic of the True Cross has been taken, and from the port of

Tyre a black-sailed mourning ship has brought us news that Saracens, the followers of Satan's Prophet, lair in the Holy City!'

'Sarcens!' Jos swatted at the gnats that plagued the Lewes shore. 'Ninety nine of every hundred Sarsens want bolts shot through 'em front to back.'

He wrinkled his freckled nose and grinned. 'And after that if it were left to me I'd go an' shoot some more.'

But through my fuddled mind flashed images of Christ's own patrimony, of *Outremer*, the wondrous land the old knights spoke of when they pointed at the severed hands and strings of Sarsen ears they'd brought back from croisade and hung as trophies on the barrack walls.

'*Urbs Jerusalem beata!* Jerusalem the blessed has been ravaged by the hosts of Satan – by Saladin the Antichrist, the beast incarnate!'

The archbishop's thin voice was straining with the effort. 'The Holy City's brave defenders, all are slain, her women violated before its altars, her children put to the sword. Dogs lap our Christian blood! Oh Lord that we should live to see Your Sepulchre used as a stable for the horses of accursed infidels, Thy Holy Cross dragged down, befouled with their excrement!'

'How graceless of them,' Hugh remarked, 'to disrespect a Roman instrument of torture.'

Behind us we could hear applause for some feat of archery or combat on the meads. But no one paid it heed.

'Shame! For shame!' a voice cried from the crowd. 'Death to the Antichrist!' another, and sensing a response the old archbishop yelled the louder.

'Hearken to the word of God. His judgement stands as high as mountains, deep as oceans, sharper than the sharpest sword! I tell you that in God's judgement we are undeserving, brothers. You may be sure He never would have suffered our defeat by infidels except to prove to us the folly of our sins.'

For a moment the old man was silent, shaken by the force of his own words. Then he began again so suddenly that half a dozen seagulls flapped from their roosts on masts and mooring posts with wild cries of alarm.

'The Christian prince who by the grace of God I am to crown next month in Westminster, has taken up the cross himself and pledged to save Jerusalem,' he shouted hoarsely, then told us that the kings of France and Sicily were also pledged. The German Emperor was already on the march with at his back a force of twenty thousand men. And even as he spoke I saw them rising from the river, an Emperor and three wise kings with principal among them the shining prince to whom I'd sworn an oath of fealty.

The picture in my mind was glorious. I saw the promise of adventure, conquest, Syrian gold, exotic eastern women. I saw the holy city of Jerusalem as a kind of paradise on earth, with pure white churches, strutting peacocks, raiments of bright silk – and streets of gold if all we heard was true. But principally I saw myself with sword upraised beneath the banner of King Richard, the greatest hero of our time!

'A knight who isn't skilled in arms can count for nothing in this world, remember that. It is your destiny to fight.' My father's voice rang in my ears.

But how? How must I do it, Father?

'Delay no longer. For love of God take up the cross and join us in this just and holy war to liberate Jerusalem and regain the True Cross of Our Lord,' Archbishop Baldwin shouted from his boat. 'Follow in the steps of Christ's apostles if need be at the cost of your own lives. Join us in the greatest cause the world has known. The Pope himself offers remission of your sins and promises salvation to all embarking on croisade.'

Sir Wolstan gave a mighty fart. 'Pass us the wineskin, will ye Haddertun,' he begged, 'before the godwit talks us sober.'

For months the plans for the croisade had been discussed in every castle ward and marketplace and tavern in the land. For two years past our manors of Haddertun and Meresfeld had paid an annual tithe towards the enterprise.

49

And dear Lord, of what account are games of war and victor's crowns, I thought, *when THIS is how a real man earns salvation?*

'An interesting proposition,' Hugh considered. 'His Grace of Canterbury preaches salvation, demands the universe of all we have of wealth and strength and manly vigour for the recovery of an empty tomb – asks nothing less of us than life itself. And offers what? The promise of eternal life? A thing we cannot see or feel or put to proof and hope in any case to gain by true repentance on our deathbeds? My Lord Archbishop strikes a narrow sort of bargain, don't you think?'

'No, since you ask I don't,' I told him mulishly. Yes, looking back quite like a mule.

'You simply don't think, boy, let's leave it there.' There was amusement in my stepfather's dark face. A trace of pity too maybe, if I'd the wit to see it?

'That dent de Bolbec gave you must have done more damage than I imagined. But even so, a sore head is no reason to embark on such a crazy venture.'

'You're right, it's not the reason,' I said hotly. 'There's such a thing as faith Sir after all. Perhaps you've heard of it?'

'Ah faith, blind faith the triumph of emotion over sense.' Hugh gave the laugh that always made me want to hit him, take a running kick at him and knock him sideways!

'Now on my soul whatever would we do,' he asked, 'where could we hope to find ourselves without blind faith to guide us?' He hated, he went on to add, to introduce a boring note of caution. But did I realise that my chances of returning from the enterprise were less than even? Had I thought at all where I was like to be six months hence?

'Shipwrecked, my poor Garon, and at the bottom of the Grecian Sea? Or lying on some desert battlefield the other side of nowhere with your head between your feet?' He jerked a forefinger across his throat and smiled unpleasantly.

'What then of faith, when even God laughs at the vanity of your pretensions? Where then the fine ideals that bat about in that thick

50

skull of yours – when fish swim though its empty chambers and worms make porrays of your brains? Listen boy, what you need now's a woman not a war.'

And of course I should have listened.

Is it time itself, or what's happened in the time since then that's changed me? I hardly need to ask. I should have seen then what I now see clearly. I should have seen that Hugh was serious for once. I should have known that I misjudged him. But I didn't.

In his attempt to save me from a folly I'd regret, the man stepped close enough for me to smell him – and once again to throw sense to the winds of instinct. Yet even then, confronted by my stubborn chin, it's to his credit that he tried again.

'I can see you're hugging yourself with excitement at the chance of killing people with God's blessing, Garon. But aren't you afraid that when you leave her your new bride will be at risk from ruthless men like me?'

'Should I be?'

'Well I'm a bollocked male and manifestly she is not.'

'My mother will protect her for me.'

Hugh sighed. 'And if you're spared to see more summers, will you eventually acquire more grains of sense do we suppose?' He held my stare for once without his mocking smile, then shrugged and turned away. 'No, I see that you will not. I see that you're the kind of militant who has no use for understanding.

'Devil protect us from idealists,' he added to the cloud of gnats above his head.

'Delay no longer, arm yourselves and join us in this just and holy war!' Archbishop Baldwin cried. 'Join the General Passage now assembling to drive the Saracens forth from the Christian Orient. Take up the cross for God and your new king!'

'And clap your hands together, let your voices ring,' Sir Hugh misquoted from the mummers' show we'd seen on Lewes meads two days before. 'For Christ, for King, for England and a bag of moonshine we joyfully will sing!'

51

But all my thought by then was on the further bank where bishop's chaplains were already labouring with shears and copper pins, to fashion strips of linen into crosses for their new recruits.

'This cross will cost you nothing.'

The old man clambered from his boat to fetch a sample of their work and hold it up for all to see. 'And yet consider that this scrap of cloth will guarantee a Christian victory and all the treasures of God's Kingdom to any man who has the courage to receive it.'

But what I saw was not only a white cross. As the sun lit the piece of fabric which he held aloft, I saw it as Escalibor, a silver sword surrounded by a shining light, and I was dazzled!

What else was in my mind? I am ashamed to own it, but I think that more than anything it was de Bernay's disapproval of croisade – the thought that I would go and he would stay behind, that finally made up my mind. I might have failed to beat him in the tourney. But in this adventure I'd succeed. My father would be proud.

'My Lord Archbishop, I've the courage. I will take it!' A seagull laughed.

So what was done was done. If I could live that day again, undoubtedly I'd live it differently. But at the time it seemed I had no choice. My aches and bruises and my woolly head entirely out of mind, uplifted by by vision of the sword – and very much aware of how I looked from where Sir Hugh was standing – I backed three paces, took a run, and jumped.

Jumped out of one life clear into another!

In fact the splendour of the leap was somewhat lessened by the saturated state in which I reached the further bank, to be presented to Christ's Deputy in England on muddy hands and knees.

'Most Reverend Father, I will take the cross,' I said, and laid my life before him like a dog who runs to fetch a stick and drop it at his master's feet. That's what I was, an eager dog retrieving an idea.

'*Dieu le veut,* God wishes it.' The old man smiled as he removed a strand of duckweed from behind my ear, then grasped my wrist to help me stand.

'My son, I bid you welcome to our company of crucesignati,' he pronounced. 'Take up thy cross and make this pledge as I enjoin thee...'

'I give myself to He who as a victim surrendered His own body by dying for my sake.' Repeating the croisade oath, I stared up like a man in love into the archbishop's saintly face. 'I reject hereby the trappings of this world and scorn it's fleshly pleasures, praise the Lord!'

Of those who watched us from the further bank, only my stepfather and the two squires seemed unaffected. All about them men were whooping with excitement – Sir Rob, Sir Dickon and Sir Mark le Jeune, tearing up the bank toward the river bridge, or leaping down as I had done to splash across the muddy stream. With giant Sir Wolstan braying like a jackass and daring everyone to cast themselves into the bishop's trawl.

Jos told me afterwards what happened next.

'Well Joscelin, we all of us look better by comparison with fools,' Hugh told him drily. 'So I'm guessing that you're not about to trust your soul to an old churchman who's too frail to lift a sword?'

'My Lord, if that's your best guess then 'tis well adrift,' Jos dared to tell him. Or dared to tell me that he had.

'God strike me blind if I would leave Sir Garry – an' to tell the truth Sir, I'd as soon split Sarsen skulls in Pallystine as fleas at home in bed.' Which said, he sketched a bow and loped off to the river crossing.

From where I stood dripping in the grass, I saw his foxy mop bob down the further bank toward the bridge at Cliffe. A long way round for my poor Jos.

And yet an all too short route to disaster.

CHAPTER FIVE

Westminster: September 1189

CORONATION

If you'd been present five days later on the north bank of a much larger river a mile outside the walls of London town, you would have seen a long procession move between two structures built of stone; its slippered feet protected from plain earth by a long ribbon of red fustian, four hundred ells of it, to join the Palace of Westminster to the monastic church from which it takes its name.

Inside the Abbey in a gallery erected for her special use, the Queen of England awaits the ritual she's ordered to confirm her son a King; a thing she's planned and plotted for almost two decades.

Her most puissant majesty, Queen Eléonore of Aquitaine, is not only the most cultured woman in all Europe, but the vainest, toughest and most self-willed princess of her generation; as ruthless in pursuit of her own ends as any of her ruthless sons.

Queens in every age contrive reputations for beauty by maintaining good health and posture – by constantly achieving splendour; and Queen Eléonore has never in her life looked less than splendid. A big handsome woman still, despite her three score years and seven, she wears a crimson gown and surcoat of an imperial style which flatters her big frame. Her wrinkled cheeks are subtly rouged, her pale brows plucked and darkened, her hooded eyes extended with a narrow line of khol. She knows the power of artifice, of colour and of polished surfaces to catch the light, adores jewels and collects them. Her arms are ringed with bracelets. Her veil is held in its place with a Byzantine diadem, its gems repeated on the hanger of her girdle. Her braided, brindled hair is wound with strings of lapis beads and river pearls. The pulses of her neck and wrists are scented with Egyptian perfume.

Taut-strung and energetic; it's only by an act of iron will that Eléonore refrains from craning forward in her seat. On her right hand sits the French King's pallid sister, Alys, who's been betrothed to Richard for more than twenty years, and on her left his aunt by marriage, the Countess of Warenne; three females privileged to witness the otherwise entirely masculine performance of a coronation.

The Queen's long fingers drum her knees while she keeps turning to the Abbey's great west door through which her son will enter, impatient for the sight she has so long – so very long awaited.

'The cheering's louder, Isabel. So are they here at last?' she demands of her sister-in-law in a voice as gruff as any man's and quite as deep as some; her days as the soft-spoken Rose of Aquitaine long gone, if not forgotten. 'Yes, here they come, and here's the Litany to bring them to the altar.'

The Queen supplies the answers for herself, a habit she's acquired from years of close confinement. 'Here's Canterbury with Rochester and my old friend of Rouen, and there's My Lord of Winchester who bears the cap for Richard.'

The clerical vanguard proceeds in orderly succession; their censers wafting aromatic smoke through all the aisles and apsidal chapels of the Abbey; their candles striking colours from its painted columns. Behind the bishops and archbishops the new king's brother, John, and David Prince of Scotland hold the rod and sceptre, symbols of royalty more ancient than the crown itself. Six further earls, amongst them Hamelin of Warenne, carry the Royal Vestments, the gilded swords of State and Justice and the Confessor's broadsword, Curtana, blunt-ended in token of Royal Mercy.

But Richard walks alone, as only Richard may, immediately behind the earl who bears the jewelled crown of Alfred and Saint Edward. When Eléonore came to her coronation, she'd clasped a live white dove in the manner of the ancient queens. Richard's hands are empty. And yet for any disappointed by the unimpressive figure of his brother, the appearance of this prince accords exactly with his legend; his broad face positive in all its features, burnt dusky red from long exposure to the sun, his form heroic, powerful as a viking's.

Clad in a purple tunic trimmed with miniver and embroidered on one shoulder with the white cross of his mission, he strides stiff-legged with belly taut and shoulders back; a gait that he's perfected to show his outsized figure to advantage; his only cap a peach-gold mane of hair, his only jewellery a pair of gilt wire rings hooped through his ears. As they sweep down the ranks of grand seigneurs who bow their heads on either side, Richard's green eyes are fierce with pride; his status validated by universal approbation.

Out of my flesh, thinks Eléonore. *I made him and I made him what he is, the Golden Hope of Christendom!*

'He is the pick of all my brood,' she says aloud, her bracelets clashing and her old joints cracking as she bends the knee to her third-born but eldest living son.

'There is a prophesy of Merlin attached to me which promises great things from my third nestling,' she tells My Lady Isabel, ignoring the three dynastically irrelevant princesses who preceded Richard in the royal nursery.

'And now it seems his day has come.'

'Your Majesty, the whole country is rejoicing with you.' The Countess of Warenne moves just too late to help the old queen to her feet. 'One only has to look at him to see he is a leader natural born, a very paragon of kingly virtue.'

And that he'd better be, thinks Eléonore while her great nestling struts the Abbey nave towards the Shrine of the Confessor, where she herself was crowned with gold when God was still a boy. First undisputed claimant to the throne of England since before the Conquest; an emperor in all but name, by God's good grace Richard's to rule the greatest Christian power in a millennium; an empire it takes months to ride across from one end to the other.

In the eight weeks since Henry's burial at Fontevraud, a new die for the Great Seal of England has been struck, to show the King on one side riding out to battle and on the other solemnly enthroned, with action and judgement thus confirmed as aspects of his majesty.

Although he'll need to be a paragon of both, his mother tells herself, *if Dickard is to take Jerusalem and still hold fast to all our western acquisitions.*

Above the central crossing of the Abbey, its famous tower rises a hundred feet into the sky. Domed and gilded, the great glass lantern spangles the chancel pavement with a thousand jewels of coloured light. A sacred grove, a sunlit clearing in a forest of stone columns, it is the place where every king since the first William has been crowned; where presently the latest of the line lies face-down before the shrine of the Confessor to crave forgiveness for his many well-attested sins.

Archbishop Baldwin, waiting to grant Richard absolution, has set himself for once to outshine the royal sinner. In place of his stark habit he's assumed a jewelled mitre and a cope of flame and tawny silk, to make up what he lacks in height and clash deliberately with the royal purple; a garment that's so heavily embroidered with gold wire it might have stood up without a man inside.

As Primate of all England, Baldwin's required to be more opulent, essentially more powerful than its king. Yet as a Devon man it's near impossible to play the gilded emperor without feeling absurd. Remembering a pedlar's monkey he'd once seen dressed in crimson satin, he cannot help but smile at his approaching monarch, and pray to God to stop him laughing outright.

'In the name of God I undertake to all Christians subject to my rule, these three things: First that I will strive to help the Holy Church of God, her ministers and people to preserve true peace.'

Richard's polished golden head is raised to take the triple coronation oath as he stands face to face with Baldwin. His voice, the kind that only an outsized pair of lungs can possibly deliver, is sonorous and passionately sincere. 'Secondly,' he booms, 'I swear that I'll forbid rapacity and all iniquities to all degrees. Third, that in all judgements I will grant justice and true mercy in emulation of Almighty God the Merciful and Clement.'

While the congregation add Amens, Duke Richard applies his leonine moustache to the jewelled cover of Saint Edward's bible and is led by his archbishop – looking this time, Baldwin rather fears, like some little fair-day fiddler leading an enormous bear – led north, south, east and west to each side of the Abbey crossing, to ask those in the chancel, in both transepts and the body of the church if they are willing to accept him as their Sovereign.

'We will and grant it so!' Four times the thunderous response. Then Richard kneels before the altar to demonstrate his own mortality, is stripped by his attendant bishops of every article of outer clothing, to stand at last before the congregation barefoot, bare-legged, in nothing but his shirt and drawers. Born to the purple, heir to the greatest monarch and richest doweress of the western world, the new king strides in his underclothing to anointing.

'Let us anoint these hands with holy oil, as kings of old and prophets have been hallowed.' Tentatively Baldwin dips his thumb into the ancient, evil smelling essence to daub an oily cross athwart the smooth white palms of one who's never ridden but in gauntlets. He fumbles with the clasp at Richard's shoulder to free the shirt and pull it down around his waist for the anointing of his upper body.

'In nomine Patris et Filii et Spiritus Sancti...' He traces lines like glistening snail creeps across the massive pectorals and barrel chest – the heavy pulse, the humid texture of perspiring skin, the multitude of gingery hairs beneath his thumb, all evidence of fleshly weakness, Baldwin struggles to believe, for all their male vitality.

'In the name of the Father and of the Son and of the Holy Ghost...'

A fourth cruciform marks the pale expanse of Richard's back beneath the sunburnt collar line. Two more bless the fleshy saddle of each shoulder, a further two the elbows he lifts helpfully for unction; a movement in the kneeling prince which wafts the mingled odours of male sweat and French perfume to the unworldly nostrils of his archbishop.

'In the name of the Father and of the Son...' Disturbed and disconcerted by the man's immense virility and something of a worrying response within himself, Baldwin makes the sign a ninth and final time across the royal brow, then wipes his hands, perceiving as he does so another kind of nakedness and one still more disturbing in Richard's gleaming eyes.

With shirt replaced and Cap of Maintenance set on his head, the anointed monarch rises for his investiture in a brilliant shaft of red and purple sunlight from the Abbey lantern. He stands with legs apart, chin up, chest out, to be enfolded in a Florentine silk tunic and sensational dalmactic of cinnamon and gold brocade.

Girded with a jewelled braiel, armed with his father's Sword of State, he steps into a pair of scarlet buskins and then waits splendidly aloof while two earls kneel to fit his golden spurs; whilst lesser constellations move around him. As each sacred item of adornment is brought to him from the altar, the Abbey choir fling alleluias to the vaulted roof. The archbishop bids the King receive the bracelets of Sincerity and Wisdom in token of his God's embracing and winds the ancient torcs round Richard's bulging biceps.

'Receive the yoke of Christ by which you are subjected to the laws of God.' A stole of purple China silk is looped round the royal neck and tied securely to the bracelets in a symbolically restrictive gesture, which Baldwin hopes against all likelihood the new king will take note of. But Richard can see nothing now beyond his own predestined pathway to the throne.

As each new vestment touches his body he reacts with a pleasure that is physical. He takes a breath, sucks in his belly for the buckled braiel, holds arms out for the torcs, while in his fleshy, handsome face there blazes a look of triumph which calls to Baldwin's mind, uncomfortably, the pagan rites that underlie a Christian coronation.

'Receive this pallium, formed with four corners, to show that all four corners of this universe are subject to the power of God,' he recites with blatant emphasis as Richard dons a mantle of terrific value, inches thick with gold embroidery and studded with cabochon gems.

'This vestment serves as a reminder that no frail mortal, be he king or emperor, may reign without authority from God, who is the *King* of Kings!'

Yet Richard stands, as frail as a bull elephant, as freighted with bullion and precious stones as any monarch of the Indies; glittering and coruscating; incandescent, radiating sparks of light; barbaric in his gaudy splendour. So dazzling that Baldwin has to blink.

His most Serene Lord Richard, by Grace of God first king to take that name in England, with half of Europe at his feet and the Holy City of Jerusalem in prospect, turns slowly in his scintillating train to set his sumptuous back-end on a throne flanked like the Chair of Solomon by life-sized gilded lions. As an anointed monarch he's already half divine; already seated, if not on God's right hand, then on a level close approaching His celestial knees.

The King's bearded chin is up, his eyes are blazing.

Archbishop Baldwin draws a breath. *'Lord forgive him. He is eager for the chance to prove himself,'* he reasons with the image of Divinity he keeps inside his head. *'Given time and proper guidance, I'm certain, Lord, he will acquire a sense of balance.'*

60

'AND WHO *PRECISELY WOULD YOU EXPECT TO GIVE A KING OF ENGLAND GUIDANCE IN SUCH MATTERS, IF NOT YOURSELF, ARCHBISHOP?*' the uncompromising Voice of God enquires. '*MY SERVANT BECKET WASN'T SLOW, YOU MAY RECALL, TO BRING KING HENRY TO ACCOUNT.*'

Which is a fair point, the archbishop thinks; and before his courage can forsake him, Baldwin takes the plunge.

'King Richard take good heed,' he warns in his best sermonising tone. 'A king is only fit to govern others while he governs in himself the vices of vainglory and impiety which ever have beset the princes of this world.'

The hollow spaces of the Abbey lend depth to his thin voice. 'King Richard I forbid you by the bones of the Confessor to assume this honour in a state of pride.'

King Richard's sandy lashes part. Two furrows of displeasure crease the royal brow. Green eyes lock with grey.

'*Forbid*, Archbishop?' he stonily enquires.

Even standing in his mitre, scarce taller than his monarch firmly seated, Baldwin speaks for once without apology.

'By the Power of God that's vested in me, I say you will assume the crown in true humility,' he states flatly. 'Or not at all.'

He waits, and for what seems an age to all attending there's silence in the Abbey. Church over Crown? Crown over Church? Which is it to be?

And still he waits.

Then Richard's overtaken by a spasm of pure rage that blanches his knuckles on the throne and leaves him shaking with the effort of control.

'With God's grace, Baldwin, and by my mother's womb I will uphold against all hazards everything I've sworn,' he finally asserts, 'And that's how I will be crowned – if not by your hand, priest, then by my own!' With which he rises, seizes Saint Edward's heavy crown and swings it high above his head; the purple stole drawn with it looping from his outstretched arms.

As the King stands poised to crown himself; godlike, oblivious to any power or glory but his own, Baldwin's reminded of the old dark legend of Anjou – sees not a Christian prince, but the descendant of a fallen angel. He thinks of Lucifer in the Book of Isaiah: *'I will raise my throne above the stars of God!'*

By the power that's vested in me, I forbid you to assume this honour in a state of pride!

Eyes closed, he says it silently this time through God's own agency of prayer. *Remember, at at coronation a new king must become the virtues that he swears to.*

'No please...' Willing Richard to believe it, he extends his own thin hands to take the crown, when all at once the little bells suspended from its golden arches begin to ring.

A muscle twitches in the crimson flush across the King's well covered cheeks, and it becomes apparent that he's shaking like a jelly.

'Well then get on with it, you pious fool,' he growls.

> *'O Lord, the King rejoices in Your strength;*
> *How great his joy in the victories You award!*
> *For You have granted him his heart's desire*
> *And have not denied the prayer of his lips;*
> *You have endowed him with the richest blessings*
> *And set a crown of purest gold upon his head!'*

The choir exults as Baldwin, with gravity and even more pronounced relief, reclaims the shaking crown to set it, gold on gold, on Richard's head. But when the King resumes his throne his face is bathed in sweat. He shakes so violently that two earls have to climb the steps to hold the crown from either side and stop it falling to the floor.

'Christus vincit! Christus regnat! Christus imperat!'

A thousand voices batter the stone cliffs of the Abbey walls. Its bells announce King Richard's crowning to the populace beyond. Then all the bells of all the other churches in the square mile of London jangle their response; disturbances which in their turn set every city dog hysterically barking, clatter pigeons from the Abbey roof – and finally dislodge a sleeping bat from some tenebrous crevice high up in the lantern. Disorientated, the tiny creature flutters down a rainbow shaft of coloured sunlight to circle round and round the trembling figure of the King in Majesty upon his throne.

'There's nought amiss. You cannot think he is afraid. My son fears nothing of this world or out of it. His courage is a legend.' Queen Eléonore's deep voice. 'It is the soldier's malady of quartan malaria that makes him shake,' she says emphatically. 'We southerners are subject to it, as anyone could tell you who's campaigned in the swamps of the Guienne.'

But behind the choir, the bells and Eléonore's defiant statement, Baldwin can hear the echo of King Henry's curse.

'*I call on heaven to curse Richard's soul! May God deny it its eternal rest until I am avenged!*'

Above, behind the bat which circles Richard's head, there flickers through the old archbishop's mind the arcane spectre of Angevin beginnings; a story whispered in the shadows.

With a sense of deep foreboding he recalls the superstition that King Henry's line derives, not only from Anjou, but from a fallen angel. From Satan's daughter, Mêlusine. From a black witch who, in sight of Christ's Own Sacrament, was commonly supposed to have changed herself into a bat and flown in terror from the altar.

CHAPTER SIX

Yes well, I'm thinking. But the more I think the less I seem to know what's best.

I've never found it hard to make my mind up in the past, and no one's ever called me indecisive. But when I listened to Sir Garon trying to explain why he must join the Kings' Croisade, I simply couldn't think what was expected – if I should back him in a cause that everyone calls glorious and noble, or keep him home, as Maman says I should, by any means I can?

My Lady Isabel had given orders for her furnishings to be left in place for their return, when she and the Earl left Lewes for the new King's coronation. So we were in her solar by the window at our usual occupation when Sir Garon and his mother came to see us.

I spin and weave proficiently if I say so myself. But Turkish-point embroidery and I have never quite seen eye to eye – and when I took up my frame that morning, I found my roses had turned overnight into pink cabbages, my little bluebirds into fat blue hens!

'My goodness, what a climb!...'

My Lady Constance came in talking, went on talking nineteen to the dozen as she came across the solar from the stairway with her big son and little daughter close in train.

'Come Edmay, stand by me. Do something useful, Garon, find us something firm to sit on. My Lady Blanche, you're well I trust? Elise my dear, may I admire your work? But how unusual. What attractive colours! Poultry in a cabbage patch, is that the theme?' (Confirming my worst fears.)

Sir Garon placed the bench for her and she subsided, putting back her veil. 'Heavens all those stairs, I am exhausted,' she confided with a kind of desperate pleasantry that anyone could see was false. 'You know I am to bear another child by Candlemas, God willing. We're hoping it will be a boy.'

So OLD! And pregnant to that dreadful man! (That's when I pricked my finger on the needle.)

In her next breath My Lady Constance told us that her son had further tidings that must certainly surprise us. Which was when Sir Garon ducked his head, performed his 'I'll-look-anywhere-but-you' thing balancing on one foot then the other, uneasy as a dog with fleas – then cleared his throat and blurted suddenly that he must fulfil his oath to join the Kings' Croisade.

'But be assured I will survive,' he told the floor. 'My knight-service is but for forty days. So when the Holy City's taken I'll return.'

'Unless you're slain, to leave your wife to moulder in the wilds of Sussex!' In her distress Maman looped her girdle up into a knot that I could see would take her ages to untie.

For me the knot was on the inside while my future was discussed – and still I can't think what to do.

But was it really just this morning we were married, united in the sight of Holy Church? It didn't even feel quite real while it was happening – exchanging rings and pledges with Sir Garon's big moist hand supporting mine (and eyes determinedly elsewhere), the vows he made to seal the bond before the castle chaplain sounding anything but joyful.

'Have you the will to take this woman to wedded wife?'

'Aye, Father.'

'To have her and to hold yourself to her and to no other to life's end?'

'Aye Father as I trust in God.'

'Then take her by the hand...'

A bride should feel important at her wedding. But I did not. It seemed a hasty, patched-up thing, too soon begun and even sooner finished.

We stood together in the doorway of the fortress chapel, attended in their absence by my Lord and Lady's Constable, by Lady Constance and her daughter. But without Sir Hugh who was away at Manor Court. (I'm pleased he wasn't there, no really.) Maman was of course – and Hod, who'd thought to bring along a toad she'd found to make sure that the marriage would be fruitful. Sir Garon wore his sword and spurs. His red-haired squire stood by the door – and I suppose I should be grateful that they didn't bring the horse!

I wore my campion gown to match the bright vermillion of my veil, with ripe ears of barley wound in my hair beneath it. The wedding mass and the repast in hall were fixed for the third week of September, to fall 'twixt harvest and Plough Monday, with the moon already waxing (and according to old Hod who claims to know a good deal more about my body than I do myself, my monthly cycle just approaching its most fertile phase).

So now we're on the move again to start our honey-month at Haddertun, Sir Garon's home and mine for all our future life – together or apart.

The sky is clear, a tang of autumn in the air. It's good to be outside again away from town and fortress. I can smell water mint. Long-legged gran'father flies are blundering about the horses. A pair has drifted into Nesta's mane cemented end-to-end – a symbol you could say of what's about to happen to her rider!

The great fields of Sir Garon's manor run from the forest almost to the bridge and water-mill – darker, redder than they really are, seen through my wedding veil. A moorhen dashes head-down for the reeds. An elm tree towers above his village; clay and wattle, huddled in the shadow of the downs. Another church, more patchwork strips and the chalk gables of the manor, standing as they've stood for more than forty winters.

And here they all come tumbling downhill; a parcel of excited whop-straw peasants, flapping homespun like a gaggle of brown geese. Peasant wives in caps and aprons grasping nosegays, patched skirts tucked into waistbands. Piefaced, tow-headed children, barefoot and half naked. Elders, lame or stooped from years of labour – all crowding round Sir Garon, smelling strong and shouting salutations. Daft grins on every weathered face.

How could I not be pleased to see them, folk struggling to make the best of life as common people do in every land and circumstance from Alfriston to Acre? As their Seigneur I liked to hear them call my name and wish me well, villeins, cottars and free tenants who'd known me as an infant and followed my advance through all the years from my first toddling steps about the manor to my return a married man. Despite our differences of birth we understood each other. And even if it seems a strange thing for a lord who had the power to sell them off the land to say, the manor folk had always treated me with kindness.

'God bless, Lord Garry Sir, an' send ye joy in wedlock.'

The hayward's wife, Dame Martha, was the first to greet us. 'Hayward here has fetched up combs from our best hives, to give ye strength all through yer honey-month an' see ye plough the furrow like a good 'un.'

'Aye, an' harvest what ye sow, to swell yer lady's belly as a fact,' said Adam Hayward, panting up behind and pulling off his hat. 'Or leastways make a tidy job of trying, eh boy?' He stuck a grubby finger though a hole in the straw crown and waggled it, and grinned to show more gum than standing teeth.

Dame Martha laughed and told us both, as if she thought we needed telling, that however menfolk wanted sense, whatever else we might be doddlish about – 'Ye're all as smart as dogs at rat holes when it comes to hornwork, every Tom an' Jack!'

And what was I to do but laugh back at their impudence? I liked the sound of their old language with its stops and starts and stretched out exclamations, knew all they said was kindly meant, and that I'd have to hear much more of the same sort before the girl and I were bedded. The mating of their lord was village business, and I found their interest in me as a stud beast almost reassuring.

Yet even as I smiled into their tanned familiar faces and gave the peasants my good day, my mind was elsewhere, most of it, on how to raise the cash for armour, food and a sea passage for my men and horses. And if I'd been unready for a wife before, God only knew how much more so I had become since I enlisted for croisade. With the girl already here in Sussex and the Countess standing sponsor, it was too late to break the contract. My mother was insistent. But if I could, I would have done it in a flash.

That was half my problem. The other half was my own ignorance of women. As far as I could tell they all were daughters of the temptress Eve. According to the Church the path to hell lay straight between their thighs. Carnality was sinful unless it be for procreation, and nothing I had seen or felt suggested otherwise. During my years as page and squire I'd seen men jerking out their seed. Or humping whores. Or buggering each other, sights commonplace in barracks – and monasteries as well if all we heard was true. The need was animal, at best a gross form of enjoyment like drunkenness or gluttony, at worst degrading to all parties. The Devil teased men with temptations. We had our morning stands and frantic fumbles, spring and autumn surges, noon and midnight cravings. But God had the last word in the end by giving us remorse. By leaving us with nothing more to show for sudden thrills than sticky voidings, weakness of the limbs and lingering regrets.

I'd never been a man myself to take a bondwoman by force or chase a serving girl for sport, as I knew that Hugh did frequently behind my mother's back. When a base urge became too strong, I'd simply tamed the beast by taking it in hand. Or else paid Lewes whores to do it for me at a basic price for something brisk and businesslike, believing that the haste reduced the sin. And yet. And yet despite it all – despite my ignorance and my obsession with croisade, thoughts of the girl began to chafe at me like burrs inside my britches. When I beheld her riding legs astride, or pictured them astride without the horse, I couldn't help but think, and revel in the thought that she would soon be mine to get an heir on. To fuck repeatedly and legally in sight of God and all his blushing angels.

It had taken the best part of two hours, nonetheless, to satisfy my squire that I was ready for my matress duty. I'd cleared my bowels. Jos set a tub before the kitchen fire in view of half a dozen smirking serfs, de-loused me, scrubbed me, shaved me, cleaned my teeth with salt and willow, even plucked my nostrils. He washed my hair in almond oil and trimmed it, combed the tangles to lie in meek waves on my neck, then showed me my reflection in a buckler. He groomed and polished every inch of me, but for my *arme de combat* which I attended to myself.

'Long as life, eh Sir? Soon stretch her understandin' that will!' someone shouted from behind the pastry table.

The way Jos beamed as he held up a fur-lined pelisson to clothe my gleaming limbs, you might have thought he'd earned the compliment himself. With any more encouragement it wouldn't have surprised me if my squire had stuck an apple in my mouth, a sprig of parsley up my arse and served me to the woman on a lattice of crossed leeks!

Flowers in the rushes on the floor – herb robert with fluellen and blue scabious to bring the grassy fragrance of the field into our chamber.

They've lit me in with torches made of hawthorn to bring fertility into the house. The fire is scented with sweet rosemary, and even Maman must appreciate an upper chamber with a chimney hearth, a thing unheard of in the north. Candles are everywhere – a chest, a hutch-press, perches for my clothes, a bench beside the hearth, a pisspot by the window. On the sill in a brown jug, Hoddie's set a bunch of wilting harebells, one of the peasant women's bouquets. The bed, near wide as it is long, stands open to the fire and Maman's tactless observations.

'But how wise to leave Sir Garon's better sheets for later,' she's pretending to believe. 'These wedding stains can be so stubborn – with first rate Irish linen hard to come by, I suppose, down here in Sussex?'

'We weave and bleach our own linen and to a standard we have reason to be proud of,' Lady Constance frigidly informs her.

'And cat fur for a counterpane – do look Elise! How quaint it seems beside the marten we've been spoiled with up in Lancaster for all these years.'

'I think the tabby's lovely, Maman.'

And for Lord's sake can't she see I'm nervous – that the very last thing that I need just now's another demonstration of her disapproval. Hod sees it, makes a sympathetic face while I squat on the pot beside the window. But Maman's off again on a new tack.

'We'll put the candles out, and range the curtains round three sides of the bed-celer,' she says to no one in particular and all of us in general. 'That way Sir Garon's first glimpse of my darling will be by firelight.'

'Unless he falls and breaks his neck in his attempt to find her in the dark.' Lady Constance gives a mirthless smile.

'In my experience the method never fails in its effect on bridegrooms.' Maman's reaching up with both short arms to arrange the indigo-dyed curtains in the manner that she recommends, as Hoddie brings my night shift from its warming place before the fire.

'It's how we got Elise's sister Cecily with child, when she was barely fifteen and her husband barely had the sense to tell his middle finger from his middle leg.'

'Perhaps in his case,' Lady Constance says caustically, 'they were of the same size?'

Of course I know about these things. It hardly could be otherwise when you sleep with your parents half your life, and spend so much time stumbling over couples in the other half – in the long grass, in passageways and under tables – anywhere that they can find the space! You'd have to be blind, deaf and very stupid not to know what men and women do to together when they get the chance (although I do remember thinking as a child that if God extracted Eve from Adam's body in the first place, it really should be women who are eager to get back into men and not the other way about).

After so many years of Maman's teaching and of Hoddie's, I think I know enough to be the mistress of a manor. Weaving isn't difficult to learn and nor are spinning, baking, curing, brewing – none of them too hard to master once you know the way. But to be the mistress of a man in bed is something you would think, like Turkish-point, that needs some aptitude and quite a bit of practice – and although I've grasped the basics well enough I'm still a little hazy on the detail. I mean, how's it going to feel to have that gristly thing pushed into me? And what should I be doing while he's pushing? There's bound to be some kind of trick to it…

Elise, unseemly! Stop at once!

'The sheets have been well cleansed with Jordan Water. I saw to them myself,' I am assured by Lady Constance.

'And even if they're still a little damp, please God the heated bricks I've brought will dry them in a jiffy.' Maman's wiping both hands on her skirts.

'I've slipped some lavender and tansy leaves between them – and if I were you, chérie, I'd lodge a sprig or two under your shift as well.'

'But see to it he asks you more than twice before you grant him sight of what's below,' Sir Garon's mother offers as I climb into the bed. 'You may believe that men will never set much value on a prize, my girl, unless they have to make some kind of trial to win it.'

70

'Nor hit the target truly neither, the precious awks, without a woman's hand to set them in the way.' Hod pops a sugured violet in my mouth to make my breath smell sweet,

'But don't keep him waiting for too long dear,' is Maman's next advice. 'Men can be generous enough and kind. But not when they're denied.'

Hod's sponged and scented me with lily water. She's used carnation on my cheeks and lips, and even on the soft skin of my belly. I'd like to wriggle down in bed. But that would never do, because I have to be propped up on pillows while they spread my hair around me like a halo. The bolster smells of lavender and starch, has parsnip seeds pressed underneath it for fruitful union – and I can't move my head for fear of ruining the look.

'You look quite beautiful, my treasure.'

The pride in Maman's voice is touching, until she spoils it with another caution. ''Tis best to leave your hair unbraided for the honey-month,' is what she recommends. 'It helps the man to think you maidenly each time he comes to bed – a virgin fresh and whole, you see, for him to conquer every night.'

But now at last it's over – all the fussing, tweaking and instruction – and they're leaving. Maman's pinching out the candles…

'I say the devil has the right of it, a woman looks as well undressed by firelight as in the costliest attire. Try not to think too much, my dear, it makes you frown and that's so unattractive. And while you're waiting it would do no harm to say a rosary.'

Her very last advice – 'Or if there's time, a prayer to Margaret of Antioch who blesses all our bellies.'

Hoddie's trying to tiptoe away on feet three times too large to manage it. Her chin recedes. She's dewlapped like a bloodhound. But her grim smile as they pass through the chamber door tugs at my heartstrings.

So I'm alone and shivering despite the fire – interlacing fingers, wriggling my toes and sucking on the violet muscadin. It's been a strange, momentous day, and nothing stranger than this moment, now.

Afraid? I know I must be because my heart is beating on my ribs like something in a cage! There's no escape, nowhere to hide – what's been a game before now all too real.

71

What can I do that's calming? 'Ave Maria gratia plena... Hail Mary full of grace, the Lord is with thee...'

The glass beads of the rosary are something to hold onto. Above the beam that ties its outer walls there's nothing but a film of cobwebs to separate us from the men. They're laughing out there. Someone's playing bagpipes. The fire has been attended to and has a good red heart, its flames embracing seasoned wood, gleaming on the bedposts. Dancing on the wall.

Silence now beyond the beam. But there's the latch. He's coming in! 'Sancta Maria, mater Dei...' Surely your Joseph was a gentle sort of man who wouldn't treat a woman ill?

Holy Saint Margaret, please help me do it right...'

'Knees up little lady! Best way to say yer prayers tonight,' a drunken voice cries through the open door. 'Give thanks for what ye will receive 'afore ye taste the flavour!'

Low comedy which isn't funny, not at all (although what about the knees? I wish when Garda listed all the ways she's tried it, I'd paid her more attention.)

Will he speak first? Or shall I do it? Surely anything is better than a silence?

The hinges creak. The door latch drops a second time. He's shooting the top bolt, and now the other...

Time to set the rosary aside. 'Dear God, defend me with Thy mighty power, and remind him if You will, that I'm an untried virgin.

So eyes tight shut and all my other senses straining...
Can he see how my hair's spread on the the pillow?

I hope that Maman's right about the firelight,
but now wish I hadn't closed my eyes.
Because I can't see
WHAT HE'S
DOING!

CHAPTER SEVEN

It was difficult to see what I was doing when I'd shut the door and shot the bolts. But of course I knew what was expected, knew I had to do my duty as a husband before I came to open it again, to prove myself a natural man in the most obvious way on earth.

I felt excited, agitated, hot as hades, cold as Ice. No one, I told myself with one hand underneath my robe, would call me 'soft-sword' – least of all my wife.

I found her in the bed where I was born, eyes closed, hair rippling across the pillows like ripe corn in the breeze. I knew she couldn't be asleep because behind me Martin Reeve was either torturing an jackass or playing something on his bagpipes.

Then Jos began to sing about the law of cock and how it goes. 'Take it as a truth from one who knows. The more we use the thing the more it grows!'

A burst of laughter followed, along with all the usual hints for threading needles, planting roots and imitating randy livestock. That's how it is at weddings. All brides the same. All waiting for a husbandman, or bull, or ram to fuck them. That's how it was with us. And as she waited for me with her eyes closed, my new wife must have seen herself as I did. As a ready cunt.

OW! OW! OW! Garda told me it would hurt the first time – and it DOES! So thick and hot it burns like fire!

But Garda didn't say how HEAVY he would be, how far he'd ram that alien thing inside me – jarring, pounding, crushing me into the mattress, forcing my legs wider with each furious thrust! He didn't ask me, hardly even spoke. He just looked baffled for a moment, then made a frantic dive to sieze me like some kind of animal. I swore I wouldn't scream or cry – eyes on the canopy above us, mouth tight, tight shut. But I can't BREATHE! No air! Can't take the weight! His fingers hurt – tight round my neck as if he thinks I might escape. I have to STOP HIM! Have to try to heave him off before…

'Ahh-aaa-oo-aaaah!!!'

Convulsion. Yeasty, beery breath gusting from his lungs into my face. And someone cheering, chanting something lewd about Jack and planting orchards – more cheers. More catcalls, drunken laughter…

But thank the Lord, he's off me – hot and slimy and SO WET!

It's all SO VERY WET AND MESSY! I know that this is not the time for squeamishness. But Jésu, what a stink! (And who'd have thought that it would smell of ivy pollen, and so strongly?) And what a clumsy, painful, messy sort of business altogether! I didn't even feel it spurt as I expected, only heard the fuss he made.

So is this IT? Is THIS the thing men boast and sing about so endlessly? Because if it is, it's going to take a lot of getting used to – that's all that I can say! He's dribbled on me and there's blood – down here and on my fingers where I've touched it…

But oh dear, a sudden picture's flashed into my mind of Everlasting God with grey hair and a long grey beard, peering through the clouds to see me flattened and spread-eagled, sticky with Sir Garon's seed! God speaking in my father's sternest tones.

'I TOLD YOU NOT TO EAT THE APPLE, TOLD YOU IT WAS BITTER TO THE TASTE! BUT THEN YOU HAD TO HAVE IT DIDN'T YOU, MY FOOLISH CHILD. AND NOW SEE WHAT IT'S BROUGHT YOU!'

I hear The Everlasting's voice. But not Sir Garon's, not a peep. Only pants and groans, a huge yawn and a series of deep breaths – because, I wish he wasn't but he's already snoring like a hedge-pig – fast asleep!

While I am bound to lie here wide-awake for simply hours!

Muffled birdsong, distant cock-crow, dawn light through the window, ashes in the hearth. So here are we a married couple, and joined last night by rather more than hands and vows!

See here's a bloodstain on my shift, another on the sheet. Maman will be gratified to see them, and that's something I suppose. Anyway the worst is over and I didn't cry aloud. And there he lies, my untamed ravisher, flat on his back across the ruin of our bed – a Samson shorn, a naked man asleep – eyes shut, chin sticking up, mouth open, snoring still 'though not so loud. We make our faces work so hard to tell our stories while we are awake, and look so different when we aren't. It's true. He looks much better doesn't he without the shifty eyes.

The cat-fur's on the floor, the over-sheet bunched up across one thigh and twisted round his foot. Those arms and hands – last night they felt like iron bars! He has big knuckles and broad fingers, a hairy crucifix imprinted on his chest – yellow bruises, traces of old scars, outlines of bones beneath the skin and two red fleabites on his neck...

So long as he's asleep I have him to myself, to smooth his hair if I so choose. To feel the ragged edge of his sliced ear. And yes Elise, admit it – to take a good long look at what he has down there while you still have the chance!

It isn't that I've never seen one. But glimpses of pink sprouts in hair – of men on hot days in the water, or pissing against tree-trunks – can hardly count as decent views. Well, can they? In chansons the male member is a force of life, battling with death to fountain seed into the world. In verse it is the mythic horn – the unicorn that's bound to women by a golden chain.

But now I can look his fiery engine in the eye, I can't say that I find it all that wonderfully impressive. What does it remind me of – shrunken, limply wrinkled, lolling drunkenly across a shiny slime-trail on his thigh? Much lesss a unicorn I'd say than a defenceless turtle squab hatched out of hairy eggs! And puny actually, beside a horse's or a mule's. No honestly, it doesn't seem to go with any other part of him, looks added on somehow, and strange for something quite so commonplace and universal. I mean all men must have one...

But I've just thought, if God made men in His Own Image, He must to have one too! (Stop it you wicked girl – that's more than quite enough! But the Everlasting with a pizzle. What a fantasic thought!)

I know I shouldn't smile, but it's so silly, all of it – the legendary unicorn, the songs men sing obsessively about their own peculiar bodies, and in the end the unimpressive thing itself. To look at it you'd think that butter wouldn't melt – the only mystery how men can ever hope to be taken

*seriously with that arrangement dangling between their legs or standing up
and sticking out in front...*

But Holy Godfathers, HE IS AWAKE!!

It's said the way you feel when you awake from your first engagement
with a woman is like to set the pattern for your future with her, and if
that's true it didn't bode too well for ours!

I'd seen her smile before I quite remembered where I was. And when
I did, and caught her smirking at my cock, my confidence was shattered.

The night before, I'd acted as I thought no worse than any man
confronted by a virgin bride. Squared my shoulders. Boldly pulled the
sheet aside, and muttering '*Victoire*' beneath my breath, lifted her shift
to bare the target and make my charge against its maiden shield. No
sense, I thought, in wasting time or looking doubtful. She'd flinched a
bit and cried a little afterwards as I'd been told she would. But by then
I'd dropped into the blameless sleep of any fellow who's successfully
performed his matress-duty.

At dawn I'd planned another onslaught, knowing they expected me
to do it twice at least within the first hours of her breeding cycle. And
'though I'd wilted sometime in the night, to wake as limp as a slit
pilchard I would have risen to the task and willingly.

I would have done. I'm sure I would. But for the girl's unnerving smile.

'I can explain,' she said. But when she tried she only made things worse.
I can't recall the words she used to make me think that she admired my
body. I wasn't in a frame to listen. Instead I broke all records for
jumping out of bed and dressing, stumbled on the hutch beside the bed
and stubbed my toe, but didn't care and wouldn't stop not even for an
instant. With boots in hand I freed the chamber door and bolted
through it.

The lamps had guttered in the dormitory beyond. The place smelt
comfortably of sleepers and stale beer. The shutters were still open and
the pale dawn light revealed the form of Martin Reeve, snoring hoarsely,

hugging his bagpipes to him like a lover. Others sprawled or hunched into their cloaks, if not unconscious next thing to it. All but one.

'My lord?' A tussocky red head, a shine of eyes reminded me that I could seldom move however stealthily without attention from my squire. But I told Jos to go back to his sleep, that I'd take Bruno in his place, and saw his mop-headed shadow slip down the wall.

Beyond the outer door an open stairway led into the manor ward, and I'd barely time to stamp into my boots before my dog came bounding up it. A half-grown pup who'd unaccountably attached himself to me since my return, he licked my hand and squirmed for my approval with every part of his uncleanly body wagging. I called him Bruno for his colour, but might have called him Pongo for his smell. We looked about us sniffing the raw morning, scenting pigs and cowpats, straw and stables through the stink of fox-shit coating Bruno's ears. The grooms were out already leading horses to their tethers. I stopped to piss into an elder by the gate and Bruno did the same. Between the grass stems spiders' webs were strung like rosaries with beads of dew, and the sky out to the east was washed with yellow.

Our corn was harvested and safely in. The manor barn cram-full of hay and barley. Wheat and rye stooks ready for the threshing. There were fat pigeons in the cotes and coneys in the warrens, the fowls were laying and the cattle flush with milk. Our manor fields were tended. Cottage gardens overflowed with kale and leeks, the mill and sawmill, smithy, brewery and the bakehouse all functioned as they should. In short, the domain prospered as I'd known it prosper in my mother's care all through my childhood and my years of training at the fortress and on every visit since.

Haddertun. Why wasn't it enough? Why couldn't I have understood that men do best in every way when they are left to work and bring some order to a limited existence? To make a gift to life of all they have to offer? I knew it later in Khadija's house and in the olive groves, have found it with the Bérgé. But back then at Haddertun contentment on so small a scale was not a thing I valued. Back then I was a fool.

What else is there about that morning to recall while I am looking down upon the fool who knew he loved the woods and meadows of his childhood, yet was determined still to leave them? Up here beyond the toils of man, I shake my head but cannot change my foolish past.

Look back, look down then Garon to see the poor fool and his dog walk out to Shaws beyond the village crossways, scattering a flock of geese...

A two-yoke oxen team, afield already, was ploughing Hobbe's half-acre strip for winter wheat. Real ploughing. Not the sort a bridegroom does in bed. As the son of a free tenant who owed me rent instead of labour, John Hideman knew the business better it was held than any in the village, ploughing in exchange for boon work on his father's holding. As little lads we'd played like cubs together, John and I, wrestling, spearing fish and frogs and shooting ducks along the millstream that we called *the mudsquelch*. Now I watched him plodding steadily from balk to headland with his following of gulls – bare-headed, whistling to the oxen, an upright figure on a huge expanse of field. His was a skill that called for steadiness and strength. It was the reason why I'd come.

'John!' I called his name in common Engleis to stay his team before the goad-boy could attempt the turn.

'Who-a-a!' John waited for me at the plough-tail, leaning on its handles. As I approached him through the stubble with Bruno dancing on before, the sweet, rich smell of fresh-turned earth engulfed us.

'Aye Sir Garry, I'm fit an' thank ye,' he replied to my first question. But as a man who liked to set his thoughts in order before committing them to speech, he paused awhile before he gave an answer to the second.

'Aye sir, I'll train to be a soldier right 'nough. Reckon I've the sprawl for an adventure justabout,' he added after further thought.

John Hideman's face, as broad and brown as earth, showed no concern at leaving Haddertun and two small brothers from his father's second wife, to fight a race of Saracens reputed to eat roasted Christian babies for their breakfasts.

78

He asked no questions, offered no objections.

How easily he pledged his life!

At the time of the Empress Mathilde's War our manor had supported half a dozen men-at arms. But at present there were only four.

'And I'll be needing three to stay behind and see my lady safe,' was what I told the ploughman. 'Then three more freemen to be trained with Jos and me for the campaign.'

'Now then I'll tell ye what. Young Alberic 'ud be middlin' handy with a pike, Sir Garry,' John offered scratching a gnat-bite on his arm.

He had the peasant's habit of looking anywhere but at you when he spoke. As if it would be rude to meet your eyes. 'Rare ol' boy is Albie. Sound as any roach I reckon. If ye could do with two lads from the village, ye couldn' hardly hope to have a better man longside of ye. Exceptin' when the kiddy's drunk.'

'And what does he do then?' I had to ask.

'Gen'rally-always mortifies yer ears by singin' like a wounded crow,' John said. 'An' then tells anyone who'll listen that Sussex is God's Country, an' more'n likely Adam came from wealden clay.'

Later in the manor guardroom, Bertram Glynde, a balding man of forty summers who in his day had served my father as a squire, was ready to make up the band of four who'd join me on croisade. I was his lord, he said, and could command him. But if the choice had been his own, he'd still have gone. He didn't see why sticking Sarsens otherwheres should be much different to sticking pigs in the weald forest, Bertram said. And nor just then did I.

The first English fleet had already left the port of London to cross the Narrow Sea before the autumn storms. Yet it was clear that with an army to equip still, the new king wouldn't follow until spring. That gave the rest of us six months in which to train. But we could not begin too soon. I spent the rest of that day helping the men clear an area behind the barn to make a training ground. So it wasn't until after Vespers that I climbed the manor stairway to resume my duties as a bridegroom. And in the hours between? Had I thought even for a moment of my bed? Or of the bride I'd left there in the tangle of its sheets?

The truth?

The truth was that I had thought of little else. Each time I cut the hard stalk of a thistle or a dock, or thrust a spade into a molehill, I'd felt a sharp thrill of anticipation. Knowing what was still to come.

Jos took my cloak and boots from me outside the chamber door. Inside I found her with her hair unbound, spread out across the pillows as before. Except that this time she was wide awake and waiting.

'Would you think me unladylike if I should bid you welcome, Garon?' she asked with her unsettling smile.

Unladylike? Or did she say *immodest*? It hardly mattered which. Because what mattered was that she said *Garon*, the very first time she had used my name. The next thing she said was that our mothers had examined our bedsheets together to confirmed the union.

'And you would think the way they talked that they could read our fortunes in the stains.' She stunned me with her frankness.

I know that I was stunned, because I have a picture of her looking up at me and waited for an answer that was slow in coming. I can see it now, Elise's face. Her smile no longer certain. Her bright eyes searching mine.

Grey eyes, of course. Her eyes were grey!

I stared into them while she waited. Then stared some more, began to sweat – and finally said... 'Ah, yes good.' Can I believe that I said anything so *FEEBLE*?

It's not that I feel less than other men. It's just that when I am embarrassed, words tend to get clogged between my brain and tongue. Or squeezed into a muffled croak as my throat closes round them, so when they finally do emerge they're generally the wrong ones. '*Ah, yes good.*' My God, it was pathetic! Even thinking of it brings me out in a cold sweat.

But what if I could change the tongue-tied bridegroom of that night to what I have become in this place, here and now? Given all that's happened since

and given one more chance? Could I do better with Elise? I honestly don't
know the answer. Or haven't found it yet.

'I thought you would be glad,' was what she said next as if she hadn't heard my blunder, and if the smile she gave me then was less assured, it was nothing to the awkwardness I felt at having to undress by firelight with her watching every move. I kept my back to her as long as possible. For 'though I mostly don't care how I look I could have wished myself more handsome in the face; and yes, regret as all men do at some time or another that what I have between my legs is nowhere near as fine to look at as it feels – the dragon that reduces to a worm. I had already given it a furtive tug. A quick waggle to improve its length. But still felt the need to shield the thing from her with one hand as I climbed into bed.

We lay unmoving side by side, although it wasn't long before she told me I could touch her. That she wouldn't bite. 'Or if you're lucky even scratch.' She gave a nervous giggle which didn't help at all.

I didn't speak, then couldn't as I watched her sit up to remove her shift. I saw the flutter of a vein in her long throat. Rosy nipples. The shadow of her navel. But above all – or rather well below it – the delicate, the secret hairgrown centre of my need closed softly on the promise of what lay inside!

'Lady, how white! How beautiful you are!'

The words that time were mine, all seven of them, which had to be some kind of an improvement. I muttered them into her neck as with relief I felt myself expand.

'Elise...' My own first use of her baptismal name, and after it, 'I want, oh God I want...'

To start a speech is one thing. To finish it is something else, and by that time I could no longer separate the words from feelings or the feelings from the action. At no time is a man more totally a man, I have now come to think, than when he feels the need to be joined to a woman.

At first it was my body I was riding, not Elise's. My thighs on her. My hands on her. My own flesh hard as iron in her and hot as fire! *ME,*

MINE! MY FLESH, MY NEED! I was the destrier, unstoppable in action, thundering full stretch to the attaint!

Then all at once and to my great surprise I found myself the rider not the horse. A man apart, astride my own unthinking body, hauling on the reins, demanding I should feel what *she* was feeling underneath me, to make a gift to her of what I felt myself. I sensed a movement not my own. I found a skill I had not trained for – and finding it, I heard her moaning, mooing. Heard her cry of sheer astonishment as her womb-head closed round me like a sucking calf.

To prompt the spur. The gallop to the finish. Close to pain and unresisting.

'Mon Dieu!' Her eyes were full of tears, her smile ecstatic.

I forced myself to smile as well, and thank her. But looking back I see that I still wasn't sure what we'd just celebrated. And at that moment lying blugeoned, sandbagged, empty of emotion, all I wanted to be honest was to sleep.

Upward, upward wings the lark,
Singing out his heart in flight...

Parts of me are floating, other parts unable and unwilling to escape. Things happening about me and inside me – surprisingly delicious tingles, the great thumping heartbeats of a creature trapped within my ribs. Something dizzying and stronger than my will – sucking at his shoulder as if my mouth needs what I'm getting elsewhere. Feelings moving, changing, bunched like sheaves and bristling like spines, as slippery and silky as a loosening girdle – unravelling and opening as if my bones have melted. Blissful! Yes, oh yes! And twenty-thousand times more thrilling than I'd hoped!

Now lingering in long repeating echoes.

And not just there, but everywhere – in every part of me right to the end of every finger, every boneless toe!

No other place but this. The world has disappeared – and how could I have ever thought him brutal? How could I imagine that anyone so clumsy could release such glorious, delightful feelings? (And if we weren't heard that time by the men beyond the beam, then all who lie there must be deaf!)

Mon Dieu, I know that I need practice – but then I never guessed… I'd say it felt like heaven if I didn't think the Devil had a hand in it somewhere. If this is the forbidden fruit, 'tis hardly any wonder Eve was tempted!

He is asleep already. It seems that men can't help it afterwards. He smiled to thank me in the middle of a yawn, then closed his eyes and in two shakes began to snore.

Perhaps it's better after all without too many words?

So am I now in love? And if I am, is it with him?
Or rather more disgracefully WITH IT?

CHAPTER EIGHT

Well Garon's not the only one with a campaign plan. I've one as well. I lay in bed this morning staring at the dark folds of its curtains and worked it out most beautifully while he was still asleep.

'Your best plan for keeping him is to make sure he gets a child on you as soon as possible, chérie,' was Maman's best advice while she saw to the packing for her journey home.

'Of all the knights who take the cross, I am persuaded more than half will end by paying an amercement to forswear the oath and stay where they belong,' she said. 'The cost of the journey will show most of them the error of their choice. But add a warm wife with a swollen belly to the argument, and it'd be a cold sort of man who'd turn his back and ride away.'

'Be sure I'll always think of you, Elise, and be there when you need me,' was rather what I wish she'd said before we parted. But she didn't. What Maman did was kiss me soundly on both cheeks, remind me that too kind a mistress makes for idle servants, then turn her own back on me to ride out with her laden mules.

And Maman will never know, because I've never told her, how much I'm going to miss her bustling backside and her endless good advice. Hod calls me things like 'duck' and 'lambkin' – but never 'chérie' or 'petite'. There's no one now that Maman's gone to use those names to me, and that's so sad!

I'd felt as happy as a queen that second night when Garon showed me what marriage could be like. I smiled into my mirror the next morning, a finished woman as I thought. But nothing's ever finished really. There's always more to come, if not from Maman then from Hod who has her own ideas of how to start a child.

'His fetch stinks. There's your first good sign,' she said with one hand on my shoulder while we strained for a last glimpse of Maman's palfrey from the window. 'But mebbe too much on the sheets for choice an' not enough inside ye?'

She chuckled grimly. 'Eat all ye can of quinces, honey and sweet almonds is what I say. An' keep 'im at it while 'e's hot. I've never 'eld with them as think ye shouldn't take it in too regular – an' if you'll listen to ol' Hod, ye won't be too particular about Church-rulings neither, duck, for all the days ye ought to be at prayer. Bless me, if priests could 'ave their way you'd only do it thrice a week!'

She tucked a tuft of iron grey hair into a coif which never has and never will contain it. 'Time enough for prayers, I say, when you've a brace of 'ealthy boys at foot.'

Nor was I spared a lecture from My Lady Constance on the subject, before she left to join her husband at their Meresfeld manor an hour's ride to the north.

'You should know that my son is an exuberant young man, who'll never walk if he can run,' she said. 'They say King Richard would sell London to finance his expedition if he could find a buyer for it, and you will find Sir Garon much the same. When something captures his attention he embraces it entirely – be it a competition, an archbishop's cross. Or a marriage bed, my dear.'

She nodded when she saw I understood, for however she'd defended Garon's actions at the fortress they clearly weren't her own idea of any kind of sense. He wouldn't be the first young man, she pointed out, to fall beneath the spell of a new bride. And if that happy circumstance should chance – the benefit, his mother was convinced, must be felt by us all.

Which brings me to my perfect plan. (Well if not entirely perfect, it's workable at least.) In the first month I act on Maman's, Hoddie's, Lady Constance's advice to make myself attractive to my husband. I know a little now about the method – and judging from the way he acts it shouldn't be too hard to get results.

I was amazed at first that anyone as incoherent as Sir Garon could be so desperate about his wants, although having seen him on the tourney field I suppose I might have guessed. He called me white and beautiful that second night, which came as a surprise. And whether he intended to or no, his body's taught me something even I had not expected.

Well then when I've reduced him to a trembling husk in bed – say by the second month, I'll please him out of it in any way I can devise. Find ways to use the guarderobe and pick my nose without him seeing. Serve him delicious food to tempt his appetite. Weave spotless linen for his shirts. Change everything inside his manor for the better – and sing for him, he likes it when I sing – and make him to smile a little more.

Then by month three, as Hoddie's most attentive pupil I'll astonish him with news that I'm with child (if that's not already obvious by month two). Which leaves me with three months in hand to show him that a lively bedfellow, a well-run home, the promise of a son and heir, are worth a good deal more than an amercement of six shillings to free him from a thoughtless oath!

I don't say it will be easy. But I'm sure that I can do it if I try.

The day his mother and his little sister left us, our first day on our own, Garon told me that henceforth his squire and man-at-arms would sleep with us in our chamber. And when I mentioned that in Lancaster no married lady would submit to such indignity, he just said things were different in Sussex and bedded both down by the fire. He even brought his verminous excuse for a dog inside, and all of them laughed at the shriek I gave when Bruno poked his wet nose through the bed-hangings.

A battle lost. But I've a war to win and will not be disheartened. Although we've yet to ride the outer boundaries of the manor, I have explored within and found a deal in need of my attention. The house is bigger than I'm used to, and even with the fires lit there's a chill about the hall. Limewash is flaking from the walls in several of the storerooms. They shutter the east chambers to keep out the flies, while anyone with half a brain can see they need to move the dungheap from the yard below them.

The whole place could do with freshening and scrubbing, and I'll not to hang my tapestries until it's done. We need more cats. There's mouse-dirt in the kitchen. We need more greenery and lavender for every room – fresh rushes every fortnight (I love that grassy smell!). I want a private garden like the one at home with shingle paths and strawberries and fruit espaliers

– a trellised arbour and a cushioned bench and lavender and gillyflowers –
and yes, a painted statue. We have to have a statue! Cupid with his bow?

The sour steward and that hatchet-faced old beldame, Agnès, who was
here with Garon's father, may need some telling what to do. But the other
servants all seem willing and I've old Hod to help me.

Meantime this afternoon... Heavens – in the next half-hour if that's Sext
the church bell's striking? – we're all to ride to Lewes, to see about a loan for
Garon to finance the enterprise that I'm determined to prevent!

'Hod, are you there?'

I'll need my watchet gown (the blue-green suits my colouring), my riding
cloak and something quick to eat while I am dressing.

'Hoddie! Hodierne!' Where in the name of mercy has that woman got to?

The steward said we'd find the moneylender's house just off the town's main
thoroughfare before we reach the fortress, in one of the steep cross-streets
that run down to the Saxon wall. In fact, it's little more than a dark cleft
between two lopsided buildings whose upper storeys all but touch above our
heads – a lane so narrow that we've had to leave the horses at the inn with
Bertram and make our way to it on foot.

'There then, be sure to take a rosary with you into that tatterdemalion's den,'
Hod warned me while she helped me dress. The Jews who crucified Our Lord
are known to be in league with the ungodly powers of darkness, she insists,
and can walk backwards with their eyes shut if they choose. Their stores of
gold and silver come from mortgaging their souls to Satan.

'True as Holy Writ, as anyone 'ud tell you,' Hoddie told me.

'Good faith, such goings on! 'Tis blowed about their Jewish rhabbis only
drink the blood an' cut away the podskins of poor little Christian lads in
their abuseful rites! Ye'll need to take some amulets along an' all,' she
thought. 'A black cat's paw's a certain-sure protection 'gainst any kind of
curse.'

Old Agnès in the background offered similar advice. 'A bag of clover tied
under-skirts 'ull save ye from ol' Nick hisself if ye should chance to rub
against the man,' she said and made a sign against the evil eye.

I told her I would think about it, which Hoddie rightly took to mean I wouldn't.

'Leastways wear your crucifix, my lamb – look 'ere 'tis, you'll 'ardly know you 'ave it on.'

Her lack of chin makes Hoddie's whole face wobble when she's agitated. But still there is something comforting about the way she fusses.

Inside the passageway, at shoulder height, someone has chalked a crude graffito of a hook-nosed Jew in a cornatum hat beside a rough-planked door.

'Depend on it, 'tis shabby by design.'

Steward Kempe's a tall, stern kind of man of more than middle age who must have had the pock at some time in his youth, his skin's so marked and pitted. He has a jutting lower lip, lank hair and a singularly long face on a long body. And yet he knows his business one would think.

'These Asrelites will never show their wealth for fear of thieves,' he scoffs. 'They'd skin a flint if they could sell it for its hide and fat.' But now he's rapping with his dagger-hilt on the plank door. 'Ho there, Jacob ben Aaron!'

Gracious, I can hardly wait to see inside.

'Ho, Jacob! Open to Sir Garon and his lady, who would do business with you.'

Part of the upper door frame is damp and rotten. Below where it is sounder, a shuttle-shaped container's nailed up at an angle with some kind of a strange sign on it like a three-fingered hand.

I wonder… But how odd, I feel somehow as if I've been here before – as if I know exactly how the Jew will look and what he's going to say. Oh, I can hear the tumble of a lock and hinges creaking…

For an agent of the Devil the old man who opens it looks remarkably benign. But not as I imagined. He's wearing gabardine and a close bonnet, both expensively dyed black without a tinge of green. Beard's sparse and grey, curled into ringlets (but I mustn't stare).

'Ah, Master Kempe, shlomot.'

He speaks in heavily accented French. 'Come in, come in!' He hurries us inside and locks the door, begs us excuse the times and the necessity to be discreet.

'Thirty of my race were slaughtered by the London mob but three weeks

88

past for daring to approach the new king at his coronation. We are confused with Saracens and are not safe abroad,' he tells us with a shrug.

'My lord knight, I already know something of your affairs. Come, let us be comfortable. Mistress, you're welcome.' He motions to a fringed and padded stool. 'Be seated if you will.'

The old Jew lifts a curtain that conceals a stairway. 'Sara, yakirati! We have a Christian lady in our house who has need of refreshment.' He looks this time in my direction and smiles within his beard. 'If only to convince her we're not cannibals entirely in our tastes.'

His voice is rasping, nasal. Teeth crooked and discoloured. But when he smiles, his sad little eyes are near-submerged in wrinkles. It seems to me that Jews are not so different in the end to other men. Christ after all was raised by Jews, was born a Jew himself – and I'm sorry but I really think I like this old man. Which is why I'm smiling back at him to show a friendly face.

You couldn't say his room is large. But such furnishings, I've never seen their like! Brass and silver, polished wood lit from a window high up in the wall – Turkey carpets, satin cushions, damask cloth and fine Venetian glass. It smells of dusty fabric, of some musky perfume I can't put a name to, and one whole wall is honeycombed with racks of parchment – scrolls tied with scarlet ribbons, nested like pigeons in a cote.

'Now Sir Knight, and Master Kempe – how is it I can help you?' old Jacob asks.

'I'm sworn to join Archbishop Baldwin on the Kings' Croisade next year.' (When you hear Garon speak it isn't hard to tell he's at a disadvantage.)

'You seek to free Jerusalem of Saracens?'

'Yes naturally.' My husband's arms are crossed – big hands tucked into his armpits.

'Yet when they first captured it your Christians slaughtered everyone within the city – Muslims, Jews and even those of their own faith. It's said that sixty thousand perished. Whereas we're told that Saladin permits men of all faiths to worship there in peace.'

Garon gives a snort of laughter. 'And you believe THAT – when we know, when everyone has heard they skewered babies, stabled horses in Christ's Sepulchre?'

The old man contemplates him, seems about to argue then heaves a sigh instead. 'There's no future in disputing rumours neither of us can be sure of,' he remarks. 'But I think you were about to tell me why you've come?'

'To raise funds for the undertaking.' Garon tells him bluntly.

'So? We talk of finance.' Jacob leans across his table to a sand-glass and turns it up to show the business has begun. 'It would be idle I suppose to think that anything but finance would induce a Christian knight to knock on a Jew's door. So tell me, have you calculated the sum you'll need to fund the venture?'

The old body, Sara, who must be his wife has brought in a tray of sugared fruit, with wine and silver goblets to set beside him on the table. She's small, round shouldered, with full breasts the distinctive profile of her race – wears a chemise, and over it a carsey-perse striped gown, primrose and cinder grey with a plain yellow sash. A length of green silk's wound about her head and knotted at the brow. Gold pendants swing from both her ears. And now as she's about to leave, she smiles – eyes black, intelligent as Jacob's and as kind. (I really like her stripey carsey-perse.)

'Fifty marks.' The way that Garon says it sounds more like a challenge than a reasonable request. 'That's what we'll need to fund a year's campaign with transport for two horses and four men besides myself.'

"T'is a realistic calculation,' the steward's anxious to confirm, 'taking every circumstance into account.

'A guess, in other words.'

Jacob brings the goblets, careful not to touch us as he sets them down. 'Our faith permits us to share a little wine on working days, although in moderation.' He smiles again into the spirals of his beard. 'A small cup clarifies the mind they say, even as a large one clouds it.'

I sip the wine. It's very sweet.

'You wish me to advance you fifty marks? A prodigal amount by any reckoning. The problem is...'

'You haven't heard what I can offer as collateral.' The interruption Garon's.

'You are about to tell me I believe?'

'I would be willing to offer you a mortgage on my land at Haddertun against the loan.' He tries to make it sound like a concession.

90

'My dear young man, I was about to point out that your Church prohibits you from pledging property to members of our faith, against a pilgrimage or any other Christian undertaking.'

'Officially.' Kempe dares to place a cautious hand on Garon's arm. 'But you and I have dealt before, Jew, and you may be sure we'll honour any reasonable terms.'

'Reasonable terms?'

Old Jacob sets his goblet back upon the cloth to wipe his beard with one long ink-stained finger. 'But there you have the heart of it, my friend. We both of us are men of business, are we not? So let's be plain, as men of business we must weigh all the risks before we make a heskem – a contract, as you say.'

'The manor prospers, Jew. The risk is slight.'

'Not from where I stand, Master Kempe. You will forgive me, but what if your young Lord should meet his Maker overseas – or mine if he's unlucky? What if the crops should fail at Haddertun? What if its livestock should be visited with murrain?' He nods. 'Oh yes, it happens.

'What if, for no fault of your own, you were unable to repay me interest out of revenues? Do you imagine that the King's Court, or your Church's, would uphold the claim of an accursed Jew excluded by all English laws from croisade usury?' He spreads his hands and shrugs again expressively. 'No, no my friend. Much as it grieves me to decline, I tell you by the Holy Shabbat that I'm unable to do business with a crucesignatus.'

An uncomfortably long silence.

Old Jacob's looking, not at Garon but at me – and all at once I see his point. I know what he is thinking!

Maybe, just possibly…

More silence, endless. My husband and his steward dumb as fishes!

It's not for me to speak. (I know I tend to do things the moment I decide them. But not this time – I can't!) You're only a spectator here, Elise. For heaven's sake don't let the wine go to your head!

I'm fidgeting, but mustn't – mustn't say it. Not a peep…

'But what if the agreement should be with the lady of the manor?' (And in the VERY MOMENT I decided not to!)

91

Worse still, I'm holding out my goblet to be refilled.

'What if the bond is in my name?' My voice, sounding shrill and far too loud.

All three heads turn. Three pairs of eyebrows raised in blank astonishment.

And, oh damnation – WHY! Why do I DO these things? Why couldn't I have kept my silly mouth closed, instead of blurting the first hasty thing that popped into my head?

So sure when I am speaking. So foolish when I pause to think!

Oh, what in God's Own name can ever have possessed me
to so forget myself as to destroy my perfect -
well maybe not so very perfect – plan?

I AM A HOPELESS CASE!

CHAPTER NINE

When I look back to those last months before I left for the croisade, it's not the preparation, not the training in the field beside the barn, the purchases of arms and armour that concern me. The thing I think about – and must think more about – is what Elise said, what Elise did. Above all what she did to me.

To take the day we rode to Lewes to the moneylender's house, I'd known from what she'd said in bed that she was not afraid to speak her mind. But how could I have guessed what she'd agree with the old skinflint? I know he must have heard about her kinship with the Countess, whose patronage secured his business in the town. But how to guess what she'd propose? Or that he'd see her as a safer risk than me?

If the loan should be recorded in Elise's name, he said, for her domestic use, then yes he might advance a sum, but not considering the times as much as fifty marks. And although he'd smiled and bowed and poured more wine, he wouldn't budge from his best offer of four hundred silver shillings – a little more than thirty marks, repayable within five years at a usance rate of one percent a sennight.

'Which, as you will have calculated, Master Kempe, is six and twenty shillings to be paid every quarter-year,' he told my steward, blowing off the chalk to roll and tie the document for storage.

Less than I had hoped, it was enough to arm us and leave something over for our transport on the ships. Archbishop Baldwin was offering a shilling every day besides to all who entered his battalion. And if the worst came and our funds ran out, I didn't think a man of God would let his people starve.

We left Lewes Borough on the afternoon we saw the Jew, by the old wooden bridge that spans the river. Riding before my wife with Kempe behind by way of the chalk road which skirts the salt pans to climb Ram's Combe hill, I reined my horse where the track widenened to let Elise draw level. As she rode up a flock of water birds rose from the river flats below. Their wings flashed like a thousand blades against the clouds, and watching them I wished I had the gift of words. Hugh would have found some charming way of thanking her for what she'd done.

But, 'Thank you, Lady,' was the best I could come up with.

She'd missed the birds, was frowning at the ruts that ridged the track. 'I don't suppose I ever will know why I did it,' she said. 'I speak too often without pause for thought. Perhaps I've caught it from my maid.'

Which was the moment that I found my voice, to say how fortunate it was that she had spoken when she did. To tell her the agreement served us well, and then go on to spoil it by repeating the lame 'Thank you, Lady,' words I'd used before!

'The agreement might serve well enough if I was ready to become a widow,' she said bitterly. 'Can you explain me to myself, My Lord? Explain why should I help you leave when I am bound by vows to keep you close and serve you as a good wife ought, at board and and in our bed?'

The breeze blew strands of hair across her face, and even as she fumbled to secure them, the invitation in Elise's clear grey eyes was plain enough to send me down another track entirely. I saw the tip of her pink tongue dart out between her lips. It felt as if she'd licked me. And by then of course I was in no fit state to answer. The eyes, the hair, the tongue, the talk of bed had unexpectedly enlarged the situation.

They say a man with an erection thinks only where it points. Mine pointed on toward the manor and our curtained bed.

> Goosey, goosey gander, whither shall ye wander?
> Upstairs, downstairs or in my lady's chamber...

I took a special meaning from the nursery verse in those first weeks of marriage. Yet up here and in my present state it's hard to see how anything as commonplace as frequent copulation could have had such a shattering effect.

94

'Love is a fool's game,' was what I'd heard in barracks. 'It leads a man to ruin.' But in truth all men are libertines by nature, and now I see that what I fell in love with was as much or more to do with me and my own body as it was to do with hers. It's said the liver is the seat of the hot humours. But I was governed by another part. To put it crudely I was governed by my own insistent cock.

It wasn't sense but madness. That's what I thought in the first moments of release; the thing I always thought when I had finished with a whore or eased myself with my own hand. But with Elise it was a madness of a different kind. The stale feeling of remorse I felt those other times lasted for days or even weeks. But each time I spent myself inside Elise, as soon as my heart stopped pounding and my blood subsided – in the mere space it took to close my eyes and tell myself I'd had enough, the tide swept in again. I needed more!

I might be judged and damned for it, but was no longer in control. I had succumbed to lust. The Church that claimed me for croisade could never have condoned it. Mine was a fall from grace, the sin that priests warned men of constantly – the carnal snare of Eve, or Jezebel, or the black sorceress, Morgan. They'd claim the woman tainted and bewitched me, blocked my path to virtue. Yet still I gorged and gorged again on the forbidden fruit. 'If this is sin,' I thought, 'then I'm a sinner natural born!'

Even when I sought relief in open air and in the training that we undertook each morning in the muddy field behind the barn – in oaths and laughter and exchanging blows with other men – I had this *wanting* feeling all the time. Burning in my belly and my throat. Goading me like a tormenting gadfly. What can I say? I was a beast in rut, a wolfhound with a juicy bone! At the mere thought of bed and of Elise my entire body hardened. I longed to lay my hand against her hand, my arm against her arm, my leg against her thigh. Sharp thrills stabbed through me chest to groin, to burn like wounds and damp my under-drawers. In all my dreams, whatever I was doing I was hard as wood! Even the act of straddling to piss teased me with untoward sensations…

All right, I mustn't wallow in all this. Not here. How can it help me now?

I started to reward myself for tasks achieved in training. For targets truly struck. Or just for riding home. If it took Raoul more than four hundred hoofbeats betwixt the orchard and the stables, I told myself I'd do it in broad daylight. I'd make her stoop to show me all her secret places. There were no limits to my fantasies although I never told her of them. How could I tell a gentle girl like that how frantically my body clamoured for an entry into hers? How much I wanted to be uncontrolled and brutal, to take her standing up or lying down, or on all fours if she'd submit to such indignity?

Well I couldn't. Instead I rode about the place in a wet trance so hard in front you'd think the thing had grown a backbone... That's how it was and how it feels when I recall what it was like to be inside her filling her entirely, cleaving through her wet, warm flesh towards a lightning strike of pleasure...

Oh God, I knew this wouldn't do me any good. It can't be what the Bérgé can have meant by learning from my past mistakes. Where am I in their catalogue? I need to have it clear.

I'd say the long and short of it is that I was too stupid at the time to see our union, the thing we both enjoyed so much, as anything but an unwarranted distraction. A blighted urge. The temptings of the Devil – Satan's game.

But that of course was all before Khadija.

> *Fair gentle lady of my dreams,*
> *With form so shapely, yet so slender;*
> *The Lord God made you this, it seems,*
> *With flesh so fair, smooth, soft and tender,*
> *To keep you for my eyes alone;*
> *No joys from others I have known*
> *Whilst I possess you in my dreams!*

Elise's voice was like a linnet's, soft and clear, and that song chimed with my feelings for her. Each night the Church permitted it we were conjoined as man and wife. And often in the morning too. And not infrequently at twilight. I only had to touch her and like dry tinder I was set alight.

My gratitude for all she brought me in our curtained bed made it difficult for me to deny her, and at her bidding I sent Jos and Bertram, even Bruno, to the outer chamber.

'I would have thought that you'd prefer me to yourself,' was how she put it, 'without the ears of half the manor cocked in our direction.'

That autumn when we rode together out to the manor fields, along the fordroughs, up onto the downland ridges to view the changing colours of the sea beyond, she commented on everything. Found everything delightful. She talked a great deal, smiled sunny smiles and laughed without apparent reason, throwing back her head to let the sound fly free. Her laughter made a lovely sound like water over pebbles. Everything about Elise was lovely. The shade of her grey eyes, pale in the centre, almost sandy, dark at the edges almost blue. The shape of her mouth, shape of her breasts, the straight line of Elise's neck, the softness of her hair, the clean smell of her skin. But there was more to her than loveliness, as I would soon discover.

Increasingly, when I came in upon my wife from hawking or from weapon practice with the men, to find her at her distaff or her loom, Elise surprised me with suggestions for improvement to the manor. As if we needed more than Haddertun could offer. With quite a dozen stools and chests to stumble over in the house, it seemed she wanted more. At her behest I had the stable dungheap moved to make a pallisaded garden for her in the yard. Another time I let her hang in our bedchamber her tapestry of a fat woman bathing. And although to smell a bit of sweat and shit is no more than man's natural state, I took to bathing too for her in a tub before the fire.

'They say a husband's like new linen,' she declared. 'They both improve with washing!'

Because she said she'd like me with a beard I gave up shaving for a while, until the stubble grew too itchy to be borne. I let her trim my broken nails. I let her take on Jos's work to comb out nits and trim my hair – and brushed her own long hair myself until it crackled. But when she begged me, as I'd known all along she would, to abandon my croisade, I smiled and told her nothing would be ventured until springtime – and then reached out to take her in my arms.

In my simplicity I thought that I could please Elise as much as she pleased me. But I was wrong.

In fact the more time I spent in my wife's company, the less I seemed to know her. She was a mystery to me, a whole book of mysteries.

Who can understand a woman?

One moment she'd comply with all I asked, as sweet as sugar. The next she'd swing round like a wind-vane, to tell me what I must do as if she were my equal. Complaining when I overset things. Even when I farted. Her voice when she was moved to raise it gained a hard Lancastrian edge. She wanted linen on the tables; shutters on the windows, benches strewn with cushions. She acted by no rules of deference I recognised, as busy as a bedbug round the place. Creating a commotion; confounding everyone's ideas of what was fitting for a wife.

But, be honest Garon, is that really what disturbed you most in those first months of marriage? Think about it.

With no one but yourself to deceive, there is no point in calling up the past if you can't face the fact that it was when she seemed less interested in your body – when your storm of climax came without the lightning strike – that you felt mostly cheated by Elise.

'Are you asking me to place our marriage above my trade of arms, above my honour as a soldier?'

He's truculent, nonplussed.

'Heavens, what has honour to do with this croisade? Do you think I can't see that's just another pretty word men use to women when they wish to leave them at their sewing and go off to kill someone or other – like barnfowl cocks and forest bucks, fighting for the sheer pleasure of the thing!'

(I do like the kind of pretended conversations you can have in daydreams. I usually indulge in them when I'm at the loom, or spinning yarn from carded wool. They give one such a chance to be decided without unpleasant consequences. To say just what you like and get away with it!)

'So tell me what it is, My Lord, that makes men seek to hurt and kill each

other? Why they won't be satisfied until they've scarred another's flesh or broken half his bones?'

That's what I'd like to ask him to his face. It's what all women want to know. Why must men SPOIL things so? Do they consider anyone except themselves? Has any woman in the history of the world ever really understood a man?

'Lady, you know full well that we are summoned to a Holy War, blessed by the Church. It is the highest duty any soldier can perform.'

'The truth wrapped in clean linen is still the truth, My Lord.'

Or maybe?: 'You men are worst than beasts, for beasts have never found it needful to justify their lust for blood as honourable and holy.'

(All things I'd like to say, if only I dared voice them!)

We had our worst exchange, a real one, last Tuesday evening after Vespers, when I begged him to put Archbishop Baldwin and King Richard and the Holy City of Jerusalem out of his mind for once, and think instead of all we had in Sussex. I let my tongue run on too readily, I know I do. I shouldn't have provoked him. But having gone so far I somehow had to venture further, and ask him to consider if he'd not been happier with me at Haddertun than anywhere, with anyone, in his entire existence? Why could he not forget his wretched oath, I asked, and stay where he belonged?

He doesn't say much as a general rule. But he surprised us both on Tuesday by finding all the words he needed.

'Forget? How in the devil's name do you think I can I forget?' he shouted. 'Do you expect the Kings' Croisade to wait on your convenience? Do you think I'd break my pledge, to cringe at home like a cur in a kennel?'

We'd been sitting on a bench before the fire in our bedchamber with goblets of heated wine cupped in our hands. I nursed mine like a fledgeling while I listened to the wood crackling in the hearth – and told him that if God could not protect His own most holy city, He hardly should expect our Englishmen to do it for Him.

'Never tell a man he's stupid,' Maman counselled, 'even if he's silly as a snipe, because it's not a thing he's likely to forget.'

So – 'I think you should uphold your other pledges first, to honour your contract to love your wife and cleave to her to your life's end or hers,' was *how I put it to him, resting my free hand on Garon's appealingly. 'Do you not see, My Lord, that it is easier to go than to remain? It takes more courage to stand out against men's expectations than to prove yourself a hero? Sir Hugh at least has the consideration to stay at home to guard your mother and their child.' I tried, intended to sound reasonable.*

But here's the thing. It wasn't clever of me was it to compare him to Sir Hugh.

'What?' He said it twice as if he didn't understand. 'WHAT did you say?!' Then made it quite clear that he did.

'CONSIDERATION? Is that what you imagine keeps that man at home?' He made me jump by yelling it right in my face, and then sprang up so suddenly the bench upended, to land me with a thump on the hard floor. 'A faint-hearted coward. That's what de Bernay is. And is that what you'd have ME BE?' he shouted at the tapestry of David and Bathsheba. 'To make me into a castrated wether bleating in the fold?'

It was the first time I had seen him in a rage. I thought that he looked silly with his hair on end where he had raked it and his dog-brown eyes ablaze – knew I looked silly too, sprawled on the floor and soaked with wine.

And so I laughed. Another big mistake.

What I regret about that night was that it was the first, the only time I lost my temper with her. She said it took more courage to stand out against men's expectations than to prove myself a hero, and in the need to tell her she was wrong I found my voice. But not the voice I would have chosen if I'd been less agitated.

'Your business is to get a child. You can't say I have shirked *my* duty there,' I shouted at her with a cruelty I'm ashamed of. Even at the time I knew it was unfair. And then I lost control and overset her in the rushes, and noticed even as I did it that the wine which soaked her night-rail showed the outlines of her belly and her nipples.

She laughed. I was the craven cur again afraid of being mocked. Although looking back I almost have to share the joke of that confused young man's confused emotions. Outraged yet stimulated. Angry but frustrated. In love with what her body did to his and his to her. Hearing what she said and yet denying who she was, and what she needed.

Did I come even close to knowing her at all before I left the manor? And would I now given the chance? Would there be room for understanding now? Think about it, Garon.

I think that was the time. The moment that I could have turned back from the brink, but didn't. And I think what makes it even worse is that I knew, but wouldn't face the fact that she was right.

I spent that night with Jos and Bertram in the room beyond the beam, the first time that I'd done so when the Church permitted otherwise. Hard words are hard to swallow. So neither of us tried. Out in the training field next morning I was glad of someone else to fight, and if I'd ever wavered in my undertaking to be part of the croisade, the thing was settled from that moment forward.

Early in November on All Hallows Day my mother brought prematurely into the world a living child. A stepbrother who might have stood as a reproach to us for failing to conceive a baby of our own, had he not proved too weak to thrive and died within two days of birth.

As soon as news of it reached Haddertun, I left in sheeting rain to ride the four leagues to Meresfeld. Jos saddled up two mounts, my gelded rounsey and a little Powis mare. But being in no mood for company, I left him scowling at my horse's arse. Even sent the dog back from the outer gate.

Down at the mill I passed a number of our bondmen perched on ladders, lopping willows on the mudsquelch with split sack bonnets on their heads to shield them from the rain. Some of them downed tools when I rode by, and Jordan Smith called out a greeting as I crossed the bridge into the forest.

What I remember mostly of the ride is how the woods felt in rain. With water dripping from the trees. The smell of decomposing leaves. Dank tunnels of contorted limbs and webs of twigs already bare. There were still tales of wolf packs in the wealdwood. But nobody I knew had ever seen or heard one. Smoke rose from sodden hovels in the clearings. Ponies whinnied from their pickets. At Uckfeld Ford beyond the pale of Ashdowne, my horse was forced to shoulder through a herd of wet red cattle up to their hocks in muddy water, and at Ringles Cross where ash gave way to birch, we were caught in a downpour.

I stood beside my mother's bed in her small upper chamber, waterlogged and dripping like a faulty bung. My little sister, Edmay, came to hold my hand.

'The baby's dead,' she told me with a woeful face. 'It was too small to play with me, and then it died.'

'I'm sorry,' I said awkwardly. I've never been quite comfortable with children or known how to please them. 'So sorry,' I repeated to my mother, blotting my wet forehead with a sleeve.

'Does *sorry* mean you will go back on your decision to leave Haddertun without an heir?'

She'd changed her view. Her child's loss made the difference in my mother's mind it seems between my staying and departing.

A little more than two score years of age, that day she suddenly seemed older. Her face was haggard and her voice was cold. Both cheerless as the rain. 'Or have you brought me news that your wife's managed to conceive?' she asked.

I said I hadn't, but that we were still hopeful.

'Then for the present I'd remind you of your duty to remain. You were raised from the cradle, Garon, to protect our Haddertun domain, and God alone knows nothing good will come from leaving it.'

And as she spoke I saw mortality in the pinched lines of my mother's face, and for the first time faced the thought that she might even die while I was off abroad. But what I told her was that for my very life I'd not forswear my oath to the archbishop.

'While I'm away Elise will need your help to keep a watchful eye on Haddertun and Steward Kempe,' I added, dropping to one knee beside her chair. Hoping for her understanding and affection. Waiting for her hand to touch me. Remembering the time she took me on her own knee – was it only once? – before they sent me away to Lewes to be trained.

But then a door slammed, followed by the sound of footsteps on the stair. My mother sighed and closed her eyes as if to banish me from sight.

'Grown man you may be. But I'd slap you if I thought that it would serve a purpose, Garon,' she said wearily. 'If you would only listen.'

'My dear, you waste your patience on him.' Sir Hugh de Bernay interrupted from the doorway, appearing in a draught of damp air. In hunting gear and mud-caked boots. He crossed his arms, and so at once did I.

'Much as we all admire his enterprise, I fear Sir Garon's proof to argument,' he said, 'more suited as he is to action, than to any kind of reasoned thought.'

I'd come prepared to tell him I was sorry he had lost a son, but took the bait instead.

'So tell us pray what suits *your* brilliance, Sir?' I burst out – knowing he was taunting me, knowing what he wanted from me, but unable to resist the challenge. 'Are hunts and tourneys the most dangerous enterprises you'd consider? And are you now become a carpet knight, so craven that you'd rather hide behind a woman's skirts than risk your life where men are, fighting for Jerusalem?'

'Ah, *for Jerusalem*? Is that what so attracts you? A place you've studied, I suppose, to understand its history and guarantee its future as a Christian kingdom?'

'That is enough, the pair of you!'

The harshness of my mother's tone sent little Edmay into a scrambling retreat. 'You know as well as I do, Garon, that Hugh's needed to defend the manors in King Richard's absence against his brother's claims. There's no one in the land who'd trust Earl John as far as they could pitch him.'

She turned to Hugh. 'And My Lord it would be best I think if you refrained from goading my poor son into worse manners than he has already shown.'

At which de Bernay bowed, as bow he must to she whose fortune governed his. 'Do not concern yourself my dear. The thing is scarcely in my power. For as far as I can see the only course that's like to make Sir Garon's manners worse, is that which he's embarked on.'

103

His black eyes glittered. 'Give the whelp a month of camp life with King Richard, and by comparison with what he will be then you'd judge him now the very soul of courtesy.

'That is, if you come back alive, boy.' He arched his brows at me with deliberate provocation.

I had a savage vision of the man in the tournament with my spear stuck through his gaping mouth, wished that it could have been Sir Hugh – and wished him onward to damnation!

'Oh I'll come back, you may be sure of that – and come back fit and ready to defend what's mine.' My deepest most emphatic voice.

'We'll wait with bated breath.'

'I'm not a whelp Sir, neither. You misname me. Nor yet *your boy* let's have that clear. Nor have been since I won my belt and spurs.'

The lamplight gleamed on Hugh de Bernay's teeth. As ever, humour was his chosen weapon and as ever it struck home.

'Not *my boy*? *My dear young man* then, if that is what you've grown to be? I'll treasure the idea of your maturity for every day you're absent. I vow I'll and take it out and polish whilst praying for your safe return.'

Long after I had left the manor, I could hear his jeering laughter ring in my head. If I listen I can hear it still.

CHAPTER TEN

'Every day muhibb, a page of story.' That's how Khadija put it in her moonlit garden. Her words alive in me when so much else has died.

'I'd recommend you make another climb through your own memories. Your history if you like. Climb that long path and then look back to see if you can't learn from your mistakes.' That's what the Bérgé said.

My head above the clouds, adrift from the world of men as I set out my memories in order like tallies on a board, to see what they add up to.

I see King Richard's citadel across the Narrow Sea above the River Vienne in the Touraine, see it clearly in the pale sunlight of early spring with yellow banners mirrored in the water and fruit trees flowering in its courts. Wheels trundle constantly across the river bridge an arrow's flight from our camp in the water meadows. Stacked carts labour up the steep approaches to the fortress, pass both ways through the town below. It seems so real, King Richard's citadel.

More real than I do, looking back.

We never saw the old queen, Eléonore, although we heard that she was in the Chinon fortress – and only ever saw her son the King but once on horseback in the distance. Across the river there was space enough for all of his recruits, and more besides. For knowing what healthy males with cash in hand are like, King Richard brought in whores, a second army of them, shipped in by wagon-loads from Tours and Angers to keep his soldiers out of mischief.

I shared my tent with Jos and Bertram. Alberic and John slept with the horses in the canvas stables they'd erected for them near the river – where the pair of them proceeded to reduce the scale of the great muster to something they could cope with, and compare unfavourably with Sussex.

'Pon my carcase, I've seen a tidy sight more *sheep* 'un this at Lewes any fair day,' said Albie in field Engleis of the huge tent city.

'Ye'r not wrong there boy,' John Hideman thought, 'an' better managed too. We'd be ashamed back home I'd say to waste so much good grazin' for the want of wattles an' a likely dog or two.'

'If only soldiers were as good as sheep at doing what they're bidden,' considered Jos, who'd come with me to see how Raoul was faring. 'Same goes for whores,' he added with a wink to make the others laugh.

Although in truth we none of us had seen so many people gathered in one place, and thinking back I am amazed how quickly we became accustomed to live with such a multitude of men.

But I am running on ahead, and wasting time on Richard's muster in Touraine – when what I should be thinking of is how I left Elise that spring, of how things were between us when we parted. Of whether we were joined by more than church vows and a warm rod of flesh? Of how much we'd gained from one another in six months of marriage – and of how much I destroyed?

There'd been no further arguments the day that I returned from Meresfeld. There would have been no point, because by then we both knew that the die was cast.

The winter that year was mild and wet. By Christmastide the field we used for training had turned into the kind of quagmire Sussex folk call *winter butter*. We rode to Lewes, Kempe and I, to make our first payment of interest to the Jew out of the manor tithes. I took the men for game drives in the forest, fought them against each other in the manor courtyard and practiced archery at butts.

'*The manor squad*' I called them in my own mind. It had a working ring to it I liked. And by and large they all did well. Bertram and Jos competed with me for the best scores in our contests. John had a good seat in the saddle. And Alberic, though bandy in the leg department was still a hulking lad. A big fair fellow with a flaxen beard, he waved a sword as lustily and flung a spear as far as anyone could ask. Yet like a plough-steer bred for gentleness, remained too kind to make a first class soldier.

106

"T'ud be a shame to tell a lie,' young Albie said when he was shown how to disable an opponent with a left kick to the groin. 'To say the truth it don't seem nice to do that even to a Sarsen,' he believed. 'I can best him the kiddy right 'nough, make no mistake o' that. But I'm no one for gelding bullocks, never was. Reckon I'd as soon hamstring 'im in the ord'nary way. Or else take off 'is head.'

He fumbled at his shirt strings with fingers like flag tubers, convinced like every other villein that he'd never change. 'Aye Sir, the short an' long of it same as I said, is that I'd sooner kill the bugger dead than tarrify 'is nutmegs.'

The days by then were short. Spending more hours in the house together than out of it apart, Elise and I preserved a kind of truce. There are few things more warming on a winter's night when it comes down to it than a live woman in your arms, and the least of our encounters in the bed were still better by a league than any other indoor pastime. For her part, Elise avoided any mention of croisade, while I made nothing of her failure to conceive, when every month unwelcome as confession her red courses sent me out to sleep beyond the beam.

I swear I've eaten enough honey and sweet almonds to rot all my teeth. Which would suggest the Devil's sent me a barren tail, as Maman warned he would the day she found me with my hands up underneath my shift? Is that why I can't make a child – to show Garon I'm a true wife after all, and put him in the wrong?

'So what ye do is work 'is codsack while 'e's sleeping, gently lamb like flaking suet, to thicken up the seed.'

'Really Hodierne. You shouldn't say such things!' (I had to hide a smile though.)

'Now then, 'tis best to lift yer hips soon as 'e's done to stop the juice run out,' was her next offering. 'Ye may believe it takes a good sight more'n fitting ends an' yowling "geemenay!" to make a firstborn child.'

But still it hasn't happened has it? – not by the usual method or any other Hoddie can devise. Now time is something else that's running out!

I rode again to Meresfeld at the end of February when I knew Sir Hugh to be away on service with the Earl. To find my mother bodily recovered but in no better frame concerning the croisade. She offered me her cheek to kiss. She asked me why young men embarked on folly imagine valour to be worth more than sense, and afterwards refused to bless me.

'The war's in Outremer. Not here, Mother,' I told her miserably.

'I've so far lost four sons to God,' was all she said by way of a reply. 'How can you think I'd willingly send Him another?'

That's how we parted.

We left Sussex in early March before the Lenten Fair, to meet Archbishop Baldwin's main force on the Dover road and join the streams of soldiery converging on the seaports. We knew so little of the journey we were facing beyond our summons to a muster at King Richard's citadel of Chinon in Touraine. They said that it would take us many weeks to reach Marseille, a seaport none of us had heard of. They said a ship would carry us across the Middle Sea to fight the enemies of Christ somewhere about Jerusalem, eighth wonder of the world. It was to be a great adventure, our chance to battle for the right and prove our worth for once and all.

That's what they said and how we saw it at the time.

On the eve of our departure, a solemn mass was offered for us at the manor church of Saint Peter ad. Vincula, which had been cleared of sacks and kindling for the purpose and thoroughly limewashed from flags to rafters.

I knelt before the altar with my little manor squad, five brothers called to Christ to hear prayers for our salvation and receive the host from Father Gerard's old, unsteady hands. Outside the church three cottage lads begged earnestly to join us on our quest. But even if we could have taken bondmen, I'd mouths enough to feed.

So I denied them. Saved their lives.

There had been times as I lay close beside Elise in our cocoon of duck-down, when I'd acknowledged all I felt for Haddertun and those within its bounds, felt tenderness and gratitude toward the woman in my arms. But that last night she turned away. She wasn't in the mood, she said, refusing me the comfort that I needed.

It wasn't what I'd planned. I wasn't to be thwarted. So yes, I forced her. There's no other way to view it – pulled her over, pinned her with the weight of my own body. Punished her for making me feel guilty. Afterwards we lay in silence without touching. And when she slept I left the bed to dress. Disgusted with my own performance.

Beneath my weather cloak I wore an unbleached linen tunic sewn with a white cross. Jos knew I was abroad and met me at the stables. Our baggage was already packed, had only to be loaded. Together in the lamplight we saw to the harnessing of mules and horses, sent Bertram down to fetch the fellows from the village as the stars paled in the sky. We took two rounsey geldings, my stallion Raoul curvetting on a lead-rein, with three big mules for coffers and equipment.

And I was here and there and everywhere. Fretting over lists and loads. Issuing instructions. Wolfing down the breakfast that Jos served me. Overseeing tasks that barely needed overseeing. Doing anything that I could think of to distract myself from what I'd done. What I was about to do.

Mist from the millstream seeped across the fields and round the the village houses. Muffling the church bell tolling Prime. Beading fabric. Wetting hands and faces in the manor yard.

Elise stood hunched into her warmest mantle by the gateway with her maid and Steward Kempe, and Father Gerard in his soutane waiting to bless us on our way. I can see her face this moment in the pale dawn light. Upturned with droplets in her hair and desperation in her eyes.

'You can rely on Kempe to help you and to pay the interest on the loan.'

I spoke it bleakly like a stranger, when I should have tried to reassure her. Should have told her I was sorry for my clumsiness and violence. Should have told her as I'd told de Bernay I was certain to return. Instead I frowned at her to hide my feelings.

Oh lord, what made me such a fool? And there is worse to come.

'I'm not afraid to die in service of the cross,' is what I told her next.

'I'm not afraid to die. But if I should then you'll be honoured lady, not disgraced.'

My words of comfort and apology! But I was desperate by then to be away.

White-faced, she stood against my stirrup to hand up the flask of wine and pack of salted fish that were to be my first meal upon the road, and said...

What did she say as she held back the tears? How did she did she frame the thoughts that I could see in her too-brightly-shining eyes?

'Pray for me before Christ's Holy Sepulchre, if you should ever reach it.' She paused to breathe. And then – 'God save you and protect you.' That was all.

I stooped to take the flask and basket. Sought acceptance in her eyes but failed to find it. Kissed her. Heaved a breath and rode away. As awkward at our parting as our meeting.

I looked back once just once to see her in the gateway. Rigid as a statue. Straight-backed with small hands tightly clasped. I waved. The others raised their hands. But not Elise.

The creepy steward's creeping closer as if to demonstrate his loyalty – as if to show that he, not I, is in control! All men think women cannot do without them. But that isn't so – and Garon isn't even looking. Old Father Gerard's blessing him, with Joscelin behind him grinning like an ape. He bows his head. He claims to know exactly what he wants – but I have never seen a man with such confusion and remorse stamped on his face!

How could I have ever thought that marriage to a knight could be other than hard, crude and violent? Or that he'd value me enough to change his mind? All men are children who break things without compunction – things like their pledges to love and hold themselves to their true wedded wives!

I don't feel lucky any longer to be a part of Garon's life. Or to be left behind him with a swollen quim and debts to be repaid. He can't have ever cared for me as he pretended. If he had he couldn't leave – and even if he manages to stay alive, who knows but that he may not win himself a new domain in Outremer and take for wife some dusky Sarasine who'll bear him swarthy sons?

I've failed to hold him here in any case. Failed even to hold in enough of him to make a child while he is gone! Failed, Elise, in every way. Failed, failed, FAILED, FAILED!

He gives a little cough to clear his throat. 'I'm not afraid to die in service of the Cross,' he's mumbling.

Then you're a fool, that's all – is what I'm thinking and should be brave enough to tell him. Because you should be, Garon, ought to be afraid. Anyone, the meanest vagabond, should value life and fear to die.

'But if I should succumb,' (another nervous cough) 'then you'll be honoured lady, not disgraced.'

As if I care for honour! As if honour ever warmed an empty bed, or held a fief, or paid a silver penny of a loan! Husbands ride out to test their faith and prove their courage, fighting to the outer boundaries of creation for the delusions they call 'destiny' and 'honour'. Wives cheated of their dreams must stay behind – their only trials to be for qualities of patience and obedience, and other so-called feminine accomplishments.

I can't even tell if I'm more wretched to be left alone than fearful of his death. I twist the handle of my basket wishing hopelessly that I could go as well – riding pillion, clinging to him like the goose-grass. Holding onto him for all I'm worth!

'Pray for me before Christ's Holy Sepulchre, if you should ever reach it.'

But I cannot think he will. It seems so far away – remote, fantastic, utterly unreal.

What else to say?

'God save you and protect you, husband.' *I made up my mind last night to speak as little as I could, in case I said too much.*

He's leaning down to take the wine and salted trout, to grip me by the shoulders. His scars have healed. His hot brown eyes, direct for once, are searching mine – searching them for tears which I refuse to shed. Now kissing me – too clumsy and too hard!

Someone's shut his dog inside the kennels with the hounds to stop him following his master. The poor thing's howling like a soul in purgatory, and I know how he feels! I am constrained as well, shut-in, with a door closing on my life. We could have been so happy here. I could have tamed him, taught

111

him how to laugh with me at the absurdities of life. I know I could, if only there'd been time.

But he's already through the gate and turning in the saddle, while I stand like a block of stone to watch the mist close round him. Hopeless.

I wondered if I would cry after all. But in the end I haven't. Loneliness will to be a new experience – if not a pleasant one then something new at least. And if you think, my friend, that I am going to spend the months or years that you're away moping round the place in widow's weeds, then you can think again!

No tears. There is a shiny yellow celandine in flower against the wall. And I'm left talking to his back-turned cloak!

Of course I had to go. Of course I did. It was what I'd always wanted, wasn't it? To champion the right?

There are times on the other hand when being certain of yourself is no great help. If I could change my memory of how I left Elise, I'd have her waving. But that isn't how it was, and when I try to think of how it felt to see her, set-faced standing in the gateway, all I can feel is what I'm feeling now.

It's not as if her hands had been bound like Khadija's. She could have waved. *She* wasn't bound!

I looked back just once. I waved. Kempe and the others raised their hands. But not Elise.

BOOK TWO

CHAPTER ONE

Vézelay, France: July 1190

DEPARTURE

In common with most enterprises involving multitudes of men, the Kings' Croisade of 1190 is subject to innumerable delays.

Since Richard first received the cross two years before, the war he'd fought against his father for control of Aquitaine took precedence over all else. Old Henry's death, the new king's coronation and subsequent fund-raising tours detained his armies for a second winter in the West, while those of Frederick Barbarossa, the German Emperor, had already reached the Hellespont. In March another death removed the King of Sicily from the affray. By then the French and English monarchs had decided on a new date after Easter for a joint departure. (For in an age when kings must personally defend their borders, it was advisable for land-hungry neighbours to leave their realms together.) But fate had one more obstacle to cast into their path; and on the day Archbishop Baldwin and his knights rode into Richard's camp at Chinon, the Queen of France chose selfishly to die in childbed, and defer campaigning for a further period of mourning.

So one way or another, it's the beginning of July before the Christian army finally assembles on the granite scarps around the town of Vézelay, a three-day ride south east of Paris.

The night before they leave, a congregation of two thousand fill the newly-built basilica of Sainte Madelaine, to call upon the Risen

Christ to bless the holy quest. Two thousand men, but not a single woman.

The last time a great army marched from France against the infidel, some forty years before, King Richard's mother Eléonore had taken up the cross herself, declaring she would strike a blow for Christendom with her own hand. Encouraged by her fortitude other women followed, riding in linkmail like amazons to form their own battalion beneath the Fleur-de-Louis banner. But not on this croisade. For this croisade the Pope decrees that only males of stainless character can save Jerusalem. Laundrywomen past the age of childbearing will be the only females to join the expedition; ill-favoured dames who'll keep its soldiers' linen and their souls both free from stain by being too old to attract them. Who but a celibate could make so obvious a mistake?

'Holy Sepulchre assist us! Let not uncleanliness, base thoughts or fornication distract us from our enterprise to free the Holy City! *Sanctum Sepulchrum adjuva!*' is what the Abbot of Vézelay has to say in Latin on the subject. 'Be strong, put on Christ's armour. Stand fast against temptations of the flesh!'

That night two thousand men, bare-headed, cram the aisles and narthex of Sainte Madelaine to hear his sermon and receive his benediction. Outside the building twenty times that number crowd the town and occupy the slopes around the village of Saint Père, the lights of their flambeaux spangling the Morvan landscape like galaxies of stars.

'Sanctum Sepulchrum...' Men's voices on the parvis relay the chant. 'Sanctum Sepulchrum adjuva!' They're proud to be men with a taste for war bred in them – trained into them from childhood. The irony of using a religion born of opposition to one military culture to fuel another is lost on the crucesignati. Gentle Jesus urges them to battle for the right to re-erect His cross and cleanse His tomb; invites them to see violence as a virtue.

'*Sanctum Sepulchrum adjuva! Holy Sepulchre assist us!*' Their paean rises to the vaulted roof of the basilica, spreads as ripples from a stone flung into water, resounding and rebounding round the hills and through the twilit valleys.

Dawn breaks over Vézelay. Its townsfolk wake from dreams of thunder to the reality of trembling earth and rank on rank of tramping feet. Platters rattle on their shelves. The sentries on their walkways feel the town walls tremble. Others who have risen early to stand at first light on the valley slopes, watch forests of raised spears move steadily along the Moulins road. Wood creaks, harness jingles, metal shoes strike sparks from stone. Dogs bark. Commanders bellow orders. Excitable young riders crow like the roosters as by degrees the sun penetrates the dust of their departure to paint colours onto fields of banners. Pennons buckle in the breeze, and from the hill behind the town the bells of the basilica ring out in noisy celebration. Cue for black cats to cross the road ahead and bats to leave their belfries. The great folly of the Kings' Croisade is underway at last.

Some few days before, the marshals of provision have ridden ahead to commandeer supplies. Now in the darkness of the early hours the highest échelons of kings and prelates leave their lodgings in the town.

Now the first French contingent begin to move preceded by two bishops, the Counts of Nevers, Fontigny, Clermont and Blois. Each with his own battalion. Each jewelled and perfumed, barbered to the ears and signed with a bright cross of scarlet silk. Behind on leading reins prance destriers in tasselled housings, with hooded gyrfalcons, peregrines on perches, smaller birds in cages and dogs in couples – greyhounds, lymers, tracking dogs and pacing dogs for running down gazelle. Behind the dogs come chamberlains and pages, clerks, heralds, surgeons and physicians, astrologers, cartographers, and chroniclers to record the valour of the enterprise and set down the history of its conquests. Then swarms of common fletchers, farriers, fewterers, smiths, scullions and pastrycooks. Packhorses and hide-covered wagons bear plate and coffers, battle helms in pinewood cases.

117

Documents on parchment. Raiments layered with lavender against the moth in solid cedar chests. Marching in their tracks come companies of soldiers – squires on foot and knights on horseback. All faces stamped with eager smiles. All bodies branded with red crosses.

Behind the French are men of Burgundy; brothers in Christ who also wear red crosses on their shoulders to strengthen their right arms. Then Mosans and Brabançons out of Flanders, riding six-abreast on Flemish horses under the green standard of their leader, Jacques d'Avenses. Then black-crossed Teutons from the Rhineland who missed their chance to leave with Barbarossa. Then cavallieres and troops of crack Italian routiers – rank on rank, with crossbows on their shoulders and yellow crosses on their cloaks. Until at last all cruciforms are drained of colour; lily-white.

More numerous than those of France, of Burgundy and Flanders, Germany and Italy all set together – too many to be counted as they pass, or calculated later for the annals – few in the white-crossed army of the English King have any clear idea of where Jerusalem might be or what Muslims believe. Within their ranks they speak eight languages and twice as many dialects. A third perhaps are mercenaries. The rest are believing Christians who are convinced they're in the right – that Saracens are in the wrong and bound for hellfire and damnation.

Then naturally the greatest Christian hope since Charlemagne rides as you might expect well to the fore; his reputation vitally enhanced by what is borne before him. For on a sumpter in a specially constructed casket bound with bands of brass, King Richard carries nothing less than Arthur's elf-made sword, *Escalibor*. Not as it happens handed to him from the surface of a lake, but risen from the earth.

His heralds spread the story up and down the lines that prophesy foretells the coming of a worthy king, within whose hand an ancient sword, cast all of bronze in a stone mould, will guide his Christian force to victory. By curious and happy chance the very sword, *Escalibor*, has recently been found within the grave

118

of King Arthur and his Queen at Glastonbury, and sent across the Narrow Sea by Abbot Hugh de Sulli for Richard to take with him *en croisade*. An inscription and a tress of Gwenevere's exquisite golden hair confirm the blade's identity, or so the criers claim. And clearly when it comes to omens of success or failure – Escalibor or Melusine's black bat? – there is no contest. The legendary weapon wins hands down.

Unhelmeted, the King of England's dressed much less for comfort than effect. Mounted on a milk-white Spanish stallion, dazzling in silver linkmail with his lightest, brightest golden crown set on his tawny head, he rides beneath the heraldic lions – the *leopardés guardant* of Normandy and Maine Anjou unsheathing claws across the scarlet waves of his royal banner. Chin up, chest out, with all his soft parts under iron control, he looks more than magnificent. He looks the very image of a hero.

The King of France, by way of contrast, is slightly built with small squint eyes and thinning hair. *Philippus Rex Francorum* looks commonplace and doesn't care. Crowned at fourteen and not yet twenty-five, his serious perceptions make him seem older than his years. Attended by a single page, bareheaded, dressed like a penitent in a plain black surcoat astride a hackney mare, he moves almost unnoticed up the line to take his place at Richard's side.

'Well now, Philippe, have you come to see how differently the road looks from an English point of view?' King Richard beams and reaches with a large gloved paw to slap the King of France on his thin thigh. 'Or are you going to tell me that you've changed your mind about Jerusalem, and want to spend the summer interviewing for another queen?'

'You know that I'm in mourning still,' the younger man says coldly.

'Which means?'

'Which I should say means that it's you, not I, who needs a wife.'

'Quite so,' Richard concurs. 'But is that your suggestion, Philippe? Or your sister's?'

119

'If you will recall, your contract with my sister has brought you, amongst other things, the territories Gisors and Châteauroux.' King Philippe shrugs his narrow shoulders looking less than pleased. 'So if it's true as we have heard that you are looking elsewhere for a queen – that land must be returned to France the day that you break faith with Alys, along with Issoudun and Graçay.'

'I'll grant you that her dower lands are one of Alys's best features. But don't ye think our noble houses deserve a little respite now and then from fucking one another?' The English King turns in his saddle and smiles to see the colour drain from Philippe's face. 'God's blood, I swear 'tis hard to tell when you are bedding France if you're performing a dynastic duty, or committing incest.'

As both of them and all the world's aware, for years the political and copulatory affairs of France and Acquitaine-Anjou have been hopelessly entangled. King Richard's mother, Eléanore, has been both Queen of France and England; married at fifteen to King Philippe's father and after their divorce to Richard's father, Henry. What's more, at around the time that Richard's brother consummated *his* marriage to Philippe's sister Marguerite, their father bedded Marguerite's sister and his fiancée, Alys, to get a child on her.

But there was more... in Paris three years earlier the princely cousins, Richard and Philippe, have also shared a naked bed – and if no one outside the sheets that night can say what happened underneath them, it's known that in his taste for adolescents of both sexes, Richard shares the carnal habits of other military commanders. Of Alexander and of Caesar. A big hairy man himself, he has a penchant for unripened flesh.

Some people, like the King of France, blanch with emotion. Others, like the King of England, darken; and only they know if it's righteous indignation or an unwelcome memory that accounts for Philippe's sickly shade.

'If you want France's support in this campaign,' he speaks

120

between clenched teeth. 'I'd recommend you save your insults for the Turks!'

King Richard laughs. 'I'll bear the point in mind.'

Thereafter the kings ride in studied silence, knee to knee, acknowledging the cheers of those who leave the fields to see them pass, or run to kiss their stirruped feet. Both bowing from the saddle. Both smiling affably in all directions but the one that brings them face to face.

Later in the afternoon, to cries of admiration, the King of England with his guard moves past the sumpter carrying Escalibor to take his rightful place as he perceives it at the very forefront of the cavalcade. He rides beneath his lion standard, his long cloak rippling across the haunches of his Spanish stallion.

The King of France, who's had enough of riding for the day, returns to rest and to reflect upon his litter.

A living mass of men and beasts snakes backward to the far horizon. The riders' long forked pennons stream and flutter in the wind like vanes of sea-kelp in a current. Some sewn with verses from the Bible. Not all of them the right way up.

Between the military divisions, herds of goats and grunting pigs and red and white milch cows keep drovers busily employed. Vans made to look like gabled hutches house the old laundresses with their washtubs and their soap. Long trains of mules and donkeys carry lighter freight. Wains hired from local carters for the journey south are stacked with camp equipment – horseshoes, chests of nails, with provender for livestock, cheeses, sides of salted pork and sacks of beans and grain. Others large enough to bear the main beams and components of siege engines and their missiles, are dragged by teams of oxen whose slow progress sets the pace for all the rest. Indeed so ponderous is their advance, that Richard at the head of the migration has crossed the winding River Nivernais three times to pitch his cloth of gold pavilion on its western bank, before the final remnants of his English army strike tents at Vézelay some six leagues to the rear.

Archbishop Baldwin, who's declined an invitation to ride forward with the Archbishop of Rouen and his *avant garde* of jewelled grandees, climbs painfully onto his mule to await the marshals' signal for departure. He's had a tiresome, tiring day including more than he can take of fussing chaplains and purposeless complaints. The journey east from Chinon has worsened his old troubles with his joints – and if he's honest with himself, as Baldwin almost always is, he feels no relish for the trials ahead. It isn't that he doubts the need for the croisade. God only knows how fervently he's advertised it as a *bellum sacrum* to Christians from Wales to the Touraine.

'It's simply, I'm sorry – but it's simply that I'm getting old, Monète,' he tells his riding mule; an animal that's busily employed stripping a sallow of its shoots and at the other end in making an unpleasant smell.

'I am too old in body for a military adventure.'

Adventure? Baldwin glances back to see if anyone beside Monète has heard him use that word. '*A just and holy war. A service to all Christendom. An enterprise to win back the Holy City for Christ's own greater glory!*' is what he should have said, and how he'd always put it in his sermons.

Just then his eye alights on a small group of men and sumpter beasts led by a mounted knight; a group advancing to the line exactly like a thousand others, except for the squire's red hair. So typical, so much the same as all the others, chattering like starlings on a roost, excited to be on the move, bright-eyed with expectation.

God bless them for their simple faith, their Primate thinks benignly stifling a yawn. The tall knight with the malformed ear looks strong and energetic. *But young, so young – why hardly out of boyhood;* his ardent face the face of all such innocents. The face of the croisade.

122

As Baldwin stoops to rub his aching knee, he thinks of Richard's face in Anjou and Westminster. Alight with pride. Consumed by greed. At Fontevraud Duke Richard spoke of guarding trade routes, building a new empire great as Alexander's, boasting he'd annex the Latin Kingdom for himself. There is a rumour circulating in the camp that in despite of his betrothal to Ays of France, Richard plans to wed the Palestinian Queen's younger sister, Isabella.

And if that's true, thinks Balwin, *it would suggest we've all been duped – me in my sermans, the crucesignati in their faith and trust. To make of us tools in the hands of those intent on gain, not for Christ's glory but their own.*

The Kings' Croisade is on the move, unstoppable in its intent. *But is it God's design or that of an avaricious prince? Am I naive to think that Christ is with the enterprise,* the old archbishop asks himself. *Or even* (terrible suspicion) *that He is here at all?*

With a feeling of dismay Baldwin acknowledges a lapse of faith; one of those abrupt descents from firm belief to honest doubt which all too frequently assail him. Sometimes he feels that he knows less about himself and his relationship to God than when he was a novice no older than that tall young knight, with a full head of hair still and a young man's embarrassingly carnal inclinations.

Mea culpa, mea culpa, mea maxima culpa…

Baldwin signs the cross, puts up his cowl and takes a breath; a little ritual that he's evolved which sometimes seems to help. 'Oh Lord, sustain me in my faith!' he cries fervently, to the surprise of all in earshot and the flat-eared consternation of Monète the mule.

CHAPTER TWO

'Oh Lord, sustain me in my faith!' You'd have thought a man who was first-cousin to a saint could never doubt his calling. But if what the old archbishop cried surprised us, I've learned since then that faith can be stretched – stretched until it breaks.

Our journey south to the seaport of Marseille took us four weeks including the delay at Lyons. On the first day we covered less than a league, which hardly seemed to justify the effort. 'If you and I had lain abed to Vespers an' then doddled on at a slow snail's gallop,' I overheard Jos telling Bertram, 'we'd still have caught the yellow-crosses at their breakfast.'

We none of us saw either of the kings that side of Lyons. Nor any of the *preux chevaliers* of Christendom, save for the old archbishop on his mule. What we saw chiefly were a line of horses' arses moving through a pulp of mud and dung and trampled vegetation. Smashed copses. Flattened fields of rye and buckwheat. Ruined harvests. Wasted hamlets. Mutilated cats and dogs. Every poultry house was silent by the time we reached it, every barn stripped of its hay. The fields of Burgundy were empty of their cattle, its woods of game and swine. We saw our Christian armies cut a swathe of devastation through the land, yet all the time thought only of ourselves. It's true. To be a part of that great enterprise, to make a gift to it of everything we had, was all we wanted in the world. That's what I told myself. I told myself that anything I still felt for the wife I'd left behind was no more than a distraction from my destiny to serve. They say that absence strengthens bonds. But with each league I put between us, I could feel Elise's hold loosen. Away from the sight and smell of her my feelings ebbed and slackened like a watercourse in want of rain. Even the guilt I felt for what I'd done on our last night had dwindled to a trickle.

Horns sounded night and morning up and down the line, to tell us when to halt and when to rise, and most days we sang as we broke camp the best of all the croisade hymns, bellowed high into the summer morning air:

'Wood of the True Cross before
Royal gonfanons of war!
Christian trumpets proudly sound;
Never have they given ground,
By their oaths of honour bound,
Strengthened in God's Holy Law!'

God smiled upon the enterprise. Or so it seemed to His believers.

My forty days' knight service ran out while we were still at Chinon. So from thenceforth, like the men I led, I was paid as an archbishop's soldier.

My little Manor Squad were on the whole a cheerful band who belted out the verses of the hymn as readily as I did. Along with other ruder songs in Engleis. They trusted me and I was proud to be their leader, finding tasks for each of them that met my expectations. Beyond his duties as a squire, Jos shared the cooking with John Hideman and helped him with the horses. The ploughman's natural gift, his reassuring whistle, made him the best groom for Raoul – a thing decided after my high-tempered destrier had bitten Albie and stamped on Jos's toes more times than anyone found helpful. Alberic and Bertram pitched the tents and picketed the mules. The elder giving orders, the younger doing most of the hard swearing. It also fell to Bertram as the senior man to guard our coffer of four-hundred shillings, all in silver pennies, marching beside the mule that carried it with one hand on the coffer-lid, the other on his dagger.

When was it that it rained so hard?

I think it must have been on the third or fourth day of the march that the heavens opened – and opened wide enough as Jos would have it to wash away our sins twice over! The dyes ran in the nobles' priceless garments, to stain them underneath we all supposed, all sorts of interesting colours. Our own were plastered to our bodies. Water trickled down our necks, sucked at our horses' hooves. Ruts cut into ruts, and in no time the way was churned into a mire that forced us into detours through the fields.

It was on the outskirts of the town of Nevers that we happened on a laundry van embedded axle-deep in mud. While John and Alberic and Bertram set shoulders to the wheels to push it back into the road, the old laundresses shouted their encouragements from beneath its looped-up canvas. The stoutest of the sisterhood came from the port of Deal in Kent, where fifty years before she told us she'd been baptised Guillemette. In addition to a hairy mole on her flat nose and grey brows thick as ropes, she had three chins – one hammocked in a tight barbette with two more underneath. To call the woman pot-bellied would do the pot a favour. But she had some good features – two of them, a massive pair of breasts networked with purple veins, and resting on the tailboard of the cart like pumpkins on a shelf.

Young Jos, who'd always been as randy as a rabbit, blew out his cheeks and whistled at them rudely. 'Give us a feel, old love,' he begged when they had set the cart aright. 'You never can tell lest ye feel if the fruit's ripe or blown.'

'Ye want to feel? Raw as a peeled onion, that's how you'll feel when I've adone with you!' the washerwoman gave him back in Engleis.

'Then here's a chance to wash my braies out, mother. I'll whip 'em off, shall I, to show you where they're marked.' Jos flashed a smile at her, and then his woollen hose, straddling short legs to thrust his stained crutch up at her obscenely.

'Belike I'll scrub 'em with you still inside, ye raddle-pated tiddler – an' see if we can't shrink what you have there to somethin' even less worth lookin' at!' And when she laughed, fat Guillemette's best features quivered in the lacings of her bodice like jellies in a net.

'Then pull it out and wring it dry? I'm ready if you are, my flower.'

My squire had never been too nice about a woman's looks above-the-girdle as long as he could come to terms beneath it. So none of us were much surprised when he crept back that night with a grin on his freckled face that squeezed his blue eyes into slits.

'She let me do it for a bishop's shilling,' he told us proudly. 'Managed it by covering her head up with a sheet. But take my word she still came close to swallowing me live. I swear I barely touched the chapel walls, an' took the Sacrament ye may believe a long sight from the altar!'

It wasn't quite the tale I would have chosen for my bedtime. Not with the image I still carried of the town whores of Varzy at the roadside two leagues back, hoisting their skirts to show us what they had to sell... Well, anyway it wasn't long before I felt the need to part my cloak while I lay on my bedroll and shake hands with a faithful friend. Then afterwards when I had fumbled for release, to fumble for forgiveness in my prayers. To put it to The Lord and any saint who might be listening, that such a thing was less a vice than a handy means of keeping vice at bay. Handy is the word. Jos had a name for it. He made it female – called it *'Fisty Flora'*. And in my own defence I have to say that at such times it was my wife's soft body I imagined. Upside down and back to front in every possible position. (Less. I said I thought about her *LESS;* I didn't say not ever.)

Somewhere about the sixth day of our march we reached the great beech forests of the Bourbonnais. A sea of treetops stretching to the far horizon. For hours we wound between their dappled trunks, and afterward through scorching heathland which grew hotter with every league we journeyed south. We found water for the horses where we could, slept where the column halted. Built fires. Cooked meals. Crept off into the brushwood for a shit. Breakfasted at sunrise to be ready for the onward march wherever and whenever it began.

We'd all grown beards by then to shield our lower faces from the sun – excepting Jos who still shaved daily, boasting that when he wanted something red and curly round his mouth he'd find himself a ginger whore. Many of the host, including John and Albie, rode stripped to hose and breeches. My nose and Bertram's burned and peeled. Jos's freckles multiplied. But John Hideman's weathered skin had simply darkened. At Thiers the skies scummed over and the heat became oppressive. Through silent villages, through rocky granite country, boulder-strewn and shrilling with cicadas, we hauled ourselves across the Massif. A place as old as God. And then we came to Lyons.

Lyons-sur-Rhône was founded, someone told us, by the Romans, standing on a goose-necked pendulum of land where two great rivers met to flow together to the sea. I'm not sure even now what made me want to view it from between Raoul's ears. Unless it was a premonition of disaster?

The wound my destrier sustained at tournament had healed long since. It barely showed beneath his glossy coat, and I remember something of the pride I felt astride his back, cheered through the city streets by crowds of Lyonnais. Its chief thoroughfare, the *Mercière*, was crammed with men and horses. Marshalls shouted from the pavements, even from the first floor windows of the houses either side. But in the end there was no choice. We had to wait while those ahead edged slowly forward to the bridge across the Rhône.

Of all the watercourses the kings' armies have to cross, the Rhône's by far the most impressive. Supplied by Alpine streams from distant parts of Barbarossa's empire, swollen by melting glaciers and recent summer storms, it moves past the city's quays and through the arches of its bridge at frightening velocity. The latest in a series that have served for a millennium to link Lyons to the eastern trade routes, the bridge consists of thirteen spans supported by enormous oaken piers. But if its architects assumed the greatest threat to its stability was represented by the Rhône in flood, then I'd suggest that no bridge in the city's history (not even in the days of Constantine and Hadrian) had been designed to bear a burden comparable to that of the great cavalcade of hooves and wheels and stamping feet that cross it now – and are to go on crossing it for three days in succession.

Six spans behind Archbishop Baldwin's plodding mule, Monète, an eight-wheeled oxen dray transports the beams and armatures of a dismantled *mangonel á tour*; a huge siege-catapult which

128

on its journey down from Rouen has managed to exhaust four teams of bullocks, destroy a shrine near Moulins and demolish most of the old bridge walls at Balbigny. Now as it lumbers out across the central, seventh span of the far wider bridge, the weapon inflicts its worst damage yet, in peacetime or in war.

One iron-shod wheel is all it takes to crack the forward brace of an oak pier, just as the bells of the basilica of Saint Martin d'Ainay at the ramped entrance of the bridge begin to ring for Prime.

The sound of splitting wood is hardly louder than a whip crack. The mangonel moves on, to leave the rest to gravity and those who follow it across the weakened span.

The second crack, much sharper, is clearly audible above the ringing bells. Rails snap. Planks splinter and an unsupported crossbeam gives way beneath the weight of the next rank of mounted knights.

'Dear Lord in heaven preserve them!'

The wild commotion on the bridge wrenches Archbishop Baldwin on the further bank straightway from the responses of his *offertorium* to more immediate demands of the Almighty.

'Oh God be merciful to those engaged upon Thy business!'

An alarm horn, sounding like a cow in pain, blares twice and then is silenced.

A pillar of the bridge, unbalanced, jarred by the descending beam and subject to the full force of the current, turns slowly to break free of its supports and crash sideways with predictable effect against its neighbour – to strike and fell it as one ninepin fells another.

I wish that we could cross that bridge as safely in my memory as those who'd already made the crossing. I wish that I could land our Albie safe and dry beside them. But I can't.

It happened suddenly, almost without a warning. And yet when I look back it seems as if we moved like men in dreams, with heavy limbs and stupefied reactions.

We'd had to wait all night to cross, felt nothing but relief when finally our column was pushed forward down the ramp and out onto the bridge. The church bells were already spooking Raoul. Then when he heard the hollow sound of his own hooves and felt the wooden boards beneath him tremble, he fought the bit, side-stepping, crabbing, forcing Jos's rounsey out against the rails.

It was all that I could do to hold him, even with John's hand firm on his bridle, and we were near halfway across before I knew that something else was wrong. The goad-boys and drovers were forever shouting at their beasts. So their yelling voices told us nothing. It was when we felt the impact, heard the horses screaming, that we began to understand. But by then it was too late.

We watched with a kind of horrid fascination while ranks of horses disappeared, dropped out of view. Twenty horses up the line – then ten – then five, and then but two!

I saw Sir Mark le Jeune go down, as a whole section of the bridge swung back to shoot its living cargo thirty feet into the river. Cascades of bodies, mounts and riders, flailing and colliding with each other's bodies. Frozen into attitudes of desperate effort. Somersaulting in thin air. And all the time the tail of King Richard's army kept pushing forward. Pushing us relentlessly, with nowhere else to go but into the abyss.

I saw John skid and fall. Then Jos's rounsey, jerking sideways to dislodge him from the saddle.

I felt Raoul quiver underneath me – and then, great-hearted when it counted, bunch his haunches to leap forward while he had purchase on the boards.

Then all my pulses leapt and pounded in the way they do when you anticipate an action. With no more time to think, and trusting to my instinct, I screamed, *'Victoire!'* and kicked the spurs in hard. To launch us both out into space.

We flew! For one unflinching moment I sat a flying horse!

We soared above the churning wreckage. Free-falling. Galloping on air... until the icy water of the Rhône rushed up to swallow us.

I hit the surface with both fists wound in the reins. Legs straight. Both feet braced hard into the stirrups. We bore the fear, the impact and the pain of it down with us to the icy depths. The shock was total, stunning, blanking all else from my mind.

Then silence. The cool darkness of a world without a top or bottom, or any way of knowing where they ought to be.

Then sheer, bloody-minded anger forcing me up to the surface. Spluttering and cursing. Breathing air and gulping in great quantities of river.

Raoul was there before me. Saddle gone. Reins trailing – and automatically I clutched his mane. Shouting heads and flailing arms were all about us in the freezing water. Alive with physical excitement, my first thoughts were of pride that I'd survived. Then gratitude that Jos and John had too. For two of the wet heads were theirs, my squire's red hair in rat-tails round his ears, John's dark and shiny as an otter. I offered thanks to God and providence for our good fortune.

'Fuck!' Jos couldn't keep his mouth shut, never could. Not even then when it was threatening to let in the Rhône and take him to the bottom.

'Fuck the Virgin! Fuck Saint George! Fuck! Fuck, fucking, fucking fuck,' he gasped – in the belief as he explained it afterwards that a whole bunch of rude words could be helpful when otherwise things weren't too clever.

The three of us were paddling to keep afloat in the fast-running current. Trying to avoid the rocks. Horses strained to hold their heads above a debris of wooden boards and splintered rails. A huge beam close beside us nudged the floating body of a mule, turning in the water like a great dark fish. Before long boats were bumping through the flotsam, throwing lines to those who clung to spars and rafts of planks. Or clustered round remaining piers.

A helpful inward current where the two rivers merged was probably what saved our lives, and John had hold of Raoul's bridle by the time that we made landfall. I ached all over and had twisted my right ankle. Jos hobbled in one boot and nursed a bleeding arm, his shirt ripped from the shoulder. John had a black eye and a graze all down the left side of his face. Raoul was shivering from head to foot as he was led to firmer ground. But at least we four were whole and living.

Of Betram, of Alberic, the geldings and the mules there was no sign.

Later in the afternoon, while wounds were dressed and dying animals dispatched, Archbishop Baldwin offered up a special mass beneath a canvas sheet that someone had rigged between the trees, in gratitude for the delivery of all who by God's mercy had survived.

For those the damaged bridge had stranded, the river crossing was completed in three days – in skiffs, on rafts, and finally by means of a pontoon of barges linked with ropes and topped with every piece of timber the city could supply. Our King himself directed its construction. From our makeshift camp on the far bank we saw him frequently in boats or striding up the river bank. A lofty figure in a long silk tunic glittering with gold. Everyone could hear him shouting orders. His oaths, they said, would shock the Devil into silence. To me he was magnificent.

It was not until the second day that we knew Bertram had survived, along with the locked travel chest which I'd gloomily assumed to be somewhere at the bottom of the river. He found us in the end by following directions to Archbishop Baldwin's tent. Advancing flat-footedly between the trees. Hatless, with his bald head gleaming and his precious burden wrapped in a concealing cloak.

'Happened quicker'n a dog can lick his arse. I had the chest safe though an' no mistake, afore the mules went in,' he told us, breathing heavily as he set down the coffer in the sand.

'I found the rail, thanks be. An' hugged it to me like the kindest friend I had. An' cried out *"Lord God an' Mother Mary save me!"* An' blame me, so they did.'

Bert blew his nose into his hand and wiped the voiding on his tunic. Then told us that he'd seen poor Albie hit a jagged beam-end as he fell. Which as he said, was a hard lesson for the lad from the Almighty and gave us little hope of finding him alive.

We'd lost both geldings. Lost the mules, and with them all else that we'd brought. Arms, harness, tents, my helmet and my father's precious hauberk. But thanks to Bert we had the means to buy replacements from the merchants and horse-traders who saw their chance to make a killing in the camp. We bargained for an old camsteery hinny, two scrub ponies, a pair of boots for Jos and four bed-rolls – along with rope and harness, a pair of battered saddles, some javelins and kidney daggers and quite a good two-handed sword. The rest I'd find, so I was told, at armourers and metal-shops in the port of Marseille.

I lay awake the night before we left the camp at Lyons and thought of Alberic's round hairy face, imagining his bloated body floating in the river. Hoping that it would be found and buried decently. I'd always felt, unfairly, a feeling of contempt for anyone of my own generation who failed to make it. Failed for any reason to survive. But when it came to Albie, what I chiefly felt was guilt. I thought of his poor mother, Ida, back at Haddertun, and how she'd be the day I rode down to her cottage to hand her the archbishop's mort-pay for her eldest boy. The day I told her how I'd let him die by accident along the way.

I saw her standing in her garden with her grown sons and her two small daughters at her skirts. I saw the mossy thatch behind her. Heard her geese announcing my arrival. Could even catch the scent of Sussex mayweed crushed by Raoul's hooves. But I couldn't picture Ida's face. Maybe because I didn't want to?

The rest of our long journey south is harder to recall than either of our chevauchées from Chinon or Vézelay. What's happened since has driven so much from my mind.

King Philippe's army, along with its Burgundian and yellow-crossed Italian contingents, branched east from Lyons to cross the mountains to the port of Genoa, where ships awaited them for their sea crossing. The rest of us left when we could. No longer in close-order or in sight of Richard's vanguard. Straggled down the east bank of the river with wide gaps between battalions.

I joined Sir Dickon Waleys's party, riding Raoul with John beside me resolutely whistling. Jos took the larger of the ponies. Bertram led the hinny and the second pony with the baggage. Footsore, hoofsore, plagued by the stinging flies the peasantry call *shimmeroys*, we trudged the dusty road. Each day we watched the sun rise in the heavens and sink into the crags. Too hot and tired to find the heart for croisade hymns. Backs turned on all we'd left behind, we were drawn south relentlessly like migrant birds to Marseille and the Middle Sea.

CHAPTER THREE

I do think the scent of fresh-made hay is one of the best smells in the world! It's so good to see things grow and be a part of life's great cycle. Even if it isn't happening inside you as it ought.

I knew within a week of Garon's leaving that I'd failed to catch his child. But why do we women have to bleed each month? I've never understood it. It can't be that the flux-blood's of a child that's failed to form, like churned milk that refuses to make curd – because I bled for years before I took in Garon's seed.

Maman always called the reds 'the curse of Eve', sent as a punishment for what she did to Adam. But I can't see why the Everlasting would decide to make us bleed and suffer pain as a part of His great plan – when He could just as easily, and far more usefully, let women yield a quart of fresh milk every month. Or a hogshead of red claret? Is that too much to ask of He For Whom All Things Are Possible?

'Glory lamb, I don't see as ye've any call to blame yourself,' Hod offered me by way of compensation as she wadded moss into the linen diaper I have to wear. ''Tis one thing less to fret about, that's eyeproof.'

So that's that, is it? A fault without a remedy? No baby, or means of getting one without a mortal sin or an immaculate conception?

For some days after Garon left I found myself in a completely hopeless state. Angry frequently. But more often listless and lethargic, unable or unwilling to perform the simplest tasks – forlorn; a bolster-case without its feather stuffing. But then you can get used to most things given time. It's very rare for me to keep a feeling going for more than five days at a stretch – and by the end of the first week I was quite well enough to ride to Lewes with my husband's steward to pay the old Jew his March interest.

Sometimes, it seems to me, my marriage is all in the past. As far away as

135

Lancaster. As unreal as a story in a chanson. Sometimes I hardly mind that he has gone to leave me to my own devices. (That's with my busy 'lady-of-the-manor' head on, when regrets aren't worth a pauper's groat. Although with my other 'Eve-cast-from-the-garden' head in place, I tend to find I want him back.) I'm really not sure what I feel. Do I still love him? Did I ever love him? Or did I just love what he did when things were going well?

SIR GARON. GARON, GARON…

I like the sound of it, his name, enjoy repeating it – it somehow makes him seem more real. And if only he'd come back, I daresay I'd forgive him. Men can't help what they are, Hod says. He's probably no worse than any other – however rough he was, or clumsy in the way he used me.

He forced me that last time – but never struck me. You'd have to call him gentle in that way. On the other hand I never got to know him well enough to guess what he'd do next, and can't guess any better now he's gone. And now I come to think of it, I can't say I've known any man that well. Father hardly counts. I've yet to spend so much as a full day with either of my sisters' husbands. As for Sir Hugh – he's far too busy trying to impress to let any woman know what HE'S about!

But I still miss him (I mean Garon). Despite the way he treated me, the way he left, I miss him telling me I'm beautiful. I miss his grunts and groans in bed, his open mouth, the joyful bellows that burst out of him – the sounds, not of a man's power over a woman, but of a woman's over him! Is it a sin to miss that kind of power the most?

Oh Mary Mother, Mater Dei, protect my Garon from an injury, or worse!

Shall I count a thousand Aves as I say them? Would that be enough to see him safe and bring him home? My lady-of-the-manor head tells me that he's unlikely to return, and that I wouldn't be the first or last to lose a husband to a stupid male idea of enterprise and conquest. Yet still I stand and stare at the ash path that leads up to the manor gate, to picture him appearing in the distance. Or think of him surprising me at my loom. Or on my palfrey in the meadows, casting up my little merlin. Or in the laundry or the pantry, to see how well I've settled down to managing the manor in his absence. I even catch myself in conversation with him, asking his opinion, finding things for him to say which he would never think of. Almost expecting to look up and see him – I've had so strong a feeling that I might.

What if today, this very moment, he should come upon me hatless in the meadow with my hair up in a simple net – chewing the sweetness from a juicy grass-stalk, sunlight playing on my neck? How would it be if I looked up to scent the new-made hay, and found him standing here. Right here before me. Staring at me in my pale blue fustian and white chemise – he'd have to think me pretty wouldn't he?

The hay's very late this year. The fair weather held for sheep-washing and shearing, and for the shearing supper in the village. But then three days of rain put mowing back another two, and July was on us before Steward Kempe came up to see me in my chamber.

'The laid-off meadowlands are fit, Mistress. An' Hayward knows because I've told 'im, that you'll want the domain hay cut first before they think of lookin' to their own.'

As if it was Kempe's place to take control instead of mine! I let him ride to pay the interest loan last month without my help, and now see where it's got me! What's more he had a note of confidence in his deep voice, a look of certainty in his long monkish face, which made me almost bound to contradict him.

'That as it happens is the contrary of what I have decided,' I said loftily. 'You should have asked me first.' And then of course I had to find the reason – and told him that the village hay was thinner, would make quicker than our own.

'We'll wait until the weather is more settled,' I declared, 'before we think to mow the manor fields.'

'Now then an' with respect, Mistress...' (Why is it when they say that, that people always show so little of it?) 'With the greatest of respect we always cut the Lord's hay first soonasever it is fit. We never change the rule.'

And perhaps if he'd smiled a little, shown some deference or made it clear that it was not for him to have the final say – well then I might, just might, have changed my mind. But old Sobersides Kempe's never troubled to hide his disapproval of me, hardly ever cracks a smile. He simply stood there like a block of wood to add, ''Tis ready now, My Lady, surely.'

So naturally I took it as a challenge to change the silly rule. Which you could say put me in the wrong when, after all the peasants' hay was made and carried to the rick yard – when after they'd cut no more than half the manor share, it rained again. And not just rain, but a tremendous summer storm, with great peals of thunder and savage hail that tore the petals of the briars and turned the cart ruts into streams.

'A little wet does no real harm before the hay is turned,' I told Master Know-it-All Nick Noddy Kempe, when he came back with the kind of 'told-you-so' look on his face that made me want to kick him!

'The sun's out now,' I pointed out. 'It'll dry through in next to no time.'

That's why Hoddie and I are out afield this afternoon. To save the hay and prove that I was right.

'Ye're never going out like that into the spiteful sun?'

Hod was scandalised. 'Nice thing that 'ud be, my lambkin!' (the name she uses when she wants to get around me) 'Good sakes, I've told ye times unnumbered 'aven't I? My Lady Blanche 'ud have me fleed if I should let you burn.'

Then, having failed three times to cram a rush hat on my head, she settled for a pair of kerchiefs for my hair and shoulders. (They're off already – who is there to see or care if I end up as freckled as a quail's egg? I'm bored to tears with looking like some pallid thing that's crawled out from a stone!)

We walked, it wasn't far. The frightful Bruno – Garon's verminous excuse for a dog, the one with feathers like a moulting hen's – perforce has come along. He always does when I walk out or ride abroad, trotting jauntily ahead. I think the silly cur believes I need him to protect me.

The sun has dried the surface of the grass that's mown. So that's good, anyway. The cattle fence is down and the huge meadow's like a painted image – molehill shapes of haycocks, moving figures, men and women, gleeful children, dogs for mine to bark at – with swallows overhead and warm soil underfoot and everywhere the malty smell of making hay. All the greens have quietened now the summer is so well advanced. The long grass tickles my bare feet and pollen rises from the seed-heads as the swathes fall to the mowers.

I've often thought our bondmen boorish fellows – Adam Hayward, Jordan Smith, old Hobbe – not one I would describe as handsome. Yet there's a kind of grace in the smooth swatching of their scythes – blades flashing in the

138

sun, mowing as they've mowed since history began for aught I know, in Rome or Babylon. I like the way they move, the line of hairy arms and thighs. Strong legs, when you can see so much of them, are rather the best bits of men. Even short ones aren't unpleasant. Father Gerard's... But they've seen us, stop with one accord to turn their heads and stare like moggie-owls, the women with the rakes as well. As if I had no perfect right to visit my own fields!

'Bon Joy, m'lady.'

The hayward's changed his scythe for his peeled ashwood staff of office – lumbers over with a sailor's rolling gait, red-faced and smelling like a badger! He's doffed his frayed straw hat to show a straight brim-line across his brow, and hair like mouldy thatch with ears that stick out through it like the handles of a pot. But now he's drawling something else in Engleis, looking to the steward to translate.

'He says you've lost some seed, but there's a tidy bit of bottom grass come up to make the crop.' (And you'd think from the expression in Kempe's face he'd just as soon it hadn't!)

'Hayward says they'll finish this bout presently and then start carryin' what's dry. He thinks the sun'll come again tomorrow.'

'Then tell him that my maid and I are here to help take up what's made.'

I'd really only thought to watch. But why should they have all the fun? And 'though I shouldn't laugh, the way the hayward gawked at that, you'd think that Kempe had told him we would do it naked with our hind-parts painted purple!

'She says a fork's a pretty thing in use, but using it wants method more'n muscle if ye get her meaning? She says there's no sense stooping down to pick up nothing. She says ye'll need to put in less an' git more out – or otherwhiles, she says, ye'll be fair frazzled afore ye've hardly started.'

While Kempe translated everything she said, the haywards's goodwife, Martha (who seems less of a grout-head than her husband) showed me the way to turn the wet side of the hay with my long ashwood fork, ready for the others to rake into windrows and then pile into haycocks when it's dry.

'There's no sense in going at it end on,' is what she's saying now according to the steward.

'She holds there's but two ways to do it, right and wrong – as she told Hayward at the harvest feast, when he got hopeless drunk and ate a tallow candle wick an' all.'

I said I shouldn't laugh, am doing all I can to avoid the twinkle in the woman's eye whilst imitating what she's doing. The movement of her brawny arms. The way she balances the fork. The lightest flick – she makes it look so effortless despite her thickened shape, a trick you have to learn.

I'm stronger than I look. But my left hand and the other elbow are aching horridly and perspiration's dripping off my chin. The meadow is so big besides, with so much to do.

Brisk as a bumbledore herself, Hod won't be told or shown the way to rake the hay up lightly in a series of short jerks. She hefts her rake instead as if it were an axe, and brings it down so hard and far away from her bare toes that five times out of six she has to stoop to free it from the soil.

'Plaguey thing won't go where 'tis instructered,' she mutters in disgust while dragging grass that's plainly green into a flattened heap that looks more like a magpie's nest than any kind of haycock. (I've never really thought of it before. But it's only when she is attending me that Hoddie's ever gentle or exact. In all else I'd say she was as awkward as a sowpig in skirts!)

The little clouds have somehow managed to meet up and scum over half the sky. But it isn't going to rain. It won't, I'm sure of it – and here's the wagon come to carry what's already made, with six red oxen yoked in pairs to draw it to the manor barn.

I'd like to see if Hod fares better, now that she's changed her hay rake for a fork – marching off to show the peasants how to pitch (as if they didn't know!). No one on earth looks quite like Hoddie from behind, I'd know her back-end in a crowd of fifty-thousand – the way she stalks, neck-forward, arms akimbo, white legs stretching her loose kirtle (goose-turd green, a colour I would never wear). Feet like dinner plates – thin rump stuck out and slapped at every second pace by one or other of the wiry tassels at the end of her grey plaits.

The other pitchers all are men. But the old besom's undeterred, and 'though I dare say I have always known, I've never quite admitted until now how very like a man my Hoddie is – how little like a woman in the way she strides about, so very independent and immodest. It's what she's always been (the reason I suppose why Maman was forever telling me to be more feminine in every little thing).

Hod's watching keenly as each pitcher forks up his hay onto the moving wain. Her first attempt draws every eye as she intends it should. The men stand back while she steps forth with careless ease and hurls her fork-load high into the sky – to clear the piled hay in the wagon by at least ten feet, and land on the astonished head of Martin Reeve beyond.

Pride goeth before destruction and a haughty spirit before a fall. Or so the scriptures tell us. Hod runs the back of a large hand across her gleaming brow and glances back uneasily to see if I am watching.

'If any of ye smart lads 'ave a fault to find, p'raps you'd 'ave the nicety to say it to me 'ead?' she says indignantly in French – just as the living haystack that's poor Martin Reeve gives an almighty sneeze!

There is no help for it – no really, I can't think I've laughed so hard since the time I gave myself the hiccoughs! The time the Reigate butler lost his footing on the castle stair and fell tip over tail into the dungheap!

The clouds have pulled apart again into long wisps like carded wool. The sun is westering, no longer visible except as fiery splinters shimmering between the branches of the trees – rooks cawing, flapping to their roosts – colour seeping from the land into a sky that looks set fair... I said it would be fine tomorrow and was right!

The hay we're perched on's like a shaggy golden raft, creaking through the shadows, swaying up the track to shed a litter of untidy stalks on either side. When Hayward set the ladder for us to climb up, Hod likened us to currants on a dumpling, riding home in pride of place atop the load with lines of plodding peasants for our escort. We've cleared all the hay now that was cut before the rain. The mowers each have carried off what they can balance on their scythes, as is their right and due, and still we have two wagons stacked to overspilling. Kempe says the quality is poor. But that's sour grapes. It's bound to be, because I know I made the right decision – even if it nearly killed me!

I can't remember ever being quite so weary – or so grimy, with dirt caked in my hair and lashes, tickling my nose. Gritty in my mouth. My arms are *burned and covered in small scratches. But I feel wonderful I really do! I haven't felt as good since... well not for months at any rate. I've had a perfect day and so has Hod.*

I glanced up from my windrows every now and then – to see her working grimly to perfect her skill, spurred on by the men's loud cheers each time a fork-load landed more or less where she intended. Excepting Father Gerard in his hitched-up cassock, the haymakers all are bonded, owe me labour. And yet each time I stood to rest my back and look along the rows, it felt more like a favour on their part than mine to be allowed to work amongst them.

And now we're loaded ready for the barn. There was moment when Hod missed her footing on the ladder, when there flashed across my mind an image of her falling backwards, yelling, with her white legs in the air. But 'Stupid blessed ladder, danged rungs are set too close together,' was all she had to say as she regained her balance and climbed up beside me on the hay. (Is it callous to feel disappointed?)

From our high perch we're looking down on elder trees, red backs of oxen, Bruno keeping pace. The women with small children have gone home. Others' hats push up like faded cockles in a field of rakes – voices, laughter, comfortable and friendly – a man's voice singing, joined by others for the chorus in the high warbling Sussex style. Someone's brought a tabor to beat out the rhythms...

'What is it? What's the song, Hod? Can you hear the words?'

'They're caterwaulin' something of the plough an' scythe and mowing in a line. And every Jack of 'em plain out of tune!' She says it gruffly with a mild expression of approval on her battered face, as the last words of the ragged chorus float across the breeze.

Silence now, but for the creaking of the wagon and the oxen's rasping breath. The hand-beat of the tabor – and now another voice and others taking up the theme.

'What is it this time, Hoddie? Tell me as they sing it.'

"Ah love's a pretty thing, a pretty thing is love! The love of the earth for the leafy green that fills her valleys fair. There's love, m'lads, there's love!

"Ah love's a pretty thing, a pretty thing is love!" (An' that's the chorus, see?) "The love of a maiden for the spronky lad who fills 'er belly for 'er."

(They sing it ruder, lamb, ye may b'lieve!) "There's love, m'lads, there's love!
Ah love's a..." *(Same chorus, just said over.)*

"The love of a mother for the little babe who fills 'er cradle nicely. *(An'
same again.)* There's love, m'lads, there's love...

"But the love of love, the greatest love, m'lads, is the love of a drunkard
for the understandin' man who fills 'is cup to overflow. There's love,
m'lads....'"

Hoddie's choking, snorting up the dust too hard to take it further.

But here we are already at the manor gate – and Bruno barking, hackles all
on end. The gate's open and unguarded. Through the arch the gleam of
harness, horses in a group.

God save us! have we been invaded? Has Count John sent his ruffians to
take the manor into Mortain lands?

Bruno's yelping, someone's hit him with a stone.

It is for me to go and see, it has to be. 'Hayward! Hayward, bring the
ladder!'

One horseman's turning through the arch towards us... Is it? I can't see...

It is! – that plaguey man again, Sir Hugh!
And must I, do I have to face him?

Oh Lord, MUST I?

CHAPTER FOUR

You have to be exhausted to sleep in stifling heat on rocks which jab you through your bed-roll, while whining insects work in relays to sting you anywhere that isn't covered by your clothing. And if our camp above the seaport of Marseille gave us a good view of its harbour, it offered little else. You couldn't drive a tent peg into its stony soil. Or dig latrines. Or find fresh water anywhere nearby. So when the morning after our arrival a bishop's chaplain came to tell us that King Richard's fleet had been delayed, he wasn't happily received.

'D'ye mean to say they've gorn an' lost a hundred ships?' John Hideman asked in disbelief. 'To leave us up here to feed the shimmeroys until they think where they mislaid 'em?'

'Word is our troops went on a drunken rampage when the fleet put into Lisbon, and mostly ended in the gaol.'

The chaplain frowned at us beneath a hat shaped like a chafing dish that served to shield his tonsure from the sun. 'The King of Portugal has sent to ask King Richard for redress before he'll let 'em out. But our King shouted that he'd see them all in hell before he'd lift a finger – called 'em witless shitheads, scurvy ship rats – told the Portugese to do a thing with his king's missive which I can't in decency repeat, and went so red whiles he was shouting it they thought his veins 'ud bust.'

'Not overpleased then,' Jos vouchsafed.

And it was left to me to discover that Archbishop Baldwin was already busy hiring vessels for our crossing from the merchants of the port. If all went well, the chaplain said, they'd be equipped within a sennight to carry us directly from Marseille to the Christian port of Tyre in Palestine.

The orders were for knights to take just one mount and two sumpters each onto the transports. So two days later, at a horse fair in the city suburbs by the Roman aqueduct, I traded the old hinny with the ponies for a couple of strong mules – and took the larger of them down to the port next morning, to carry back the purchases I'd still to make.

Jos came along to lead the mule. John stayed to mind the other with Raoul, with Bert to brood our padlocked coffer like a hen on chicks, sitting on its cover with a spear in one hand and a dagger in the other. 'If any care to try the lock, they'll very soon learn how a stuck pig feels,' he said without the glimmer of a smile.'

The city, even at that early hour, was thronged with crucesignati, housewives and street urchins, and every kind of merchant conversing in a harsh patois that we could barely follow. The shops and stalls that lined its cobbled ways were busy selling anything that could be worn, consumed or used to ease your life or shorten someone else's. To our distaste we saw black Moors and Moslem Saracens amongst the traders. But when we asked how they could deal within a Christian port, were told that wars were the affair of soldiers. Not of honest men with businesses to run.

I'd brought enough to buy myself an only-slightly-dented steel pot helm with a slit visor, and a linkmail hauberk second-hand – and that was was just the start. In a street full of ironmongers and armourers I acted like a child among the sweetmeats, and bought a baselard, a crossgrained buckler, nearly new, and a fine-balanced shortsword with curved quillons and a fantastically engraved Toledo blade – the kind of sword I'd wanted all my life. For the men I found three gambesons of quilted buckram, kettle hats (of a new type the trader called '*chapel-de-fer*') and three well-seasoned shields. In a street market further down the hill we purchased twenty ells of Spanish sailcloth, with all the cords, waxed thread and needles that we'd need for tenting.

Then I left Jos with the loaded mule to kick their heels beside a horse trough at the foot of the church steps, and paid five silver pennies to have a mass said for the soul of Alberic. I set a candle for him in the church before a statue of the Magdalene, and watched it flame and splutter into life – and pictured Albie stomping on his bandy legs

145

through hosts of angels, determined to be unimpressed by anything they had to show him in the realm of Heaven.

"Tis all very fine I dessay, an' lor' forbid I'd ever say what's false,' I could hear him patiently explain. 'But not bein' funny, I've seen sights back over Sellin'ton Strand an' otherwheres in Sussex as valiant as anything in this 'ere Perridise – an' blamed if I don't think so.'

From the Church of the Magdalene, we followed the steep streets down to the water to see if we could find where our sea transports lay. In lock-ups set against the harbour wall and numbered to match galleys moored along the quays, shaved-headed convicts of every faith and colour waited to serve out their sentence on the rowing benches. On the stone flags before them, mongers sold roast capons, vegetables of every sort, and more tubs for live fish or stalls for dead ones than I'd ever seen or could imagine.

The harbour taverns overflowed. Beggars and cut-purses, stevedores and harlots all plied their trades amongst the crowds. A tightrope walker balanced on a hemp line strung between two stacks of barrels. A bear danced upright to some sailors' shanty tooted on a flute, while an enterprising whore contrived to take in three men all at once, and then a rampant jackass. A thing involving too much careful management to be at all exciting. (Or so I said to Jos, with one hand casually depressing my raised tunic.)

'My Guillemette 'ud take 'em slippy as ye like,' he boasted, as the men with heavy frowns of concentration, fed in the donkey inch by careful inch. 'Those three – bear an' donkey, tightrope man, four stevedores, an' a couple of bench slaves to make up the round dozen – easy.'

Among the red and white-crossed soldiers shouting lewd advice at the performers, we happened on a man from Caen in Normandie, who told us that King Richard had already left Marseille with all his retinue. The news in port, he said, was that the German Emperor had died by accident before he was halfway to Palestine – and that King Richard, hearing that the German croisade was confounded, had sworn he'd wait no longer for his fleet, and sailed straightway for Genoa in ten rented galleys. With fifteen more to follow as soon as they could be equipped.

Marseille, he said, was never short of galleys, or ship-owners ready to supply them.

Larger vessels jostled with flotillas of sardine boats stalled like cattle all along the quays. Sleek taride galleys with banked oars and pointed metal rambades at the prow, lay side by side with broad-beamed merchantmen – with esseneques and dromonds for the freight – each vessel brightly painted in the colours of its owner.

It was not until the order came to strike camp three weeks later that we knew which ships we'd sail on. In a dock by the Templar's wharf which stank of sewage, four merchantmen had been refitted for Ranulf de Glanville, Bishop Hubert Walter and their troops, to voyage in convoy with our own archbishop's flagship galley for the port of Tyre.

The cost of passage on the tarida for myself, my horse and squire was eight silver shillings, with six marks more to pay for places on a dromond for the others and the mules. By then I judged it safest to divide some of the silver between the four of us, in wallets tied beneath our tunics. Or wrapped in rags and wadded into body-pouches sewn into their linings. Although before we sailed, I'd had to part with three marks more from my own share, to pay for all the damage caused by Raoul when we came to embark him.

At our first attempt to lead him up the ramp into the galley's hull port behind Sir Ralph of Stopham's destrier, Raoul put his head down, planted all four hooves as wide apart as he could place them on the slatted boards – refused to budge, as obstinate as a stone donkey. The second time we tried, I rode him to it at a canter. But that was a mistake as well, because the moment that he heard the hollow sound of metal shoe on wood, he tossed his head and rolled his eyes dementedly. Plunging. Rearing. Squealing like a weaner, before clattering back down onto the wharf on his way to kicking in a wine keg and toppling three sides of salted pork into the harbour.

The third time, we tried it in reverse with John on one flank of the trembling horse and Jos the other. I was at the head (which is to say the sharp end), risking life and limb to force him slowly backwards step by step. Until we found ourselves, all four of us including Raoul, cast violently onto our knees. Then when we had to let him up, the maddened horse crabbed, white-eyed, slap into a stack of wicker crates – to send a cloud of feathers and a dozen squawking chickens down the quay.

John Hideman volunteered to try him blindfold for the fourth attempt, with sacking bound across his eyes and more spread on the boards to soften the effect of his big hooves.

'I'd be a fool to say that I know everythin' of horses,' he admitted as he tied the blindfold. 'But chances are he'll trot up like a lamb, if he can't use his eyes an' ears to tell him where he's at.

'En't that the truth of it old feller?' he crooned into the rigid muscles of Raoul's neck – talking quietly, coaxing the big horse slowly up the ramp.

His voice was higher and a good bit louder though, by the time that he'd been bitten in the shoulder, trodden over and farted at explosively in Raoul's fourth and final bid for freedom.

'I think you'd best run up to see if they've a winch on board, John,' I told him as I gingerly removed the blindfold. 'Or else our friend's croisade will likely end as…'

'Horse meat tough as boot leather,' Jos helpfully supplied.

'Unless you'd let me have a try to help the old bugger to see reason?' he asked when John had disappeared inside the ship. And when without much hope of a result I said he might, he wheeled the sweating stallion round to face the ramp, handing the reins to Bertram in exchange for his long pikestaff.

'Let go when I say "*Now*",' he said, with one hand lifting Raoul's black tail, and with the other carefully alligning the blunt end of the pike with the horse's pouting arsehole.

'*NOW!*' he cried and rammed the pike shaft home.

John Hideman told me afterwards that from inside the hold he heard the shrill sound of an animal in pain – or very much surprised – then saw poor Raoul come thundering down the larboard gangway, to wedge himself tight as a bottle-cork into its furthest stable. But when he asked Jos later how by the Son of Mary he'd achieved it, my squire had turned from wiping the wet pikestaff on Raoul's blindfold, to tell him with blue eyes as clear and innocent as summer sky: 'Just had a quiet word in the old sort's ear. He knows I speak his language.'

It would be funny still if I could think of it without the knowledge of what happened to them later, Raoul and Jos.

But now the voyage – the time that I've looked forward most to calling back. With all the horses loaded, with the tarida's port caulked and sealed, we cast off from our moorings after Vespers on the twenty-sixth day of the month of August.

Archbishop Baldwin blessed us in the undertaking while we all knelt on the deck, invoking the protection of Saint Drausius and Nicholas, the patron saints of sailors, and calling at the last on Christ's own Sepulchre to save us and protect us.

'*Sanctum Sepulchrum adjuva!*' he cried from the poop above us, looking like a saint himself with both arms raised to the red crosses painted on our sails. Our *amens* rumbled raggedly across the deck as Marseille faded back into the haze. But Baldwin's words sang loudly in our hearts. It was the moment we were born for.

That's what we all believed.

Beyond the harbour-mouth, long herringbones of oars propelled our fleet into the open sea. Baldwin's decision to follow Count Henri of Toulouse, and sail as he had done by the direct route south of Crete, involved some element of risk. Without putting into port along the way, we'd need a fair wind and stout oarsmen both, to get to Tyre before our wine turned sour and maggots ate their way through our supplies – and even in the summer, fierce gales called *gulphs* could capsize a shallow-draughted vessel. Pirates ranged the Middle Sea in galleys which moved faster than a horse could gallop. A monstrous beast, *the Melar,* with whole trees growing from its back, was said to haunt the Barbary Coast and gobble ships for sport. Mermaids with fishes' tails and women's breasts could lure us onto rocks – and if we reached the coast of Outremer unscathed, we could expect to be attacked by Moslem warships, belching some kind of *wildfire* that only vinegar could quench.

In fact the voyage was nothing near so perilous. Or not until we sighted land. By Tierce each day the tar which sealed the deck seams was hot enough to scorch bare flesh, the space beneath the poop where we were meant to sleep too stuffy to be borne. So most nights, clad in nothing more than body linen, we'd carry our bed-rolls up to the open deck to let the timbers of the tarida creak us to sleep. Or else distract ourselves from thoughts of *Fisty Flora* by seeking out the Wain and Dragon from the multitude of stars that lit the vaults above and danced reflected in the waves – above us and below us, as if our little wooden world had left the sea to sail amongst them.

It isn't hard to see myself stargazing. How could it be when it is what I'm doing now?

Khadija told me once that she believed each mortal had their own star, which shone the moment they were born and darkened with their final breath.

Maybe I saw her star one breathless night from the poop deck of the tarida? But if I did, it isn't in this sky.

In the early mornings, when the air was cool at sea and Jos had gone below to see to Raoul, I liked to climb into the narrow space beside the mangon catapult above the galley's rambade. To perch up on the cordage, barefoot and grimy-soled, and feel the salt spray in my face. To watch the oar blades slice the water, listen to their creak and thump, and wonder with each league we put between us and Marseille if I would ever come this way again.

The galèriers who rowed the tarida were all of them convicted felons culled from gaols in Burgundy and Aragon, shackled to their benches and branded in the armpit with their terms of servitude. 'For better a repentant Christian to transport us,' Archbishop Baldwin ruled, 'than a disciple of the camel-driver, Mahomet.'

Below the rowing benches, the stabularia in the hold where Raoul was stalled were set in a long row in line along the keel. Even with the hatches open their foetid atmosphere was near unbreatheable. It tasted foul and stung your eyes and burned the skin inside your nose – and Jos, who brought his food and water and worked to massage Raoul's slack muscles, proclaimed it to be dense enough to cut up into cheese. And as for my poor destrier, they'd hung him from a canvas *cinta* slung beneath his belly with his four hooves barely brushing the esparto bedding of his stall. I hated seeing him suspended, suffocated, dull-eyed with misery, and am ashamed to think how little time I spent with him as a result.

Horses cannot vomit. But if their slings spared them some of the worst effects of sea-sickness, we human freight were left to cope as best we might with decks which even on a calm day rolled and pitched beneath our feet.

One morning as I passed Archbishop Baldwin sitting in the shade beneath his awning on the poop, I was surprised to be addressed. 'Sir Knight, I have a riddle for you.'

The old man's face in contrast to his sooty hood was sickly greenish-white. A bucket at his side contained what I supposed to be his breakfast. 'Tell me the difference if you can between a jellyfish and an archbishop,' he asked me as I straightened from my bow.

I shook my head to own shamefacedly that I had no idea.

'No please, 'tis very simple. The difference is that only one of them has too much sense to trust himself to any element but that which he was born to.' He looked at me with red-rimmed eyes and heaved a sigh. 'Regrettably, it is the jellyfish,' he said.

Many men were sick as dogs. But Jos and I soon gained our sea legs, and even the archbishop was on his feet within a week. We had been told that, with sails set and a good breeze astern, our passage by the southern route might be completed in three weeks or less – and the wind was in our favour. Most days it filled the triangular lateen sails flapping from our mainmast and the mizzen. Slower in the water under oars and often lagging far behind, the bulbous dromonds in our little fleet could hoist a third sail if they chose. Which meant that when the wind was strong they could be near enough to hail.

Jos always said that he could tell which one of them held Guillemette, and whether she was sitting fore or aft, by its tilt in the water. Although in truth we never saw a face we knew in any other vessel.

On the evening of our twentieth day at sea, with our ship's biscuit hard as stone, our water putrid, wine turned to vinegar, our men and horses dysenteric, we sighted land at last. 'There she is lads, can't ye smell her?' Our Genoese shipmaster took up the pilot's cry.

All we could see at first was a pale line to separate the sea from sky, and long before we caught a whiff of anything but tar and horse piss, our attention was called elsewhere.

'Sail! Sail out to larboard bow!' – appearing as a simplified child's chalking of a single sail, divided as the craft approached into a triple row of lateens. A flash of foam showed either side of an immensely high-beaked prow, with something brightly coloured flapping round it. I stared transfixed.

'*WHAT SHIP ARE YOU?*' Our master bawled the challenge through a hailer in the harsh Levantine French that navigators use. 'A bireme, but no heathen crescent – could be a merchantman from Venice, or a Pisano out of Tyre, yer Grace,' he called to the archbishop, who was shinning down the poop deck ladder with a surprising turn of speed.

'But he doesn't think so,' I heard the old man mutter as he hurried past.

'I've seen the like before of that there swaggin' round 'er belly.' A hush on deck as the strange vessel drove towards us enabled all to hear. "T'will be soaked in camels' piss and vinegar, to stop the hull from catching, d'ye see?' the shipmaster told Baldwin when he joined him in the bow. An' if she's carrying the fire, yer Grace, she'd 'ave to be Byzantine, or...'

'Fire?' I saw the old man fumble for the silver crucifix he wore around his neck. 'Do you mean *feu grégeois*? Is that her armament, my son? The thing they call *Greek fire*?'

'...or else she'd have to be a Sarsen fireship. *Diavolo*, 'tis all we need!' The master's weatherbeaten face was grave. 'There's none as know how wildfire's made, excepting Sarsens and Byzantines. But it sinks more vessels in these waters, take my word, than any other weapon in creation.'

He hawked and spat over the side to emphasise the point.

'Then would it be advisable to challenge her again,' Baldwin suggested, cross in hand, 'before we come within her range?'

'*WHAT – SHIP – ARE – YOU?*' Amplified by the storm-hailer, the master's challenge must have reached the other.

'*WHAT SHIP? WHERE ARE YOU BOUND?*'

But all the answer that came back across the water was the rattling sound of ratchets from its towering castles, as unseen hands winched down the slings of the ship's mangonels to load them ready for attack.

'She's Sarsen, never doubt it. A *shayan*,' the shipmaster confirmed. 'Two hundred oar if she's a dozen.'

'Could we outrun her?'

'Not a hope in Hades, seein' how this old tub's freighted.'

'Then if we cannot run, as servants of The Lord we must engage her. I suggest you signal for the dromonds to make for port, Master – and then do all that's needful to turn our vessel in her path.'

'But the Sarsen has the fire! She'll scorch us quicker than a feather in a furnace. Aye, and overtake the others too, yer Grace, to serve 'em each a measure of the same!'

Forgetful for the moment of his status, I saw the master seize hold of the archbishop's thin arm and squeeze it 'til he winced.

'Do you not see it, man? We either have to take 'er on together as a fleet, or run three ways at once and pray to Christ that two of us can find the speed to shake 'er off. *Porco Madonna!* We stand no chance against that bugger on our own!'

By then the other vessel's massive size was obvious, with turbaned figures in her waist and on her castles visible to give her scale. But none of us that day, the shipmaster included, had credited our leader with a quarter of the courage he possessed. Ignoring the profanity, Archbisop Baldwin raised his head to look around him at the sailors, at knights and squires awaiting his instruction, and gave a gentle smile. 'I do believe King Saul may have suggested something similar to David,' he said, 'when that young optimist stood up to face Goliath with nothing but a pebble in a leather sling.

'*Never place a limit on the power of God!*' His voice, restored to sermon pitch, reached all on deck. 'Our Blessed Saviour has brought us here to crush the infidel, my friends, for His own greater glory,' the old archbishop cried. 'So let us do so in His name. We are in God's hands now!'

CHAPTER FIVE

A hundred bare feet thudded on the larchwood boards. Red-capped sailors ran in all directions, scaling ladders, reefing canvas to the master's bellowed orders, cursing in Italian. Galèriers struck oars. Knights and squires collided, locking weapons, jostling for places at the rails.

'Here, Sir Garon. Here my lord!' Jos panted up with my new shield, my sword, my arbalest, my cocking belt and two sac-quivers stuffed with quarrels. 'I guessed the bow?' he said just as it slipped from his sweating fingers to clatter down between us on the deck.

Before I could retrieve it, the shayan opened fire. We heard the chok and whistle of the mangonels. Then something no bigger than a flying fist hurtled past our heads to splash into the water.

'Grenades! Look out on deck!' a voice cried harshly through a hailer. As two more missiles plummeted into the sea, I knew where I had heard the name before. A sailor in our first week out from port had warned of Sarsen bottle-bombs made out of clay to look like pomegranates, and called 'Granadas' or *grenades* after the place in Moorish Spain best known for growing those strange fruit. Another struck the belfry of our forward castle even as the thought passed through my mind. Struck, shattered and ignited! With a sound like gusting wind, a blossom of dazzling blue and yellow flame exploded where it landed.

Fire flooded the forecastle, splashing onto clothing and bare limbs. Dripping through the hatches onto the naked oarsmen. Burning, even on the metal surface of the bell. A squealing rat, its fur on fire, lay writhing on the deck. Men shrieked and thrashed, danced in the flames' embrace. Flesh hissed and shrivelled. Others ran to aid them, stamping on the fires which lapped the upper deck before they could consume the mangonel that armed it – efforts which, if anything, made

155

matters worse. For nothing, as we all had heard, could quench Greek fire, but camels' piss or...

Vinegar! I suddenly recalled the raw taste of the wine I'd spat onto the deck that morning, a vintage now so acid that few of the company could stomach it. 'Wine! Fetch wine!' I heard my own voice, and then Jos's, shouting wildly. I thrust my squire toward the forward hatch. 'Now, now! As much as they can find. The wine will...'

'Put it out, Sir Garry?' Jos hazarded

'Yes, God willing, so it will.'

And so it did. In less time than I could have hoped, a tun of sour Bordeaux was hauled onto the deck and broached, its contents slopped in buckets hand-to-hand to quench the fire in clouds of evil smelling steam.

We were too late to help one wretched human torch, who in his agony leapt from the rail to flounder screaming in the burning water, before his own weight dragged him down. But through the steam the mangonel appeared unscathed. The mangonel was saved.

By then the ships were closing, and the bombardiers lost range. As it bore down on us with single-minded purpose, the Saracen shayan looked more like a devouring monster than any kind of ship, with double banks of oars for fins, a wrinkled skin of canvas sagging from its prow – and above, what else but the great gaping head of an infuriated dragon!

'Christ's plague, the bugger's moving! They can move its head!'

Behind the shield he held for me, my squire's blue eyes grew rounder. 'Next thing they'll have it belching fire,' he breathed, as unbelievably the segmented serpent neck dipped forward.

Somewhere behind it in the vessel's prow a turban moved.

A red spark gleamed.

Then with a mighty roar, a jet of living yellow flame shot from the dragon's mouth – to prove Jos right and set the water blazing in its path!

For me the time was past for horror or surprise. The fire, the wine, the screams, the sulphurous smoke had brought me up to a killing pitch. Then when I heard the shrill whinny of an excited horse from somewhere down below, I knew it instantly, and felt a surge of pride to think of Raoul straining in his sling to join the action. With taut nerves and tauter bowstrings, we waited only for the order to loose bolts. I needed action too. My target was the man directing the fire-breathing creature – and I could see his gore already sprinkling its painted head. I needed blood!

Archbishop Baldwin standing close behind, was looking in the same direction. 'What is it underneath that man,' he called up to the master in the smoking prow, 'I mean the platform he is perched on?'

'Yer Grace, we *must* change course or we're roast meat!'

'When we're opposed, Saint Gregory instructs us to regard it as a test of faith. Is it some kind of a receptacle, the platform? A reservoir perhaps for *feu grégeois*?'

'Most likely 'tis, yer Grace. They use a pump and siphon, so they say, to spray out the petra'olea an' naptha an' whatever else they 'ave in there. But mark me Sir, they'll ram us on this course. We must, we 'ave to...'

'Of what construction is it, would you say, this reservoir?'

'Iron for sure under the timber cladding. But yer Grace you must allow...'

'And would I be correct in thinking that the liquid it contains is volatile, combustible, a mixture that is likely to explode on impact?'

''Tis 'ow they use it in grenades Sir, an' why they seldom move it but by water.'

'So if we were to strike this metal reservoir a heavy blow? Say with a sling-stone or ballista bolt, fired broadside at the closest range? Could the effect be that of a grenade of many times the size and power? To blow the Philistine apart?'

I saw the master stare at the old man in silence. And whether in his heart he thought the risk was justified or no, he acted with the swiftest resolution. In the bare time it took to shout the order, he had our steersmen hauling on the rudder, and the larboard side galèriers increasing strokes to help bring round our prow.

A warbling, ungodly battle cry rose from the decks and walkways of

157

the other vessel, to raise the small hairs on a hundred Christian necks. Already hordes of arbalesters lined its gunwales, withholding fire as we came up in range – and then the drums, a rapidly increasing beat, as with a surge of power, the shayan's oarsmen jerked her up in four short strokes to ramming speed.

Archbishop Baldwin's order to loose bolts came late, and through a hail of Sarsen darts. They sizzled inboard like giant hornets.

Steel points splintered woodwork, thudded into human flesh.

Trusting Jos' skill to shield us both, I kept my eye fixed on the man behind the dragon's head, ignoring the blood pulsing in my own. My breath was short, but nothing trembled. Remembering my practice at the butts, I aimed unhurriedly. I raised the trigger to release the string and was already bending with my right foot in the crossbow's stirrup to reload, already lining up the backsight with the head of my next quarrel – before I saw the first had missed.

Unharmed, the man behind the fearsome mask was turning its demonic face towards us. Behind him on the turret reservoir two others worked the handles of the force-pump. Perched by the dragon's arching neck a fourth man held the touch-torch ready to ignite the spurting fluid...

With a new target in my sights, I fired again and watched the spiral-feathered quarrel drill the air to find its mark – and felt a vaulting, savage thrill of conquest, as my victim with the torch still clutched in his dead hand, plunged head-first into the sea.

'Well shot, Hadderton!' My friend Sir Mark le Jeune clapped me on the back as he ran by.

'Clear the decks!' the master bellowed through his hailer while I stooped to load again. 'Up on the castles lads or in the hold, wherever there's a space.'

Below us we could hear the bos'n's mate withdraw the chains which linked the oarsmen's shackles.

The infidels shot running Christians like foxes bolting from a stand of corn. Above me on the poop-deck ladder, a dart passed through the body of a man to burst out from his belly in a fount of blood and yellow fluid. It was Sir Mark. Another missile struck the side-rail of the ladder, barely missing Jos's hand. Even before we reached Archbishop Baldwin's ragged awning, to see our straining oarsmen through the hatch, it seemed that nothing could prevent our little ship from being crushed.

Two shrills of the bos'n's pipe were all it took to show my perfect ignorance of sea warfare.

At the first short whistle, every oarsman on the steerward side raised his blade clear of water, as those to larboard executed one more powerful stroke in perfect time. To send the ship about so violently that half the men on deck were thrown onto their knees. At the second and protracted whistle, the larboard rowers to a man leapt from their benches, knelt and shipped their oars. Surprised, the Saracen had no time to warn her crew before our bronze rambade ripped through the canvas draping of her hull, snapping banks of oars like twigs, to crush the bodies of the oarsmen between their jerking looms.

Up on the foc'sle of the tarida, and through another hail of darts, the bombardiers were bringing round our mangonel for the close broadside that we needed to explode the reservoir. It was a chance that would not come again. Six men strove frantically with ropes and levers to move the heavy engine. Two more worked the winch and windlass, to drag its beam into position. Another slid the heavy fifty-pounder stone into the sling spoon. But even as they cursed and fumbled, a second torch was lit behind the dragon's deadly gape – and it moved round to find them.

No time to pray or wait another instant. The first to reach it, tripped the mangon's slip-hook. But too late! Our vessel in that very moment gave a lurch to steerboard. The catapult's great beam flew up, to strike its padded stop and shoot the stone too high, too wide. To miss the reservoir by yards.

The wounded dragon roared and took its vengeance. A terrifying flood of liquid fire engulfed our bombardiers in an inferno. To bring them death in dancing agony – and to destroy the Christian catapult completely.

Bombarded, burning, helplessly adrift, our tarida had but one chance more to save herself from immolation. Mounted at the taffrail, a pivoted ballista in form much like an outsized crossbow, waited for a last shot at the shayan's reservoir, before the fire that lapped the poop deck ladder swept up to consume us.

The range of the machine was upward of two hundred paces. So when the shayan's forward turret swung into its sights across mere feet of water, it hardly could have missed.

We saw a glint, rotating vanes of brass attached to steel. We heard the violent clang of one metal in collision with. We even had the time to judge the thing a failure... before a mighty fist of light and heat punched through our ship. To send us scudding landward like a leaf across a pond.

It's curious the way explosions work. You feel them when they happen as a single blinding force. Then afterwards they seem to do it all again, but at a slower speed. Send wood and iron and bits of human flesh cartwheeling through the smoke. Set fire to hair. Scorch skin. Blind vision. Deafen hearing. Shoot red-green colours through your brain!

Is it the sound that hits you first? Or the searing heat? Or the choking blast of sulphur? And how long does it take? How long before you know that you're alive? How long before you see that what is blocking out the light is your own hand?

How long before the pain comes as you work to quench the flames about you?

How long before you're able to thank God in Heaven for arms that work, and legs that bear you up, and all that's still intact between them?

Away to stern, the dragon lay without a head. Billows of black smoke, coiled through with brilliant sapphire flame, rose from its shattered hull to cloud the evening sky.

'Deo gratias, the day is ours!'

My Lord Archbishop's face was smudged with soot, and without his eyebrows he looked mightily surprised.

'Aye, an' thank The Good Man while we're at it for sending our mangon stone well wide,' the ship's master recommended from behind his shoulder. 'For if we'd 'ud struck 'er broadside as we meant to, I'm 'ere to tell yer Grace we'd all 'ave flown to heaven, or the other place, already cooked an' jointed!'

It had taken every man who could still stand, and all our barrels of Bordeaux, to douse the fires on deck. And even then, long snakes of flame continued to dance round us in the water while the sun sank slowly back into the sea.

That night it was impossible to sleep for the unceasing cries of those who had been burned. The archbishop with his chaplains moved quietly round the ship – salving wounds with goose fat, offering last rites and giving comfort where they could – while Jos and I sat in the poop beneath the remnants of his awning, hands clasped about our knees, to talk and talk through all the hours of darkness.

Too thoroughly excited to take heed of his burned foot or my raw neck and shoulder, we kept recalling for each other our first sight of the shayan, the first grenades, the dragon's moving head. Comparing our reactions at each moment of engagement. Re-living every movement to the point of our explosive victory.

'Except for you remembering the wine, My Lord, we'd none of us be here to tell the tale.'

I'd saved us all, Jos told me proudly, Archbishop, chaplains, knights, squires, crew and horses. All who could be saved. It was a thing to wonder at, Jos said – and I agreed.

The way I saw it on the poop that night, I'd just survived the greatest triumph of my life!

Soon after Tierce next day, in a flat calm, our charred and tattered tarida was rowed to shore. At dawn, Conrad de Montferrat, the Governor of Tyre, had sent out fresh water in two skiffs. Archbishop Baldwin and his chaplains were invited to return with them into the city. But our gallant little leader had insisted on remaining to see our vessel safe to port.

'Oh Lord, we come unto the Land of Promise, which Thou hast given us through Moses and our dear Saviour Jesus Christ,' he cried out from the prow. 'We pledge our lives this day to its deliverance!'

Built on an island joined to shore by a long causeway constructed by the Greek King Alexander, Tyre was one of few seaports in Palestine remaining still in Christian hands. Which meant that refugees were packed like herrings in a barrel in every souk and church and bagnio in the city, with those who could not get inside spread out in camps along the white sand beach. The people who came out to stare, the mongrel offspring as we understood of Christian settlers and Arab women, were bare above the waist, their women cloaked, their children naked or in rags. We'd often heard that Outremen had dogs' heads on their shoulders. Or but a single eye set in between their nipples. But these folk they called *Pullani*, were formed much as we were ourselves, except that for the most part they were small and slender with dark skin and jet black hair.

The outlines of the rocks and trees, the blue smudges of the distant hills already shimmered in the morning heat. To disembark, we berthed in the deepwater basin on the south side of the causeway, its stone flags rolling as it seemed beneath our feet as we set them on *terra firma*.

My Raoul, thank God, was not one of the horses that had died at sea. But if I'd pictured him descending from the ship with any of the force he'd used to enter it, then I was disappointed. I barely recognised the animal that Jos led through the hull port, blinking at the glare. No longer fearful of the ramp and near too weak to stumble down it, he moved stiff-jointed like a blindfold well-horse.

'Poor old bugger might as well be stuffed and drawn on hobby wheels,' Jos said as he led out a beast with jutting bones, and weeping sores attracting flies in places where the sling had chafed his belly and the skin behind his forelegs.

A black-robed deputation from Josias, the Tyrian archbishop whose pleas to Christendom had launched the Kings' Croisade, was waiting for our own archbishop before a huddle of low buildings on the causeway. Long trains of donkeys bore our freight to where a strange group of *jamal* (or as the seamen called them, *'camels'*) squatted in the sand like huge dun-coloured geese, their long mule faces set in haughty sneers.

John Hideman must have seen us limping into port and ran out along the harbour wall to meet us, a sunburned and familiar figure. He spoke at first so fast that all his words were jumbled, although we gathered he and Bert were lodged already in the stables of the Bishop's Palace with all our baggage and the mules. But all the talk in Tyre, he told us as we fell in line to march into the city, was that the Christian Queen of Jerusalem, a cousin to our own King Richard, had died of fever in the siege of Moslem Acre a day's ride down the coast.

'Ye may be sure King Guy, who lays siege to the place in our behalf is fair beside hisself with grief,' John said, 'whiles Saladin sits laughing in his camp up in the hills at the dear man's misfortune.'

The colour of the water on either side of Alexander's causeway was a fierce blue. The heat pressed in around us like a cloak. Laden camels stalked ahead on knobbled feet, their thin heels chafing as they moved. Ahead of us, the white walls of the city had been daubed from base to battlement with a limewash of crushed sea-shells which glittered in the sun.

After so long at sea I walked wide-legged at Raoul's tail. I could have wept to see him scrape and stumble on the even road, and might have thought him finished as a destrier – but for the clarions that sounded to announce our entry.

The camels belched their own complaint at the disturbance. But Raoul's head came up. His thin neck jerked. His shaky joints braced back, and snorting with excitement he once again became the warhorse he was bred to be – ready, fit and willing to do battle!

I know, because I felt the same. Because at that first trumpet blast, the sparkling walls of Tyre were of a sudden blackened and bombarded. Became the walls of Acre under siege. The Christian Queen was dead. Her widower, King Guy, had lost most of their realm to Saracen invaders. King Richard was still far away across the sea. But Saladin of Araby, the Mussulman, the AntiChrist and spawn of Satan we had come to slay, was camped that very day no more than ten leagues south of where we stood!

I pictured the ungodly Sultan mounted on a black Arabian stallion. Black-haired. Clad all in black, his mouth and chin obscured by a black veil – a prince of earthly darkness, as black as midnight's arsehole.

163

While we clattered down the causeway through the land gate of the city, we charged him in imagination, Raoul and I. Responding to the clarions, we charged the archfiend shouting *'Victoire!'* with my lance-point aimed at Saladin's black heart.

CHAPTER SIX

Tel al-Kharruba south of Acre: September 1190

THE SULTAN, ALL IN FLAWLESS WHITE

In the fourth and final week of Ramadhan, al-Malik al-Nasir, Salahuddin Abu 'l-Muzaffar Yusuf ibn Ayyub ibn Shadi; Allah's Deputy, God's shadow on the Earth, Defender of The One True Faith, Sultan of Egypt, Syria and Yemen, Ruler of Aleppo and Damascus, Prince of Believers, Commander of the Faithful, Giver of Unity and the true Word, Adorner of the Standard of Truth, Corrector of the World and of the Law – the boy his mother knew as *Yusuf*, the man all Christendom calls *Saladin* – sits cross-legged in his tent on a maqada matress, facing south to Mecca. Around him stand his eunuchs, his senior officers, his qa'ids, his emirs and tawashis, along with others of his Kurdish and Turcoman counsel who've earned his special favour.

The Sultan's camp is sited on a high and largely treeless ridge a little to the south of the plain of Acre. A well-ordered settlement; it is a place in which drunkenness and loose behaviour are accounted sins, where all kneel five times a day to thank Allah for his continued favour. Laid out in streets like a small town, its lines of tents are interspersed with limestone huts; their doors and windows canopied against the glare. One houses Salahuddin's falcons, another his Egyptian hunting cats. Behind, a partially submerged ice-house is packed with mountain snow to cool the Sultan's drinks. Asses and riding camels are roped in groups wherever there is space. Ponies are picketed. Chickens scratch

165

for beetles. Sheep graze the grey sages and ratams which sprout between the rocks.

A warrior who's weathered more than thirty seasons in the field; a man of legendary piety who knows a good deal more than most about the human state; heir to the ancient wealth of Egypt, ruler of an empire twice as large as those of the English and the French King set together, the Sultan's appearance lacks any kind of ostentation.

The face of Salahuddin Yusuf ibn Ayyub is the colour of oiled walnut, narrow and deep-lined, with the almond eyes and long beaked nose of a true Kurd. A slight figure in a qaftan of bleached cotton, he wears a turban made from pleated lengths of snowy muslin, wound round a small felt toque and pinned with a single aigrette feather, also white. His brows are dark and heavy. His thin moustache and neatly parted beard, both trimmed symmetrically, have had the grey dyed out of them with litharge and burnt lime. His hands are scrupulously clean. His feet are neatly shod in buskins. All of his eight fingers and both his thumbs are innocent of rings – the austere effect he seeks, spoiled only by the large, untidy, wildly weeping female who's attached herself to the crossed ankles of God's Shadow on the Earth.

His eyelids droop. But when he lifts them, the Sultan's eyes, black as obsidian, are lively and alert.

'Assure the woman that her daughter shall be sought and found, if she has not been sold,' he tells his dragoman interpreter. 'If God so wills, the Christian child shall be restored into her mother's care.'

He speaks with quiet authority. His voice is light but clear. 'And tell her she shall have our gentlest mare to bear them both in safety to the unbelievers' camp. The compassion of Allah is universal,' he concludes while two plump eunuchs prise the woman from his legs and lead her sobbing from the tent.

The Sultan Salahuddin Yusuf ibn Ayyub has acts of cruelty in his past. But in his sixth decade he has discovered mercy. By any standards he's a fair man and I think you're going to like him.

166

'Now, let us hear the latest tidings of the Frankish kings.' The Sultan claps his hands just once; to have admitted to his presence a broad Cilician Turk, turbaned and trousered with a bright emerald sash to span a well fed belly. The man makes his obeisance; touches heart, lips, brow, then kneels to kiss the carpet three times by the Sultan's nearest slipper and wordlessly to place a leather cylinder in the hand extended to receive it.

The Sultan breaks the seal, extracts a parchment and unrolls it. His moves are those of a trained soldier, rapid and precise; much as they had been three years earlier, in the same tent at Hattin, when with the same slim hand he'd expertly decapitated the double-dealing Christian, Reginald de Châtillon.

God's Shadow on the Earth studies the Turk's report while those about him stand or kneel in silence; the only sound within the tent, the faint creak of its cedar poles .

With courts to govern from Tunisia to the Arabian Ocean, with vital trade routes and supply lines to maintain and enemies of Islam to forestall, the Sultan's network of informants is reaching ever outwards, year by year, around the Middle Sea, across the Straits of Africa and up through Moorish Spain as far as Gascony and the Atlantic seaboard. 'My agents are my eyes and ears,' is how he's put it to his viziers to justify the cost of maintaining spies across three continents, together with their homing birds and donkeys. 'They are as keys to the unknown.'

'So?' The Sultan Salahuddin surveys the kneeling man across the parchment. 'Thou hast assembled the intelligence thyself? This is thy transcript?'

'It is, Sayyid.'

'The work is good.'

Within a single sweep of his free hand Allah's Deputy receives a bag of silver dirhams from the shadows at his back, to drop it on the mat between them. It is *sadaqa*, an act of generosity pleasing to God. Man and master understand each other; the one too mannerly to lift the sac and weigh its contents, the other too considerate to keep him waiting.

'*Allah yessallemak*. Felicitations and the Peace of God be with thee.' The Sultan signals for the agent to accept his payment and depart.

'Our scouts inform us that five further vessels have put in to Tyre with Franks, with al-Firinjah aboard.' He speaks to all assembled in the tent as he returns the parchment to its case. 'Yet neither of the kings who've sworn to drive us from this land has yet embarked on their sea crossing. We hear the King of France lies sick in Genoa. The English king sails south from thence to meet the body of his fleet in Sicily, to refit and perhaps to winter there if this dispatch can be relied on.'

'Which shows us that they're craven.' The Sultan's eldest son, al-Afdal 'Ali ibn al-Nasir Yusuf; a dark youth with an eruptive skin, dressed splendidly in Alexandrian silk brocaded with the gold crescents of Islam, steps forward to address his father. 'They sniff and dawdle at the wayside, like the dogs and progeny of bitches that they are, knowing they'll be beaten if they fight.'

'Not from the evidence we have.' The Sultan looks upon the eldest, best beloved of all his sons, the prototype for sixteen more, and sees in place of his tall figure a small boy flourishing a wooden sword and doing all he can to prove himself.

He smiles indulgently and thinks how little Ali's really changed, despite his height and blemished skin. 'From all we've heard of him, my son,' he says, 'it seems unlikely that a lack of courage is what delays the King of England. Our man in Gascony reports that the old queen his mother has already left Bordeaux to cross the Pyrenees and fetch a Spanish princess for his bride. They are to meet in Sicily when she completes the journey. It is for her, we gather, that Richard al-Malik's waiting.'

'Sayyid, may I speak?' An old man with his back against a tent pole; a stooped, grey-bearded Imam clad like his Sultan all in white, presumes to do so on the Sultan's nod. His voice has been ground down to a hoarse whisper from years of calling men to prayer. Nor is the fact that he is toothless any kind of help.

'How can we credit this report,' he rasps, 'when all the world knows that the two kings are united by the King Richard's pledge to take the French king's sister as his queen?'

'All the world does not have agents in Pamplona and Bordeaux as we do, Umar.' The Sultan smooths his very black moustache.

'But why insult his ally with another bride? It cannot be good policy, Prince of Believers.'

'We're told the old queen, Alienor, believes the French king's sister was her husband's mistress, has even borne his bastard child. If that is true, their Church must rule her marriage to King Henry's son unfitting and incestuous.'

'These filthy al-Firinjah pigs!' Al-Afdal's eyes are slanted like his father's, but wilder, less humane. 'May God confound them and destroy them! May their black souls be cast into the pit of hell for their vile fornications! May they be scourged! May they be singed and scalded, seethed in pitch to roast in everlasting torment!'

'I would advise you to seek out the metaphors and melodies concealed within the Holy Revelations before you take them all at face value,' remarks his father, who privately believes that Allah the Compassionate agrees His Prophet's range of recipes for roasting unbelievers to be both tedious and wastefully severe.

'In any case it's not as fornicators, but as invaders that they will be judged. But to answer Umar's question, the tainted French woman is past her best years and may be unable to bear further children, whilst naturally the King of England needs an heir.

'In this report,' the Sultan taps the leather cylinder, 'a servant of the old queen boasts that she has chosen for her son a princess from the warlike Kingdom of Navarre; a hardy woman from the Spanish marchlands who is likely to withstand the rigours of a military campaign. It seems King Richard would have wed his cousin, Princess Isabella, to claim the Latin Kingdom for himself, if she had not been promised by her mother to the Governor of Tyre. Instead, if our report is true, he means to bring the Navarrese with him on his jihad and make her queen instead.'

'The King of France will never tolerate it, Sayyid,' old Umar whispers through the silence which has fallen in the tent, making sure the sigh he gives to end the sentence is audible to all.

'But that, my old friend, is the point exactly.' Their eyes meet and a faint nod of agreement passes between the Sultan and his Imam. 'Allow me to remind thee, venerable uncle, that the first rule of success in any conflict is to seek knowledge of thine enemies, be it official, covert, or even anecdotal. The second to make use of any weaknesses they may show as a means of...'

'*Allah u Akbar, Allah u Akbar! God is Great, God is Great!*' The ululating voice of Islam summoning the faithful to the Temple of Salvation, cuts through two layers of tented goat hair and the Sultan in mid-sentence. '*Ash-hadu al-la Ilaha ill Allah! I bear witness that there is no Divinity but Allah!*'

'Enough, enough.' God's Shadow on the Earth rises at once to set aside his spy's report and cleanse himself for prayer. 'Allah reminds His children it is time to put away the toys.' He swiftly demonstrates why slippers are so named, and standing barefoot, signals for the tent flap to be lifted and his attendants to disperse.

They leave without a word; and when the rest have hurried off to pray in other lamplit tents and huts, or to perform the Maghrib litany beneath the stars, only the Imam remains as he is bidden to lead the Sultan and his son in their devotion.

'*Allahu Akbar*, Subhanna rabbiyal 'Azeem, Subhanna rabbiyal 'Azeem...' The old man intones, as first they stand with thumbs behind their ear lobes, with right hands over left above their genitals, then bow with palms on knees.

The three men, equal in the eyes of Allah, stand close together side by side with arms pressed to their thighs. They kneel to touch the Turkey carpets with foreheads, noses and with hands. They look westward over their right shoulders to seek the angel who records their good deeds, look east to he who debits sins – until at last, exhorting God to hear them and receive their prayers, they rise to greet each other in the certainty of His forgiveness.

During the month of Ramadhan, no nourishment may be

consumed until the time of Maghrib, sunset; fasting being one half of endurance according to a Prophet who enjoyed his food; endurance one half of true faith. So when the drum is beaten to end fast, and their repast is set before them, few words pass between the three men in the tent until the sharp edge of their hunger has been blunted.

They lie at ease on low divans strewn with silk cushions, drinking iced sherbet, eating fruit, enjoying roasted fowls and skewered mutton. Although the days are hot, the nights are cold here in the hills. A brazier of charcoal has been lit for comfort on a square hearth of tiles. It casts a warm glow round the tent, illustrating on its panels some of the other pleasures denied in Ramadhan during the hours of daylight.

Al-Afdal in the silence is studying a panel that depicts in beaten bronze a group of priapic sons of Islam and happily receptive daughters, performing four of the eleven recommended attitudes for copulation – before he realises that both the older men are watching him and smiling.

'Allah is beneficent. They take their pleasure without guilt, which is as He intends.' His father's tone is playful. 'Praise be to God, who hath directed husbands to take their pleasure in the natural parts of wives, and hath designed their zabbs to give equivalent delight. Wherefore He blesses fleshly union as the source of life, and at its climax bids us to behold His face. It is the moment, is it not, that every worthy man would choose to enter Paradise?'

'Thy speech before Maghrib was of a dispute between the Kings of England and of France.' Al-Afdal's rapid change of subject, reflects the distaste of the young for any idea of their elders still engaged in carnal recreation. 'Thy thought is that this quarrel could be helpful to our cause?'

'Truly it is said, that knowledge is chief of all things, my son. It allows us to see clearly what we may achieve. Conjecture is no substitute for fact.'

The Sultan Salahuddin tosses his wooden meat skewer into the brazier to watch the flames consume it, the planes of his thin face suffused with rosy light. 'Empires are built on the imperfections of mankind, not on its virtues. We learn that Richard Malik al-inkitar is a violent and ambitious man who fought his father to the death. He treats war as a sport and has forgotten all the peaceful preaching of the Christ whose cause he claims to represent. He is concerned with glory in this world and is indifferent to the next. King Philippe on the other hand is Christian and pious.'

'Can anything be done about it?' the Imam enquires.

'Everything we can discover of the Frankish kings will be of use in our campaign,' the Sultan says. 'If all we hear of him is true, the King of France is also sickly, cold in temperament and acute of mind, which renders him the more dangerous of the pair.'

Al-Afdal grunts. A eunuch sets a chased silver bowl of scented rosewater before his father and the Sultan dips his greasy fingers. 'The characters of the two men oppose each other,' he continues, dabbing his hands on the towel provided. 'They see the art of kingship differently. Add to this disputes over the territories they rule, and over one's rejection of the other's sister, and I'd expect them to be at each other's throats before they even reach our shores.'

'But they are both pledged to jihad, Prince of Believers. Neither could abandon the invasion without loss of face.' Umar, at his master's invitation leans across to rinse his hands in turn.

'Abandon? No, my friend. But we know that they cannot sustain a campaign so far from home for more than two winters, three at most. They haven't funds enough to feed them. Nor may their vassals leave their lands for longer. All things considered, I'd expect King Philippe, who has no appetite for war, to look for a good reason to return to France when Acre falls. So with God's help, I would suggest we make sure that he finds one.'

In the act of passing a soft towel to Umar, the Sultan looks directly at his son, in time to catch him choke on a ripe fig. Al-Afdal's shocked, incredulous. 'When Acre falls? By light and fire that cannot be!' he splutters. 'The city cannot fall to unbelievers!'

He is already on his knees, but is detained. 'Be still Ali and listen.'

172

The young man shrugs impotently, unwilling or unable to disguise his outrage. With both fists clenched he settles back upon the cushions.

'We are in private, can speak plainly – and alas the city must surrender in the end, however we may strive to save it.'

'It tempts ill-fortune, Father, even to consider failure.'

'Yet we must be realistic. The Franks have been encamped outside the city walls for a full year, withstanding all assaults. We may surround them on the landward side. We may break through the siege by land or sea to re-provision Acre. But every month, more ships arrive with Christian reinforcements.' The perceptive dark eyes beneath the turban engage his son's and hold them. 'If the kings do not come this year it will go hard with the al-Firinjah over winter. But by the spring we too will have lost half our army. And they will come, make no mistake, with engineers and siege machines and all their multitudes of knights. King Richard is a leader whose fame rests on his success at siege warfare, and thou mayst believe he will bring everything he needs to breach the city walls.'

'But only if we let him, Father. What honour is there in defeat? How often hast thou told me that God loves those who fight His cause with zeal, and fight to win. Give me command. Allow me to take but two divisions of mamluks to meet their armies as they land; strike down the kings before they ever reach the city. Wilt thou not trust me Father? The way to kill a serpent is to cut off its head, and I say I'm the man to do it!'

With the balled fist of his right hand Al-Afdal punches his left palm. 'Leaderless, without the loyalty they owe to kings, without pay from the royal coffers, is it not obvious what will happen? The Christian armies will disperse. They'll melt like winter snow to leave us in possession of the city.'

The Sultan sighs and thinks how much his son has still to learn. 'Thy bravest thoughts are beaded on one string, Ali. I told King Guy when he was at my mercy at the Horns of Hattin that kings should never slay each other. As I answer to The One True God, I

173

tell thee that we need both kings alive. Thou speakest of serpent's heads. But consider the Greek fable of the Hydra. From each of its nine heads the monster had the power to grow two more. A man could sever three necks, only to find six more sprouting from their stumps. When he dealt with those, twelve more appeared – and so would the Christians multiply if their campaign should end in grievance. Be sure that spilt blood never sleeps. The armies they would mobilise against us would be legion if we made martyrs of the Christian kings.'

Al-Afdal is still frowning, pimply face in hand. 'But Acre's only the beginning, Father. If we should spare the kings this time and Acre falls, how can we stop King Richard marching on al-Quds, the place he calls *Jerusalem*, to crown himself its king?'

'By playing out a waiting game, Ali, to delay the fall of Acre for as long as we are able. By understanding there are more than two sides to a conflict and exploiting the kings' dislike of one another – to help the one decide he's had enough of warfare, and convince the other that he cannot rule two kingdoms separated by an ocean – and by preserving Richard's legend, to grant him enough success to send him home a hero, whilst weakening his army to the point that it lacks force or will to take al-Quds. In other words, my son, by using intellect, diplomacy and the minimum of violence.'

The Sultan's words are measured. 'Time is on our side. We have it in the East, the Westerners do not. So long as we defeat the al-Firinjah they'll return. The wiser way will be to give them something we can spare. We may not allow them to besiege the Holy City of al-Quds. But – I say this for thine ears alone – it may still suit us to award them a remnant of their petty kingdom. Give them a handful of seaports which deal in any case with traders of all faiths. Give them a taste of victory and a puppet king. Give access to eastern trade routes, a safe passage to the holy places for their pilgrims – and let the dogs bark as they will, my son. Our caravan will pass them by.'

There is a further silence while the speaker pulls the silk tassel of a cushion through his fingers, contemplating the red embers in the brazier. 'It's held that a sound policy is like a strong tree, firmly rooted, yielding fruit in every season,' he says reflectively. 'Our policy must be to treat for lasting peace on our own terms and strive to make a better world for all who follow.'

'Is it not written that he who mediates between men for a worthy purpose shall be the gainer by it.' The pious Imam draws a look of irritation from the Sultan's son. 'Needless brutality is repugnant to The Lord of the Seven Heavens. I pray He will prolong thy life, Hakim.'

'May Allah hear thy prayer.' The Sultan smiles.

'By the Lord of All Goodness, thy heart is as the ocean.' The Imam casts his eyes up to a distant heaven, only to encounter the much closer goat-hair ceiling of the tent and cast them down again. 'Thou wilt be praised, Sayyid, this day and to the end of time for thy fair judgement.'.

'My Father, thy fame rests rather on thy victories,' the disgruntled al-Afdal interrupts. 'Thou hast fought all thy life and now is not the time to rest thy sword.'

'I fear thou hast the right of it, Ali. That time is not yet with us, and for the present we must continue to delay the kings by force of arms,' the Sultan adds with quiet regret. 'God knows I've done my share of killing. But how powerful is a state whose people know only how to shed blood in the name of one faith or the other? All warfare is ugly, clumsy and destructive and evil comes of evil. Is it not possible that as Children of the Book we may still sink our differences and live in peace together?

'As Salaamu 'alaikum wa rahmatullah.' He touches his breast, his lips and brow. 'That is God's benediction, is it not? The blessing we bestow on one another when we part? Indeed we must defend al-Quds. But I believe that lasting peace will be achieved by patience and negotiation, and not by endless bloodshed. "My words are the law," the Holy Prophet held, "my actions are the way."'

The words of Sultan Salahuddin Yusuf ibn Ayyub reveal a crucial difference between his view of justice and that of the King of England. A difference which in course of time will decide the outcome of the Kings' Croisade.

CHAPTER SEVEN

They're skating on the meads where I saw rows of coloured tents the day before the tournament – oh let's think, it must be fourteen, sixteen months ago? Hard to believe that so much time has passed.

The children skate on mutton shin-bones, from here look like brown birds, fluffed-up in serge with waving woollen wings to flutter them across the ice – and even from this distance I can hear their cheerful little voices, shrieking with excitement. They have no thought of me and my business in the town, and wouldn't care a jot about it if they had.

What fun though to be a child again and make a game of winter weather! We had another fall last night. I caught the scent of it before it came, but was surprised still when I threw the shutters back this morning to see the fields and hillsides blanketed with snow. The view my window gave me of the world made white and new was magical, enchanted – until its cold chill reached me, and I suddenly recalled my brave intent to ride to Lewes.

But was it brave, or foolish after all to say I'd come myself to pay the Jew for the last quarter of the year? God knows I'd not have promised it, but for Sir Hugh.

We were the first from Haddertun to cut fresh tracks to the frozen millstream, on untrodden snow that squeaked underfoot. When I looked behind I saw the manor mantled in an ermine coat with black tail-streaks for windows – the downs as sugarloaves, the stream a murky serpent snaking through the white. The harsh beauty of the landscape caught my breath and frosted it in icy plumes before my face.

There was that sense of quietness that always seems to come with snow, muffling the squeaks and crunches of the horses' feet, when at Ram's Combe we crossed the prints of other hooves and wheels. At Lewes the fishing nets looped from the willow spinneys by the river were all frozen, rimed with ice.

But the way across the bridge into the town was slippery with trampled slush, and at the east gate we dismounted to lead our horses up the hill.

I've sent Kempe on ahead to clear the way – follow with Nesta (not too close, in case his rounsey slips and falls), with our two sergeants at my back to shield me from attack. Hod would have come despite her dread of Azrelites, and wasn't pleased to be told a third time I could manage with the steward.

The payment's safe enough with me. Heavens, I hardly know myself where we have sewn the pockets to the fox-fur lining of my cloak. And thank you very much, I've worked too hard to risk its loss to vagabonds and thieves! The last time I came myself to pay the interest on the loan was back in March, a bare fortnight after Garon rode away. In June I sent Kempe on his own. Then in September, quite against my wishes, Sir Hugh had made a point of carrying the dues to Lewes – determined as he ever has been to set me at a disadvantage.

When he and Lady Constance came in July to see how I was managing the manor, I did my best to show them what a careful eye I've kept on industry and waste. I have the capabilities, Maman made sure of that – and the morning after they arrived I showed My Lady all the looms and everything we'd woven. We solemnly inspected the bake ovens and the cheeses in the dairy, then toured the storerooms and the dyeing vats, the tanning sheds, the saltings and brewery. And 'though she made a point of brushing a stray cobweb from a chamber doorway – although she thought the fowls at breakfast over-cooked – the fact that she could find no more amiss than that, must prove me a success as Lady of the Manor. (Why wouldn't it, when that is what I am?)

But it's not Lady Constance, it's her wretched husband... What is it that so maddens me about that man? His voice? His oily looks? Or is it how he manages to catch me out so often and make me feel uneasy?

At haymaking, when I climbed down the ladder backwards, looking like a peasant I've no doubt, he'd laughed so heartily that I'd no choice but to smile back. 'I bid you welcome Sir.' (About as welcome as a slap across the face with a wet herring!)

'I take it you propose to stay?' I added hastily to cover my mistake.

'Take anything you like, my dear. I do at every opportunity.'

And when he laughed again, I smiled again – and lost my chance again of keeping things between us on any kind of a safe footing.

He was no better when he rode with me to view the kine, the standing corn and all our barn reserves. I'd swear he barely listened when I told him how much flour, how many bales of wool we'd sold, or when I listed all the rents and tithes that I could call to mind. (Kempe reads me all his latest dealings each Monday after breakfast, and my memory is excellent with figures).

But – 'Have you considered what you'll do if our brave soldier of the cross dies of an excess of hard steel in Palestine?' was what he asked me first. And determined that time to do nothing further to encourage any kind of inappropriate response, I turned away to stare across the fields and tell him woodenly that I knew what to believe.

'Is that so, my dear? Then put it into words. I am all ears – or I would be if I didn't know the answer.'

'Liar! You can't know,' I thought. Then asked him how he did.

'I see it printed in large characters across your charming face. I see that you believe, because you want to – not only that our Garon is alive, but that he will return to you a changed and better man.'

I felt his eyes on me but wouldn't meet them. 'And if I should tell you that we'll all end catching larks when the sky falls on us,' he said cynically. 'I don't doubt, if you wanted to, you'd find a way to think that very probable as well.'

Imagining he planned to tease me further, I moved a short way up the laine towards the fallow land at Shaws.

'But even if against all likelihood he manages to cheat the worms, d'ye think that a young man obsessed with military prowess will ever leave off questing once he's started on that course?' Sir Hugh persisted. 'How can I put this to you gently? The boy's a perfect bonehead and you know it. Surely it has crossed your mind that if he lives, he is as like as not to gallop into service with some local baron who'll employ him killing Saracens so long as they're in plentiful supply.'

'I don't know what you mean,' I said.

'I think you do – and you may as well face facts, my dear. There's scarce a dog's chance he'll return.'

'I'll face facts when I have to Sir, and not before,' I told him haughtily.

Then realising how thoroughly ill-bred that must sound, erred on the other side by becoming too polite.

'Our barley is already ripening – see over there.' I pointed to the West Field crop, fenced off against the cattle. 'We'll have the sickles out before the next moon if the weather holds.'

'My dear child, cut the barley. Shock it, thresh it, grind the corn – do anything you like to pass the time. It makes no difference to the fact that in the end you're bound to run to me for what you need. Now what d'ye say to that?'

'Nothing that you'd want to hear,' I told him rudely. (And wasn't quite sure what he meant – although I don't suppose that he was talking of the harvest, was he?) I knew that if I turned to look I'd find him grinning horridly.

But I'm not a fool, however he might think it, and don't believe that man is all that he pretends. I see that it amuses him to play with women's feelings. But that's not to say he likes us… I mean as people, rather than mere bodies. (It first struck me that he doesn't much, when Agnès told me he was swiving little Edmay's nurse behind his lady's back – and I saw in his face that he despised the silly creature, even as he used her.)

That was when the picture I now have of him began to come together – slowly like a piece of coloured stitchwork, thread by thread. A little clearer every time we meet. He acts as if there's nothing in the world that discommodes him. But more than once I've heard a note bitterness in that light voice of his, and caught a glint, the flicker of a flame in his dark eyes – heard something hollow in his laugh, which first I took for simple knavery, but now begin to see as anger and frustration. Anger at his circumstance. Frustration with his dependence for position on a thin old woman who has borne him nothing but a daughter.

Which means I've found a weakness in Sir Hugh de-Perfect Bernay!

I took my chance that day out in West Field while he was giving his impression of a heartless charmer, to turn my mare's head back toward the manor – and Nesta set off at a trot which with a little heelwork turned into a canter.

'You will need help, and when you come for it, ma chère, be sure you'll find me waiting.' He shouted it after us to have the final word.

'AS IF,' I thought! Because I didn't need his help, and wouldn't trust the man to give it freely if I had.

That was in July. But when in September Sir Hugh returned to warn us that the anti-Jewish riots in the eastern counties were in danger of infecting Sussex, and to suggest it was too great a risk for any Christian lady to trade openly with Jews – I was persuaded to allow him to take the usance for the quarter in my place. Even to thank him for the offer – like a fool!

'I put it to the old man that with affairs so dangerously unsettled, he'd be lucky to retain his licence as a lender,' Hugh dared to boast when he strolled in from Lewes four hours later, with six shillings of the twenty-six still in his pouch. 'I told him that his rates were scandalous, and had but to lift my cloak to make him see the point.'

He showed me the dagger in his belt just as he'd done to the poor moneylender. And when I informed him stiffly that I'd sworn an oath, could not in justice see Sir Garon's debt defaulted, he'd laughed at me – again – that maddening, infuriating laugh!

'Life doesn't work like that,' he said. 'To make the best of it, my dear, you have to do – not what is seen as just by others, but just what's needed to survive.' (Although something in the way that he looked through me as he said it, gave me the feeling he was talking less of my life than his own.)

A sharp wind's blowing, north-east through the gaps between the houses. Despite the hood, my face is frozen – feels as if some devil's sticking sharpened icicles into my chin. Thank God, I say, for warm boots and sheepskin lining. The shutters of the shops are closed. Nesta's snorting though her whiskers at the drifting woodsmoke from the inn – and I hope to heavens that the Jew's house has a brazier. A group of ragged destitutes huddle at the castle gate and all across the bridge, in hope of something warm to fill their bellies – withered faces, pinched with cold (the only mob, poor things, that we are likely to encounter!).

We had to have a bullock killed at hay-homing for Lady Constance and Sir Hugh; a beast I'd hoped to keep back for the Lammas feast. Considering how drawn and ill she looks, the lady's appetite surprised me. But I'll be ready for her when she comes again at Christmastide, I am determined. If my Lady Constance thinks to find me unprepared for banqueting after the salt-fish fasts of Advent, then she will have to think again.

Jésu, how the beggars gawp. (You'd think they'd never seen a lady lead a horse through snow!)

The sky looks yellowish and heavy. If there's to be another fall we'd better be sure not to stay too long. The men have taken Nesta with Kempe's palfrey to find shelter at the inn yard, blowing in their fists to keep them warm. I've told them I will have them whipped if they so much as wink at a town whore... But what on earth have those three ravens found to make them so aggressive? – grisly birds; they call them 'gallows-crows' – has someone left a dead cat in the street?

They've swept the loose snow from the door sills, all but the Jew's. But is he in? A row of icicles hang down across the entrance and I can't see any smoke. We stamp our feet. Kempe's rapping with his dagger hilt just as he did before.

'Who's there?' (Old Jacob's voice.)

'It is the Lady of Haddertun!' My words freeze in the air.

'And remember Kempe,' I whisper, 'this time I'll do the talking – the business is between the Jew and me.' He's frowning, has an unattractive habit of pushing out his lower lip to show his disapproval. But I'm giving him no option to refuse.

The shuffling feet again – the grating lock, more snow, an endless fall of whirling flakes blotting out the roofs. The door swings back... He's swathed in woollen shawls against the cold, all grey – long nose and rheumy eyes, a bleary creature peering from its burrow. And hard to see into the shuttered room after the glaring whiteness of the street.

He greets us warmly nonetheless with, 'How do you, Mistress? Master Kempe?

But inside it's chilly, odorous as a spice coffer, steeped in shadow, misted with a bluish haze.

'I fear this chamber is too cold for you, My Lady.' Old Jacob's gesturing through all that drapery toward the rusty curtain I remember at the back. 'If you can bear a little woodsmoke, we'll be more comfortable within.'

He holds the curtain back for us to pass behind the narrow staircase. A central fire glows through a fog of smoke in the small room beyond. His old wife, Sara, nods a greeting, hooks an iron pot to a tripod straddling the flames. It's hard not to cough, and Kempe isn't even trying. (Our clothes are going to reek of smoke!)

182

'There is too little space between the buildings – so hard to get a good cross-draught.' The old man's pointing to the vents above the shutters. 'A south-west breeze is what we need. But as things are – My Lady, Master Kempe – I believe you'll find the smoke less tiresome if you sit.'

Sara hurries in with cushions for the bench. I tuck my cloak in and reward her with a smile. 'The recent persecutions of others of your faith? They do not touch you here in Lewes I suppose?' (No more than courtesy to ask.)

'More of our race have been slain in Norfolk and the counties to the east, despite King Henry's charter. Some of the rioters were fined, but not a single Christian hanged.' The old man is looking sorrowful as well he might.

'But thanks to God, and to my Lord of Warenne, we are safe here for the present, Lady. So long as we agree to stay indoors and never think to venture forth in daylight.' His smile is painfully awry.

'I'm glad of that.'

I've practiced what to say – pull off my gloves, talk rapidly and fumble for the drawstring bags within the lining of my cloak. 'Sir Hugh, and my man Kempe here, were greatly in the wrong to withhold any part of the sum we've agreed. I wish to tell you that they acted on their own without my knowledge – and now I've come to make amends.'

I have a purse in each hand, both chinking fatly. 'One pound and fifteen shillings for you, Jacob – four hundred and twenty silver pennies divided into two. I think my calculation is correct, but count it if you will?' (And what a huge relief to have that said and done.) 'The sum should cover all the interest to the year end, with three shillings of the principal included as a gesture of good faith.'

'Mistress, I have to say...'

But Kempe doesn't have to say it, does he? There are times when I could cheerfully divide him with a meat-axe from his lank crown to horny toe. But this time merely glare him into silence. He scowls morosely, gnawing at his lip – and serve him right for being such a niggard!

'My steward knows as well as I do that we can afford it from our sales last month of grain and beanflour,' I state firmly, 'and a good price for our lambswool in July.'

Although I have to smile, as my hands fly up the moment Jacob takes the heavy little sacs into his own. He's saying that he has no need to count the

183

coins. The scales will show the sum to be correct – and he's grateful plainly, hugs the bags of silver pennies like lost children to his woolly chest. The wine that Sara hands me is warm, red, spiced this time and welcome. We're steaming gently at the fireside like a couple of salt hams.

'Sir Hugh is not a man I care to deal with.'

Jacob pauses by the staircase on his way through to the scales. I give a little nod across the goblet to show I understand. 'You will perhaps forgive me for presuming, Lady. But I would advise you to be wary of him. In my experience, a person who proves treacherous in business may not be trusted to act fairly in his other dealings.'

I nod again – as if I needed telling!

The last patches of snow have thawed, and it is raining hard. I've had the puddled courtyard strawed and planked across to let the maids walk dry-shod, with more planks in the yard behind, to reach the milch cows and the poultry. The ivy garlands are already wilting on the walls. But, thank the Lord, the Christmas feast is over.

We ate in silence at the high board, Sir Hugh and I, with Edmay and her nurse, Odette – and Hoddie doing all the talking, describing every feast she could recall, and who was drunk and who was sick, and who attempted liberties beneath the cloths. 'Glory, some soul had to speak,' she told us afterwards when Hugh had left the board. 'We can't all sit like stuffed fowls in gravy with our necks across our backs!'

Last Christmas, after a church mass to celebrate the coming of the Holy Child, the Yule log was brought in at the commencement of the feast to be set amongst the fragrant juniper and crabwood on the fire. We'd all cried 'Yole!' and 'Joy! Joy! Joy!' and begged God to increase our number, while Father Gerard crossed himself and blessed the celebration. But this year, before the log was flamed the priest was upstairs chanting paternosters by My Lady's bedside. This year there's no cause for joy, or reason to believe our numbers will increase – rather the reverse, considering that Lady Constance is about to die!

On Christmas Eve, Sir Hugh brought her to Haddertun in a closed litter. She was too weak to walk. He had to lift her out, and he and Fremund carried her upstairs – her clothing wet with rain and little Edmay crying out pathetically to tell her not to die.

184

'She started on the coughing fits at Martinmas,' Sir Hugh said, as he laid her by my own instruction in the bed I share with Hod. 'But it was not until we'd passed the ford at Uckfeld that she became distressed.'

He seems disturbed, and at the same time angry with his wife for giving him the cause – and maybe will decide to love her after all when she is dead. He's only three or four times entered the bedchamber since he laid her there, each time so stumbling-drunk and thoroughly impatient with her case, that the poor woman begged him to depart and leave her to her prayers. She's asked for the little girl to be kept from her too – and as the dim-witted nurse can only think of weeping (which is no help to anyone, least of all a frightened child), Edmay's with Hoddie, learning how to twist a yarn (a thing, Hod says, her mother should have taught her years ago).

So here am I. And there lies Lady Constance propped up on pillows and close to paying her last debt to nature, for the fever is malignant. I know that she's in pain and struggling to breathe. The poor woman's laboured to give birth to Garon and to Edmay and the child that died, and now must labour to deliver her own soul.

A candle burns beside the bed, and has done day and night since she first came. It's guttering already (I'll have to light a new one, and the rushes on the floor need changing). Here on his knees is Father Gerard, who's shriven her and hopes to speed her into purgatory before he falls asleep – and here am I beside a woman I've no reason to be fond of or to mourn when she departs – sitting at her bedside like a faithful daughter while her husband drinks himself into oblivion.

Hod says that like as not I'll see the Callydus fly in before she dies. 'A big white bird that flaps in through the window, to perch on her bed tester, an' turn 'is 'ead away from 'er to show 'er time has come.'

I'm trying to recall what Mother did when Grandmère died? The coffin's ready. I have the linen band for tying up the chin. But should we wash her first for decency? Should we clip some hair and fingernails, as Hoddie recommends, to keep her son from harm? Then when we close her eyes, is that the time to place the coins on them to stop the lids from rolling up? Or does that all come afterwards when we have laid her out? Old Agnès, who was here when Garon's father, Sir Gervase, gave up the ghost, will know what we should do. They say the soul stays near the body, watching for the space of forty days.

Would it be right to stop the villagers from revelling on Twelfth Night?
But she's speaking!

'My son...' One thin hand's raised – and now falls back to where her rosary coils like a snake across her wasted breasts. I take it in my own. It's burning hot.

'My son – wait, wait seven years for his return. Full seven years, d'ye hear?'

Her lips are dry and cracked, her voice so faint that I must needs bend close. Her breath stinks with the foulness of infection. 'If he fails ever to return...'

'He will come back.' (Whatever I may think, it is my duty to convince her, or at least to try.) 'Believe me, Lady – your son will return.'

'But if he fails,' she croaks. 'Don't, don't...'

A fit of coughing overtakes her. I wipe the slime away with the soft cloth that lies beside her. It's green-blotched and disgusting!

But she has more to say, braced back against the pillows – another painful breath that rattles in her chest. 'Don't let him have you' – panting, gasping like a landed fish. 'Not Hugh, don't let...' Her pale blue eyes are open, desperate. Bony fingers clutch my hand – surprising strength dragged out from somewhere for a final effort.

'The Church will not allow it – nor will I, my girl,' she whispers with the faintest echo of her old severity. And then subsides like a pricked bladder.

So that makes two; two warnings that I've had against him – although it's wrong for her to think such things at such a time, and wrong for me to hear them.

Forgive her the transgression, Lord. Forgive me mine for listening to her fear and jealousy, for watching the poor creature die while part of me is wondering what I should do – how I should act when it is over. (And pardon me for yawning while I wonder.)

A sudden screech!

The Callydus? With his head turned backwards as he flies? Or just a night-owl in the stable yard? I'm shuddering, it gave me such a start. But Father Gerard bends his head to start another paternoster, pretending it means nothing.

I'm bound to cry when it is over, when her soul has fled. (I'm almost certain that I'll cry.)

But should I kneel beside the bed, or at its foot? How many candles should we light? Are we to douse the fire? And should we have the death knell rung down at the church?

We'll have to send a message up to Lewes fortress to My Lord and Lady of Warenne...

But what beasts should I have killed for the funeral repast?
(Thank God that we have fodder for the livestock.)

So will I have to wail and beat my brow?

Is that what they'll expect of me
when Lady Constance dies?

CHAPTER EIGHT

Death. Nothing could satisfy its greed for human flesh however many died, and it's impossible to guess how many thousands did. But all that was later, after our first sight of Acre.

Our little convoy of five vessels sailed down the coast from Tyre in mid-September, to pass through a fleet of Pisan war galleys blockading the old port. The city of St Jean d'Acre was built out onto a promontory above a long sand bay, surrounded on three sides by water. During their former years of occupation, the Latin Christians had enclosed its port and fortified the city on the landward side with high walls and a moat.

According to our Tyrian pilot, the Saracens managed twice within a year of siege to breach our sea blockade – and a third time, back in June, had used trickery to bring a quantity of grain and a whole flock of fat-tailed sheep to the starving Moslem garrison. Egyptian sailors disguised as Christians had shaved their beards and sewn red crosses to the sails of their supply ship, so the pilot claimed. They'd even set a crate of live hogs up on deck to signal that they brought relief – not to the Moslems, for whom pork was forbidden, but to the Christian camp. But then as soon as they were near enough, they'd raised the chain that sealed the city harbour, shot through its gate and tossed the pigs into the water of the inner pool. As the poor creatures swam about the boat, they'd stuck them full of arrows, except for a single hog, which somehow managed to escape and paddled to Christian shore.

'Which only goes to prove,' said Jos when I told him the story, 'that Mussulmen and even pigs have more wit than Pisanos.'

We docked alongside a wooden jetty built into the bay. Behind the towering walls of Acre, a second city of Christian tents completed its encirclement – with, less than half a league behind them, another crescent-shaped assembly of pavilions clinging to the slopes above the plain like limpets to a rock. And the men-at-arms sent down from camp to help unload our cargo, could hardly wait to point out for us the individual camps of Bedouin, Egyptians, Mamluks and Turcomans, which taken as a whole made up the army of our enemy, the Sultan Saladin.

In Tyre we'd rested, stuffed ourselves with food and wine – and now, refreshed and spoiling for a fight, we had expected stirring sounds of battle outside Acre. Screaming voices. Pounding catapults. The clash of steel on steel. Yet all we heard above the normal din of disembarkation were the shrilling of cicadas in the dunes and mewing seagulls overhead. And when I asked the reason for the lull, a weathered little orderly who drew a wage from Count Henri of Toulouse, said frankly that he'd wager we had missed our chance of any kind of action before the autumn rains confined us all to camp.

'We came to Acre in July with orders for our young Count to take command of the whole friggin' Christian army,' he told us, 'being as 'e's blood related to both kings.'

All hands were needed for the landing. So Jos and I were hefting sacks of dry stores from the tarida for the orderly to load into a waiting mule-cart. 'Thousands upon thousands of 'em out there on that plain,' he said, 'an' all the use King Guy could find for the poor sods in near a year of siege, has been to fill the city moat up with their stinkin' corpses!'

'But then your people came,' I prompted.

'Aye, and brought the beams for two great rams, an' all the parts for five siege engines – torsion mangonels, Venetian make, with punch enough to knock a window through ten foot of stone!'

'So why aren't they in action now?'

Backturned and busy with his load, the carter took his time to answer. 'We wheeled 'em out along the ditch for an attack at dawn,' he said at length, 'and would've breached the wall an' smashed the city gate for sure. But in the darkness Sarsen-Jack dropped men down the walls, didn't 'e, with nets of fire-bombs in clay pots around their friggin' necks. We spit 'em down to the last man. But not before those bastards 'ud set light to all our mangons and both rams – wildfire, an' no piss to save 'em. An' no wood anywhere in this forsaken place to make up so much as an axe-haft.'

'You would have thought the Sarsens' harbour would be the place for an attack.' An idea rising through a mop of red hair from the far side of a haunch of salted beef. Jos heaved it in and mopped his freckled forehead with a sleeve. 'For sure our ships could force a way in through the gate?'

The orderly looked doubtful. "T'ain't feasible,' he said, scratching his crotch. 'Matter of fact, Young Count sent out three fire-ships full o' pitch to burn the old light-house they call the Tower of Flies, as guards the entrance to the port. But Sarsen-Jack was there before us wasn't he, with wildfire an' hand-pumps.'

'You don't say?'

'Aye, an' scorched our oarsmen to a crisp 'afore they could jump clear.' He chuckled grimly. 'Pitiful, the way them buggers shrieked.'

'Then why not use our manpower to build a ramp against the city walls?' I asked, remembering a tale I'd heard somewhere about a Roman siege.

'What, with ten thousand arsewipe Sarsens inside the wall, an' forty thousand at our back? No chance!'

The man stooped to lift a walnut from the body of the cart where it had rolled from a split sack, and held it up for us to see. 'Listen boys, suppose this nut is Acre, see?' He waited for agreement, then clenched the walnut in his fist. 'Oh aye, we 'ave the sod in hand aright, but so 'ave they.'

He brought the other hand across to clamp the fingers of his own fist still more firmly round the nutshell. 'So's what we 'ave is Sarsens holdin' Christians holdin' Sarsens – deadlock, see? No one moves an' nothin's gained.' He lobbed the nut into the sea.

'So how much longer can the garrison hold out?'

The orderly shrugged bleakly. 'No friggin' idea,' was all he had to add.

It was late in the afternoon before we'd landed all our men and mules and horses and the stores we'd taken on in Tyre. The route ashore already taken by Archbishop Baldwin and the other leaders, led up across the plain between the two opposing armies to King Guy's hill camp of Toron. By then Bertram and John had joined us with the mules. And Raoul, fed all the oats that he could eat in Tyre and freshly shod, was once more fit to ride.

So how did I feel mounted up and at the head of my own little squad again, knowing that we'd somehow managed to survive and reach the Holy Kingdom?

I can remember almost everything about our landing in the bay, can still see the half-breed Pullani children holding out their hands for alms as we passed by, but strangely can't recapture what I *felt*. I think I must have turned at some point on the track to look back at the city ringed with ships and congeries of tents – because I have a picture of it standing like a crown of ivory against a sea shot through with the warm colours of a westering sun. But what I *felt*? I can only think that anything of triumph or achievement that I felt the day we joined the siege of Acre, was blotted from my memory by what we found in camp.

'*Toron*' was an ancient word for 'castle', we were told, and I suppose the ruined hill town King Guy had chosen for his base was at least moated like a fortress, rising from a stagnant ditch through a series of uneven mounds and terraces to the gold-crossed banner of the Christian Kingdom flying from its summit. Otherwise it looked more like a maxon heap than any kind of castle we had known. Dilapidated campaign tents like those arranged in ranks out on the plain were pitched on level ground about the moat, and at the top amongst the broken fangs of masonry that ringed the King's pavilion. Elsewhere, a chaotic shanty-town of huts contrived from wattle, reed-thatch, hides of goats and asses and every kind of patch-worked fabric, clung to slopes and ledges and straggled through the ruins, roped or staked or propped against each other. Grown up like mushrooms sprouting out of filth.

Archbishop Baldwin had sent a guide to find space for us on the far side of the hill with Rob de Pierpoint's men. Gabbling in some kind of broken French that was impossible to follow, he led us by a sloping thoroughfare between the shelters, passing leaking dung carts set along the way in place of drains. Through doors and openings on either side, we saw men sprawled on pallets, sleeping, drinking, rolling dice. Some called to ask where in Hades we had sprung from. One eager lad begged Bert to tell him if he'd seen the Kings of France or England on their way to save us. A rowdy group of soldiers in ramshackle tavern with a sage bush on a pole outside, whistled at Jos and his red hair and called him poison-pate and rusty bollocks – and shouted after us to bid us welcome to the arsehole of the world.

'Wondered what the stink was?'Jos held his freckled nose and rolled his eyes outrageously to make the point. 'Don't tell me boys. Were you the last turds to be dropped?'

Flies rose from every surface. Rats scuttled, crows and seagulls probed the piles of refuse littering the alleyways between the shacks. But what springs first and last to mind when I recall the day we came to Toron – the sight I can't forget – was that of two men struggling together in the shadows of a ruined wall. They both had crosses on their tunics, to show they were crucesignati, as if there could have been a doubt. And they were grappling, the one man searching for a hold upon the other's neck.

Or so I thought, until I saw the way the man behind was moving. Until I saw exactly what the one in front was doing underneath his crumpled cross!

The sight would not have shocked me elsewhere. It was commonplace in barracks where men are close confined. I knew – of course I knew – that given the right circumstance, almost any man will fuck almost anything that moves. But the cross of Christ – the sordid thing the man was doing to our holy symbol of croisade... that's what I found it hard to take.

The Archbishop of Canterbury is even more appalled than Garon by what he finds in Toron; and he writes to say so to King Richard on his way to join them at the siege.

My Liege it grieves me to report the Lord is not in Toron. In this camp there is no chastity, sobriety, faith nor charity. The army in this pestilential place is given up to sloth and sinful practices, and I cannot think that God will grant a victory to Christians so far sunk in vice. Moreover there is sickness in the camp which has taken the lives of your most estimable cousins, the Queen's Grace Sibylla with, her daughters, may God Almighty have them in His keeping, and is most like to spread throughout the host this coming winter. They die like flies, or so the saying goes.

But here men die and flies survive in legions, his secretary records to Archbishop Baldwin's slow dictation in his tent at Toron. *Meantime the King of France's kinsman, the Marquess Conrad, who is commander of the Port of Tyre and cousin to the King of France, proposes an illegal marriage with the dead Queen's royal sister...*

'Your Grace, we have to stop him!' had been the first words spoken by King Guy himself, when all the formal greetings were completed and his guest had shown a proper sympathy for his bereavement. A strikingly good looking man, clean-shaven and magnificently clad in a striped robe of black and tawny silk, his pale eyes encircled Eastern-style with khol, King Guy de Lusignan descended from the dais of his royal pavilion to seize the old archbishop by the hand.

The King's slurred, Levantine mode of speech served only to accentuate his anger. 'If that rogue, that feather-bed adventurer Conrad dares steal the Princess Isabella and get a child on her, with my dear Queen scarce cold within her tomb,' he growled, 'well then this Kingdom is as good as lost to de Montferrat, Your Grace. As good as lost, I say!'

The archbishop's own loss of eyebrows in the fire at sea had suggested a level of surprise he didn't happen to be feeling. He had been told King Richard's vassal, Guy, was arrogant enough to think this marriage was what threatened his authority in Palestine – rather than the fact that nine-tenths of his subjects saw him as an incompetent pretender who never should have been crowned in the first place. But naturally he was too polite to say so. Baldwin won a grateful smile instead from Guy de Lusignan by simply stating that the Catholic Church could not and never would support a canonically incestuous union.

193

On the instructions of King Guy, a chair was set for the archbishop before his dais.

'As I understand the case, Conrad's brother and your own Queen, Isabella's sister, were also married in the past,' Baldwin continued when he'd eased his painful joints, 'and if we credit all the rumours that are rife in Tyre, their Governor already has a wife – no please, two wives still living – which must make the union bigamous as well.'

Not that kings ever lose much sleep over such technicalities, the old man wearily acknowledged to himself, *considering the antics of Queen Eléonore, King Henry and their kin, within the bonds of wedlock and adulterously outside them!*

You will be gratified to hear that I am planning to enlist the support of Archbishop Josias, Bishop Hubert Walter and Archdeacon Ralph de Hauterive in forbidding Conrad of Tyre to embark upon this marriage to the hereditary Latin princess, Archbishop Baldwin now dictates to Richard on the Isle of Sicily. *We cannot fault the man as a commander and governor. For as you know My Liege, he has successfully defended the Christian port of Tyre for more than three years now against the Sultan and his armies...*

In view of which, the King of France's cousin doubtless has the makings of a better ruler of the Kingdom of Jerusalem than the King of England or his peevish vassal, Guy de Lusignan, could ever be. A thought that Baldwin will not share with Richard, recalling as he does the grey-haired, battle-scarred Piemontese Italian he's met at Tyre and rather liked. King Guy described Conrad de Montferrat as a rogue, a feather-bed adventurer.

But naturally it takes a rogue and an adventurer to know another, the archbishop cannot help but think, considering Guy's own beginnings as a simple knight from Poitou.

He pulls at his ear lobe thoughtfully, choosing his words to resonate with Richard of all princes...

Whatever his achievements in the field, I judge that Conrad de Montferrat's past history and present situation must render him unfit to wear The Holy Kingdom's crown.

He instructs his secretary, Anselm, to begin a new line on the scroll.

My Liege, there is another great affliction likely to beset the Christians of this land. They say there are some eighty thousand soldiers encamped upon the plain of Acre, with horses, beasts of burden and the folk who wait upon them. Our armies seek to starve the Turks inside the walls of Acre. But if their own supply lines fail, they too must face starvation. Neither King Guy, nor Count Henri of Toulouse who now commands the armies, believe they can rely on Marquess Conrad to send supplies from Tyre. So they commission Genoese and Pisan merchantmen to purchase victuals and fodder from the Moslem Caliph of Morocco and ports along the heathen coast of Africa...

Anselm's goose-feather quill scratches and squeaks its way across the parchment. Within a yellow pool of lamplight he bends to the task with total concentration, frowning slightly, tongue thrust out between his teeth, delicately angling his nib to form the letters. Each word a minor work of art.

And how could I expect him to react? Why should a scribe confuse himself with morals, when consecrated churchmen are here to do it for him, thinks Baldwin. *A missed word now, or an unsightly blot of ink. These are the things that bring scribes out in sweats. What is it to Anselm if Christians who fight Moslems to the death at Acre are happy to rely on farmers of the same impious faith to grow the food which keeps them all alive? It is for kings and bishops, not for scriveners, to say how far they will allow their own beliefs to be distorted by the demands of war.*

'Begin a new line, my son, and with a bold M for My Liege,' he says aloud.

His secretary adjusts the lamp to throw more light, with ink-stained fingers dips his quill once more into the horn. The shadow of a bat flicks past the open tent flap, and Balwin thinks of Melusine.

He turns away to pass a dry palm over the sparse remnants of his fringe and stroke his thoughts into another channel.

My Liege, we trust to greet you and the royal fleet before the winter storms render the Middle Sea too hazardous for vessels with a shallow draught...

Some time before the end of September, we heard in Toron that a large fleet of Egyptian ships had broken through the Christian cordon in the Bay of Acre to bring supplies to the beleaguered city. Two ships had foundered on the rocks. A strong wind drove a third ashore. But twelve had made it past the Tower of Flies into the Moslem port, to save the city from starvation. By that time it was near certain that the Kings of England and of France would not arrive until the spring – although three weeks later, in October, a remnant of the German force trailed in from God-knows-where; five thousand men to swell the Christian army. Or as its commander, Count Henri, was said to have complained: 'Five thousand mouths to feed, five thousand arseholes and five thousand pricks to spread the flux and pox through all the rest.' And then just when we least expected a relief, the orderly who wagered that we'd lost our chance of military action this side of wintertime, was proven wrong.

For two months we had been kennelled in the filthy stews of Toron. So when at Martinmas Archbishop Baldwin came in person to recruit us, we were like lyme-hounds baying for the chase.

A fragile figure leaning on his chaplain's arm, His Grace limped out into the open area beside the Toron wells to tell us what was planned.

'Brethren, Count Henri is to lead an expedition to the town of Caiffa by Mount Carmel, with God's help to surprise the Sultan Saladin's supply ships in the harbour and relieve them of the grain that we so badly need.

'This is The Lord's work surely,' the old man cried, 'and I would judge myself unworthy of my calling if I were not to ride before you in the enterprise. My friends, take courage in the knowledge that the worst God's enemies can do to us is separate our bodies from our souls. Not even Satan can deny you your reward in heaven, where every one of you is promised an eternal life.'

A piece of memory, a picture bobbing to the surface of my mind – the same man in a different place, the old archbishop with his arms extended reflected in the River Ouse: *Delay no longer, arm yourselves and join us in this just and holy war!*'

He bade us bring our carts and pack-mules with us to be laden with the spoils of victory, and offered safe-deposit for our valuables within King Guy's own almonry, to free as many of us as were fit to march.

'And I'll see action with the arbalesters if it's the same to you, Sir Garry,' Bertram offered, 'an' leave the mules to Hideman, who's a safe hand with any beast.'

His worst decision, looking back. The worst poor Bert had ever made.

We set out on the morrow of Saint Martins in November, surging like a river... No, much broader than a river, rolling out across the Plain of Acre as a living carpet, glittering with light reflected from our helms and spearpoints. Steam rose from us, attracting insects with its stench. Even without the kings, the Kings' Croisade was once again a fact, a Christian horde that no one could restrain.

In place of Guy de Lusignan, perched like a spare cock on the dungheap of Toron, the army was commanded by Count Henri of Toulouse, a fresh-faced man in pristine armour who we glimpsed in the muster on the plain. Behind him in Christian fellowship, rode knights from every European race – Theobald of Blois with half the chivalry of France in train, Duke Frederick of Swabia with his remaining Germans, King Guy's own brother, Geoffrey de Lusignan, to lead the Latin Franks – with at the rear, behind the block of mules and muleteers that included my John Hideman, the military orders of Knights Templar and Hospitaller, who were committed to God's service, along with Danes and Friesians, Sicilians, Pisanos, Flemings, Hungarians and Lord only knows what other countrymen besides.

Alongside each cavalry division, our infantry marched ten abreast to shield us on both flanks against attack. From where I rode with Rob de Pierpoint's horsemen, near the centre of the host, I sometimes caught a glimpse of the red scarf Jos wore beneath his kettle hat, and knew that Bertram must be close at hand amongst the marching soldiers. Ahead, the banner of the Blessed Martyr, Thomas Becket, showed where Archbishop Baldwin sat his mule in company with Bishop Walter and the old Justiciar, Ranulf de Glanville.

There were six hundred horse to our division. All less than sleek, for

197

provender was scarce. Yet all as game as we were. Nothing I had experienced since leaving England had altered what I was or what I wanted. I needed action. So did Raoul. He knew as he sidestepped and fought the bit, we all knew it was coming! You could hear it in the soldiers' jokes, in the strident sound of their excited laughter.

'How do Mussulwomen like it?' one man demanded of the host. 'On their knees and facing Mecca!' half the army shouted back.

The summer heat had passed. With the first rains, stiff blades of grass had pushed through the stony soil to turn the plain pale green. In the distance to the south, the jutting rampart of Mount Carmel, the place our little hill at Lewes took its name from, stood out against the blue mass of the sea.

Shoulder to shoulder we crossed the River Belus, streaming through the bottleneck of its stone bridge. We passed the road to Nazareth where Jesus Christ was born to Mary, no more than six leagues as the crow flies from where we rode. We passed the hill of al-Kharruba, where Christ's enemy, the Sultan Saladin, crouched like a spider in the centre of his evil web. Yet everything was in our favour, so we thought. No one in their senses, least of all Count Henri, expected the Sarcens to ignore the gauntlet we'd cast in their path. But we had the numbers, the formation and the level field – and best of all, we had twelve hundred destriers shipped out from Europe in the certain knowledge that no one and nothing could withstand a charge of heavy horsemen trained and primed and armoured to the teeth.

What they had were Turcoman archers.

Screaming the hair-raising battle cry we'd heard on the shayan, the Sarcens' light horse, the Turcomans whose very name we learned to dread, had waited only for the sun to sink behind the hills to show us how they dealt with armoured knights.

Allahu akbar! Allahu akbar! In twos and threes and scores and hundreds, they whirled in from the wadis, shadows out of blackness, to engage us in a game played by Moslem rules.

Bastards! Devils! Dark-faced little men in plated armour topped by turbans or steel helmets, they crouched with shortened stirrups and bent knees on ponies half the weight and twice the speed of our great horses, turning in the saddle to draw their little recurved bows and loose their arrows in a stream too fast to follow. Giving tongue like staghounds. Then melting back into the shadows as quickly as they came, and never still for long enough to let us to charge.

War isn't like a tournament, I know it now I've fought one. In war, men seek to kill as much as possible from a safe distance, as little as they may in close combat, hand to hand. In warfare all are governed by their orders. And ours, bawled down the line, were to defend ourselves – to shield our bodies and our mounts, maintain a close formation, and trust to our archers and our spearmen to return the Moslem fire.

Advance at a walking pace. Give arbalesters time to load.

Arrows whickered in around us in the failing light, bouncing from steel links and helms, finding marks in shields or living flesh – aimed for our horses mainly, knowing they were harder to replace than men.

Dawn found us in the same condition, dared by the Moslems to break ranks, unable to attack. We halted twice during the night to water horses, shit our shit and bolt our rations, but otherwise kept on the move. Now and again a Sarsen fell to a steel bolt or a flung javelin. But mostly they were far too swift, and it was our men and beasts who suffered, stuck like hedge-pigs full of quills.

I saw one French knight, taunted as we all were near to madness, ignore Count Henri's orders and suddenly charge through the lines. They brought his horse down first. Then as he lay with one leg pinned beneath its body and his hauberk rucked around his waist, they shot four steel-tipped arrows in succession through his under-linen into the fork of the man's groin – before his screams were silenced with a final shaft through the eye-socket to his brain.

The sun by then was warm enough to make a ride in battle dress uncomfortable to say the least. Running with sweat and raging with frustration, I kept on turning back to seek a glimpse of Jos between the shields he and the others held above their heads. Each time I lost sight of his scarlet scarf I feared the worst. Of Bert, or of John Hideman trudging somewhere down the column with the pack beasts, I saw no sign at all. I was consumed by anger, by concern for my three men. But not by fear, not then. Because I had the skill I needed – or maybe just the luck – to stay alive. A strong left arm's as vital to a soldier as the other, and I caught two arrows on my buckler that second morning. A third passed through Raoul's knotted tail to wound another horse beyond. A fourth removed the tip of his right ear to spatter me with blood each time Raoul tossed his head. But that was all we suffered.

Along the way we passed the empty houses and mud walls of villages. If we were told their names I have forgotten them long since. They were deserted all of them, but for a mangy dog that ran out barking, to die on someone's spear. Green melons from their fields were kicked about as footballs in the ranks. Until the scouts Count Henri sent ahead to Caiffa, returned to spoil their game with news that the Sultan's ships had been and gone already. The port was empty of supplies, and long before we reached it, we saw and smelled the evidence of its destruction. Clouds of acrid black smoke cloaked Mount Carmel, drifted out across the water. Anything the townsfolk could not herd or carry they had burned.

Faced with nothing but a smoking ruin, we had no choice but to retrace our steps.

For all that afternoon and night and most of the day following, the Turcomans circled and tormented us like hordes of stinging gadflies in pursuit of hapless cattle. During the day, we'd had to push up in the stirrups and contrive to piss without dismounting – as if it wasn't difficult enough arranging our soft bits to suit the saddle – and Raoul disliked it, flinching every time he felt the splash of urine on his flanks.

During the hours of darkness, the enemy set brushwood fires to light us for their arrows. And when the sun rose from the mist, it showed us we were riding through our own excrement. Or worse, through the bodies of our dead – men, horses, mules and camels – attracting carrion birds and multitudes of flies.

'Bring any of the wounded who can walk or may be tied to saddles,' had been the order that came down the lines. 'Collect the weapons of the fallen. Leave corpses where they lie.'

By then we rode bloodshot and bleary. Our limbs were stiff, our thighs rubbed raw. Our horses tripped and stumbled underneath us, dozing as they walked. And half awake and half asleep, I dreamt of Sussex – of the green depths of the forest, the scent of wild thyme in the downland turf, the dusty, chalky roadways and long summer twilights. I saw Elise's face and smelled her hair. I touched her milky skin. And saw her at the manor gate too proud to raise her hand.

It was at the Belus river in sight of Acre and the hill of Toron, and while the centre of our column stopped to water horses, that the Sarcens, shrieking like women and ignoring the first rule of warfare, mounted their attack.

It was a sharp encounter and a bloody one, armed as they were with falchion blades like cleavers, which in one flashing stroke could joint a horse or separate its rider's head and shoulders. Up on the bridge and in the river shallows, in water churned to mud and red with gore, mules brayed. Men shouted hoarsely. Weapons clashed, destriers reared screaming, cannoned and collided. I snatched a javelin from someone in the pandemonium and hurled it at the nearest Infidel with scarce a pause to aim. No time for anything but instinct. I was the hunter, he the quarry.

And *yes!* – *a* score, a kill! The Moslem's name was on the weapon and he was skewered like a capon. An exultant surge of triumph pieced my vitals as the javelin pierced his. I felt *elation*, if that's the word? – and heard a bellow, deep and animal. And realised that it came from me.

But if I killed a single Moslem at the river, his fellows took a terrible revenge. We lost more infantry and mounted knights in a single hour that morning, within sight of our own camp, than in three days of fruitless quest.

Among the dead was one from Haddertun in Sussex – a balding veteran who had survived one bridge disaster, only to fall victim at another. As Jos related it, before they reached the bridge and in the act of stooping to reload his arbalest, Bertram took an arrow through the neckbone between his helmet and the plated collar of his gambeson.

He died before Jos reached him, and like the others was abandoned where he fell – like a dead sheep on a bostal, to be torn by crows and vultures. To have his guts pulled out and fought over by jackals. To be reduced at last to little more than shreds of flesh and a jumble of stained bones.

As if poor Bert had never lived and breathed and eaten food and dropped his turds as we do.

Five manor squad men, if I count myself. Five brothers called to Christ – reduced to four, and now to three, with more deaths still to come.

Had I learned anything from Caiffa or from Bertram's death, when I prayed for his soul? I'm sorry to admit I hadn't.

CHAPTER NINE

The Hill of Toron; November 1190

QUIETUS

One further casualty of the ill-fated enterprise to raid the port of Caiffa results, not from a Moslem shaft, but from the final loss of one old man's belief.

It may be that Baldwin guessed the outcome of the war. Certainly he knew the price that men and women, children and dumb beasts on both sides of the conflict would have to pay for a croisade confronting a jhad, to set one aspect of divinity against another.

In any case, somewhere on the long march back from Caiffa – bone-weary and cadaverous, supported by his chaplain on one side of his mule and Bishop Walter on the other – the old archbishop lost the will to sanction human suffering, or to stand as judge to any man; and with it he lost any wish to see King Richard Ramsbollocks arrive at Acre as the embodiment of Christian virtue.

The will to live (or on that coin's reverse, the fear of dying; *timor mortis*, the thing that makes us cling to our mortality at any cost) has slipped away from Baldwin before he's borne into his tent at Toron. He's urged so many men to join him in a just and holy war – has bribed them with the offer of salvation. And has lied. The knowledge strikes the poor old man with a greater force than any of the inspirations he's received in all his years of service to the Church. He sees men suddenly as children, nothing more –

occasionally loving, more often greedy, violent and confused. He's led them and betrayed them, threatened them with Hell and Doomsday, as if he knew for sure that they existed, and seen them fed to Moloch.

Now Baldwin understands that hell is what men make of places like the hill of Toron; and Doomsday, now that he approaches it, no longer seems appalling. As we've already seen, it's not the first time he has lost his faith in the Almighty. But given his condition, it has to be the last.

It comes as a relief to Baldwin to know he will not have to go on seeking proof of Christ's divinity, or explanations for God's uncaring nature. All is illusion. Death holds neither fear nor the anticipation of delight. He has dispensed with Christian fortitude, with grace, humility and love, and simply seeks escape from pain. A place to sleep, to be enveloped in the warmth and safety, the soft darkness of the womb he's left so many years before.

He feels only regret for what has passed and a deep longing for oblivion.

'When My Lord of Canterbury saw Christ's army in retreat his spirit was afflicted greatly,' is how his secretary, Anselm, chooses later to describe his dying master's state of mind.

'He complained of cold and stiffness in his limbs, as if the vital flame of life had left them. Within but a few days of returning to the camp, His Grace received the Body of Christ and yielded up his soul.'

What Anselm has omitted to record are the Archbishop's final words. So I'll supply them.

At the very last, it seems to Baldwin that he has no body; nothing but a shrinking skull, a gradually reducing brain with everything drained out of it but his remorse.

'My fault, my fault, my own...

'I am so sorry.' He struggles desperately to force a smile for the benefit of those about him. 'I must... You see I must – I have to leave. No please...?'

He dies apologising.

When I recall our sodden winter in the camp of Toron, with so little to mark one day from another, it seems that time itself has seeped into the mud.

The rain began in earnest on the day they buried our Archbishop, lashing our leaking tents, fouling the lanes between them with sewage overflowing from the shit carts. The River Belus, swollen to a torrent, washed rotting carcases into the coastal marsh to spread their stench across the plain. Damp penetrated everything. Our stores. Our clothes. Our very bones.

The Marquess Conrad took his chance when Baldwin died to get the Bishop of Beauvais to marry him to Princess Isabella – a girl much less than half his age, forced to the altar by her mother. That's what they said in Toron. They said the Marquess laughed at King Guy's challenge to a combat, to decide who'd rule Jerusalem when it was taken from the Turks – laughed at his emissary and returned his gage, and from that day refused to send supplies from Tyre to feed his army on the plain.

By January, our rations were reduced to a handful of dry beans, a spray of millet and a small loaf of twice-baked Toron bread per man. The waterlogged camp gardens had been stripped of greens. The last of the salt meat had gone and flesh of any kind was at a premium. Without the provender to feed them, asses, camels, sumpter beasts and even riding horses were being killed and eaten. Duke Henri's destriers and hunting dogs were under constant guard. Knights with peregrines and goshawks flew them tirelessly until the rainy skies above the plain were empty of small birds – then wrung their necks and plucked the hawks themselves for roasting. When we could bring them down, we even ate the carrion crows which hoped to pick our bones.

In February, when they were least expected, one moonless night a force of Saracens had swept down from the hills. They killed the guards before they could alert the camp, and entered by the Maledicta Gate to reprovision Acre. By then a hen's egg sold in Toron for as much as sixpence. Rats and seagulls or a bunch of netted sparrows cost two shillings. Destriers were making higher prices dead than living, and most of us existed on a dreary diet of millet porridge, and boiled carob beans that made our farts smell foul. The only thing we had enough of was wine that tasted like horse liniment, and a raw spirit called *al-yazil* that was rough enough to strip the paint off a church saint, and doubtless killed as many men as it consoled. Jos, John and I drank it to heat the blood and held competitions afterwards to see how far across the tent lanes we could piss.

Cooped in by rain, we festered in our tents for weeks of misery, defending our beasts and our remaining silver, playing dismal games of dice and backgammon with Dickon Waleys' men across the way, picking at our flea-scabs, juggling our balls inside our braies, and moving on to Fisty Flora when that itch wanted scratching.

'Or maybe *Fisty Fatima* if you're Sarsen?' Jos joked to cover my embarrassment when once he caught me throttling the thing. 'An' never worked right-handed like a decent Christian, eh Sir Garry?'

At night we dreamt of banqueting – of all the courses in the hall at Lewes, only to wake with empty bellies. *And if up here I can't recall exactly how it felt to starve, I do remember how it felt to shiver under dripping sailcloth, because I'm trembling now.*

They say it's a lean common where ne'er a goose can find a bite, and John said he'd heard that Friesian soldiers on the plain were eating tallow, and stewing leather harness up with worms to fill their aching bellies.

'Take my word, they'll even scrape a camel's guts for what's inside when all the rest's picked clean,' he told us. 'Tragical. An' worse'n that, Sir Garry – 'tis held if you will credit it, they're payin' the Pullani to pick the grain from jackal shit to use for makin' bread.'

Out of the damp and filth and meagre rations, came dysentery and fever to take their daily toll. Until it became impractical to bury anything less than a dozen corpses piled into a grave-pit at a time. Amongst the great men who died, were Ranulf de Glanville, along with Theobald of Blois and his brother, Stephen of Sancerre. Frederick of Swabia, who led the German forces, fell sick the twelfth night after Christmas and gave up his soul soon after. Even our Commander, Count Henri of Toulouse, seemed like to follow – confined to bed with leeches stuck all over him and raving like a madman. Some men turned renegade, deserting to the Moslems when they heard that Saladin had given orders for his Christian captives at Kharruba to be fed as much as his own soldiers.

Meantime, we ate what we could find, shat goat pellets, and somehow managed to survive until we had to kill first one mule then the other – bartering their guts and hooves for millet seed and mouldy chaff in the camp market. We lived off those old mokes for longer than we ought, and sinned by eating flesh in Lent, supposing we'd already done our fasting one way or another.

'But 'though I've smoked 'em 'til they're black, I reckon that we're chewin' worms now more'n hide,' John told us ruefully in Engleis. 'An' when they're gone, Sir Garry, I'll swear there 'ent enough in camp to keep a mouse alive.'

'Aye, 'tis cruel to all dumb beasts,' said Jos.

'Leave alone enough to feed a big ol' horse,' John added quietly. At which the pair of them turned pointedly to stare at Raoul.

'*NO!*' The first word I'd spoken for awhile – it came out frayed, much louder than expected and for once without its echo from my squire. 'No listen both of you, it makes no sense,' I told them. 'The winter's almost over. They say the grain ships may already be at sea, and after them the royal fleets with everything we need to leave this cursed place, and...'

'Occupy the city? 'Tis not what we've heard blowed about, Sir Garry.' The flesh had melted from poor Jos' face. His blue eyes looked enormous. 'What we've heard tell, is that our precious kings have been a deal too busy picking fights and fornicating along the way, to spare a thought for Acre and us poor starvelings outside it. They're saying in the French camp that a priest's hair turned as white as chalk last Advent, when our King Dickard came to make confession on the Isle of Sicily. The man's too happy adding to his score of sins, is what they're saying, to be in any haste to get here.'

'For God's sake Jos, you know as well as I do that such falsehoods are spread about by spies and infidels to undermine morale.'

'And if you think...' I turned to John. 'If you think for a moment that I'd sacrifice the horse I've brought here at such cost to ride in battle

207

with my King – then I can only say you've failed to grasp what this croisade's about!' We were standing as it happened in the rough stall that he'd shared with the two mules. So I laid one hand protectively on Raoul's bony neck, and scowled at the two men I'd brought with equal thoughtlessness into the living hell of Toron.

'Then we shall have to scratch hard, Sir, I'm tellin' ye, 'afore we find another scrap to swallow,' had been John Hideman's last word on the subject.

I sat unmoving in the dripping stall for the third part of an hour, listening to the patter of the rain – then spent the other two thirds sharpening my dagger on a whetstone. I'd seen Raoul born at Haddertun one Easter on a visit from the fortress – recalled his wobbly legs, his small hammer head, his soft pelt black and shiny as a chessboard knight – recalled him later on another furlough, racing madly round the paddock, rolling like an outsized puppy, sidling flat-eared to snuffle in my collar with a velvet nose. He was a beast without a soul, yet seemed to me a person I had loved and brought to ruin. And stood for me already hobbled, slack-hipped and with drooping head – trusting me, the poor old bag of bones.

'Now then, I'll do it for you Sir an' gladly,' John offered without his usual pause for thought. But I shook my head, and frowned and clamped my mouth tight shut to stop my teeth from chattering. I felt my horse's skin twitch as I stroked him with light fingers. I felt the hard scar of his tourney wound, his ragged ear. Poor Raoul, if only I had left him to cover mares on the green meads of Sussex, instead of dragging him across the world, to starve and suffer an ignoble death.

'I know. I know you're weak, old fellow, weak and weary.'

His ears flicked, listening – as quietly, very gently I secured his halter – feeling for the artery with my left hand – murmuring with the soft voice I'd used to tame him, calm him, win his confidence when we were both still colts.

But Raoul the high-bred, Raoul the temperamental, no longer had the fight in him to pull away. The poor beast simply stared at me with patient and defeated eyes.

'Head up – that's it, old friend. That's it.' I had to blink to see what I was doing, make sure that I had the place. With trembling right hand clenched hard on the dagger hilt, I wrenched the blade across his throat. Deeper than I needed to be sure.

A violent jerk! Surprise and terror. Pain. Betrayal. A buckling collapse – and blood, *so much* of it!...

It was the hardest, hardest thing I'd ever had to do, hard even to recall it. But there was worse to come.

RELIEF

Near the end of March, when native chrysanthemums spring up between the tents to cast a golden net across the Plain of Acre, the first sail is spotted out to sea; and the first Italian grain ships anchor in the bay to end the famine in the camps.

Duke Leopold of Babenberg, another cousin of the King of France, sails in soon afterwards to take command of the siege army, while Count Henri lies sick abed. Then, as a further insult to King Guy perched on his mound at Toron, the French King himself makes landfall at the Port of Tyre – to set his own seal of approval on the union of its Governor, the Marquess Conrad, with the hereditary Princess Isabella. Although in truth, Philippe's support for Conrad in place of Richard's vassal, Guy de Lusignan, has more to do with his contempt for Richard than any special virtue in the Governor of Tyre.

When they rode out so splendidly from Vézelay, the Christian kings had sworn a public oath to act as friends and allies for the course of the croisade. But nine months later when they separated at Messina, their oaths were of a different kind and their intentions every bit as hostile as the Sultan Salahuddin predicted. In Genoa they'd argued over transport for King Philippe's troops. Later both fleets were delayed in Sicily, where Richard started a small war in defence of his sister, Jehanne, the widow of the island's king. He demanded her return into his keeping – and crucially her dowry; receiving both eventually by conquering Sicilian Messina, and (I mention this in passing) by selling its new ruler the onetime talisman of his croisade: King Arthur's fabled sword, *Escalibor*.

By then the Kings of England and of France had spent the winter bottled up together in the harbour of Messina, playing chess – dynastic chess with princesses for pawns.

Following his cousin's unsuccessful ploy to secure the Latin princess Isabella, King Philippe's first move in the game had been to offer for King Richard's widowed sister, Jehanne of Sicily, together with her dower lands of Agenais and Quercy. When Richard, who had other plans for her, countered by moving Jehanne across the straits to the Italian mainland, King Philippe challenged him again to honour his betrothal to his own sister, the Princess Alys. At which point the King of England coolly introduced a new princess into the game – the queen's pawn he had up his sleeve.

'The world is full of delusions, Philippe, and my marriage to your sister's one of them,' he put it to the French King in his lodgings by the harbour. 'There's no other way to tell you, Cousin, but to say plainly that the Queen my mother is on her way here as we speak – to bring me for my bride the Infanta Berenguela of Navarre. The ladies have already crossed the Alps to spend the Christmas festival in Pisa.

'Perhaps I should have mentioned it before?' He raised his sandy brows. 'At any rate, as soon as we're betrothed I plan to send the girl before us into Palestine, to wed her at the altar of the Holy Sepulchre when we've secured it from the Turk. From what His Grace of Canterbury reports, I hear we have no time to lose.'

The muscles in the French King's cheeks showed that he'd clenched his jaw. 'The Holy Father has expressly forbidden women en croisade.' Startled into speech, it is the first thing he can think of.

'A sick old eunuch in a gilded palace?' We hardly need to consider his opinion.'

'And I hardly thought you'd break your contract with my sister?' Philippe countered bitterly.

'Ah, did you not?' King Richard's turn to show surprise. 'Hell's bells man, did you really think that Eléonore would let her within a half-league of the throne? A girl who's borne her husband's bastard?'

'I warn you, Richard – if you scorn Alys for marriage with a Spaniard, you'll forfeit any claim on Gisors, Châteauroux, Graçy or Isoudun, and with them the goodwill of France. My word on that.'

'Which brings us back to that other word of *incest*, does it not? Dear man, you know as well as I do that Henry's is not the only prick that stands between me and your sister. Or if it comes to that, between you and my dear sister's quim.' King Richard showed his teeth. 'We have an interesting history, Philippe, you and I. And have you thought – maybe this Advent we should go further than avoiding drink and bum-boys, and purge our souls of sin before the bishops? The Pope has spies in every port, the Sultan too I hear – we'd have the ears of all the world to hear us in confession, Cousin.'

'You wouldn't dare!'

They weren't the best words Philippe could have chosen to respond to someone of Richard's reckless reputation; and within a day the King of England proceeded to make good his threat – by summoning a group of French and English bishops to the harbour chapel for a sensational performance. Dramatically stripped naked for the scourge, crowned with a garland of blue periwinkles to denote repentance, he'd beseeched their Graces at the altar to absolve him of the sin God abhorred above all others – the act of sodomising a young man in Paris three years earlier.

It was a statement he'd be willing to repeat in public from the steps of the Cathedral, Richard said – and in the next breath (with more frankness than was strictly necessary) supplied the co-respondent's famous name.

The embarrassed bishops hastened to lay on the whip (backhanded and slack-wristed to spare the great man pain), to smother the unpleasant nature of the sin in euphemistic Latin, and grant the royal repentant absolution. Queen's pawn checks king in other words – to leave Philippe with no choice but to retract all his objections to the Spanish marriage

To all appearances the two Kings parted amicably in Sicily when Philippe left for Tyre. But no one aboard his flagship could fail to gauge the King of France's temper on the long sea voyage. Bleary-eyed and seasick, hunched in his cabin like a moulting pullet, he plotted his revenge on Richard – spitting chips.

In April at his camp of al-Kharruba, the agents of the Sultan report the arrival of King Philippe at the port of Tyre with near three thousand men and fifteen hundred horses. In the guise of a silk merchant, Salahuddin's trusted emissary, al-Harawi, gains audience with the King of France and his cousin, Conrad de Montferrat, in a closet of the Tyrian Palace. No witnesses are present to record their conversation. No documents are signed. But four hours later, al-Harawi leaves without the heavy chest he carried in with him (supposedly containing samples of silk fabric); and it's further notable that when he moves his army down to Acre ten days later, King Philippe seems in no great haste to prosecute the siege – remaining mostly in his tent, due it is said to a recurring sickness.

In his celebrated masterwork, 'Discussion on the Stratagems of War', al-Harawi is later to record: *A Sultan may beguile his enemy by offering whatever he most earnestly desires, and guaranteeing its accomplishment with oaths upon his honour –* and as he writes, the secret bargain struck between the Sultan Salahuddin and the King of France is what he has in mind.

In effect, the Sultan's offered to spare Philippe the effort and expense of a long campaign by guaranteeing its fair outcome in advance. He will support Conrad de Montferrat as ruler of the Latin kingdom, in place of King Richard or his vassal Guy de Lusignan. He will allow the Arab caravans from Egypt and Damascus free access to the port of Tyre, from which Conrad may readily supply the court of France with all the eastern dyes and spices, gems, cotton and brocade they need within a mutually beneficial alliance. Alas, the Sultan cannot yield the Holy City of al-Quds the Christians call Jerusalem. But he will continue to extend protection to any Christian pilgrim who may wish to worship at its shrines. Then, after Richard has exhausted his resources taking Acre, he will negotiate with both kings for a lasting peace.

To honour his part of the bargain, all Philippe is required to do is to delay the siege until the English King arrives, and when the city falls to ensure a fair exchange of prisoners as part of an agreement to cede further territory to Conrad de Montferrat and Princess Isabella.

It's not a bargain that will suit King Guy de Lusignan of course, and on the very day he hears from his own spies of Philippe's dealings with the Marquess and the Sultan, he sails to intercept the King of England on his way to Palestine and beg for his support. They meet offshore, where Richard is already making headway with his conquest of the Holy Land by capturing the strategic isle of Cyprus. And while they fight to bring the Cypriots to heel, King Richard and King Guy agree their own plans for the resolution of the Kings' Croisade.

In the words of his official chronicler, the very hills rejoice the day that Richard comes to meet his destiny in Outremer.

'Pen could not write, nor words describe the people's rapture,' the annalist enthuses, before proceeding to describe it anyway in vivid purple prose. *'Horns resounded, trumpets rang out and pipers added their triumphant sounds,'* he scribbles in his notes for the Itinerarium of King Richard's Palestine campaign – and then improves the line with an alliteration (cross out *triumphant* and add *shrill* – *'Shrill sounds'* is plainly better. *'...pipers added their shrill sounds. Drums were beaten, the deep booming of war clarions were heard. But it was as though all these discordant notes combined in perfect harmony; and there were few indeed who did not add to the general tumult of praise and jubilation. To show the gladness of their hearts they toasted one another in the wine that was distributed among them, recounting tales of ancient heroes.*

'In unalloyed delight,' writes Richard's chronicler, *'they sang and danced the night away, lighting the darkness with their fires and torches, until the Turks believed they'd set the Plain of Acre all aflame.'*

The spring flowers have long since faded and summer entered its fifth week of drought, before the English fleet put into Acre. One of the first barges to drop anchor in the bay contains King Guy and the royal ladies, sent on ahead as entrées for the pièce de résistance that's to be King Richard.

The Sicilian Queen, Jehanne, coined from the same mint as her brother – large, roseate and handsomely well-padded – sails down the jetty in her flamboyant samite silks and muslins and her feathered turban, with King Guy de Lusignan himself to hold her parasol and shade her from the sun. A child of eleven or twelve summers trots to keep pace with the Queen's ladies; identified as Béatris, Damsel of Cyprus, daughter of the island's former ruler and now captive to the English king.

To the general disappointment of the multitudes who've come to see her land, the fourth member of the royal party, Queen Bérengère, is glimpsed but for a moment in the distance as she's carried in her stockings from the ship to her conveyance on the quay – which some might say was the best way to view her. For although the decorations of her curtained litter suggest a form within to match the loveliness of her new Latin name of Berengaria, the Queen's in fact a stocky, broad-hipped woman with a dark complexion and a long Basque chin, selected by Queen Eléonore less for her looks, than for her stamina and childbearing potential. The romance which has preceded them to Acre, tells of King Richard's passion for his Spanish bride; an infatuation which compels him to marry her in haste on the enchanted seat of love itself – on Cyprus, birthplace of the Goddess Venus. The truth is more prosaic. His mother is the only woman Richard loves or ever listens to; and in the days she spent with him in Sicily, Queen Eléonore impressed upon her son the need to bed the Princess of Navarre as rapidly as possible to seed

214

in her an heir for Aquitaine and England. She hadn't brought a royal mare for him across the Alps, she said, to see the royal stallion baulk at mounting.

'You could be killed or gelded in the conflict,' Eléonore told Richard baldly. 'You never know in warfare, Dickard; and if you've the sense God's given you, you'll go to work on her this very night.

'Then seal the contract later,' Eléonore advised, 'when you are sure the mare's in foal.'

Which was precisely how her son had acted, in despite of his own taste. For Bérangère was rather too brown and mature to suit his appetite. So far from home and unprotected, the Spanish princess had no choice but to submit; and when in Cyprus six weeks later her maids reported that she'd missed her monthly course, King Richard married, crowned, and left her – all within a single day. God willing, they'd be in the Holy City of Jerusalem for the child's deliverance, he told her. Meantime she would be wise to rest and keep it safe within her womb. Her husband smiled on Bérangère indulgently, then waved a meaty hand and rode away from matrimonial drudgery to amuse himself amongst the youngest of his captive Cypriots – female and otherwise.

The royal smile is once again in place when Richard's Genoese war galley, *Piombone*, comes into view at last around the sea wall of Saint Jean d'Acre. Victorious in its encounter with a Saracen troop-ship in the roads to Tyre just sixteen hours before, the galley's decks have since been cleared of wood-splinters and Arab blood, its bows and gunnels scalloped with gold and scarlet silk to match the colours of the royal banner. Long ranks of oars sweep it ashore. King Richard's born for great occasions. He shares with other charismatic conquerors of Acre – with Julius Caesar and before him, Alexander – a genius for personal display. As with his coronation at Westminster, as with all his entries and arrivals, he comes to demonstrate that kings are not as other men.

But if he seems a god to those who crane over each other's shoulders to see the English King, some hours at anchor up the coast and out of sight have something certainly to do with his magnificent appearance. His entourage of groomsmen, hairdressers and keepers of the royal vestments have all worked ceaselessly that afternoon to massage, to manicure, and to enrich the rosy tints in Richard's hair. To polish, perfume and bejewel him. Shirt him in silk. Envelop him in velvet – rings on his royal fingers, bells to his royal toes. Over his silver-link parade hauberk (which since Vézelay has come to seem a trifle tight), he wears a supertunic brocaded in the eastern manner and signed with a white cross. His crown's an areola in the sinking sun. Gilt threads woven in the French style through his tinted hair and beard ensure that they too glitter, underlit by their reflection in the waves. Despite the heat, a cloak of Lincoln scarlet ripples from King Richard's shoulders, blazoned like his escutcheon with guardant leopardés.

The reborn Once and Future, now very present King, who's sold Escalibor in Sicily for twice its weight in gold, now flourishes a new sword as a symbol of his own invincibility. He stands, legs wide-astride (the boastful pose that men adopt to show the muscles of their thighs, and maybe the uncommon bulk of what's between) – rampant in the prow of *Piombone:* Richard as Redeemer!

The King's reception on the strand is as his chronicler describes – although it's doubtful if the words of triumph and encouragement he shouts across the water are audible to anyone above the cheers, the drums, the blaring horns. Thousands on the shore applaud him in a fever of delight. A little short of sight, and as ever focussed inwardly upon his own achievement, the King sees those who await him simply as a moving blur. The picture that he makes with sword upraised and legs astride; larger than life, dressed gorgeously to maim if not to kill – backed by a fleet of white-crossed sails against a gold leaf sky – is just the image history needs to confirm his legend as a Christian saviour.

Seagulls circle *Piombone* through the warm salt air.

No bats this time for Richard.

CHAPTER TEN

So many people on my travels, hearing that I was in Acre, have begged me to tell them what I saw there, and how I managed to survive. But always I refused to satisfy them, said it was too painful to remember.

Until the Bérgé dal becce taught me otherwise.

The whole world knows how King Richard came like Joshua to trumpet down the walls of Acre and win the city back for God. But that was how it ended. Not how it was to be there.

Guillaume, the arms-master at Lewes who taught us all we knew of warfare, ticked off the crucial stages of siegecraft on his fingers – beginning with *Blockading* on the smallest, and counting through *Bombardment, Escalade* and *Mining,* to finish with *Terms for Surrender* on his stubby thumb. He was a hard taskmaster who punished inattention with the knuckles of same five fingers clenched into a fist. And yet, perhaps because he had so little use for it himself, Guillaume quite failed to mention what we needed most at Acre – which was *Patience.*

After the grain arrived that spring, we had been ordered out of Toron, Jos, John and I, to join the Salisbury bishop, Hubert Walter on the plain – although even after four more months of service, we were still novices in the pursuit of siegecraft. For there were many thousands in the Christian camp who had already waited for three summers and two winters to starve the city to submission. On our first tour of the lower camp we were astonished by its scale. It had become a canvas city through the years; its occupants a plague of locusts who'd long since consumed the fields and gardens of the port. In districts beyond the reach of missiles from the Moslem garrison, King Guy had set the tents in squares, with roads between for horses and wheeled traffic. The outer camp was bordered on three sides by earthen ramparts, with sentry posts at intervals to warn of Saracen invasion. But closer to the walls of Acre, the army had moved underground.

Everywhere amongst the rubble, tunnels led into a labyrinth of dugouts, reinforced with bolsters of bagged sand and cribbed with olive wood. Soldiers and Pullani squeezed past each other in narrow, rush-lit passagways, connecting caves where everything was sold from water skins and salvaged weaponry, to rows of human ears on strings – even Sarsen heads with eyes and brains removed, hung by their hair as Christian trophies.

Jos said he'd like to take one back to Haddertun, to use as a lantern to frighten maids with at All Hallows. But I forbade him such a gruesome souvenir.

Compared with many on the plain, the Bishop of Salisbury's encampment near the eastern ramparts was orderly and clean. A tall man, dressed more like a soldier than a churchman, His Grace saw to it that any of his men caught fighting, gambling, sodomising or consorting with Pullani whores were flogged and sent to work a fortnight on the shit carts. He personally called the rolls and supervised the rotas for sentry, siege and mining duties, refuse disposal, earthworking and water-carrying. He sent round barbers to ensure that we were trimmed and shaved. He issued combs and jars of horse-sweat to counter lice and fleas, and made it his daily business to inspect his laundry and infirmary and the latrines, to satisfy himself that all was as it should be for his soldiers.

It was at the washing lines outside the Bishop's laundry that we ran into our old friend, the washerwoman Guillemette. Not that I knew her at the first, so thin and lined she had become. Her plain old face was hung with empty sacs of flesh, the mountains of her breasts and belly flattened into molehills underneath her homespun gown.

But – 'Guilly, my treasure!' Jos cried out the moment that he set eyes on her. 'I'd know ye anywhere, you pretty thing!'

'An' bless ye, Tiddler. I'd of picked that ruddy comb o'yours from any flock o' roosters!' The old woman flung the shirt that she was pegging back into its basket, and ran across to sweep my squire into a crushing hug that lifted little Jos a clear foot off the ground.

218

'Show up? I'll tell ye, that red knob 'ud stand out like a cock-stand in a convent. An' prove as welcome too, I wouldn't wonder!'

If they'd been made of sugar, the pair of them could not have found each other sweeter – and were off to risk a Bishop's flogging in the laundry van as soon as I gave them the nod. In return, we were allowed, all three of us, to bath in the grey suds of Guillemette's last wash. But when Jos whispered later that she'd be willing to relieve me of a little more than sweat and grime, I found that I was able to resist. For somewhere in the deprivations of our Toron winter I'd lost my carnal inspiration, and even *Fisty Flora* found it hard (or actually the other thing) to get a grip.

John Hideman made his own arrangements for relief, I never quite knew how – although there was one laundress by the name of Maud, who sometimes helped us when we bathed and was a shade less ugly than the rest. I saw her wash John's back for him. But if she ever moved round to the front, he never mentioned it, and I was careful not to ask.

There weren't too many chances for us to to flex our military muscles either during those final months of siege. Sometimes I rode with other knights at cavalry manoeuvres in one or other of the camp parade grounds. Sometimes before the sun was up too high for comfort, I'd find someone – if not a knight then ever-faithful Jos – to help me practice swordplay and tone my muscles as I put on weight. But there was little room between the tents, and bouts ended all too often in some kind of an unpleasantness involving severed guy ropes and torrents of abuse.

On Lady Day towards the end of March, the bishop sent me off with Jos for sentry duty on the outworks, and for fourteen days and thirteen nights we strained our eyes for signs of movement in the scrubby hills. From behind a hedgehog fence of sharpened stakes, we scanned the Saracen positions – prepared for, even hoping for an action of some kind. But we saw little other than cloud shadows in the daylight, or passing squalls of rain. At dawn we watched the sunrise. At sunset there were wisps of smoke. Each night while the cicadas shrilled, an arc of red sparks in the hills encircled galaxies of Christian campfires on the plain. But that was all.

At the end of our guard duty we marched back into camp with nothing to report.

Another fortnight brought the French fleet into Acre, and with it a disturbing rumour. We heard from Guillemette, who had it from the Bishop's chaplain, who'd spoken to a merchant, who by chance had overheard a conversation in the harbour – that suggested Sultan Saladin was treating with the King of France behind King Richard's back. They had a plan – the sailor told the merchant, who explained it to the chaplain, who boasted of the knowledge in the laundry – to cede the ports of Tyre and Acre with some other coastal towns to the French King and his vassal Conrad, in exchange for their agreement to abandon the croisade and leave Jerusalem in Moslem hands.

'Which even if it's quarter true could mean we're home by Christmas,' Jos said cheerfully. 'Or Shrovetide at the latest.'

'How could it possibly be true? Why would the King of France come all this way, simply to trade the Holy City for a handful of old ruins and a port we occupy already?' I demanded. 'And wouldn't you expect Conrad de Montferrat to come to Acre, if he thought....'

'...That it was ready to surrender?' Jos helpfully supplied. 'I think he will, My Lord.'

But when we heard that Conrad had indeed left Tyre for Acre, and that King Guy de Lusignan had gone to meet King Richard on the Isle of Cyprus, I had felt bound to draw my squire's attention to the siege engines King Philippe was assembling outside the walled city.

'Now why would he do that,' I asked, 'if he already knows the garrison is close to a surrender?' (And as I asked it, hoped to heaven that he didn't.)

In May, the three of us were sent down with the rest of Bishop Walter's force to the mine workings, where sappers burrowed constantly like moles to undermine the city walls. Duke Leopold, who'd led the siege before King Philippe took command, believed the city's weak point to be the gate-tower known as *Maledicta*, which jutted like a ship's prow from an angle of its wall, and could be mined from both directions. The ditch which once made an island of the place, had been drained early in the siege. In course of time the tunnels on the Christian side were deepened, lined with timber and pushed out beneath the putrid heaps of refuse and disintegrating bodies which filled the empty fosse, until they reached the footings of the tower – where picks in place of spades were needed, and fresh teams of miners with arbalesters in support. Which was where we came in.

But if we'd hoped our tour of duty at the city walls would coincide with some fresh action on the part of the French army, we were soon disappointed. The King of France's illness still confined him to his tent. His trébuchets flung rocks at Acre's towering walls, inflicting no more damage than a few more pocks and pits to add to their already pitted surface. In retaliation, the Moslems' petrary – nicknamed *God's Evil Cousin* – tossed blocks of masonry the size of cottages down on the Christian camp. But since its range was known and it was far too cumbersome to move with any kind of stealth, its missiles almost always fell in areas already cleared for their reception. Otherwise exchange of fire was limited to crossbow bolts; and by and large the casualties were slight – a tent destroyed with those inside, a bolt that found its way to earth through human flesh, a cry behind the merlons of the curtain wall – and cheers were far more often for near misses than for strikes.

Early in the year, when the Saracens had broken through our cordon in the night, they'd flayed two Genoese alive, and suspended a Pisan soldier from the city wall as a target for Christian archers who thought to end the fellow's misery. From the target's point of view, that hadn't worked too well – and in revenge, a group of his countrymen had burned a captured infidel alive in sight of the Pisan's perforated corpse. But on the whole such acts of cruelty were exceptions. At Christmastide, to mark the birth of Jesus which even Moslems honour, they'd flown a flag of truce and let down some little Saracens in baskets from the walls to run races and hold wrestling matches with Pullani urchins from the camp. And then on Easter Sunday, while Jos and I were on the outworks, we'd heard that the Bishop of Évreux processed barefoot to the Maledicta Tower bearing a silver cross and chanting psalms, and that the enemy had set their bows aside to call out friendly greetings from the pentises above.

In many ways the siege seemed less of a real war, than some kind of a laborious game with scores to tally and acts of prowess to perform.

Our task had been to cover the retreat of Christians coming from the tunnels with rubble from the tower's foundations, and to return the fire of Moslems up on the walls whose own task was to prevent them. John Hideman laboured with the miners. Jos held the heavy shield we'd been issued from the Bishop's armoury to catch the bolts as they flew in, while I sought groups in place of single heads along the walls to give my arbalest shots the best chance of finding living marks. Repeatedly I stooped and loaded, aimed and loosed the quarrels. Repeatedly Jos used both arms to raise and angle the steel mantlet. We worked together as we'd always done, as any tradesmen work to do the best job that they can, and while we worked at our own trade of arms we talked of anything that crossed our minds.

'Well Jos, what have I brought you to?' I asked one noontide, when the sun was like a hammer pounding at the rocky anvil that was Acre, and every inch of us inside our clothing ran with sweat. 'I'll warrant that you little thought that as my squire you would be dragged through rivers, fried on shipboard, carried half across the world to starve in camp, and then be roasted in...'

'My jacket, Sir? No more I did,' Jos agreed. 'A country boy like me? I never looked to travel further than from Haywards Heath to Lewes as a fact. Nor thought to see a sight more wonderful than our smith's daughter, Fat Hamanda, on her back and serving us a raspberry slice with both her knees 'longside her ears!'

He pulled a face and wiped his hands on the grey buckram of his gambeson, collecting more dust than he shed. And that was Jos the jester, who never would be serious if he could make you smile.

'So wouldn't you as soon have stayed home, now that you can see how many soldiers we have out here to uphold...'

'...The Christian cause, Sir Garry? Well every little helps, as Jack the sailor had it as he pissed in the sea.'

222

My squire's blue eyes were on the battlements. 'Not being funny,' he added while the mu'adhdhin's third wailing call to prayer inside the city signalled an end for us of that day's duty. 'But I'm your man, Sir Garry. That's the shape of it, an' ever will be I daresay so long as God's above the Devil.'

It was in so many words what he'd told Hugh when I took up the cross at Lewes, and in spite of the familiar grin I knew he was in earnest.

The mu'adhdhin were silenced, every one, when we moved into Acre. But when I heard them at his graveside, and later on the road to Joppa, I recalled what Jos had said.

King Richard's coming with the queens and Guy de Lusignan changed everything completely.

At first sight of his fleet of ships, all loaded to the gunwales with men and horses and the latest instruments for breaking sieges, it was clear to all – to soldiers and Pullani, friends, foes and everyone, that Acre had not the faintest hope of holding out against him. And everyone was right. The King of France rose from his sickbed to welcome the royal party. A huge area was cleared behind the Templars' tents for King Richard's gold pavilion and the Queens' marquee – for their household offices, an armoury, a barracks and a stables, and for five thousand soldiers. Then, while his sappers visited the mines beneath the moat and his artillery began assembling petraries and calculating ranges, and all in camp got drunk at his expense, the King declared an armistice in which to send the Sultan his own terms for treaty.

The gossip in the laundry was that what King Richard chiefly sought from Saladin was acceptance of his vassal Guy de Lusignan as ruler of Jerusalem, with Queen Jehanne (herself descended from a Latin king) beside him on the throne. It was the reason, all supposed, that he had brought Jeanne from Sicily and kept Guy at his side – to add the client Kingdom of Jerusalem to his empire. King Richard offered to parley in his person with the Sultan, and sent him as a gift a handsome black youth from the slave market in Messina.

'Used him as a bum-boy while they were on the seas,' said Guillemette, 'an' likely thinks ol' Sallydin 'ud find a black arsehole a nice change from the pink.' And when I told her sharply not to spread such falsehoods, she'd blessed me as an innocent and winked at Jos.

The King's terms were refused in any case, and after two more days of peace he launched his main attack on Acre.

What happened to the black boy no one knew.

In its last weeks, the siege moved from an unreal sort of order to something close to chaos. Having started arse-first with *Terms For a Surrender*, the King's approach to siegecraft was to throw all aspects into it; redoubling the sea blockade of Acre whilst at the same time sending his own sappers underground and increasing the bombardment of its walls. For every ballistic engine the King of France provided, King Richard set up two or three of twice the size and range, and had torsion mangons from the castles of his ships remounted onto wheels to batter at the cracks that were beginning to appear. Twelve tall sling-trébuchets like children's see-saws on a massive scale tossed quicklime, burning pitch, baskets of scorpions and bees, and buckets of infected faeces over the battlements into the city streets. King Richard threw everything he had at Acre, and what it could, the Moslem garrison threw back.

King Richard sent out the towering, sixty-foot siege castle he called *Mategriffon*, with men inside it like the horse of Troy – an edifice assembled from the beams and sections he'd brought with him and covered with wet ass-skins drenched in urine to protect it from Greek fire. But the Moslems simply siphoned *feu grégeois* in through the space beneath its roof, to consume the tower with all the shrieking men inside it in less time than it took to roll it to the city wall. Their charred flesh smelled of roasted pork. Then through the smoke the garrison sent mirror-signals to the Sultan's cavalry, to bring them from the hills in their defence.

Our orders from Bishop Walter were to hold the south defences of the camp against a Saracen assault – and looking back, the hours, the scores of hours we spent exchanging fire with Moslem horsemen galloping from left to right down to the city, or else from right to left back to the hills, all seem to blur into one hot unending day.

Others rode to battle, wielded swords, gained reputations. Others, not us. Ours was the dull duty of holding a position that we knew was safe. And while we manned our barricades, exciting news came up the lines of actions elsewhere in the fray. Word was that *Saphadin*, the Sultan's brother, had been forced into retreat with his Egyptian cavalry by none other than the Marquess Conrad, who'd lately joined the French King's army. We heard King Richard had a fever, but rather than allow King Philippe to command, had had himself wrapped in a quilt, and carried on a stretcher to direct the fire of the great mangonel á tour they'd fished out of the Rhône. Then finally we heard the news that we'd so long awaited. As King Richard's sappers fired the timber stanchions of his mines, a gaping crack had opened in the north face of the Maledicta Tower.

'*The Cursed Tower is breached,*' his criers shouted through the Bishop's camp. '*Richard, King of England, Duke of Aquitaine and Normandy, Count of Poitou has authorised the offer of three gold bezants for every stone that's drawn out from the city wall and carried to the trébuchet known as The Lord's Avenger!*' And because, in real life as in chess, a king outranks a bishop, it was an offer we could not refuse.

It's well known to all commanders that sober soldiers are less willing to take risks. So in addition to the gold, they gave us each a long pull on a skin of burgundy for every stone we dropped behind the trébuchet. The wine was full of sediment and tasted of corroded metal. But it helped.

'And if they're giving us a choice, then I'd as soon go with a skinful of the red stuff,' Jos confessed, 'to meet Saint Peter with a blithesome face.'

But that was early in the piece; and after three hours in the blazing furnace of the fosse, we had been anything but blithesome – dry as dust as grey as ghosts and drunk as Munster's monk.

It's easiest up here to see things from a distance, looking back and looking down from high above the city, soaring like an eagle above the fleet, the

225

yellow strand, the vast blue mantle of the sea. Easiest to see myself as I was then, a tiny insect in a seething mass of thousands, climbing over one another in the dust to move the debris from a broken nest. Up here in Heaven I've become a god, poking at an anthill with a stick. It crushes, smears the insects. Kills some, leaves others writhing. One staggers sideways with a flattened abdomen. Do ants make sounds that can't be heard by human ears? The injured ones will die and shrivel in the heat – their death, the death of ants, the death of men from this high viewpoint miniature and unimportant.

But now I'm back amongst them – to feel the stone dust boiling round us, gritting in our lashes, clogging in our throats, even with our cotton scarves tied round our faces – and to see the sun glow through it like a firebrand.

With both eyes closed, I can still feel as much as hear the blare of the King's clarions, the din of voices beating in my ears, the odd sounds of people coughing and convulsed with sneezes. Figures loom and disappear. It feels as if we've entered hell to suffer all the torments of the damned. I see a lump of masonry scythe down to punch a red hole through the mayem to our left. Ahead of us the city walls are streaked with blood and pitch. The enemy hurl rocks into the breach as fast as we can haul them out. The sky is raining rocks.

Yet still the tower holds.

Our world is made of wall – rising sheer above us, strewn about us, falling from one state into the other. I catch a glimpse behind me of Jos' curls. No longer red but powdered with grey dust, and know that John is in the same disguise. We are no longer warriors with enemies to charge, but moving targets, climbing through the rubble and the bodies of the fallen. It takes all three of us to free a single block of rough-hewn stone, to haul it out with blistered fingers, push it, pull it, guard it jealously from others who would steal it from us, manhandle it across the littered surface of the ditch.

So many make the crossing with us, to queue for our gold pieces and our wine, that in the end the press is such that none of us can move at anything but a back-breaking shuffle, with nothing to distinguish knights from common soldiers or Pullani. Stooping as we shuffle. As if a crouching posture could protect us from an arrow or a falling block of stone.

Will she mourn me if I die?

Was it the third time that we climbed leaden-footed to the breach? It could as well have been the fourth or fifth. I only know for sure it was the last.

I had just slipped and nearly fallen, felt John's hand beneath my elbow, just regained my feet. As I looked up a shadow crossed the red eye of the sun. And I will never know if it was instinct or the downrush of hot air that flung me to one side. Then all at once a mighty crash, an acrid cloud of dust. And pain!

It took a moment more to know that I was on my back with something sharp and heavy on my foot. More pain, intense and burning as I wrenched free, rolled over. Tried to rise. But it was only when I used the slab to haul myself erect, that I saw what it covered.

Death stands at every soldier's shoulder. I should have been prepared, but I was not.

His feet were kicking, fingers clutching at the air, as if he was – as if he could have been alive still with that great block of limestone crushing his poor head! For some reason that I can't explain I had half-drawn my dagger. Then I was shouting, screaming for John Hideman to help me move the block – cursing, weeping as we fumbled, sickeningly dropped it, raised it with the help of others, rolled it back.

The flies were there before us, alighting on the pulp of shattered bone and brains. On traces of red hair and bubbling blood where Jos' freckled face had been. Crushed now like an eggshell.

I was too shocked to think or speak. The muscles of my stomach clenched and heaved. I fell onto my knees beside his body to vomit in the dust.

CHAPTER ELEVEN

When you lie flat on your back the sky fills all your vision, blue as a throstle's egg and limitless – as if such things as clouds had never been and never will be in the future. The blue goes on forever.

You have to squint, the sun's so bright. You think of silence, but there's no such thing. The air is full of sounds – of buzzards whistling, and of a skylark somewhere singing like an angel.

> *Upward, upward wings the lark,*
> *Singing out his heart in flight,*
> *Cares abandoned to the dark...*

If only I could fly. If only I could fly with him into the dazzling light, instead of feeling earthbound and so heavy and so weary. I could be anyone, a nun, a dairymaid – a body in the sun...

There's scarce a breath of wind and we have had no rain. The plums are ripening; crabs and cobnuts swelling on the bough. It's going to be a record harvest, bound to be.

They're out there now in Middle Field, an army of them – neatmen with their boys, their wives and daughters and their cousins and their aunts. Their figures shimmer in the heat. The boys crouch with their longbows by the wall of uncut barley, waiting with the dogs to take any hares or foxes that run out. Hod's out there somewhere in the stubble helping to set sheaves up on their legs, with little Edmay and Odette, and Bruno – which is lucky for he'd never let me lie here otherwise in any sort of peace.

It's like the day last year when we came haymaking, but hotter much. The earth looks tired as though the heat has sucked the goodness from it. The shadows are all shorter, greens all darker now the sun's so high. I came to help, not to be idle. I should be out there with them shocking down, making sure that all is as it should be – but can't find the energy to do it.

What's wrong with me? Why DO I feel so tired?

Is Garon out in blazing sun like this? (It's always hot in Outremer, or so they say.) Is he alive and in the sun? Or buried in the earth and in the dark? We've had no word, which is to be expected. All news of the croisade is stale. We only heard the other day that King Richard's married a princess with an outlandish name and taken her with him to queen it in Jerusalem (if they should ever reach it). But no one knows what battles have been lost or won, and I have almost stopped believing he'll return.

Is that what's wrong with me? Have I lost heart?

Is it the prospect of a life trapped in the manor that depresses me, with all the endless dairying and baking and preserves – with one day's tasks so like another's, knowing that I'm weaving dower sheets for daughters I may never bear? Or is it worse than that? Am I afraid of losing what I have, a woman unprotected in a world of predatory men?

Unprotected? Come, that's hardly what you are, Elise, with face-ache Kempe and three trained sergeants at your beck and call, besides your bondmen and My Lord and Lady of Warenne (and if the very worst came, I suppose Sir Hugh?).

He left the manor soon after we laid Lady Constance to rest in the fenced burial plot beyond the orchard – before Epiphany, before we'd even sung the first mass for her soul – and left us with his little daughter. On Plough Monday we heard he'd gone to join the Earl at Conisbrough for his knight service, saw neither hide nor hair of him through Lent or Holy Week.

The blackthorn was in flower before he finally returned. I was at my chamber window as it chanced, shouting to the maid Berta to stop her foolish chatter at the manor gate and bring the milk directly to the pantry – when she looked up, and I looked after her to see who it was on the chalk track.

'Look Edmay, here's your father on a courser,' I called out to the child behind me on the settle with old Hod. 'He's come to take you home for sure.' And it touched both our hearts to see the joy in her thin little face as she jumped down and ran to see him for herself.

She took a little while to understand, poor poppet. But I knew in a day that she was not the reason why he came. I was.

He wouldn't dream of taking her to Meresfeld with him so long as she was so contented here, Sir Hugh pretended to believe. He would prefer to visit her at Haddertun, he said – but when he came, spent little time with her and too much altogether plaguing me. (And if anyone knew how to make a thoroughgoing nuisance of himself, it was Sir Hugh!) Wherever I was needed in the household, he somehow managed either to be there before, or to intercept me on my way – in courtyards and on stairways, descending to the laundry or returning from the yards. He'd interpose himself between me and my purpose, raising insolent black brows in query, smiling his infuriating smile!

Spoken or unspoken, its message was the same: 'Why trouble to pretend, my dear, when we both know I have the remedy you seek?'

He was here at Whitsun and again at shearing. I never know now when he'll next appear. But at least I've learned not to return his smile – at all costs not to meet those dangerous dark eyes. I am disdainful, haughty as My Lady of Warenne; a look I've practiced and perfected in my mirror. (Definitely unenticing!) I tell the man repeatedly, monotonously, that I know Sir Garon is alive, I know he will return – that I am bound to wait for seven years in any case before I wear a funerary badge. It's well-trodden ground between us.

At shearing time I thought to add that if I were ever to remarry, at some time in the far distant future, Sir Hugh de Bernay could be sure he'd be the last – THE VERY LAST MAN IN THE WORLD I would consider!

At which he'd dared to wink at me across the pens, and say in the full hearing of the hayward and the rest, that frankly the idea of marriage had never crossed his mind. But as I'd raised the subject, he would give it all the serious attention it deserved. And when I stamped my foot for sheer vexation, had laughed his bitter, ringing laugh and called me hypocrite and fool.

'Admit it Lady, you were purchased for Sir Garon just as I was purchased for his mother – and ask yourself what either of them knew or cared about our feelings in the matter when they bought us,' he said drily, 'a withered heiress and a numbskull boy.'

I heard the heavy thump of his dismounting and knew I must escape. But before I could get back to Nesta, he'd reached out to grip my arm – his

230

movement swift, his aim precise. 'D'ye think I don't know that you want me? D'ye want to hear me say it – that we men know just as dogs do when a bitch comes into season? D'ye think that I can't smell it on you?' he asked me with his mouth against my ear.

'No. No I don't!'

'No twice? Does that mean, no you doubt that I can smell it? Or, no you'd rather that I couldn't?'

And when I wrenched away from him to fumble for my jennet's stirrup, he made a show of stooping with cupped hands. 'I'd show you ways of doing it that would not make a child, d'ye see?' he whispered – then threw me up into the saddle.

'I see the devil in the thought Sir – that's what I see!' I spoke to fill a silence that might otherwise imply I understood – and I turned my face away.

'But is the prospect of the devil, now you recognise him, fearful or exciting?' he said softly. 'Surely you know, ma chère that when the ram draws back 'tis only to strike harder. Why not say yes, admit it and be done?'

I put moist fingers in my ears and wriggled them, to make a noise like woodblocks striking one another that drowned out every other sound, including his insulting voice. It's obvious men like him think that we cannot do without them – which simply isn't true – and even if I have considered how it might feel to be with him in that way, I've only done it once or twice to pass the time – and to convince myself that it could never happen!

I raised my head to look a little while ago and saw he wasn't there. It's strange how difficult it is to think of other seasons in these long summer days. The men are singing now to keep the rhythm – stooping figures in a lake of golden corn – the long flank of the downs – the boys, the dogs their pink tongues lolling... (But no one on a horse, and thank the Lord for that!) The glare's intense – the sun so hot that I can feel it burning through my gown – so stuffy in the house, I had to be outside...

A bright green grasshopper clings to a grass stem, so close I only have to reach to... Ah, he's up and gone! I should have let him be. When you lie back, flat in the clover, to feel no larger than an insect... Oh God, I feel so weary – limbs so heavy, hot and heavy, hard to move. And there's no need – why try? – why not simply...

*Silvery larksong, wingbeats, dancing dust motes, mindless patterns –
swirling, turning shapes as all the drowsy sounds of summer fade...*

*I'm looking not up into sky but into water – stewpond-gazing, Hoddie calls it –
watching fishes darting just beneath the surface, gleaming silver, weaving
through the lily pads – the green spears of the reeds – sun on water, rainbow
hues as if it's filmed with oil. I'm floating, spinning like a leaf, breaking the
reflection... But there's a frog – oh, beautiful! I've never seen a green so pale and
clear! It's like a jewel. I hear the little splosh his body makes as he springs from
the rushes – have to follow, need to touch him, have to catch him, have to...*

*He's on the bank and leaps again – now in a sandy hollow just ahead. I
think that I can reach him... But now he's curled with his long legs tucked
up against his belly – and fat, not green, but living pink; a fat pink baby!*

*I reach to touch him, feel his warmth... He leaps away through tall green
grass. So green! I have to tell him, tell him to come back!*

He runs so fast, a child, a naked running child...

*Where are we? I have never seen a place so beautiful, so green! Long
ribbons, ropes of pink and white striped trumpet bindweed hanging from
the trees. Magic colours – pale bright green, sky blue, lavender – the colours
of the glass in the new windows of the church at Lancaster, with sunlight
shining through them!*

*I'm brushing through the ribbons, through the weeds... Banners, silken
banners, banners of Damascus silk. A scent of watermint and nectar. I know
it now, have always known this place of Outremer, of course I have!*

*And there's... why, it is Garon – so close and just ahead! But not a child,
a naked man. Sun on the pale skin of his buttocks – and in the distance,
shining; the shining pinnacles of his Jerusalem!*

Come back! Oh wait for me!

*He's gone. Lost in the ribbons... (Sleeping. I'm asleep and dreaming.) But
not waking – don't have to wake when I can reach him though the colours –
touch him, catch him... Wait, oh wait!*

But one eye's already open, and now two.

*The light's so bright I have to squint. My throat is dry – arm numb where
I have lain on it – awake and back in the long grass at the forest edge...*

232

Was it the sunlight on my eyelids that made those lovely colours?

Across the field they're sharpening their blades. I can't see Hod or Edmay, but – ah, there they are, up in the furthest corner by the horse. They're...

Lord, I should have known it – they're talking to Sir Hugh!

Hand's tingling, pins and needles. (Move the fingers and move slowly backwards.) If I crouch – edge back behind the hawthorn, straighten, sidle into shadow...

He's looking up. (But can he see me? How does my pale linen look in shade?) I'm screened now by the trees in any case – and he's hardly likely to ride over. What reason would he give?

The path into the forest bears the prints of cattle baked in clay. A bramble catches at my skirt – ahead the rising trunks of beech trees, smooth as flesh. Tangled limbs above and twisted cords of clematis – ripe summer smells of foliage and dry grass. But cooler, so much cooler shaded from the heat and glare.

Something rustles in the undergrowth. (A bird or some small woodland creature, searching like me for a place to hide?) Where trees have fallen, sun still penetrates. Brown-speckled butterflies dance in the shafts above the brambles and field roses – vibrating crickets, the men's voices fainter with each step I take.

One leaning branch has red hairs in its bark, dry blood. Some cow has used it to rub off a tick. A red-breast robin flits out of nowhere, tilts his head, a bright black eye, and flits away. And here a clearing trampled by the cattle – flies buzzing on fresh dung. (Another world – but real, not like my dream.) Here logs grow moss and flowers fail for want of sun. Still air, the richer scents of cattle, leaf-mould, rotting wood, a pecker drumming on a distant tree trunk. The vastness of the forest.

There is a thing they call wood-madness. Is that what I have, what I'm feeling? Suddenly alive! An urge to take my clothes off, swing from branches! Hoist my skirts to urinate – become a creature of the wood!

Is that what makes my hearing so acute?

What was it that I heard?

A twig? A fluttering of wings?

Suddenly I'm listening, alert!

I hear the drumming pecker – and a blackbird closer chattering his warning. But it isn't my imagination. There's something's moving – something large. A stag? Or…

There! Between the trunks, across the clearing – a dark shadow. Halting. Listening like me.

They say that there are spirits in the woods – Jacks-in-the-leaf, green-clad, green-skinned from head to foot…

It's turning, moving out into the open, to see me and be seen. A shaft of sunlight through the branches gleams on a black head of hair!

Stay calm and hold his gaze. Don't let him see for God's sake that you are afraid!

Say something normal, anything. (But what, oh what…?)

'I saw a hare run in and followed, but I couldn't catch her.' (That sounded lame, ridiculous!)

'I rather think that it was I who saw the hare run in, and now it seems I've caught her.'

He doesn't smile, I wish he would! His voice is soft but far from gentle. And what always seemed a kind of game is now in earnest, all pretence forgotten. (Why did I think that I could ever call him to my aid?)

I search his eyes for signs of mercy, indecision. But they're fierce, relentless, hard and black. I see a wounded violence in them – subjugation that's intended for us both.

Outside the wood they're setting stooks, forcing sheaf butts hard into the stubble…

He's already passed the point of turning back – and what for me felt safe, has now become a trap!

He's right, I am the hare – nowhere to hide – and he's the predatory stoat, braced ready to cut off my first attempt at flight. Wanting – daring me to move. (Dear God, I think he needs my fear. It's what excites him most!) My best, my only hope is not to let him see it. His face is gleaming, wet with perspiration; charm peeled away to show the animal beneath.

I see his throat move as he swallows. He's panting, red-mouthed…

234

So am I, my own mouth dry and sticky with saliva, gulping air – need more, can't seem to breathe in fast enough...

'PLEASE!'

'Please what? Please spare me your uncouth attention? Or please to use me like a bitch on heat, knowing I've been begging for it this twelvemonth?'

Too late for him to change his course. Too late for me to run.

I won't look down to where the state of his excitement's obvious. I have to meet his eyes, to hold them – hold him from me...

A greenfinch twitters through the silence in the wood.

'Men can control their urges.'

'Puny men with feeble urges.'

'You will be punished.' *(But my voice sounds pitifully small, the bleat of a trapped lamb.)* 'My Lord of Warenne...'

'Is away in York until after Michaelmas, My Lady with him.'

'I'll not allow you to betray my husband.'

'Your husband is not here.'

And, Jesus crucified, he's creeping closer, step by step!

'I'll scream!'

'But won't be heard by anyone but me.'

Too late – he's here! Burning eyes above me, merciless, wide open, hideously blind...

Oh God, I'm down! He's on me – heavy, hard and heavy – rancid, sweating, ramming at me with his knee.

Push! Push back! Both hands, frantic as a bird in lime – wings beating but can't fly...

No good, my little knife. But he's seen it, twists my arm...

Aah! Flings it... But I have teeth and can bite – and bite again – hard in the neck!

Aaagh, Jésu! Did he have to use his fist?

Warm blood – I'm tasting blood... Lady of Mercy, Queen of Heaven, you're a woman – don't, don't let him, Holy Mother...'

The finch can fly, but sits up in the tree instead – sounds like a rusty gate –
wrenched open and slammed shut...
Rasping, tearing – wrenching open, slamming, wrenching, slamming...

I have no will. There's nothing I can do
but listen to the bird...

CHAPTER TWELVE

Afterwards when it was over, I watched him leave the wood. Disgusted, with himself, with what he'd done – and certainly with me. And he said nothing, nothing when he left me.

What could he say, and what could I? I lay there like a broken doll.

With harvest in, and in twice more since then, I've re-lived every moment of my degradation. Week in, week out. Day and night, awake and in my sleeping nightmares. I've re-lived how it felt to be defoiled, torn, bruised, abused!

God forgive him, for I never will. Or will forgive myself. Or can escape the knowledge that I fuelled the fire that finally consumed me.

For two full years I forced myself to think of it, remember what he's killed and what he has created. What has changed.

I had my own good reasons through those years.

NOW I HAVE ANOTHER.

BOOK THREE

CHAPTER ONE

The city of Saint Jean d'Acre: July 1191

SURRENDER

'As the defences of the city weakened, the Saracens lost hope and treated for a peace,' King Richard's annalist records.

'The terms agreed were that the Sultan should restore the Holy Cross and release one thousand and five hundred Christian captives who were held in chains through his dominions. Thus was the city of Saint Jean d'Acre surrendered to the kings with all the riches of the Moslem garrison, who saved only the clothes they wore and their own lives. 'With peace restored, the King Philippe purposed to depart from Palestine against the wishes of his people and King Richard, who offered to him half of all the gold and silver, arms and horses he had brought if he would but agree to stay. But the King of France would not be gainsayed in the matter, and to the outrage of the Christian host, took ship with but a few companions to sail home to France.'

I'd put it differently.

The original conditions for surrender, agreed in Tyre between the Sultan Salahuddin and King Philippe, allowed for the Marquess, Conrad de Montferrat, to take charge of the captive Moslem garrison until the Sultan could discharge his soldiers' ransom and exchange them with an equal number of Christian captives. In the interests of a lasting truce, the Sultan would return the Holy Relic of the True Cross, captured four years earlier at Hattin – in addition to allowing Christians free trade in Moslem ports and access to the holy places of Jerusalem.

It was a plan for all the *People of the Book* to live in peace together, whether they be followers of Jesus or of Muhammad. A plan that suited King Richard and his vassal, Guy de Lusignan, about as snugly as a saddle suits a sow! A negotiated peace? Is that what Richard has journeyed half across the known world to achieve? A hero who has boasted of a Christian victory? A monarch who has set his sights on a new client Kingdom in the East that owes allegiance to Anjou?

Is it likely he'd be willing to save lives by settling for a bloodless compromise agreed in secret with the King of France? Well, what would you imagine?

Despite the onset of a fever, which improves his patience not at all – on his arrival Richard makes a series of deliberate moves. He declares an armistice. He has a carpeted divan installed in his pavilion. And then, deliberately excluding King Philippe and his kinsmen, he summons to its side the other Christian leaders – Count Henri of Toulouse, Robert of Leicester, Duke Hugh of Burgundy, Andrew de Chauvigni, Theobald de Blois and Bishop Hubert Walter – to seek their views on which of the two claimants, Guy or Conrad, is best qualified to wear the Latin crown. But when, sprawled like a potentate amongst his cushions, he hears from every mouth a firm intention to back Philippe's man, Conrad, in place of his man, Guy – King Richard blasphemes on every intimate anatomy of Father, Son and Holy Ghost, and tells them all to go to Hell!

Next day, he takes advantage of the truce to have his siege machines assembled for a final and victorious assault on Acre – then lays a snare to catch a Sultan.

The Church of Rome absolves its followers from all oaths made to unbelievers. So when King Richard's emissary bows before the Sultan Salahuddin Yussuf in his new camp of Shefa' Amr – to tell him in mangled Arabic that his master cannot travel due to sickness – but to assure the Lord of Egypt and Damascus that he may come in perfect safety to treat in Richard's tent for the lives of those within the city – to all intents and purposes he has his Christian fingers crossed behind his Christian back.

242

But Allah's Shadow on the Earth is far too old a jackal to be deceived by such an obvious trap and turns his tailbrush from its jaws.

'It is a sad condition of our station that opposing kings may not meet at times of war without relinquishing their right to opposition,' he declares. 'There is a Christian saying, I believe, that a long spoon is needed to sup with the devil. Alas, I do not have one. But by all means let us be civilised. I will send my own physician to thy master, may God preserve him in his affliction. From what I hear of the malady, he suffers from a sailor's diet, lacking khudhar-leaves and fruit, the condition that the Christians call *scorbutus*?'

Eyeing him uncertainly, the emissary nods.

'It may be then that something from our orchards will restore his health.'

The Sultan claps his ringless hands. 'Pack citrus, *khushaf* and fruit sherbets in snow from one of our ice-houses,' he orders an obedient eunuch. 'Our noble adversary, Richard Malik al-inkitar, hath need of them as soon as they may be conveyed.'

But as the servant turns to do his bidding, his master is reminded of another matter.

'The boy?' He indicates the dark-skinned slave the King of England's sent him as a gift. 'He is entire and functions as a male?'

'He does My Lord.' On surer ground, the emissary risks an unctuous smile.

'Unfortunate.' The Sultan sighs. 'So shall we let him choose whose service he prefers? King Rikhad's – as a catamite with, shall we say a well-worked passage; but with all that God hath given him still in its proper place? Or in my service as an *emasculatus* – with the source of his discomfort and the attachments for participation both removed?'

God's Deputy bestows a look of fatherly compassion on the youth whose fate is in the balance. 'As Allah lives, we all know, do we not, what men most value after life itself? Thou mayst return the boy with my felicitations.

'And tell His Majesty,' the Sultan adds with a fine sense of Kurdish irony, 'that the son of Najmuddin Ayyub ascribes his own good health and that of his descendants to prayers performed five times a day – also to citrus fruit and the embrace of wives, both taken regularly but in moderation.'

The spurned gift and diplomatic snub serve to spur King Richard into violent action, much as Salahuddin has expected. The final stages of the siege take longer and demand more Christian lives than he himself anticipates. But the crucial gate-tower finally collapses. The dust cloud clears. A white flag of surrender appears above the rubble, and four envoys in snowy turbans, servants of the emir Baha-uddin Karakush, climb through to offer terms.

The troop detailed to guard King Richard's gold pavilion, are kept busy for the best part of two days and one long night with the continual entrances and exits of his couriers, his secretaries and Christian allies. It is the time of *khamsin*, when hot winds from the southern deserts scorch the plain. Pullani water-carriers work ceaselessly with siphons to soak the outer fabric of the suffocating tent – to cool the bodies of the men inside, if not their tempers. Three are kings; and the Marquess Conrad, summoned from Tyre to help decide the fate of Acre, has made himself a prince. They shout. They pace. They all but lock the golden fleurons of their crowns, like rutting stags intent on gaining territory.

Twice – once in daylight, once in darkness – they send an emissary to the Sultan's camp. Constantly the Bagdad pigeons fly with messages from God's Shadow in the hills to His defenders in the city, whilst those outside it wait to hear if the Moslem prisoners are to be spared or slaughtered.

On July the 12th, the first morning following the feast day of Saint Benedict, the chain is lifted in the Moslem harbour, and the grizzled veteran commander, Conrad de Montferrat, enters Acre with his Italian bodyguards and a platoon of Tyrian soldiers, by means of a makeshift bridge thrown over the dry fosse. Expendable to Richard but trusted by King Philppe, his task is to accept the garrison's surrender and prepare the city for re-occupation.

Soon afterwards, the King of France's criers ride through the camp to broadcast the armies' orders.

'Hear that the city of Saint Jean d'Acre has fallen, praise be to God! Henceforth it is forbidden by order of the Council of Christian Leaders for any man to strike the city walls, or to revile by word or deed the conquered infidels. The ransom for their lives, to be paid within four weeks of this day, is two hundred thousand bezants loaded onto forty camels, with a further forty thousand to be paid to Princess Isabella and the Count of Montferrat. Likewise the holy relic of the True Cross is to be restored, together with one thousand Christian prisoners of high station and five hundred of a lesser rank. Those companies to be housed in the city will be informed of it by their commanders after the hostages have left its precincts.'

On the evening of the same day, the Moslem garrison of Acre files from the city to the compound that awaits them, in a long crocodile formation of six battalions led by the Egyptian eunuch, emir Baha-uddin Karakush ibn Shaddad.

'Oh Most Merciful of the Merciful, Lord of the Weak,' the Kurdish leader, al-Maktub, who leads the third battalion, commands his Imams to recite. *'We care not if we are delivered into the hands of foes and strangers, provided that Thy wrath is not upon us!'*

King Richard, recovered from his fever, rises next morning to dress as he has dressed for his arrival in the Bay of Acre. Clad in the purple and the scarlet with a gold crown on his head, he rides into the city – as Alexander rode to claim it, and Caesar in his time – with all his chamberlains, his greyhounds and gyrfalcons, his pastry cooks and household troops in train to make a stately entrance. On either side as he trots by, long ranks of Christian soldiers cast their cloaks beneath his horse's hooves. Or else kneel in the dust as if they're witnessing the passage of a saint.

The King of England's bearing when he comes to climb the

staircase of the emir's palace is regal and benign. But when he strides into its marble courts to find them crowded with the followers of the French king's cousin, Leopold of Babenberg, he becomes the beast with which he is most frequently compared. He gives a deafening roar; and shortly afterwards the shocking spectacle of Richard's troops casting the Duke of Austria's presumptuous eagle into the filthy moat, and hoisting their own king's emblematic leopards in its place, is gleefully recorded in his annals.

Duke Leopold's own outrage at the insult is accepted as the reason for his swift departure from the Christian camp with the remnants of his German forces. But when it comes to King Philippe's return to France a fortnight later, none of the motives that the chronicles ascribe to him tell the whole story.

'He professed that illness had been the cause of his pilgrimage and that he'd now fulfilled his vow,' the Royal Itinerarium maintains. *'The King said he was departing because he was sick. Well, say what you like, that's what he said!'* is the troubadour Ambroise's version of events. But the chronicle of Ralf de Diceto is closest to the truth, with: *'Once the city had surrendered, the French King proposed to go home as if everything was now completed,'* reflecting as it does King Philippe's earlier agreement with the Sultan Salahuddin and Conrad de Montferrat, to secure a French bridgehead in Outremer.

In view of Conrad's popularity and Isabella's royal status, King Richard's own next move is to propose a division of the Latin Kingdom, with de Montferrat in control of Tyre and all the northern ports, and Guy de Lusignan to rule in Acre and any land the Christians might succeed in capturing to the south. Half for France in other words and half for England – with in the English half (are you surprised?) the great prize of Jerusalem itself.

It is a scheme which Philippe knows and Conrad knows and Sultan Salahuddin knows (but Richard stubbornly refuses to accept) is doomed to failure from the outset – assuming as it does that the crucesignati will not only agree to spending two more winters on the far shores of the Middle Sea, but will somehow gain the strength and funds to siege Jerusalem and hold it in the future against the full might of the Arabian empire.

Meanwhile, King Philippe leaves hard on the heels of Leopold and his Imperial troops, to signal to the rest the folly of remaining, while at his camp at al-Kharruba the Sultan plays strategically for time. The French King sails by way of Tyre with twelve hundred of the Moslem captives, including the emir Baha-uddin Karakush. He's heard that Richard slaughtered near eight hundred Saracens aboard a captured troop ship on its way to Acre, and thinks his hostages will be safest with the Marquess up in Tyre.

Conrad de Montferrat agrees, and says he fears a dagger in his own back every time he's close enough to hear King Richard laugh.

The soft bell-music from the fold sings to the moon, brings out the stars. The sound of it is comforting when I think how we buried him, at dusk during the Moslem call to prayer – a kind of music too, that last long call to prayer before the mu'adhdhin were silenced.

I am your man, Sir Garry, that's the shape of it, an' ever will be I daresay so long as God's above the devil.

We fetched Jos back to camp. John found the strength, as I could not, to deal with what was left of his poor head and tie it in his gory shirt to keep it with the body. I wouldn't have him taken in a tumbrel with the others to the grave pits, but hired a camel-sledge to draw him to the grave. Old Guillemette was there to see him into it, dabbing with a kerchief at the streaming ruts and wrinkles of her face. For it was she who washed the blood away and fitted Jos into his grave-bag – she who handed me the silver coins she'd found sewn in his tunic.

'Poor Tiddler, he's in heaven with the angels now,' she sobbed, 'God bless 'is spotty little soul!'

But that's not where I saw him. By then I'd seen so many corpses, knew death and thought I knew the way it worked. How could I not at Acre? I wouldn't have Jos thrown into the pit, but saw him lowered gently in the boots I bought for him in Lyons and he'd worn ever since.

A lizard on a heap of soil beside the grave gave a quick jerk like something on a string, then disappeared from view. (So strange the things you see and you remember when your mind thinks it's no room for aught but grief.) I listened with the rest to all to the rites of burial.

I saw the sappers shovel in the lime and earth, but couldn't think of Jos as just another body that would rot and stink. I couldn't picture life without him. I couldn't tell where he had gone or how his soul departed – couldn't see him up in heaven dressed in white; couldn't think of Jos, my Jos, as unable to react or swear, or bounce about and make a joke of his own lack of brain or loss of face.

Am I so...? Obvious? No Sir, not by any means.

Would God appreciate the mischief in him? I couldn't see that either.

Behind us the Christian camp was celebrating victory. But I could not. *Victoire,* my chosen motto. How empty of all meaning it seemed now!

Afterwards I bought a two-pound beeswax candle to light for Jos at the re-consecrated church of Saint Andrew inside the city walls – and did my best while it burned down to hope that it would bring him to salvation.

But later, that was later and again I've jumped ahead...

When it was first agreed that Bishop Walter's troop would be housed in the city, one of his chaplains climbed onto a bloodstained tumbrel to broadcast His Grace's orders.

'Hear this, men,' he shouted. 'You'll find quarters to the south of our King's palace, and will be shown which streets are in your bounds. You will not loot or rape, but treat inhabitants with due respect. The families who house you will be issued with supplies. But gold, silver, jewels, fine fabrics and the like are now King's Property, to be collected by his agents. Any man caught stealing or concealing valuables for his own profit will be severely dealt with. You may have heard that Musselmen revenge themselves on thieves by cutting off a hand.' The chaplain smiled unpleasantly. 'His Grace leaves you to guess what they'll take off to punish rape. He looks to you to follow God's Commandments, to be steady and keep discipline as Soldiers of the Cross.'

'Sayin' we can live with 'em but musn't think of fittin' ends. Is that what Bishop's sayin'?' a man behind me muttered. 'So what the nation does 'e think we're goin' to do with 'em, play blindman's buff?'

'Only if they're fearsome top *and* bottom, boy,' another voice remarked. 'Otherwhiles, fuck any that ye fancy as know where to put it, there's the rule. So long as they've been married, it can't 'ardly count as sin. As for the maidies – we'll just 'ave to ask 'em nicely won't we 'afore we take a dive. That's all the bugger's sayin'.'

My own thoughts as we entered Acre, had been less concerned with theft or rape than with the simple competence of placing my right foot before my left. I managed it by limping on my heel to keep my swollen toes clear of the ground, but couldn't manage to avoid the feet of all the others surging through the ruins of the gate.

Each time they trod on me I yelped with pain, and would have fallen twice, but for John Hideman's steady hand.

Beyond the inner gate, a broken honeycomb of streets led north to where the King and Bishop Walter lodged in the old emir's palace. Or south down to the harbour. Every street and alleyway was dusty, potholed, strewn with splintered wood and fallen stonework. Skinny, black-eyed urchins scrambled through the ruins or perched on mounds of rubble, to watch us pass. Flies clustered round the crevices between the stones to show where corpses lay beneath. The city's dogs and cats, its rats, its pigeons and its sparrows had all been eaten in the siege. Only the flies still prospered in the blazing heat, to pester every living body and breed maggots in the dead ones.

A supply sergeant we recognised set us to following a flock of fat-tailed sheep inside the gate on their last journey to the butchers. The folk on that road to the harbour had already been supplied, he said, and knew how many soldiers they must feed. 'Then once ye'r billeted, ye'r free to fetch in what ye've left in camp.'

He showed us on a rough map where our quarters lay.

'How many to a house?' I asked.

'Depends.'

The sergeant shrugged his chubby shoulders. 'Some of 'em'll take two dozen. Quartermaster's ruled one sheep to feed six men. So they've 'ad four.'

'Sounds friendly,' John observed in careful French. 'How many to a bed?'

But by then the man was talking to Sir Rob de Pierpoint, who was behind us in the press. So, following the flock, we took a road that that led in shallow steps toward the city harbour.

'I'm sure that we'll do very well, John,' I said hardily. My function to pretend that all was for the best.

'Aye, Sir Garry, well as ever.' John Hideman's to support me in the lie.

I turned to him, the last of my brave manor squad, to show a cheerful smile – tripped on a step and fell, full-length amongst the sheep shit – flat on my cheerful face!

Even with bruised knees and broken toes, it's amazing how rapidly you can spring upright from a ridiculous position. (The cringing cur again, you see, who hated being mocked.) And I was on my feet and turning from the thoroughfare through a dilapidated arch, before the laughter even started.

I suppose I should be grateful that John managed a straight face – asked how my foot was, handed me the cloak and bedding roll I'd left in my need to be elsewhere.

'Well. I'm very well,' I said as I limped off at breakneck speed. 'Let's take a squint down here then shall we? See if we can find a billet?'

The arch was one of several buttressing the blank walls of houses, with a drain that reeked of sewage running through the alleyway between them. At the far end where the sun lit on a flaking, parchment-coloured wall, there was a wooden door. It was the only one. Which didn't leave much choice.

'We'll try this one,' I said, and knocked on it with with a clenched fist.

Some doors in Acre had grills for looking through, but not this one.

This one was blank, and there was no way that we could know what was beyond. But all doors lead to somewhere – and thinking back, I've often wondered what would have happened if I hadn't fallen on the steps and turned into that lane.

If I had found another door in quite another place?

As it was, it opened in the very moment I'd decided that it wouldn't – first a crack and then a handsbreadth.

We glimpsed a face, a pair of anxious eyes.

'Madame...?' Before I could say more, the door swung in to frame a second door beyond it. A magic trick. A frame within a frame. A view into a garden with green shrubs and a reflective pool – a view into another world!

After the dust and the destruction of the siege, the crowds of men, the stinking alley, the blank wall – a cool green garden was the last thing I expected.

No, not the last. The last thing I expected was Khadija.

Although I'd learn her story later, in that first moment I knew no more of the woman hidden by the door than that she was a Sarasine.

'Dost thou seek shelter? *Dhall, Malja' Ma'wa,* here in house?' The voice was low-pitched for a woman, blending her native tongue with the accented French the Pullani used in camp – and something fascinating in the way the Arab words turned in her throat with a soft hissing sound like tearing silk.

'If you will give us leave,' I asked the door. 'Your house has room?' *I never have been good at introductions.*

'Yes, yes Seigneur please to enter. *As-Salam Alaik,* all comes from Allah, peace and welcome.'

The woman stepped back to admit us. 'Thou art *ithnan?'* She glanced behind us down the alley before she closed and locked the outer door. 'Two men?

'Yes for the present,' I said guardedly. 'There may be others later.'

'*Insha-Allah.'* If she was afraid of us, she hid it well. The shapeless cloak which covered her from head to foot could not conceal that she was tall, and thin. Who wouldn't be in Acre? But in the moment she turned from the door and put the cloak back from her face, I saw she was unveiled.

And there she stood exposed to view. A whole live female – and there stood I, a man who'd been without one for a year!

But how should I describe her as I saw her first? Can I do better with Khadija than Elise? All faces have two eyes, a nose, a mouth, a chin, arranged in much the same positions. How different can one face be from another?

I saw that she was older than I was. I saw that she was thin. I must have noticed dusky skin and straight black brows, feathered where they all but met above her nose – a wide mouth with a cushioned lower lip and deep lines either side. Teeth crowded, less than even. But what I see most clearly when I think of that first meeting, are fingernails stained brilliant copper-red, exposed as she put back the cloak – a mass of dark hair falling loose, and eyes... great lustrous eyes, enlarged and elongated, smudged around with some kind of an inky salve. The gentlest eyes I'd ever seen.

And in that moment, in the soft depths of the woman's eyes, all my fixed opinions of Moslems as sons and daughters of perdition were unfixed for me.

The square flagged room in which we stood was bare of furniture, lit by the open door we had already seen into the garden, and containing only what was useful. From a roof beam, the flayed remains of one of our Quartermaster's gifted sheep hung wrapped in muslin to protect it from the flies. From others were suspended sacks and herbs. Stacked neatly round the walls were copper bowls and earthenware containers, with wooden trays, neat stacks of faggots and dusky heaps of charcoal – nothing out of place. At the end furthest from the sheep, a barrier of matting hid a covered drain, which, as we discovered later, was for bodily relief.

The woman must have seen me limping as we entered, and pointed with one red fingernail at my right foot. '*Qadam?* Pain, yes?'

I nodded, 'Just a little.'

But did she know? Was she resigned already to what would happen next? Looking back I find I cannot tell. All I remember is the way she clicked her tongue in sympathy.

'We find something to make it easy.'

She rummaged for a bowl, a cloth and a small jar from the assemblage round the walls. 'Thou wilt come, yes?' She motioned us to leave our burdens in the vestibule and follow her into the open court – and when she walked, she seemed to glide. Her feet just barely grazed the surface of the bricks.

Bounded by narrow paths, the garden the court enclosed was sunk below the level of the house, its small space filled with pomegranates and pistachios grown round an oval pool – a cool escape from dazzling light. An ancient fig tree trailing vines cast deep green shadows, with here and there amongst the leaves, pink blossoms – roses twice the size of our sweet briars and eglantines and of a deeper hue.

It seemed a kind of miracle, not only that the plants survived the siege, but that they could bloom at all within the dry shell of the city.

'It's beautiful!' I hadn't known until I walked into that leafy court how much I needed, or had missed, the sight of greenery and flowers.

The woman inclined her head. '*Al-Jannah,* same word for paradise and garden,' she said softly.

On one side of a second doorway, a wooden ladder led to a flat roof. On the other, a brick oven sent a thin plume of smoke into the sky. I heard a man's voice beyond the garden wall, a baby crying further off – then nothing but the steady shrilling of cicadas from the shadows.

The woman stooped to light a taper from the oven, then stepping through the door, transferred the flame to a brass oil lamp in an inner chamber.

'For *ahlan,*' she told us, 'for welcome to house.' The invitation was a bridge for me to cross. Limping after her, I felt a hopeful, fishlike movement in my breeches.

John was behind me in one sense, ahead of me in quite another. The shepherd back at Haddertun had trained two dogs to work the flock – the old dog barked, the young one worked in silence. But when the old dog died, the other naturally took on the task of barking at the sheep. Like Jos and John. Because it now seemed that John Hideman understood what was required, before I even thought to ask.

'Mebbe I'll set here on the steps a piece,' he said, and took care to avoid my eye. 'Then in a while I'll take the time to slice some mutton for the grill. If the lady don't object?'

Inside the further chamber, the woman had already reached a curtain stencilled with an interlaced design. She lifted it to show a jackdaw's nest of rugs and cushions flecked with sunlight from a lattice in the wall – and in the centre of the nest, a chick. In fact a little girl of five or six with snaggled hair, smooth olive skin and her mother's fine black eyes.

The woman set down the jar and cloth and knelt to whisper something to the child in their own tongue, then hoisted her onto her hip. 'I take her to thy man,' she said. 'He is kind, yes?' More a statement than a question.

The little girl peered round her shoulder at me, while she was borne out through the door and down to where John Hideman, whistling softly, sat on the steps above the sunken pool. Leaving me to wonder how the woman came to understand so much about us in so brief a time. I heard the murmur of their voices, saw her set down the girl and dip her bowl into the pool. Saw John pull off his silver ring to spin it for the child's amusement.

'He has small brothers of his own at home. She will be safe,' I told her mother later as she unlaced my boot.

'He tells me, yes. He hath the way, Alia understand.'

She already had my stinking, cheesy foot in both her hands, and raised the toes until I winced with pain.

'Need time to mend, but we do this.' She washed and dried it carefully, anointing it with scented ointment from her jar. A gift of service which appeared to please her near as much as it pleased me. Indeed, by then the heavy perfume of the balm, the dextrous movement of her fingers and the dark fall of her hair tickling my shin, had all combined to make an obvious point. Or rather raise one in an obvious place. I gulped, and more than once.

She only had to look to see how things were standing, and I needed her to look! One part of me at least was more than ready, knew exactly what to do. The rest, hampered by some misplaced sense of courtesy, was still unsure.

But in the end a peal of childish laughter from the garden was all we needed to decide us. The woman met my eyes across the pulsing pole-tent in my breeches and gravely nodded her acceptance. And then, almost before I knew what she was doing, moved on from offering one comfort to attending to another, setting down my foot to stand and drop her cloak, unlace a colourfully broidered bodice, step out of slippers and full Turkish trousers and finally throw off a cotton shift. To shock me again, at least as much by her directness as by the woman's form that she revealed.

I don't know if she trembled, or if it was just me.

I stared at her thin body, meshed with sunlight from the latticed window and glossed with perspiration. There were hollows either side of her thin neck, and all her ribs were visible. Gaunt bones. But living flesh. And I could see, or thought that I could see, in her broad hips and softly drooping breasts something abundant that the siege had stolen from her. She had a little sun or star, a nimbus of blue rays tattooed beneath one collar bone. I looked at it, and wondered if the roughness of my hands would scratch her naked skin.

She stood for a long moment fingering a lock of her black hair then sank onto her knees. 'Thy wish, Seigneur,' she asked me quietly. 'Yes?'

But what I mainly understood was her consent. Which meant, I told myself ungallantly, that no one afterwards could say it was a rape.

Taut as a bowstring, you might say that I couldn't move – if what I had in mind had not involved a good deal of quite violent movement. I felt my joints, my fingertips, the sweat between my thighs, the hair rise on my forearms, my tongue against my teeth. I tasted the sweet taste of my own saliva – to find that I was dribbling. (I wasn't gaping like a fish. I wouldn't say that I was slobbering exactly – I wasn't *drooling*! It's only that my mouth was open, and I'd forgotten how to swallow.) Remembering eventually, I closed it – gave my chin a furtive wipe and nodded silently in answer to her question.

The woman murmured something else, a plea containing her god's name. A thing that I remembered later, but barely noticed at the time. In a strange, fatalistic gesture she drew her coppery fingers down her face, then closed her eyes and fell back suddenly onto the cushions at my side.

Her brass anklets made a soft, metallic sound. The soles of both her feet were painted red. Deliberately she raised her knees and parted them. A frame within a frame. Another door into another universe. A coarser thing than an enchantment; the vixen-scented gate of life itself!

For once I knew that there was nothing that I could or should be saying – although I may have gasped a bit. I had the ailment, she the remedy. My need and her acceptance spoke directly to each other. That's all there was to know.

With my heart beating like a kettledrum. Panting at one end, dribbling at the other, I made a brutish noise midway between a growl and moan, and fumbled with the buckle of my belt. It felt as if someone had thrust a burning iron through me from arse to tip, which must inflame and thrust through her in turn.

She was all women. She was Eve, and I was Adam gobbling great mouthfuls of the fruit of knowledge... dripping juice!

If death itself awaited me I could not have desisted.

I was the lance and she the quintain.

I was the bull, she was the gate.

CHAPTER TWO

The woman's voice again beside the pool instructing me to see each day as a new page in the story of my life.

I want to loiter in the green bower of her enchanted garden, in that golden city at the far end of the world – lie naked in her curtained chamber. Or loosely clad upon its roof. Extend each day. Prolong each night. Halt time itself!

Considering where this is taking me, I'm loathe to turn the page and see the next illumination. Because that's what I do. I dodge unpleasant truths. It's what I've always done but can no longer get away with.

Her name, she said – the name her father gave her – was *Khadija*, in honour of the Holy Prophet's first, most favoured wife. She was the widow of a Syrian merchant, who'd brought her and the child to French-speaking Acre before its Moslem occupation, and lost his life during the siege. She had no maids to help her, and until the city fell had kept house for the merchant's brother, now a prisoner in Tyre.

All this she told us that first afternoon while we sat on her chamber floor, the four of us, on rugs set round the cloth she spread for our repast. Me with my injured foot stuck out before me. John with the wide-eyed child Alia close beside him marking every movement of his sunburned hands. We ate the skewered mutton he'd cooked in the brick oven by the door. We washed our greasy fingers a bowl of scented water and dried them on the towel Khadija held for each of us in turn. And all the while I watched the spidery lamp-cast shadows of her lashes on her cheeks, impatient for a chance to catch her eye, to show her what I wanted, and how badly.

But of course she knew. The downcast eyelashes, the flushed cheeks, a certain kind of heaviness in all her movements, an odour I could not mistake, convinced me that she knew.

I cleared my throat and shifted my position on the rug, raising the knee of my good leg to hide the signs of my conviction from the others. A man with an erection...

What drives the body of a man? What drives the sun across the sky?

It took a little while to settle her child to sleep behind the curtain, and by then Khadija had produced more bedding from a stack of mattresses and cushions in a recess of the chamber wall. John took his bed out into the garden, to sleep wrapped in his cloak to foil the biting flies.

We lay inside, wrapped in nothing but my need. I was that night as I had been in my first weeks of my marriage to Elise; impossible to satisfy. But when at dawn I tried to do again what I had done before the meal, and twice more in the night, Khadija reprimanded the most eager part of me with a light slap.

'*Al-Heurmak* hath need of rest.' She smiled at me and smoothed the loose hair from her eyes. 'I rise? You will allow?'

'If that is what you want,' I told her, stiffly in more ways than one.

'I go early. We have need of bread, Sayyid, and other things.' I gave her what she asked to market for provisions, and watched her dress and cloak herself and then perform her morning prayer.

'Holy Prophet hath decreed we cover ornaments of body, except for hands and face,' she told me when I asked why she dressed so plain. 'Hide woman's shape in street, but show in house.'

When she had gone, John grilled us mutton collops for our breakfast, and then set-to to cut up the carcase of the sheep for distribution to the neighbours. The four of us could never hope to eat a quarter of the beast before the maggots found it – and I planned selfishly to keep the house just to ourselves.

'We'll need to make it look as if it is already full of soldiers,' I said determinedly, 'and say the rest are off elsewhere to anyone who asks.'

'An' prove it with the sight of dirty platters an' bedding for a dozen,' John thought would do the trick. And grown men that we were, we sniggered like a pair of naughty boys as we ran round about the house,

258

to drag out mattresses and smear dripping over knives and platters strewn across the floor. The child, Alia, watched us anxiously with one hand to her mouth, and when she heard her mother's light tap on the outer door rushed off to hide behind the fig, with nothing showing of her but a hank of black hair and a pair of bright eyes peering round its trunk.

The woman set a large rush basket of provisions on the bricks, to view the pigsty we'd made of her neat house with sorrow.

'But soldiers will not come,' she said when I explained. 'Go see. They are too busy with bad women in the harbour.

'And Seigneur, go to hammam at Khan A-Shuna in Pisan quarter.' She made a show of wrinkling her nose. 'Time for nice bath, you think?'

The main street to the harbour seethed with figures, mostly women, hurrying up from the docks with baskets on their backs or bundles on their heads. Crowded tenements on both sides of the road were piled one on another within the broken boxing of the city wall. We could see the masts of ships, and glimpse the dazzle of the water in the pool before we reached the quay – and when we did it seemed as if the whole world and his wife was there already. Every man who wasn't Genoese or a Pisano was a drunken soldier, and every female who wasn't cloaked from head to foot was a Venetian whore.

Nowhere in our travels – not in Lyons or Marseille or Tyre – had we beheld such women. Dressed in bright silk, with painted mouths and hair dyed very red or very black or shiny golden-blonde – with loops of silver harness-bells tied to their wrists and ankles – they took their breaks from clients standing at the rails. Or else along the quays. To part their silks with frozen smiles. To sound their bells and entertain the queues of soldiers on the gangways of their floating brothels.

John Hideman, gaping like a beggar at a banquet, turned suddenly to stare at a blank wall. A sure sign he was thinking and about to speak.

'Mebbe I'll stop an' watch the boats awhile if it's the same to you, Sir Garry,' he said solemnly in the plain French he used these days more often than his native tongue. 'Reckon there's a tidy bit to learn from watchin' boats unloaded.'

I laughed and took three bezants from my purse.

'No doubt there is, but you'll need money if you want a whore,' I said and dropped the coins into his palm. 'You'll have enough there for as many as you like, and food and drink besides.

'But what will you do sir?' was all he asked.

'I'll find a church and light a candle for poor Jos's soul. Then go and have a bath as I am bidden.

'And John,' I said, as if the thought had just occurred. 'Stay with the ladies if you like. There's nought I need, and you know where to find me in the morning.'

He took the money without looking, whistling softly though his teeth. 'Then I'll see you after Tierce, Sir Garry.' He gave the warehouse wall an understanding smile. 'An' rest easy, Sir, I'll not show up before.'

I found Saint Andrew's Church in the lower town close to the Pisan Harbour, and bought my two-pound candle from a Christian chandler at its door. But 'though I knelt on the stone flags until my knees were numb, I couldn't picture Jos in purgatory or paradise. Or even in his grave.

The hammam bath-house, one of a number in the twisted maze of streets behind the harbour, was a low building with three white domes perched like huge eggshells on its roof – each pierced, as I found when I entered, with rings of little windows to vent steam from the hot water of the pool.

I stripped and paid to be allowed to wash myself amongst the other bathers with a cake of perfumed soap. But finding it a strange enough experience to show my shapes to dozens of unknown and naked men, I refused an oily massage by a hairy pool attendant wearing nothing but a breechclout, and paid the extra for a shave instead. Then I limped through the crowded thoroughfares of the Venetian Quarter, to reach Khadija's house more by luck than skill from the far end of the alley.

'Clean now?' she asked when she had closed the door and heard my news of John.

I told her that I'd bathed but had refused the massage and the oil. 'Is good,' she said, 'we do this here. Come I will show.'

While I'd been out, she had distributed the mutton and restored her house to order. Alia, would be staying with a neighbour who had children of her own.

'It is to be alone, *muhibb*.'

I'd swear my lower body heard it and reacted before she told me that the word *muhibb* meant *lover*. And then she led the way a second time into the sunken garden, where she'd laid a rug and cushions by the pool.

From a long-spouted jug she poured a drink for me which she called *nabidh*, a mild wine made from fermented dates and permitted to the faithful by their Prophet – then left me on my own to listen to the night song of the cicadas, and watch the moon rise through the branches of the fig.

Returning with a spangled scarf tied round her hair, Khadija brought me first one tray of victuals, then a second and a third. The scents she wore moved with her in the warm night air to mingle with the perfume of the roses. She served me spiced and shredded mutton wrapped in vine leaves, pigeons stuffed with almonds, and rice stained with saffron, blessing every item as she brought it. She tempted me with sugared chick-peas, honey cakes – and a strange fruit called *citrus*, with flame-coloured rind and a sharp flavour unlike anything I'd tasted. We faced each other cross-legged on the carpet, eating only with our right hands, until our bellies all but begged for mercy.

And only then, the thing I had awaited from the first.

She fetched me cotton towels and a small flask of scented oil which she'd had warming by the stove.

I had already taken off my boots. Khadija helped me out of hose and breeches, and drawing off my tunic, bent to place a kiss on my bare chest. Arranging towels for me to lie face-down with head on hands, and broken toes propped on a cushion – she started with my neck and shoulders, kneeling at my head.

I closed my eyes. But at the first touch of her hands, I couldn't help myself. My body clenched into a solid mass of muscle.

'Mmm-hrrhh!' I groaned – or something very like it.

'No, no Seigneur.' Khadija laid a palm flat on my back between my shoulder blades. 'Last night we break the dam, but now we mend,' as with both hands she began to knead my rigid shoulders.

'Now I teach what young men in Damascus must learn to please a wife.' And easing her way down, she spread her hands to smooth the knots from either side of my tense spine, exploring the healed scars she found there, pressing outwards, downwards, sliding in the oil. Each time lower. Each time reaching closer to those working parts of me which – if I could only tell her – were beckoning, were crying out, were standing up and waving flags for her attention!

'Lower, lower... Touch me, stroke me, grab me, pinch me – anything! But lower! LOWER!' I am ashamed to own, that's all that I could think.

'Seigneur, is honey sweeter in throat or on thy tongue?' Without waiting for an answer, she moved to kneel beside me, the better to work on my lower back. I felt her thumbs push hard into its hollow and then move lightly – for God's sake far too lightly! – over arse and thighs, and reach too soon the safer areas of knees and calves and after them my twitching, swollen foot (by then entirely free of pain).

But naturally I knew that what goes down must surely rise. By then my eyes were open wide – and sure enough, she was soon moving slowly, infinitely slowly, upwards. Smoothing leg hairs. Dipping in behind the knees. Rising still, still rising, back to thighs, both hands...

I gasped for air. The hands moved upward. Inward. Closer – *CLOSER* ...

Christ in heaven! Too much altogether! Next instant, with a yelp, I'd bucked and buckled. Bobbed up like an ungraceful cork! I couldn't help it! Hairy buttocks in the air. Legs wide apart – with all between them swinging wildly!

And when she laughed and pushed me back onto the towels – a picture of Elise the morning after our first night together, flashed into my mind. Complete with the humiliating smile!

How easy for a woman, I thought sourly – to mock all men as captive unicorns in thrall to their own horns. To laugh at us like dogs!

But I was wrong. There was no mockery in Khadija's laughter. Only understanding and amusement.

'Slow muhibbi, *slow!* No one will come.' She smiled at me. 'We have

262

five gifts of sense: al-*Lams, Annadhar, Ashamm, Adhdhauq, As-sam* – touch, sight, smell, taste, hearing. Now we have time for all.'

Then what had I to do but submit gratefully to all she had to teach me – things I'd never dreamt of. And if I thought myself experienced, I came to see that I knew little more of copulation than a ram does. Or a barnyard cock. Less probably, considering how often those beasts perform the act in their short lives.

'Men fight men, fight women too. But Allah makes a game for both to win. Is true, I teach you how.'

She helped me turn onto my back persuading parts of me I'd never thought of as interesting, to be interested in her.

'You see, we are not foes. Thy *zabb* is not a sword. We are like plum-fruit, we ripe better when we touch,' she said – and having shown me what she meant with my fast-ripening plums, and heard my strangled gasp, she placed my hand where *she* most needed it. To show me how to do the same for her. 'If only take, thou wilt take less. Forget thy Christian priests. Know Allah fashions man and woman, each to be good to the other.

'Taste here, muhibb,' she told me – later, when she judged that I was making progress. 'Is true all men who leave mother's breast are eager to return.'

An idea I was in no state to deny!

Then later still, and lower down: 'Taste hungry Abou beldoum,' she whispered with one hand on my neck, the other parting the soft hair to show me her most precious, secret place. 'Here kiss, ah here! Breathe, taste, is ripe for you. Yes there!'

And, when I felt her rise to meet my mouth, to enslave me with me the salt-tide oyster taste of *Abou beldoum*. And when I entered her, and saw her eyes beneath me blacker than the blackest pool – and heard her moan, and felt the hunger of her mermaid's clasp. And when I dived, and dived again with her into the tropic fathoms. Dark and deep and warm. Then I remembered how Elise had been with me, and how I'd been with her the second time we bedded – and in that moment knew that I was capable of learning. For then I understood the need in all of us to give as well as take.

And who better for a teacher than Khadija?

All my life I had been taught to think carnality a weakness. An unfortunate distraction. At worst, a sin. In camp they'd talked of *fitting ends* as if that's all it was about. Men's swords and women's scabbards. Men's pestles, women's mortars pounded with a will to grind the seed. Ways to thread a needle. Ways to peg a beam. But this woman saw the act as God's gift to marriage of the sexes, and the instruction that she gave me changed how I saw it too.

There were times, Khadija would allow, when haste in lovemaking could hardly be avoided. But the oriental virtue she called *sabr*, which in a siege we knew as patience, was what she chiefly recommended. While gnats danced in the lamplit doorway of her chamber with the red-stained thumb and forefinger of her right hand she introduced me to the skill that the Moslems know as *imsak,* to bring me to the simmering height of ecstasy without, to my intense surprise, allowing me to boil! I felt as if I must explode with pleasure, but could not. Or not until the woman let me cross its threshold – the patience being hers not mine.

I wasn't in control. I didn't have to think – just give myself to feeling. It seems ridiculous, considering what we were doing. But it was like regaining innocence. In turn she inflamed and humbled me. Sometimes both at once – and with a kind of joy that purged me of my guilt, and made me wiser in the morning. Because amongst the things I learned was my own power of speech.

Al-Samit, the Silent One, Khadija called me as I lay moaning wordlessly beneath her expert hands. 'One gift we have is hearing, so make me the words, muhibb. Say what is good in me, what makes thy breath come fast. We are God's gift, there is no shame to speak of what He makes.'

And so I did. I told her all I loved about her body. And when I saw that my rude choice of words did not displease, I used some even ruder.

Later still, while we lay at our ease in the pale light of early dawn, I told her how I loved her simple house and its secluded garden – spoke of its peace and safety after the horrors of the siege. And then, because I'd found my voice and couldn't stop I told her of the heat, the dust, the falling masonry, the screams on that last day before the city fell. I spoke of Jos's death, the sight that met my eyes when we rolled back the stone, the gaping grave, his shrouded corpse amongst the tangle of dead limbs.

'So now he's dead,' I said at last as if it were any kind of news.

'Muhibb, accept.' She held my face between her hands and kissed me gently. An act as intimate as any she'd performed.

'There is a saying of my people: *If we could find a merchant who would buy regrets, we must be wealthy all.* Death waits for us as Allah wills.' She smiled. 'We are as roses, we bloom then blow and fall in dust.'

'But he was always there beside me, stitched my clothes and oiled my armour, got my horse aboard our ship when no one else could do it – found me food when we were starving. That was Jos. He always had a joke to cheer us – and the reddest hair, you've never seen hair redder, and not an inch of him that wasn't freckled...'

She made me stop, to show her with a dotting finger what I meant by freckles, and I think pronounced them, *'namash'*.

The moonlight shining through my tears gave her thin face a silver halo. And like a supplicant before a church Madonna I just kept babbling on. 'He always knew what I most needed, even seemed to know what I was thinking. The only thing he didn't know, you see, was just how dear to me he was. He couldn't know, because I never told him,' I ended hopelessly. 'And now it is too late.'

'He is in Paradise. Be sure he hears, he understands...'

'That's not what Saracens believe,' I interrupted. 'You think as we do that all infidels must burn in hell.'

'No. Is false, muhibbi.' She raised her chin to tilt her head back in the way her people do to stress the negative. 'Only one God, Allah, makes all from Adam's rib, loves all His children – Jews, Faithful of Islam, even Christians who see Isa as a man – all People of Book who worship only one God may enter Paradise.'

'But that's not true. How can it be?' I heard myself blurt out. 'When

265

the reason for this whole campaign is for our Christian armies to take back Jerusalem for God!'

'To take back for Him? When He is there already?' Khadija looked at me in real surprise. 'Is not why you fight. You fight for land, for trade. Is always so.'

I told her I could not accept that.

'Is maybe how they bring you here?' was her response. 'You not believe. So you will fight.' And staring back at her uncertainly while that idea sunk in, I must have looked as foolish as I felt. The idea of Christians and Saracens squabbling like selfish children under the eye of an indulgent father who was common to them both, was new to me entirely. It made no sense. Or rather must make nonsense of the way that I'd seen good and evil. And of the Kings' Croisade. It was as if the world I knew, proved suddenly to be no more than painted canvas, and our campaign a mummers' play performed with wooden swords!

At any other place or time the thought must have appalled me. But that night, lying in a state of total drainage by the moonlit pool, it came as a relief. It told me what in my heart I'd recognised when I first heard Khadija's voice. That friends and foes are cut from the same cloth. That all humans share some kind of a kinship. That it's better to discuss two views of God, than kill each other to deny them.

'It is not pain, is joy. We smile at the loving gifts of Allah,' Khadija said.

And in that place and at that time, it wasn't hard to smile.

Through all the nights that followed, while the city slept we sprawled on rugs beneath the fig. Barefoot or bare of everything. Entwined or otherwise. Or on the roof, where in the daytime washing was put out to dry. Or sat cross-legged before the red glow of the oven, and talked of life and love, of birth and death and all that lay between them.

That's when Khadija told me that we each had our own star, and taught me Syrian songs and told me tales of foolishness and wisdom from Damascus and Bagdad. I taught her new French words.

And yes of course, we spent time practicing those movements and positions which in Damascus have been taught for centuries. They say

266

that the third heaven of Islam is coloured pink, the seventh is pure light.

We found them both.

On our third day in Acre, when John strolled in from his close study of the ships in harbour, reeking of Venetian perfume and whistling softly to himself – I'd sent him off to Bishop Walter's camp outside the walls to fetch the rest of our possessions and learn the latest news. He came back wearing his gambeson and kettle hat, despite the heat, and bent beneath the burden of my pot helm and link-hauberk in a sack across his shoulders.

Our orders for the present were to stay at ease within the city confines, he told us, setting down his burden on Khadija's flags and ruffling Alia's mop of curls. Troops drawn from those camped on the plain were working hard to clear the city moat and mend the breaches in the walls. But the main news in camp, John said, was that the King of France was bent on leaving Palestine now that the siege was won. Duke Leopold, who led the Christian armies before the kings arrived, had left already with his German troops.

'They're layin' bets out there that once the ransom's in, King Dickard'll be off an' all, to make an end of things.'

Then, seeing that he had our full attention, John told us all the rest. 'They're thinkin' that old Sallydin 'ud have to empty half the galleys on the Middle Sea to find prisoners enough for the exchange, which isn't goin' to happen overnight. They're thinkin' Michaelmas is like to come and go before the city's set to rights, an' askin' where we'd find the food to bait an army half the size through even one more winter.

'We en't a monkey's chance of takin' back Jerusalem. Not this year or the next, or anywhen this side of kingdom come,' John added with a shrug. 'That's what they're sayin' in the camp.'

'*Sanctum Sepulchrum adjuva!* Holy Sepulchre assist us!' That's what we'd chorused outside Sainte Madelaine's basilica in Vézelay at the start of the croisade. '*Sanctum Sepulchrum adjuva!*' the old archbishop shouted from the poop-deck of the tarida when under oars we'd left the harbour of Marseille.

'But if we end the campaign here,' I reasoned slowly. 'Who is to save the Sepulchre?'

To see our God and Allah as the same was very well, I thought. But to abandon the desecrated shrine that Popes and kings and all of Christendom had made the very centre of our quest, was to turn victory into defeat – with my poor Jos and Bertram and so many other Christian lives lost for nothing!

'You hear the Sultan ties his horses in Church of Isa's Tomb, yes?' Khadija, in the act of helping John out of his padded gambeson, regarded me with upraised brows.

'If Isa's Tomb is our Church of the Sepulchre,' I answered. 'The Archbishop who recruited me said it was made into a stable. He told us it was fouled with dung and with the blood of its defenders. He said that Christian men were slain before its altar, and women raped and children put to the sword.'

'All is untruth.' Again the negatively lifted chin.

'One hundred years past, Christians killed all our Faithful to take al-Quds, is your Jerusalem. But when our Sultan took it back he set your Christians free – gave them its treasure, left altars to be tended.'

'You're telling us we've travelled all this way for something that's a lie?' I felt like some poor bastard who'd stepped on a rake to meet the handle hard between the eyes.

'Son of Ayyub would not spoil a shrine to Isa, Son of Mary. Have we not kept a place for Him in Holy Prophet's tomb?'

'A place for Christ at Mecca?'

'Is true.'

She left John's side to place a gentle kiss, not on my lips this time, but on the brow where the rake handle struck. 'Thou hast come far, muhibb. But the way is further to the truth.'

It was another kind of way – another journey I suppose which from its start in Acre would lead me down into the very pit of hell, and out of it to take the steep path that's brought me to this place.

But not yet. Not for just a little longer…

I can spend a little longer, surely, with Khadija and the child?

We stayed on in Acre for the hottest part of summer, through Lammas to the local feast day of St Timothy in August, collecting our wage each Friday from the bishop's paymaster and duty clerks, at tables set against the gates of the royal palace; waiting for an order to embark for home, or else march on Jerusalem – an order that took six full weeks to come.

As Khadija had foretold, no other soldiers came to knock upon her door, and we were left to come and go just as we pleased. I paid for John to visit women when he chose, and share my own discovery that pleasure could be taken without guilt. But in the main he stayed to sleep in the vestibule and act as Jos had done, to keep my armour oiled and shield my left side when I limped abroad. Inside the house he helped to feed the stove and water the rose garden. He showed Alia how to play at huckle bones and make cat-cradles out of twine, and after patiently enduring several days of wet and windy puffing, taught her finally to whistle.

The little house became a playground. Shuttlecocks shot through the branches of the fig, and cloth balls splashed into the pool. We found Alia fast asleep one night with one that John had made her grasped tightly in her hand. And at the sight of it, Khadija smiled.

When John and I climbed on the battlements behind King Richard's palace, to view the reconstruction of the city walls, Alia stood between us, watching with round eyes the labourers and masons who climbed the wooden scaffolding like sailors in the rigging. Or perched with mortar boards. Or worked with rope and tackle, to haul the blocks back in place. She came with us on expeditions to the harbour and the souks, her small hand held in John's, attempting with pursed lips and an almighty frown to match his jaunty whistle.

One day she led the way herself, dancing ahead through vaulted passageways to show us where the women fetched their water from a reservoir beneath the city streets. Lit by an opening high in its rock-cut ceiling, it took the form of a huge drum-shaped cistern with stairs built wide enough to take two women with their buckets passing. In contrast to the heat above, the air down there was wonderfully cool. The water in the reservoir was clear and pure. It was the means, Khadija told us later, by which the city had survived not only for three years of siege, but on this site since ancient times. Supplied by springs fed underground through conduits from the mountains, ass-driven wheels and networks of lead pipes conveyed its water all about the city. Even to our garden pool. 'And they told us Saracens were barbarous,' I said to John in wonder, 'when all the time they have been capable of this.'

By then I'd come to see that even after a destructive siege, the life of Acre was superior in every way to anything we had at home. In the city's roofed bazaars and open markets, women with dark flashing eyes and all their wealth of besant coins looped through their veils, sold silver jewellery from Cairo and Aleppo, perfume jars of ivory and alabaster, quails, marmosets and nightingales in cages. From laden stalls there drifted through the press the smells of spices, pepper, cinnamon and cloves. Silk merchants rolled out bolts of fabric unlike anything we'd ever seen – gold-brocaded, striped and spangled, bordered with embroidery and dyed in brilliant colours. Vases and ceramics caught rainbows in the surface of their glazes.

And in Khadija's house and garden, riches of another kind. She was a woman of Islam with a wealth of knowledge and experience which it seemed to me exceeded anything our English monks and bishops had to offer. Among so many things, she taught me to see beauty in the commonplace – in the shape of a single leaf, the pattern on a lizard's back, the colour of a petal floating in the pool. I learned to feel it in the evening breeze. To smell it in fresh linen, hear it in the chirrup of a sparrow. To pause and smile, not at another's folly, but at my own good fortune. I discovered beauty – in Acre, in myself and in Khadija.

Discovered it and lost it.

Have I? Have I lost it? Or have I brought it with me? Has it become a part of who I am?

One afternoon, while I sat in the shady refuge of her chamber watching her spin out the wool she'd carded from the Quartermaster's sheep, I told Khadija that I had a wife at home, whom I'd served ill and left without support or comfort.

'It may be,' I said, 'that I have left her with a child. I have no way of knowing – and God only knows what will become of her while I'm abroad.'

'Muhibb, thou sayest right. Allah knows all and guides her feet.' With the distaff under her left arm, she twisted the carded wool onto the wheel she spun with her free hand.

'If He wills to protect, then she can take no harm. Is thy wish to return, yes?' Her eyes glowed briefly as she raised them to take in my nod.

'Be sure then when you meet that thou wilt bring her joy.'

CHAPTER THREE

There are times when any of us could be forgiven for thinking men were put on earth for the sole purpose of bringing grief to women. Yet still when they abuse us we seem to want to take a share of blame upon ourselves.

I did it after that man raped me – told myself I'd smiled too much, had led him on. (Recalling it, I'm doing it again. Does that make sense?)

I woke just now in a state of confusion – saw light through the bed-curtains, and thought that it was morning. But then I saw the outline of the cradle, understood the light was moonlight, knew I was in bed, at home. At Haddertun.

What time of night? I've no idea how long I slept – can't tell if he's asleep as well? Or is awake like me?

I'd always thought I knew myself, and what I was, and what I wanted. But what that man did in the wood changed everything. I felt as if I shared his sin and was forever branded as a sinner!

I'd always managed somehow to convince myself that I was equal to any hand that life could deal me – found something ludicrous to smile at in almost any situation. But in the wood life ceased to be a game, and I became a different person.

I crept back down the cattle path that summer afternoon, when I was certain he had gone – trod through a drift of campion flowers spattered with drops of red like blood – to see no sign of him when I peered from the cover of the trees. No sign the harvesters saw anything amiss. The reapers all backturned, intent on holding their line straight. The women and the children shocking sheaves. The child Edmay was at the far end of the field, scarce taller than a sheaf herself, with Hod beside her, working with a will.

She straightened while I watched, to brace her back and shade her eyes against the sun. But before she looked in my direction, I'd already stepped back to the shadows. No one must see me bruised and bloodied, starting-eyed like something taken from a trap. That's all that I could think.

I left the forest further down and out of sight, to cut across the common pasture and avoid the village. Swallows flashed about me catching the insects I disturbed.

Somewhere I'd lost my hat, and as I stumbled through the grass, I twisted my loose hair into a knot. I knew I had to fight the heavy, hopeless feeling pressing on me like a weight. But for the present all I wanted was to reach my chamber and to bolt the door. Saving my worst thoughts for later when I was alone.

With but a single gate into the manor, I had no choice but to march through it, with one hand gripping the torn bodice of my gown. Head down to hide my swollen face. I heard a sudden hush in conversation and felt the grooms' eyes on my back. A woman tentatively called out my name. But by then I'd passed the guardroom and the wicket to my little garden. Reached the outer stair and bolted up it, three steps at a time. Ran into my chamber, slammed the door and shot the bolt – then I positively howled!

I would have thrown myself onto the bed, but couldn't bear to pollute the quilt or sheets with the rank smell, the leavings of that man. Or any part of me he'd touched. I was tainted! Ruined! Fit for nothing but the floor!

That was where I was, still crouching with my back against the door, when Agnès knocked the other side to ask if she could serve me – and when I could trust myself to speak, I begged her send someone to the harvest field, to fetch Hoddie to me.

'And tell her to make haste.'

I wanted to scream it at her, but somehow managed not to – although when she tried the lock, I yelled for her to leave me on my own.

Then after what seemed like a long eternity of ages – before she'd even climbed the stair, Hod's jangling complaints left none in doubt of how far she'd been made to tramp in the hot sun. Or at what cost to her blamed feet.

'But as I live, I'd never think of comfort when my lamb is calling,' she assured me when I closed the door behind her. 'By Saint Jim, I'd cross a field o' starks barefoot an' gladly if...

'God a'mercy! Will ye look at the state o' your pore face!'

She stared at me aghast as I turned back into the light.

'He caught me in the wood while you were all out harvesting,' I told her shakily.

'My eyes an' limbs, ye're never serious?'

She didn't need to ask the name. But I needed to say it, give it substance. I took a ragged breath and then another.

'It was Sir Hugh,' I said. 'He hit me Hoddie. Then he raped me.' And I almost had to smile at the variety of shocked expressions chasing one another over Hod's unlovely features, while she searched for something comforting to say.

'There then!' were the first words that came to hand.

'And 'aven't I 'eld always that the devil stuck 'is bit on Adam, an' all men after 'im, whiles God was backturned makin' Eve?' she offered as she took me in her bony arms.

If she said more, I can't remember what. It was enough to let her stride about and shout at servants, have water heated and herbs fetched in from the garden. Enough to be a child again. To let her bathe me, soothe me, call me lambkin, poultice my bruises with her own concoction of crushed comfrey leaves and parsley – comb out my hair and fold me in clean linen sheets. Push pain away and filth and guilt. To let my mind go blank. To banish thought – and sleep...

'Wake, wake up my Lady!'

Hod's voice. Hod's large hand on my shoulder. 'He's 'ere my Lady, d'ye 'ear me? Downstairs in the hall.'

'Who? Who's here?' For a moment I stared stupidly at the grey plaits that framed her face.

'Sir Hugh, that's who. God pick 'is wicked eyes out, an' stuff their 'oles with salt!'

Then all at once the knowledge flooded in. I was awake and shaking like the dodder. Terrified! 'He's here? Downstairs? But why? Why is he here? What can he want?'

'Same as Master Reynolds who's bin at the fowl-yard.' Hod gave a bitter laugh. 'Sly fox 'as come back 'asn't 'e, to take another bite.'

'I can't see him, I can't! Not after what he's done!'

I heard the rising panic in my voice and struggled to control it.

'Nor shall ye, lamb. An' so I'll tell 'im to his 'ead, an' set 'im down in front of all – blamed if I don't!'

If Hoddie'd had a chin to jut she would have jutted it. As it was she used her nose.

'No Hoddie he's too clever. He'll twist your words, I know he will, and say I led him on. He will defame me, tell them I'm no better than a whore – and say that I'm unfit to hold a manor in my husband's name!'

The desperate thoughts came one upon another, while I stood beside the bed with eyes tight shut and both hands to my temples.

And all the time, at any moment he could mount the stairs... Oh God, there was so little time!

Think! Think Elise, I told myself to stem the fear. And then it came to me – and in a flash I knew what I must do.

I ran to where the keys were hidden under the loose window board, and flung back the heavy coffer lid to lift a sac of coins for Hod to see.

'There's thirty shillings here,' I said. 'I'm taking them with me to Lewes.' I rummaged for my agate brooch and garnet pin in my jewel casket – threw my summer mantle on the floor and tossed them onto it. Then slammed the coffer lid and turned the key.

'I'll go for justice from My Lord the Earl and Lady Isabel, and show them what he's done to me before Sir Hugh can fill their ears with lies!'

'But not alone, my dove. Not leastways without a stout 'and longside of ye to see ye safe.' Hod clenched a hefty fist to show me what she meant. 'Best if I come-along, ye'r never going to make it on your own,' she added staunchly.

'No Hod, you have to stay to keep him from suspecting. Tell him I am sick abed. Or that I've locked the chamber door and won't come out. Feed him – make him wait to see me. Say anything you like to keep him here. Do you understand? To give me time to get away.

'Now, help me dress and quickly! I'll need a change of linen and another gown. The blue – my stoutest boots, the burnet cloak...' Urgency, a sense of danger, sped my movements, cleared my brain. The broken creature of the wood forgotten in the need for action, whilst Hod packed the clothing in the mantle and knotted up the corners.

275

When Garon's grandsire, Sir Arnould de Stanville, fortified the manor for Mathilde's War, he'd had constructed as a means of possible escape, a narrow stairway hidden in the wall of the main upper chamber – its entrance covered by a tapestry and stout oak chest. Its exit through a poultry house in the farmyard below.

There must have been some chinks and crevices for insects to creep though. Because the candle that Hod held to light me down, cast my dark shadow on a tunnel of grey cobwebs, which wrapped themselves around me like a dusty shroud. A crack of daylight showed above a doorway at the bottom of the stair.

'Look after Edmay,' I urged her when we reached it. 'And give Kempe the coffer key. We'll have to trust him not to thieve.'

I set down my bundle, to use both hands on the rusty bolts. 'Hod, bolt this door behind me when I'm through.'

The top bolt pinched my finger when it finally gave way. But what was pain? I almost smiled again when I looked back to see the old thing swathed in webs, and looking like some kind of animated duster.

'I'll send to you when I am safe and know what's best,' I told her as we hugged across the bundle.

'Trust to me, lamb. I'll keep 'im 'ere, if I 'ave to hogtie the bugger. An' if he asks me where ye've gone, be sure I'll shut up closer than an oyster. Wild 'orses wouldn't drag a stuttick of it outter me,' she promised, unaware of the strange picture of a horsedrawn shellfish she'd just conjured in my mind. The last sight I glimpsed of her before she closed the door, was a forced smile beneath two shining tear-tracks in the dust that coated Hod's plain face.

'There then. Lor' save you an' protect ye, lamb,' she ended gruffly.

But for a pair of sitting hens in the nest boxes set along one wall, the poultry house was empty. I picked my way across the smelly droppings to the outer door and peered into the sunlit yard. The air was hot and heavy, threatening a storm. A gleaming tide of barley straw swept out across the cobbles from the open portals of the barn. That's where the busy chickens were, competing with a flock of pigeons for any grain left in the litter. Otherwise with all afield, the yard was deserted.

I could have, should have sidled through the shadows of the barn to make sure there was no one on the track beyond. But that wasn't what I needed.

I needed to break free. Do something wild and violent. Run headlong through the barn across the threshing floor. Send hens and pigeons clattering into the air – release the fear and anger, feel the power of my own body – racing, shouting, fighting back!

So that was what I did, although the madness lasted only for as long as I could run flat out. Which was no further than the outer boundary of the orchard, where a tree root brought me to my knees and to my senses, both at once. And the one, the one thought in my mind, as I knelt trembling with the effort, listening for sounds of a pursuit, was to escape to Lewes fortress and the protection of My Lord and Lady of Warenne.

Once I had crossed the millstream, I planned to leave the road and scale the long ridgeback of Caburn – which lay guarding the approach to Lewes like a huge hound with its head between its paws.

Thinking back, I have no sense of leaving the domain. The next thing I remember is the hill itself – the steepness of the bostal track, the effort that it cost to climb it in the sultry heat.

There was no sign of a pursuit the first time I turned. Nor yet the second. But the third time I looked, it was to see that God had sent the hills themselves against me. The whole long ridge of chalk across the valley surged toward me as I watched it, cresting to engulf the manor!

'Holy Mary,' I thought in a panic. 'The downs are moving!' And because I dared not trust my eyes, I closed them tight.

But when I dared to look again, I saw it was a bank of storm-clouds that was moving, not a hillside – their shadow that crept out across the land – and felt the fool I was! Next thing, a gust of wind blew back my hood to bring the smell of wet earth to my nostrils. Then the deluge, as a curtain seamed with silver came folding and unfolding while it swept across the fields – as unreal in its way as moving hills.

Then it was on me, stinging, wrapping my wet gown about me, slashing through the grass stems to dissolve the chalk beneath my feet. The trees down on the Ram's Combe road were heaving like a sea in tempest. I heard the whinny of a frightened horse. But all I could see were outlines, looming slopes which vanished into cloud before I reached them.

Buffeted and battered, blinded, stung and deafened, I barely caught myself from stumbling over the lip of a deep chalk pit cut into the hillside, and balanced on the edge of the abyss, stared down upon the wet and steaming backs of cattle taking shelter from the storm.

Beyond the pit the hill rose steeply, surely to the summit? Yet as I laboured upward, each curved horizon gave way to another. Until at last I was the only upright thing in an empty prospect, dark as night, with nothing visible but gusting rain and sodden turf on every side. Until quite suddenly a jagged fork of lightning bathed everything in brilliant light – the leaden under-surface of the clouds, ten thousand diamond raindrops, every grass blade on the hill. To show me I was standing on the very shoulder of the sleeping hound!

The next instant, thunder cracked directly overhead and rolled around the summit. My hood fell back again. My heavy, saturated plaits lifted my face into the lancing rain.

I stood alone invisible to all but God, inviting the elements to scour me, cleanse me and beat back into my body some feeling – any feeling that was not of self-disgust or of defeat!

> *A violated woman in the centre of a summer storm –*
> *the same woman safe and warm in bed.*

> *Is it what's happened in between*
> *that's altered how I feel?*

Another flash! A livid vein of lightning threw up the knotted branches of a thorn tree, deformed into a slanting shape and clinging to the bank of a descending combe.

I counted up to five before the thunder followed, and was already on the downhill track, before the next flash lit the gleaming roofs of Lewes.

The storm retreated, thumping and bumping as it went – and the rain had settled to a steady drizzle by the time I crossed the river to duck in through the Saxon Gate. I closed my ears to what the sentry shouted after me and hurried up the hill. The normal bustle of the place was dampened by the weather. But there were others sloshing through the puddles, or wrapped in cloaks like me and sheltering in doorways.

278

All of them with predatory stares and grasping hands. All capable of violence!

I kept as far away from them as possible, sticking to the centre of the road. I had rehearsed what I would say to those they'd set to guard the fortress. But when it came to it, there was but one old porter in the fortress gate-house – an aged individual in a gleaming kettle hat with brows like besoms and a forest of white bristles on his chin.

Quite as repulsive as the rest!

'If you're the one 'as got away I'd like to see the other feller,' he said in French, when he had taken in my draggled hair and bruised, discoloured face. His teeth were rotten. I smelt his evil breath – thought suddenly of Hugh above me open-mouthed. Began to shake.

'I am Elise of Haddertun,' I said as steadily as I could manage. 'The Countess of Warenne will vouch for me if you will send her word. I wish to be admitted.'

'Wish all ye like. My Lady's off abroad, an' won't be back 'til Hallowmas.' The porter spat into the moat. 'Constable 'as charge 'til then, an' 'e won't vouch for no one.'

I stared at the rude old man in silence. In all my haste to get away it had never crossed my mind that the Warennes, who always came to Lewes in the summer, might this year have made other plans.

'So what ye got in there? T'other feller's head?' The porter pointed with his pike at the wet bundle I still clutched under my wet cloak.

And why is it men imagine that a joke is all you need to set the world to rights? Why are they so convinced of their own cleverness that they can't see the pain they inflict on women with their endless subjugation. With their taunting jibes and noxious, thrusting bodies? That's what I thought of the old porter at the fortress gate.

But here alone? Am I so sure they're all the same?

The rain had stopped by then. The porter added something risible about a butcher's shop and brawn. But I had turned across the wet boards of the bridge, to cross the street and make my way between the puddles to the alley where the moneylender lived.

The one man in the town that I could trust.

279

CHAPTER FOUR

The Emir's Palace, Acre: August 1191

ABLUTION

In fact King Richard's bathtime.

Of all the many decorated courts and cabinets inside the palace of Saint Jean d'Acre, the most exquisite is a first floor chamber, once used by the Byzantine princess, Maria Comnena, and more recently by Emir Baha-uddin Karakush. The King has allocated smaller, plainer apartments within the palace to his wife and sister and the little maid from Cyprus, to save this architectural jewel for his own use.

Mercifully undamaged by the Christian bombardiers, its walls are tiled in turquoise, terre verte and carnelian, in an endlessly repeated pattern to signify God's infinite capacity. Friezed in gold with calligraphic surahs from the Qur'an, they're set at intervals with polished copper mirrors framed in porphyry, reflecting sunlight from the chamber's gilded dome. Its floor is an elaborate mosaic composition of green fronds and lily pads, with swollen buds surrounding an enormous open lily flower. Enclosed within the lily's petals carved in marble, are forty gallons of hot water, perfumed with spikenard and sweet basil – with at the very centre of the blossom, singing cheerfully and lounging like an outsized worm in an exploded bud, the nakedly pink person of Ricardus Rex.

Wallowing and wreathed in steam, as he has been each morning since he first occupied the emir's palace, King Richard in a high good humour entertains his usual press of courtiers and minions with one of his great-grandfather, Guilhem de Poitou's, obscenely graphic chansons.

> 'Eight days I fucked them at a frantic rate
> One hundred times and eighty-eight!'

The King's bass voice, roughly in tune, reverberates around the chamber.

> 'My tackle afterwards was in a state;
> Sweet Jesus it was sore!
> And I was shagged and shattered to the core –
> Shagged and shattered to the core!'

An exhibitionist like Richard is bound to shock, and to take pleasure in the shocking. So, singing still, he stands to soap his testicles; then poses with one foot on the mounting stool for ewerers to rinse him – just as his English Bishop, Hubert Walter, is announced.

'Hubert, greetings!' he booms expansively with water deluging from acres of clean pink flesh. 'Come in, come here man. Don't just stand there like some randy novice gazing at my bollocks!'

The bishop does as he's commanded, concealing his alarm at being granted quite so much of the royal presence, and carrying the smell of horse sweat though the perfumed chamber.

'So tell us, has the old fox finally agreed our terms? Come Hubert, spit it out.'

'My Liege, the Sultan Saladin of Egypt and Syria begs leave to wish you long life. He sends you salutations from his camp at Ayadiyeh with the gift of a fine ruby.'

The Bishop, with his companion envoys, de Quincey and de Préaux, makes his obeisance, whilst trying to ignore the lowest of the three thick mats of reddish fur that still shed moisture from his monarch's gleaming body.

'He bade us inform you, Sire, that a further fourteen hundred

281

Christian captives have reached his stronghold of Kharruba, to add to those he has already freed.'

'God's teeth, I knew it!'

The King, descending to a pool of water on the lily tiles, holds up his arms for pages wielding towels to mop beneath. 'Did I not say the dog would come to recognise his master given time?'

He nods complacently at the large gemstone Walter holds before him and signals for a servant to receive it. 'So what of the ransom? Tell us in plain speech, does Saladin accede to that as well?'

'He does, Sire. We are assured that payment of a hundred and twenty thousand bezants, which must account for more than half the total, has already been collected at Kharruba.'

'It is well done.' The King emerges from the towels to stride across the chamber in a rude state of nature and shake his bishop by the hand. 'I knew if anyone could carry it with Saladin 'twould be his Grace of Salisbury!'

'You have not heard it all, Sire.'

But Richard is already acting for a wider audience. 'Did I not say that Acre was the key to our success?'

He stands before his courtiers in naked triumph, head back, hands on hips, wet feet wide apart; an emperor in all but name. 'Its hostages have bought us all we need to take Jerusalem,' he boasts, 'the men, the funds, the Holy Relic of Christ's Cross to bear before us into victory – and Saladin can't do a damn thing to prevent it!'

'My Liege...'

The bishop dares to interrupt the sycophantic court's applause. 'With the greatest of respect, Sire, I beg to point out that we have but half the hostages we need for the exchange. The Marquess holds the balance up in Tyre.'

The King's heroic rearview freezes. 'But I have asked de Montferrat for their return,' he says with slow precision.

'I fear that he will not relinquish them. The Marquess says he cannot trust you with their lives, Sire.'

'Conrad says what?' The moist cheek of one royal buttock twitches.

A tall man, Hubert Walter's face is less remarkable for handsome features than resolute composure. He's of an age with Richard and hasn't Baldwin's habit of apologising for displeasing facts. 'The Marquess says he cannot trust you with the Moslem prisoners' lives, or with his own life if he should choose to deliver them in person. He says there is no man on earth he fears as he fears you, my Liege.'

'As well he might, the craven cur.'

King Richard's gratified to be feared by such a famously brave foe, and pads back to the mounting stool to have his feet dabbed dry. 'So then we'll send Duke Robert up with a detachment,' he shouts over his shoulder, 'and make it clear to Conrad that neither he nor his French cousin will see a bezant of the ransom until all their little Moslem lambs are safe here in our fold.'

'My Liege there's more, you have not understood. The Sultan has agreed to pay the first part of the ransom and release his thousand common prisoners. But he refuses to return the Relic of the Cross, or all the noble prisoners we've named, until we have set free the entire Moslem garrison from the Emir Karakush down to the smallest child.'

'Are you telling me that weasel-turd would break the terms agreed for the surrender of the city?'

The King half turns in disbelief. A kneeling page receives the full force of his naked foot and sprawls across the tiles

'The Sultan claims the terms were offered by his emirs, Sire, without his confirmation.'

'He dares to say so after five weeks of prevarication?'

'My Liege, these people measure times in other ways to ours.'

But Richard is no longer listening. 'I know what they're about,' he growls, 'the Sultan and the Marquess and King Philip; I see that all those sons of vipers mean to do is play for time. They think that with their Venice whores and Tyrian wine-ships and their endless arse-numbing delays they'll weaken and unman our Christian

283

armies, until they'll as soon crown Conrad and forget Jerusalem, as follow our command.'

King Richard spins round suddenly to face his envoy. Forgetting to brace back his shoulders or hold in his paunch, he glimpses something moving in the nearest mirror. At first sight fails to recognise his own reflection – but when he does so, is appalled.

The image in the copper is of a fat man with an open mouth and glaucous, bloodshot eyes. A ripple in the metal drags down one eyelid – distorts a powerful body run to lard through gluttony and want of exercise. Top-heavy, wider at the waist than hips, its chest sags like a matron's. Its genitals, grotesquely puce, are dwarfed by the pregnant pod of the great paunch that juts above them.

In the moment he is forced to claim the ruin as his own, King Richard starts to shout. He's managed to believe himself a naked Hercules, a Jupiter, a Mars. The mirror shows him his age and ugliness, the spectre of his father's gross red body on a slab; and he reacts as any self-deceptive man is apt to when confronted by his mortal failings – with fury.

'They dare, they dare defy me! A shrivelled Turk, an upstart bigamist!' he rants.

The veins stand out on Richard's brow. His face turns purple. His bass voice rises to a roar. 'Blasted, spit-licking, fuckwit sons of whores!'

The King's barber, who's just walked into the bathroom, walks out again. His courtiers and servants shuffle backwards, hunch their shoulders, show a sudden interest in shoe leather. (You'd do the same if you were there.)

'I'll fucking murder them, the swine! D'ye hear me, Bishop? I'll split them lousy head to crabby tail! I'll pull their festering guts out, wrap them round their scrawny throats!'

'*GRRAHRR!! AARRGH!!*'

The King's howls of frustrated rage sound through the twisting streets outside the palace. The labyrinth contains a monster, bellowing for human blood!

The monster snatches from a squire a priceless silken robe, to drag it on and wrap it round his traitorous body.

'From the devil I have come,' he roars 'and to the devil I will send them!'

Which said, with all about him shocked to silence he's no further need to shout. In a measured and deep-throated monotone – which is if anything still more alarming – King Richard issues his instructions.

They trained me to bear pain, but not how to forget it. And so it all begins again. I feel as I once felt in Lewes waiting for the tourney charge. Or in the silence at Arsuf before the battle. I'm shivering.

'Three things make thy heart live long,' she recited from her holy book, 'to look on water, on green leaves, or on the face of woman.'

But I look down in darkness from another world, and my heart's empty. Nothing in it.

We spent six weeks in Acre, John and I. So short a span. Yet looking back, the time we spent at ease within Khadija's house seems limitless. Two men, a woman and a child. We lived, not as a captor with his captives, but as a family, contentedly.

'Every day muhibb, a page of story.' Yes, that's how she put it: 'Yesterday is flown, tomorrow is Allah's to order.'

Can one man's life be seen as pages in a book, and by someone who has never learned to read?

I accepted all she gave me. Not as Adam snatching stolen fruit from Eve. Not as our Church saw men and women. But as a son of nature taking only what was owed. Six weeks of paradise – of lovemaking, of water, greenery and beauty – and of a woman's beauty, found in a soft curve, a movement, an expression in the eyes. But what is love? Do joy and true affection have to reach a certain pitch before you call them by that name?

She said, 'Al-Qalb al'Ashiq Yawa,' and told me what it meant: 'A loving heart will find love where it may.' Was that too from Khadija's Qur'an? I only knew that I'd discovered someone in me who talked more freely, laughed more, limped less, played children's games, felt strong affections. And was happy.

With autumn fast approaching, it seemed less likely every day that we would siege Jerusalem that year. Most of our men in Acre were sleeping in the open on the quays, or in the crowded khans, and weren't in any haste to leave them. The news John Hideman brought us from the harbour was that the Queens of England and of Sicily had come to join King Richard in the palace, along with the little maid from Cyprus whom he favoured over all. The Sultan, it was said, was holding back from sending us his Christian captives with the ransom payment.

"Tis held that when he heard that Sallydin won't pay a bezant of it 'til he sees our hostages with his own eyes,' John said, 'King Dickard cursed the man nine ways to Sunday. An' now he's sent the Duke of Burgundy to Tyre to fetch the French king's prisoners. An' tells the Sultan to be ready in a week for the exchange.'

Khadija heard the news in silence – and of course I should have known our time with her in Acre couldn't last. But when a few days later John strolled in to tell us that the hostages from Tyre had come – that all the taverns and the brothels had been closed, that all leave was cancelled – it still came as a shock.

King Richard's criers, shouting through the streets, summoned his soldiery to join their units at the outer harbour in the hour of Prime, and ordered every member of the captive garrison to report at first light to the Maledicta Gate.

'They have King Philippe's hostages already penned up in the pits at Hadyah where they quarry lime,' John reported, 'and plan to march the rest out there to join 'em.'

'But not you and Alia, they can't mean you,' I told Khadija. 'You are civilians, not defenders.'

'ALL, is what they're sayin'.' John either missed or wilfully ignored my shaking head. 'Men, women, children too.' He looked from face to face. "Tis true, Sir Garry. The orders are for all of the families who garrisoned the city, bearin' only what they can hold.'

The little girl was sitting cross-legged by the leathern cloth her mother spread for our repast, and Khadija bent to smooth her curly hair. 'We are 'ayla – family,' she said quietly. 'Abdallah, brother of my husband, is at Tel al-Ayadiyeh. Is as God wills, we go.'

Which meant that in a few short hours it would be over. Khadija and the child would be taken to Damascus, while John and I were bound for home. Or else to Jerusalem, if our King was still convinced that he could siege it.

On the last night before I left Elise, I'd forced myself on her. No, why mince words? I *raped* her! – to exchange a state of tension for worse feelings of remorse. But in Acre that last night, there was no time for dalliance. While Alia slept behind the curtain, her mother piled supplies onto a blanket – dried fruit, some beans, a loaf, a melon and a knife to cut it, a copper pan, a stoppered pot of oil. She filled a water skin. She packed a long cloth bag with all that it could hold. She looped a dozen silver chains and strings of beads around her neck beneath the collar of her gown, then brushed the tangles from her long dark hair and plaited it into a single braid. For our part, John and I prepared our arms and armour for campaign, fixed straps or cords to everything we planned to carry and bundled up the rest in leather sefras to be stored in camp.

Most of what was said that night concerned possessions and containers. What to take and what to leave behind. But when the sky began to lighten and the time came for her to wake the child, Khadija spoke as I had never heard her speak in all our weeks together – as if she doubted Allah's favour after all.

'We live as married, but are not. Is written of adulterous woman she must stay in house to death,' was what she said. 'Allah is merciful. I pray that for a widow who hath mourned four months, it may be no offence in war to lie with an unbeliever.'

'Offence?' She took me by surprise.

'But you believe that God approves of men and women finding joy in one another, you said so. And why would He make us like you, with the same feelings, if He saves all His gifts for Moslems?'

287

'Incha-Allah – as God wills. As He kneads us from clay, He sees our weakness.' She smiled. But something in the sadness of her smile made me afraid. 'Nothing is but as God wills,' she said. 'And all return to earth when is appointed.'

There are moments when you would stop time if you could do it. When I recall Khadija talking of incha-Allah with her hand upon my sleeve, I see three versions of myself – the Garon of the moment, gripping her and feeling fear. Another Garon staring past her to a future that will hold the memory forever in his mind.

And now a third – this Garon of the present high above the earth, groping through his memory to view the scene, and feel the fear, and live it all again.

We left her house before it was quite light. She closed the door, but might as well have left it open. For there were men already waiting in the alley to search the house as soon as we were out of it.

Who lives there now, I wonder, in Khadija's house. Who tends her garden?

In the road up from the harbour, the King's soldiers – a platoon of red-crossed Limousins as welcome as a plague of ship-rats – were emptying the houses of their owners.

'You there! What the friggin' hell d'ye think ye're doing?' a bearded sergeant bawled at us from the shattered entrance of a shop across the way.

'Orders are for prisoners to carry their own bundles to the gate.'

'If you're you addressing me, I'll thank you to mend your language,' I shouted back at him. 'These people are our hostages in durance and entitled to respect. Or are you about to tell me you know better?'

'You a knight. Sir?'

'Yes I am, with Bishop Salisbury's Company.'

'Then carry on Sir, if ye will Sir.'

The man moved backwards knuckling his forehead, motioning for us to pass – and no doubt swearing after us as soon as we were out of earshot.

I held Khadija in the circle of my sword-arm. The child Alia was half-asleep still with her cheek pressed to John's shoulder as he bore her up the stepway.

A crowd of women with their children was already forming in the ruined area between the covered market and the Maledicta Gate, streaming in from all parts of the town. Everyone was pushing, shouting, gabbling in French or Arabic. Some were weeping. Far too many seemed intent on treading on my broken toes.

A row of horse-drawn carts piled high with baggage of all kinds were lined along the roadside where the rubble had been cleared. As we approached, Khadija was required to show another squad of self-important orderlies, what she was carrying beneath her cloak.

They left her with her beads and chains, and handed back the water skin and bundle of supplies. But, in spite of all that I could say, they took the cloth bag from her and tossed it to the driver of the nearest cart.

'*Qif!* No please, I keep,' she begged him. '*Satufqad ma'al*... So many more – it will be lost!' She even reached to take it back. But the driver was already stowing it beneath the pile.

'I'll put it 'ere, my love, d'ye see, up 'ere behind the nag? I'll warrant that ye won't miss Jack, when ye come back to look.'

He pointed to a star-shaped scar on the pony's narrow rump. 'There 'en't another with a bloomin' daisy cut into 'is arse, ye may be sure o' that.'

It was an act of courtesy amid so much confusion. Or so I thought.

We stayed with them as long as we were able, beside a buttress of the wall that served to shelter them to some extent from the press of the crowd.

But in the end it was Khadija who bade us leave them for our unit – and when she did, put back her cloak just as she'd done the day we met. And this time, in sight of anyone who cared to look, she offered her soft lips for me to kiss.

'*Fi Ri'ayatillahi wa Hifdhih* – May Allah in His mercy keep thee. All things come from Him, muhibb, and must return. We borrow time from life is all, only Allah is eternal.'

That may not be exactly what she said. I was confused, upset, and felt her fear.

'I'm sure we'll pass you on the way to the exchange at Hadyah,' I said huskily. 'Look out for us, and when you see us wave your hand.'

I can't, I can't go on with this......

CHAPTER FIVE

Tel al-Ayadiyeh: Tuesday, 20th August 1191

NEMESIS

On the third Tuesday of the month, King Richard rides out from Acre mounted on the splendid Arabian horse he's had shipped over from the Isle of Cyprus; a paragon of polished copper, its trappings sewn with blue silk tassels and small silver bells. Arched of neck and bright of eye, iron of tendon, fleet of foot – the stallion's name describes a burnished pelt to match the King's own tawny colouring.

The Cid rode *Babiéca* into legend; King Richard has *Fauvel*.

They've made a special banner for the King's ride through the camp to where the Moslem hostages have been assembled in the lime pits near the hill of al-Ayadiyeh. It is of silk, stitched into a rectangle of twice the normal length, fixed to a pole of twice the normal height, and carried on a cart drawn by a pair of Syrian ponies. For Richard needs the Sultan Salahuddin, high on his hill above the camp, to observe the royal leopardés – and know that the King of England has come in person to see the hostage situation resolved.

Behind his standard ride the sovereign's escort, with two companies of the Knights Hospitaller of Saint John. (Nursing monks devoted to the care of Christian pilgrims, who pray to gentle Jesus seven times a day and kill without compunction). Behind them march an infantry battalion – and, following the hostage transports, a rear-guard of mounted knights.

King Richard evidently leads the best part of an army.

But why so large a force? And why have the other Christian leaders remained in camp, along with Hubert Walter and the bishops? Why?

The Sultan Salahuddin Abu 'l-Muzaffar Yusuf, God's Shadow on the Earth, has also asked himself why such a body of armed soldiers has been mobilised for the negotiation and exchange.

From where he stands close to the summit of al-Ayadiyeh, he watches the long snake of the approaching army wind through the Christian tent encampment on the plain. And when at last he finds its tail and can begin to estimate the creature's size, he calls for a pigeon to be flown to al-Kharruba.

'Send to al-Malik al-Adil,' he commands. 'Write that the al-Firinjah are come in strength to oversee the change. Accord to my brother his title of *Sayfuddin*. Tell him that *'Righteousness of Faith'* hath need of *'Sword of Faith'*, with all the askars and turcomans he can muster.'

The message is inscribed.

The pigeon flies.

The sun is in the Sultan's eyes. He calls for a battani observation tube to shield them from its dazzling light, and holds it up to trap the image of King Richard, captive as a cricket in a cage. The next image framed in its round window is of the lion banner on its buttressed cart – next after that, the lines of heavy horse, the polished points of soldiers' spears. And then...

The Sultan stares intently, removes the instrument to squint with both eyes through the glare.

'They're bringing out the women and the children in the wagons they use for carrying their dead.' (He graciously describes the scene to those behind.)

'Praise be to God. The al-Firinjah intend to treat our people with respect.'

I've had a rest to set my thoughts in order. The Bérgé says that I must face it. He thinks I can, and I've agreed to try…

So be calm. Do it, Garon. Take a breath – deep breath…
  DO IT NOW!

From my mare's back I could see the outline of the final tumbrel, the cart that bore Khadija and Alia, though the rising dust. And I was grateful – *grateful!* – to imagine that King Richard in his mercy was sparing them a long march in the summer heat.

I so much wanted to protect them. Should have managed to protect them. *It is with God,* I thought – fool that I was!

When John and I rejoined our unit, we found that horses were in short supply. Few of the mounts shipped over from Provence had managed to survive the winter famine. The coursers they'd brought in from Cyprus had all been allocated to high-ranking riders. To leave the rest of us with nothing but the drooping culls – the worn-out relics of warhorses that the military orders were prepared to sell.

I would have left them where they were to march with John and save the price of something useless in a combat. But my injured foot still pained me over distance. So, for five silver shillings, I bought a scabby, cow-hocked mare that looked strong enough at least to bear my weight in armour. Then joined Pierpoint, Waleys, Stopham and the rest – riding five abreast behind the transports, in link-hauberks but without our helms.

By then it was already well past noon.

We had been told the hostages would be brought out in tumbrels; our task to close about them and defend the rear in the case of an attack. And when they passed our lines to take their place in the long column – eight wagons, laden to the stades with human cargo – I finally caught sight of them in the last vehicle that passed. I saw them, see them, crouching at the tailboard, Khadija and Alia – the little girl pressed in between her mother and the rail.

293

I shout her name. Khadija hears, looks up. But not the child. I said for her to wave. She simply stares, her mouth compressed, with something in her eyes as they meet mine which I don't understand.

She moves. It seems as if she's praying. Then I see what I missed when all the others passed.

Why did they have to bind their hands?

The Sultan of Egypt, Syria and Yemen, the man whose honorific title, *Salahuddin*, translates as '*Righteousness of Faith*', believes his faith in Allah's mercy to be justified when, from the summit of Tel al-Ayadiyeh, he sees his hostages marched out of their confinement in the terraced quarries.

The faint sound of a voice is audible – someone shouting. Soldiers move amongst the prisoners as they come to an untidy halt. Some are detached and marshalled to one side.

'Goats from sheep.' The Sultan smiles. 'He means to place a higher ransom on the heads of our qua'ids and emirs.'

The Christian soldiers have been working in the shadow of a row of lime kilns, to rope off an enclosure to contain the rest – two, possibly as many as three thousand adult men. The hostages are driven into the corral amongst the broken rocks and boulders. Hands bound. Robes, turbans uniformly coated in grey dust. From the Sultan's viewpoint high above, they look like sheep at market penned in blazing sun, standing quietly waiting for their sale to be agreed.

Meanwhile, the female prisoners and the children are alighting from the wagons – jumping down or lifted by the soldiers.

The time for the exchange is fast approaching.

Oh God, if I could only lose my memory, halt time, or else jump clear from that day into this. Oh God, oh God, oh God! I'm sweating, panting – beseeching her God, my God, anyone's idea of God, to intervene and save them!

But I must look the devil in the face and enter hell. I must remember how it feels to be among the damned!

They held us back until the tumbrels were unloaded. By then the infantry were ranged on all sides of the roped arena, armed with arbalests and pikes and spitting dust.

We were not close enough to see more of the Moslems than their crowding heads. No chance for me to find Khadija or Alia. But we could hear some of the women calling for their menfolk – the high voices of the children. The sound of babies crying...

The Sultan calculates that it will take Richard al-Malik's emissary a quarter hour at most to canter up the hill with his fresh terms. Please God, al-Adil and the light horse will have left already from al-Kharruba, where fourteen hundred Christian hostages and twenty caskets of gold bezants await the pleasure of the king.

The Righteousness of Faith lifts the battani tube to his right eye and carefully positions it. Looking down.

From his position on the plain the King looks up; and when he's made sure his adversary's tents are where they ought to be along the ridge, King Richard turns to the seething multitude in the enclosure.

He's sworn that in all judgements he will grant justice and true mercy in emulation of Almighty God the Merciful and Clement. As King he is the fount of justice. The great sword *Curtana*, representing Mercy, was borne before him at his coronation. At Westminster before his crowning he swore to Baldwin to abjure rapacity and all iniquities to all degrees. But Archbishop Baldwin's dead and buried, can't remind him of it.

In the rock-strewn enclosure Richard sees Moslem mothers with bound wrists clutch babies awkwardly against their breasts. He watches men trussed up like capons with their hands behind their backs, bend forward as they move – sees children who might otherwise run freely, press closely to their parents, seeking

295

reassurance. The round, frightened eyes of a small child its best defence against most adult enemies.

But not against Ricardus Rex.

'Kill them,' he raps out to the adjutant beside him.

The young man's face is white as chalk. With all his heart he wishes himself elsewhere. 'But who, Sire? Who will do it?'

'The Knights of the order of Saint John follow the butchers' trade. Send them – and Rénier, tell them to make sure to kill them all.'

'The women, Sire? The children?'

'Have you gone deaf? Or am I speaking in some language you don't understand?'

With one gloved hand, King Richard tugs at his silk-fringed reins, to turn Fauvel towards the hill of al-Ayadiyeh – again looks up. 'Let's teach the Infidel what happens when he breaks his oath. Kill them, kill them all! Destroy them root and branch!'

I saw the white-crossed Brothers of St John, the priestly knights, dismount and run towards the gate of the enclosure.

Over a line of helmets a blade flashed. Then another and another!

The prisoners understood before my mind could take it in. I cannot tell if what I heard first were their screams, or my own.

I don't know if I called for help – can't tell if I broke rank that instant. Or if I froze in horror. Or if my feet applied the spurs before I truly knew what I was doing. The first – the last thing I remember was ploughing through the armoured lines that blocked my way. Breath burning in my throat. Arms everywhere – voices yelling – my sword drawn in my hand.

I saw the chimneys of the kilns beyond. A glimpse of sky. I heard a woman's shriek... Then something hard slammed shut the door on light and sound. On everything.

The demented young knight's fall from his horse is unnoticed, by all except the men he's barged aside and the young pikeman who runs up to drag him clear. His mare kicks free of the loose rope, regains her feet unharmed. His sword lies by his senseless body in the sand. His servant pushes through to kneel beside him, unties his aventail and searches for a pulse.

All eyes are on the Knights Hospitaller, as they advance into the prisoners' enclosure.

At first they keep together, walking steadily towards the Moslem crowd.

Instinctively the hostages move back, move in to form a human barrier, the men outside, the women and the children in the middle, some holding hands. The shrieking has quietened to a sound like wind through trees, a murmuring of prayers to Allah, surahs from the Qu'ran, whimpers of mortal fear.

The military monks are not in need of any kind of skill to massacre bound prisoners by the thousand. They hardly need to aim, scarce need to look to know that they are slicing into flesh. The qualities they need for hours of butchery – the instincts men call base or primitive and spend their lives attempting to deny: brutality, barbarity, sadistic lust – are sadly not inhuman.

A Soldier of Christ who wears the white cross of the noble order of Saint John of Jerusalem is forbidden to allow his body, any part of it, to touch a living woman's flesh. But by some perverse distortion of belief his sword is free to mutilate her. Through all their prayers to God the Father, Son and Holy Ghost the Knights Hospitaller have always been aware of their sadistic instincts; of wolves that prowl the deepest shadows of their beings waiting to attack. Their faith is pitiless; the Pope of Rome confirms it. Infidels deserve no mercy.

The monk who strikes the first blow, thrusts his sword so violently into the body of a prisoner that it impales the man behind.

It is the signal for the others to begin.

It makes no difference if they scream or pray or gape in silence, or try to hide behind the rocks. Or crouch, or kneel in supplication beneath the slashing blades. Or bolt like game towards their own destruction. It makes no difference to the Hospitallers if they die at once or slowly and in frightful pain.

Few reach the barriers, and those that do are picked off by arbalesters who surround them. A child who runs in terror from the swords is shot in the back before they separate his squealing head from his small body. A woman is released from bondage when her arm is severed at the shoulder. Babies have their soft skulls smashed on boulders, are stamped on, trampled underfoot.

Limbs thrash, alive and dead. The air reverberates with bestial sounds – with the high, inhuman cries of creatures in extremities of pain and terror – the shriek of a mother who sees her child struck down, the worst sound a human voice is capable of making.

As the afternoon wears on and sword arms tire, sliced throats become the favoured mode of execution.

It takes two hours of systematic butchery to kill two thousand seven hundred men and something over three hundred women with their children. King Richard sits his horse throughout, beneath the parasol his squire holds up to shade him from the glare – to view the carnage like some latter-day Caligula, with pitiless composure.

By the time it's over, the arena has become a mass of raw, red flesh – of saturated fabric, clotted hair and offal. With blood in rivers – streams and pools of it. More blood than it seems possible for humans to contain. Most of the carcases have been eviscerated for the jewellery they have swallowed, and for the gall the nursing brothers of Saint John will later drain from their extracted bladders, for use in treating a variety of Christian ailments.

Clouded, sightless eyes stare out of bloodless faces. Contorted bodies crouch, embrace and sprawl in heaps – among them, webbed with the blackening intestines of another gaping corpse, something which once had been a woman named for the Holy

Prophet's most beloved wife. A small blue star imprinted on its skin is visible beneath the blood. Close beside, half-hidden by its outstretched arm, are the torn remnants of a female child.

Blown flowers and rotting fruit, viscous and congealing. Destroyed for what exactly? Revenge? Strategic gain? Or for something worse? Were they destroyed to satisfy a basic human need? A flaw within the beast that regularly, and in every age, drives it to slaughter its own kind?

Flies rise in clouds. The stench is so appalling that all within a hundred paces hold their noses.

'So are avenged the blows and arrow shots of infidels,' King Richard's annalist is later to record. *'Great thanks be given to the Creator!'*

A spoiled child of a Creator who smashes His own toys? Is that the God he has in mind?

From Tel al-Ayadiyeh, the Sultan Salahuddin sees his brother's archers sweep down from al-Kharruba. He hears their battle cry. Time and time again he sees them harrying the larger Christian army.

As daylight fades he sees their frantic sallies fail, and fail again to save their dying people.

It is the time for evening prayer.

'Oh God Most High – I attest to thee there is no other God but Allah. I declare that Muhammad is the Prophet of God. Come to prayer! Come to the temple of Salvation! God is great; there is no other.'

The Sultan genuflects, looks west and east towards the angels who record men's deeds, begs Allah to receive with honour the souls of those who have been, will be martyred, beseeches Him to help His servant to countenance and to accept.

'When the sun ceases to shine, when the stars fall from the sky and the mountains turn to dust: then shall each soul be made aware of what he hath committed.

'Ya-Allah kam minal-jaraaim turtakab bismik; Allah, what evils

are committed in Thy name. Behold the soul of man in the mystery of its nakedness.'

The first to be found wanting on that Day of Judgement, God's Shadow on the Earth believes, and takes what comfort he can find from his belief, is he who hath shed blood without due cause.'

It is already dark before the last Christian soldiers leave the monstrous scene. The Knights Hospitaller slump on their horses, slack-mouthed and glassy-eyed, flushed, foetid and polluted; men who have reached and then exceeded their own capacity for violence. Every now and then one leaves the ranks to vomit, or to sit his mount and stare into the darkness.

The King's composure has deserted him. His face is hidden by a scented scarf. His body trembles as he rides.

Back in his palace, he ungloves himself, demands to be admitted to the Queen. But news of what he's done has reached her, and it seems there is less steel bred into Bérengère than old Queen Eléonore supposed. The pregnant Spanish woman screeches through her chamber door for him to leave her be.

So Richard has them find the captive child, the thirteen-year-old princess he's brought with him from Cyprus. Takes her to bed instead, and muffles her screams with a pillow.

In the early hours of the next morning, Queen Bérengère miscarries. Her maids are sworn to secrecy. But King Richard's oaths are all it needs to spread the news from palace court to city street and through the gate into the Christian camp.

Two days later, the Queen appears in public, pale and silent, with wads of bloodstained linen rammed between her thighs. No one can read her face or tell what she is thinking. But Bérengère knows, and in due time her husband will discover, that in all but name their four-month marriage has already ended.

Later the same afternoon, with their hostage problem solved, the Christian armies leave the Plain of Acre, to march south for Joppa and Jerusalem.

300

CHAPTER SIX

It's said that when God seeks to punish you, He grants you what you've prayed for. I prayed in the port of Tyre for victory and death to infidels, and was punished. How I was punished!

But not by God. Because it was as if a curtain had been wrenched aside to reveal an empty void. I realised that there was no God in heaven. No Allah or Jehovah. I saw the sky as empty of anything but clouds – saw the whole thing as a lie. There is no Day of Judgement. Payment for our sins is made in this world not the next. The Evil One is not in Hell, but here on earth in mortal form. The human masks we wear whilst prattling of love and of forgiveness are made in our own selfish image, not in God's – the faces underneath them, those of snarling devils who kill for pleasure and delight in pain.

It's said that man's above the beasts. But I say he's beneath them.

I saw their faces in my nightmares, endlessly repeated.

The mare's fall and my concussion spared me the sight, but not the knowledge of the butchery – and night after night, I woke from shrieking, blood-filled dreams to see it happening again – and heard Alia's screams – and shared her mother's anguish. I saw the sword-blades fall. I felt them bite into their flesh, and mine, because I died with them in every dream.

And when I woke to recall where I was and what had really happened – to live again, dry-mouthed and desperate. That was even worse.

It was a march of more than twenty leagues from Acre to Arsuf. It took our Christian armies more than two weeks, with halts to rest along the way. We moved, as my Jos would have said, at a slow snail's gallop – or so they told me afterwards, for I had lost all sense of time or reason.

And but for John, I would have stayed behind, refused to move a further pace for their croisade – and likely had my throat cut for desertion.

So when I woke to the familiar sight of my old tent in Bishop Walter's camp, and heard from John how he had led me back unconscious from al-Ayadiyeh tied across the saddle of my mare – and asked him what had happened to Khadija and the child – and saw the wordless truth of it in his contorted face. Well then I must have lost my senses!

I shouted, shouted anything to drown his words and block the truth in them. I felt the pressure of a wall of tears behind my eyes, a dam about to break – and something tightening around my head, and something in my throat I could not swallow. And then darkness pressing in, so close and stifling I could not breathe – and John's voice in the tone he used for frightened beasts, soothing words devoid of sense – and John's hands gripping both my wrists as I fought through the flood.

That night, the night before we marched, I woke again to griping pain and crouched between the tents to squirt out a stinking flux that splashed my braies and burned my arse and emptied me of thought and energy and all emotion.

I stank! I thought I never would be clean again. But next day, John washed me, dressed me in my helm and armour, sat me like a sandbag dummy on my horse.

'Trust to me, Sir Garry.' Was what he said, or something of the sort. 'Now then, trust to me an' jus' do as I say.'

That journey is as unclear now to me as it was then. When I think back, few details of that time remain. My memories are all in fragments. I know we only travelled in the morning, from dawn until the summer heat made it impossible to march– and in the afternoons we camped beside the track or in the dunes or on the beach, while fresh supplies were landed from King Richard's ships which kept pace with us down the coast.

Through the slit visor of my helm I see the sun, a fiery red ball veiled in dust. I see the smudge of distant hills, the salt lagoons, the sails of Richard's ships against the blue-green of the sea – long winding lines of men and horses, floating and distorted by the heat. I feel the flies bite, hear the grunting of the camels, the clanking cooking pots beneath the carts – the *tok, tok-tocking* of the kettledrums, the disembodied calls to prayer to tell us we were not alone – that Sarsen horsemen matched us pace for pace and camp for camp.

We never knew when they'd appear, and when I saw them taking substance out of haze and dust – screaming out of nowhere, to shoot and hack and batter at our lines – I couldn't tell if they were men of flesh and blood, or demons from my nightmares. Well no, that isn't true. I could tell, but I had no interest, was indifferent to my fate. I couldn't summon energy to care if I should live or die.

When I lay down at night, I hugged myself. I pulled my legs up to my chest to make myself as small as I could beneath the blanket that John laid across me. I felt defeat in every way it's possible to feel it. My faith was gone and with it everything that I believed in – and in its place a thought that terrified me. Because I knew that as a soldier primed to hate and trained to kill – knew then and know it now – I might myself have waded through the blood of men and women, even children. Because somewhere inside me as I lay there with my knees beneath my chin, there crouched the monster that is man!

Night after night I lay awake, postponing sleep as long as I was able, knowing that there was no refuge, knowing what would come. Bright rings of jagged lines like fangs flashed through my vision; and when sleep came I dreamt that we were back in Acre in a maze of streets and alleys, empty houses, broken walls with doors that would not open and stairways leading nowhere. I dreamt that they were screaming, screaming for me, Khadija and her child – somewhere behind a wall, shut in a house, up on a roof I couldn't reach – that rocks were falling everywhere to block my passage as I ran to find them, stop them screaming – anything to stop them being killed – to stop them. Stop them... *STOP THEM!*

And when I willed myself to wake, and lay soaked in sweat with eyes wide open straining in the darkness, the images inside my head refused to go away. I knew I'd helped to take them to that place believing they would be exchanged, and if I was betrayed in my own ignorance, I had betrayed them too. Even with my eyes screwed shut and fingers in both ears I heard their screams and saw the images of slaughter. I was in purgatory and on the road to hell.

How long is it since then? Weeks pass these days without the nightmares. But they haven't left me, even here amongst the stars. Their spirits haunt me. Perhaps they always will. So much I had to give them still, which now I never can.

But then the time came, as I knew it must, for me to die.

One morning after Prime we'd barely mounted up, with some four leagues to cover still between the woods of Arsuf and the port of Joppa, when the sergeants shouted for us to make ready for engagement.

That I do remember.

Far behind us, we could see the Moslems circling the rearguard of our army, like wolves attacking a migrating flock, their shrill cries muffled by the distance. Horsemen galloped up and down the lines in clouds of dust, with who knows what instructions from the King?

Until at last we heard the clarions, and wheeled about to move into position for a charge.

'Good fortune, Haddertun,' Dickon de Waleys called out from somewhere down the line.

Then, as the infantry drew back to let us through, 'Sir Garry, God protect ye!' came from John Hideman – who still believed in God and His protection ('though just to make sure on the march, had never strayed much further with his pike than a pace from my stirrup). It was the last time, I thought, that I would hear his voice.

We moved off as a squadron in a double-rank formation to the orders of the Bishop's marechal – first at a trot. Then at a canter when we reached the wooded hills which hid the main part of the Sultan's army.

A charge uphill, and over broken ground into a soldid mass of Saracens, could only end one way. I knew it was against all reason.

Which made it of a pattern with the rest of my unthinking life. The mare I rode was old, untrained for battle. The lance they'd given me was cracked, would shatter almost certainly on impact. The thing was plainly suicidal. So when the order came to charge – when I applied the spurs, I charged no longer with the heroes of my dreams.

I see my own face, pale but calm. My life had lost its meaning. Yet even now I feel a stab of panic, knowing I am riding to my death, as I had always thought I would. That's how I see it, feel it, looking back and looking down.

Death comes to all of us, I told myself. But only once.

How could I guess how it would be?

So now, the famous 'Battle of Arsuf'...

In recording his most celebrated victory on the eve of the Nativity of Our Lady, 1191, the writer of King Richard's *Itinerarium Peregrinoram* allows himself free rein as usual.

The heathen pack pressed hard the host, assaulted them and closed with them. Seaward and landward, so close they hemmed the host and with such great fury that they caused grievous loss of horses which they slew...

Then charged the Hospital, all in a body, which had suffered so long... Then had ye seen the thick dust fly! And all they who had dismounted and were shooting at us with bows, wherewith they so harassed our folk, these now had their heads cut off; for so soon as the knights overthrew them, the sergeants slew them. And so soon as the King saw that the host had broken its ranks and closed with the Turks he thrust his spurs into his horse, waiting no longer, and came on at full speed to help the foremost lines.

Swifter than a crossbow bolt, with all his household brave and eager, he smote so violently a division of the heathen that was crowded together on his right that they were all dumbfounded at the sight of the valiant men, and perforce must void their saddles; stretched out as thick as sheaves of corn had ye seen them lying all along the ground. And the brave King of England pursued after them and charged them; and so well wrought he in that hour that round about him, on either side, before, behind, was a great open highway filled with Saracens that had fallen dead there; and the rest drew back, and the windrow of the dead reached full half a league in length...

Such deeds of valour wrought Richard, King of England upon the loathsome enemy, that all men beheld his prowess with amazement. He and his horsemen drave back and held the Turks until our people could regroup around the standard. Thus were our armies able to march on to Arsuf, where they assembled to erect their tents and their pavilions.

Later in his narrative, which covers several pages, the Christian writer, who desperately needs a victory to record, takes time to summarise what has occurred.

These people, devoid of all virtue, were driven back in such wise as I have recounted. Nor were they able to accomplish that whereof they boasted to their Sultan in their arrogance, that without doubt or fail that day the flower of Christendom was to be humbled and defeated. But all was contrary! Had you but viewed it from the mountain-top the way the Turks were fleeing! For we have heard from they who saw it from this vantage that when our armies clashed, we drove them back so violently that as they fled, their camels died, with horses, mules and hinnies by the hundred and the thousand. They lost so many soldiers in the conflict, that had our armies pressed harder and pursued them further, then must the whole of Outremer be occupied by our victorious Christians!

Now listen to one of King Richard's latter day biographers, writing in the nineteen thirties, in a chapter titled, *THE VICTORY AT ARSOUF.*

   '*Richard was about to launch the greatest military enterprise of his life, and there was genius in everything he did,*' this writer blatantly suggests. '*Saladin's determination to force a battle is easily understood. He saw, no doubt, that his former harassing tactics, though very annoying for Richard and exhausting for his* men, were having an even worse effect on the morale of his own followers... Some time or other they must stand up to these heavily armed crusaders if victory was to be won. That time, he judged, had come. He chose the ground with his usual skill. Arsouf was the only point on the line of the march where wooded hills came right down to the water's edge...

'As soon as the crusaders were fairly entangled amongst the trees, Saladin launched his attack. He seems to have approached in crescent formation, with his centre held back for the final assault, but with the right horn of the crescent considerably in advance of the left, and thrown out so widely as to envelop the Christian rear... The rearguard, composed of the Hospitallers, bore the whole brunt of the battle in its early stage. The crossbowmen on the outer flank and the infantry covering the hindmost of the baggage wagons suffered terribly. They would not halt, but we are told that they marched backwards, always facing the enemy, and that their progress in consequence became alarmingly slow...

'The Hospitallers sent message after message to Richard begging for permission to charge. Half of their horses were already down they said. Might they not charge out from amongst the infantry before it was too late, and flesh their lances in this mob of insolent paynims? But Richard firmly refused.

"My good Master," he said to the Master of the Hospital who had galloped up to him, "it must be endured." He realised the primary importance of getting the whole Saracen army within range of the cavalry charge, which he knew must be his decisive effort...

'But the Hospitallers could stand it no longer. There were cries from among them of, "Why do we not give rein?" "We shall be held as cowards for evermore!" Suddenly as one man they wheeled their horses and, calling upon St George, dashed out through the broken ranks of the footsoldiers, led by their own Master... Richard's carefully-thought-out plan was wrecked. But he acted with his usual decision. Ordering the trumpets to be sounded immediately, and calling upon the Normans and English to follow him, he galloped to the rear and hurled himself into the fray behind the Hospitallers, cutting a wide path through the enemy as he went. The Saracens went down on every side, and the Christian infantry, following behind the knights, lopped off the heads of all the infidels on the ground...

'But the battle was not over. As the knights and men at arms drew slowly back towards their own line, there were several counter-attacks. There was an emir with a great yellow flag who charged almost to the foot of the Standard. But William de Barres drove him off, and Richard, with the reserve, completed his discomfiture. The King of England, being mounted on his peerless Cyprus steed, Fauvel, often got dangerously far ahead of his companions; but his tall figure and his well-known voice inspired such terror in the enemy that their one idea was to get out of his long reach...

'At last it was finished. Scouts reported 7000 Saracen dead. The Christian losses were comparatively slight... Richard's magnificent élan, and the irresistible moral effect of his presence in any part of the field, was something different from his legendary feats of physical strength. We are told that his enemies fled before him like sheep...

'The resounding victory at Arsouf represents the climax of Coeur de Lion's Crusade.'

Oh yes?

That the battle is considered one of Richard's finest hours is due to such accounts. It's quoted everywhere as evidence of his success in Palestine, and to this day contributes to his enduring legend as a military commander. At Arsuf, it seems the best man won.

But is that truth or fiction?

Bismark is said to have remarked that people never lie so much as during warfare, and I should say that he was right. The truth about Arsuf without the spin is that it's less of a pitched battle than the most sustained of a series of hit-and-run attacks on Richard's army, as part of Salahuddin's strategy to delay and weaken it; to thin out its heavy cavalry especially, and render it incapable of mounting a successful siege upon Jerusalem.

The Sultan's forces easily outnumber Richard's. He could have overwhelmed them anywhere along the road to guarantee a victory. But from Hattin four years earlier he's learned what's apt to happen when you behead a Christian Hydra; and at the age of fifty-four he cannot face a Fourth Crusade.

So his Plan A. Before they meet in battle, he sends his brother, al-Adil, under a flag of truce, to place again before King Richard the offer of a Frankish Kingdom that will include the ports of Tyre, Acre, Caiffa, Caeserea, with access to the Holy Sepulchre. To offer him a foothold in the Orient and enjoyment of its trade routes, in other words, if he'll agree to leave in peace.

But Richard needs much more than access to the Sepulchre. Through his interpreter he tells al-Adil that he is pledged have the City of Jerusalem itself or nothing.

The Sword of Faith returns empty handed to his brother's camp above the forest of Arsuf, and together they proceed to their Plan B.

Historians agree that most of the Moslem raids occur in early morning when the crucesignati are least prepared for an attack. On the morning of the seventh of September, the head of the long Christian column is already nearing the seaport of Arsuf whilst its rearguard is still striking camp the best part of a league behind; and it's no accident that the terrain in which it finds itself, between an ilex forest and the coastal cliffs, is ideal for an ambush.

Battlefield revisionists have drawn neat maps to illustrate the positions of the Christian infantry and cavalry divisions and those of the attacking Moslems, at the onset of the conflict, and later in the day. The reality, as in most military actions, is a good deal more chaotic.

Historians have trawled contemporary first-hand and second-hand accounts for their descriptions of the Hospitallers' defence;

and yet remarkably have failed to highlight why, at this point in his campaign of limited guerrilla warfare, Salahuddin chooses to attack the rear of Richard's army and with such committed savagery.

When the sun ceases to shine, when the stars fall from the sky and the mountains turn to dust: then shall each soul be made aware of what he hath committed.

How could they miss the point that only nineteen days before Arsuf, the Kurdish brothers *Righteousness of Faith* and *Sword of Faith* bore witness to the slaughter and the desecration of three thousand of their people at the hands of the white-crossed Knights Hospitaller of the Order of Saint John?

The day after that abomination, the Muslims drove away the jackals, vultures, rats and crows with carrion, with parts of men and women, bits of children in their jaws. There was not time for them to wash or to enshroud the bloating bodies, or separate them male from female, or position them correctly before the setting of the sun. But the Sultan and his brother stayed to see them shovelled into hastily-dug trenches, aligned to face Medina – to see corrosive quicklime shovelled in to speed them on their journey. To hear the Imam, Umar, beg Allah the Compassionate to receive their souls with all due honour in His green gardens of delight.

But now is the time, at Arsuf, for Allah's Shadow on the Earth to send down the faithful, with cries of *Itar! Itar!*, *Vengeance! Vengeance!* To stall the rearguard and leave the white-crossed and red-handed Hospitallers in no doubt of why as instruments of death they in their turn must die.

For reasons of diplomacy, the King who ordered the slaughter of the hostages, is to be spared to settle his own account with Allah at some future time. And later in the day, when both armies have sustained losses (significant enough, but a great deal smaller than the exaggerated claims of the Itinerarium) – when a group of inoffensive refugees from Joppa lies massacred by Christians –

and when a boil on the face of the Sultan's firstborn, al-Afdal, is recorded in the Muslim records to have burst – the tears which Salahuddin sheds are not for a defeat.

The Sultan's tears are rather for the follies of mankind – for the unending conflicts of the People of the Book, and for his own part in the bloodshed.

It isn't hard to act the hero, if you don't care whether you live or die – and from this place and in this frame I see my attitude that day, less as heroic, than as reckless, selfish, typically mortal. I knew I was unfit for battle. But I charged anyway at a stretch gallop. Charged not to victory or glory, but to oblivion.

And yet it ended in the last way I expected, or could possibly imagine.

Ahead of us, dark savage faces, bristling spears, a hail of bolts and javelins. The thunder of the hooves. The rising tempo of the drums. The blare of native shawms and crash of steel on steel. A thousand hammers beating on a thousand anvils!

Something struck my helmet. Through the long slot of its visor I saw Sir Dickon fall, and then the blade that felled him, wet with blood. I heard the mare scream underneath me, as another slashed her neck. The animal was panic-stricken, plunging sideways, impossible to hold in line...

I dropped the lance to haul her back. Fell hard against the cantle of my saddle, as someone slashed the reins. Then we were in amongst the grey-leaved oaks. As I came up, I hit a branch. Lost a stirrup and regained it. Cast a gauntlet for a purchase on the horse's mane. Came up again in time to duck another sweep of leaves...

Figures in the glade beyond fought grimly, as they fought in every other glade, and on every yard of hillside all the way down to the sand cliffs and the sea. The mare flew through them, heedless of the steel, to leap the body of a fallen horse – careered off through the trees.

Immediately ahead, a group of Christian riders galloped with drawn swords and cries of *'Dix nous aid!'* toward a solid wall of mounted Turks.

311

Their leader was a massive man, helmeted, armed to the teeth and mounted on a brilliant copper-coloured horse. His standard showed the forked tails and spread talons of yellow lions on scarlet silk – identified him to friend and foe. He was the King!

If I had dreamt what happened in that wood, it couldn't have been stranger.

'Al-Malik Rik! Al-Malik Rik!' The words swept through the ranks of turbaned Moslems as a chant.

Then in the moment that I leant to catch the trailing rein and bring the wounded mare into control, the wall of Saracens began to open and draw backwards like the waters in the Moses story. To melt away into the wood. No shot was fired. No spear was thrown – as they retreated.

The King and his escort wheeled and wheeled about, blank faced in their steel helms through clouds of rising dust.

'Fight, damn ye! Fight, you cowards!' His helm muffled the King's deep voice. His waving sword became a gesture of bravado, for there was no one to oppose him.

I watched him wheeling, shouting, flourishing his sword.

Furious! Impotent!

And when at last he stopped, the only sounds within the grove were those of the cicadas and the rustling leaves.

The encounter was fantastical. Unreal.

But later it seemed less so – when we were told the Sultan Saladin had ordered that at any cost, and wherever he might be upon the field, King Richard's life must be preserved.

Which was of course why I was spared. Riding in the shadow of the King, I lived – not by the grace of God, but at the pleasure of the Sultan.

CHAPTER SEVEN

It's warm in bed too warm. I'm sweating and I need the pot. In just a moment I'll get up and use it. But not quite yet...

What woke me? Was it the boy? Did he cry out for Mother in the dark? But listen. He's still deep asleep...

Except for Sara, I would not have known about the baby. Or not at least so early in the piece. Yet even so – it was six weeks before I could be sure I was with child. Six weeks of waiting to petition the Warennes. Six weeks of hiding like an outlaw the attic of the moneylender's house.

When they came in together from the market, the old couple found me sitting in a wet heap on their doorstep, and hurried me at once into the warm. At the sight of my bruised face Sara exclaimed, and fussed around me just as Hod had done, to make me something hot to drink and set a fire to dry my clothes. Then following a whispered conference with her husband, she led me up two flights of stairs to a small chamber underneath the roof, where I was brought clean things to wear. They were too large and smelled of cloves – and by the time I'd sashed and gathered them to clear the floor, I must have looked like something lumped up in a net to feed a horse!

His wife would not allow the Jew to see me comb my hair before the fire downstairs. But when it was near dry, she covered it with a silk veil, and called him in.

I told them everything – and the more they shook their heads and clucked their tongues, the more I found to tell.

313

When I had done, the old man Jacob looked as if he would have liked to pat some part of me, if it were not forbidden by his faith. But as it was, he asked me to forgive him if we talked of practicalities.

'I take it you seek justice from My Lord and Lady of Warenne for the injury Sir Hugh has done you?'

'Yes and I will have it too!' I said. 'Except that they are both abroad.'

'But will return to Lewes in due season,' the old man pointed out. 'Meantime, perhaps you fear Sir Hugh will find you first? Or reach My Lord the Earl with a tale of his own that might entitle him to some claim on your property and person?'

It was exactly what I feared, and a relief to hear it put so clearly into words.

Old Jacob clasped his hands when I agreed, and looked at me across them. 'The first thing you must know,' he said, 'is that you have canonical authority on your side. Your Christian Pope has stated that no claims may be made against the property of a crucesignatus, until it's certain he will not return. Depend on it. Unless it can be proved he's dead, the Crown Court will uphold Sir Garon's bond with me for the five years of the heskem – for all that it is with a Jew.'

'But you said when I signed the bond, that English laws exclude your people from croisade usury.'

'In word, but not in deed.' The old man smiled. 'It may be that I stretched the truth a little, Lady. "Hameyvin yavin," we say. It is the way that we arrange things.'

'So will it help if I continue to pay interest?' I asked. 'I have with me what's due this month, and for the quarter following as well.'

He shrugged as if it was the last thing on his mind, and said we'd talk of such things later. 'For now 'tis best if you stay here in safety until My Lord and Lady come.'

It was without a doubt the kindest offer anyone had ever made me, and looking back I see how brave those two old people were, and what a risk they took. God only knows what Hugh de Bernay would have done to them, if he had found me there.

But even so, six weeks is long enough – a deal too long – to be shut into a box-coffer of a house that treats fresh air as something dangerous. And by

314

the end of it, I no longer wondered why its occupants were both of them as yellow and as wrinkled as stored apples!

There was scarce space in my small chamber in the roof to take as many as three steps without pressing your nose against a wall! And for several days I suffered headaches in the mornings which I felt sure were caused by lack of air. A window in the thatch offered a view of dingy rooftops. Or if I climbed onto the bed and leaned out far enough, a glimpse of the river threaded like a silver ribbon through the meadows. The first time I opened it, a great mess of moss and cobwebs fell onto the bed, the casement had been sealed so long. But after that I seldom thought to close it, except when it was raining. Given a choice, I told myself, I'd rather freeze to death than suffocate!

I sometimes think the view from that small window was the only thing that kept me sane. I sat up there for hours on end to watch the summer wear itself away. To watch the pigeons on the roofs, the boats slide up and down the river, and re-live all that happened in the wood.

Plotting my revenge!

For five days out of seven, men and women from the town – merchants, burgesses, monks even from the Abbey, came to knock on Jacob's door to beg for loans or pay him interest. I often heard the murmur of their voices, but never ventured down until after dark. On Saturdays and Sundays no one came and we were quiet. And when I found that on their Sabbath Jews were not permitted to so much as lift a hand, unless it be to eat and drink, I gladly took on all the cooking and pot-scouring for that day. Old Sara showed me the way. It wasn't difficult – and at least when I was laying fires and stirring pots, I wasn't sitting on my own and feeling sorry for myself!

The old lady's French was nowhere near as fluent as her husband's. But she often blessed me in her language, grasping handfuls of her bunched-up skirts to stop herself from taking me into her arms. I learned from her that people of her race may not cook meat in any vessel they have used for milk or butter – that Jacob bought his ducks and chickens live, and killed them in his own way in the yard behind the house. I discovered that their favourite dish was chicken broth. But on the third or fourth Sabbath, had turned away from stirring it, because I found the smell repugnant.

'Is new for you? You like before?' Sara asked me with an anxious face.

Then, when one morning some days later she heard me vomiting into my chamber pot, she came to sit beside me on the truckle. To cast all caution to the winds and wash my face with her own hands.

'Yakirati, you feel it here and here?' She set the wet cloth down to place both palms on her breasts and rattle the gold chains which lay across them, to show me what she meant.

'They have the itching here? And here?'

'I thought it was the weather or the fabric of my shift?'

The old dame sighed and shook her head. 'No, no, is herayon, Lady.' Then seeing that I'd failed to understand, she told me frankly that I'd make a baby.

'In springtime, is for sure.'

So just when you imagine that things can't get any worse, they absolutely do!

If I'd felt sick before – I felt a good deal sicker when I realised that the devil Hugh was STILL INSIDE ME, threatening to sicken and distort and tear my body, and make sure that I never, ever would be free of him, or what he'd done to me! More than once I thought about the morning following our wedding, when I first saw Garon naked, and thought of his male member as a force of life. Then thought about the other man's, and how I'd like to see it shorn from him with rusty shears!

But others saw it differently even from the first. Old Sara took my hands, both hands, in hers, to cross another barrier between her race and mine while I sat rigidly with staring eyes beside her on the bed.

'Baby is blessing, she make you happy.' An idea which represented her experience, not mine. Because next thing she told me in her halting French, was that she'd left a daughter and grand-daughter back in Normandie, when she and Jacob crossed to Sussex in the Old King's reign.

She missed them every day, she said with tears in her dark eyes. And it was not too long before the dear old thing began to act as if I had been sent direct from heaven to take their place in her affections.

She served me strengthening and kosher food, to purify the blood which nourishes the womb. She cooked me fish in place of the poultry I found nauseating. She brought me quinces and ground almonds, eggs beaten up in

316

milk, insisted I abstain from spiced meats, salt and onions. I must stay quiet, she said, suppressing thoughts of anger or revenge which might affect the growing child. I must not look upon a horse, a pig or any unclean beast, not even from a distance. I should recite Psalm 20 every night, and put my trust in God to ease my pain and grant my heart's desire.

Although, if old Sara had but known it, my heart's desire just then was to be rid of the intrusive spawn – expel the cuckoo child and scream her little house down in my rage and desperation! But then how could I bring myself to hurt the poor woman's feelings, by telling her I'd almost as soon die as give birth to a rapist's child!

It was as well I didn't know until he'd left, that Steward Kempe had come to see the moneylender after Michaelmas, to pay the quarter-day interest on Sir Garon's loan – and pay it in the name of Sir Hugh de Bernay of all people – for the man, he told the Jew, who was now managing the Haddertun estate!

'I could not tell him you had paid it, Lady,' Jacob added to the news that Kempe had stood so recently downstairs, not twenty feet from where I sat.

'In part it may have been a test to see if you were here.' Old Jacob tapped his nose with a forefinger to show his wisdom. 'But I can play that game as well as Master Kempe,' he said. 'I hid the place from him on the heskem, to trace the line I had already marked, and when the business was concluded, begged to send my duty to the lady of the manor, and ask if you were in good health.'

'What did he have to say to that, the rogue?'

'He said he was surprised I had not heard his Lady had absconded with the profits from the manor harvest.'

'He dared accuse me of a theft?'

Damn the man and blast him! I knew he'd never liked me!

'He said you'd left the manor and abandoned all depending on your management. He claimed it was the talk of all the district.'

'But I was raped, attacked! I wasn't safe. How could I stay?'

I fear I shouted at poor Jacob, as if he was the one I must convince – while Sara hurried off to bring a stool, and make me sit before I did myself a mischief.

'They must know what Sir Hugh has done? They saw my injuries. My maid must surely have accused him?'

'Master Kempe said nothing of it,' the old man told me gently. 'He said Sir Hugh has paid the interest from his funds at Meresfeld, and plans to manage both estates until My Lord the Earl rules on the matter. He said your maid believes you may have travelled north to Lancaster from whence you came.'

And in the middle of it all, I took a moment to thank Hoddie for that piece of inspiration – guessing that she'd had to keep the peace for Edmay's sake, and knowing how she must be worrying. I could hardly wait to send for her, but had to. I couldn't send for Hod until I'd seen the Earl and Countess, and was sure of their protection.

The Countess came at last in the third week of October, when the leaves of all the oaks outside the town were turning bronze – as was, to my disgust, the skin around my nipples.

Jacob had it of a debtor that the Earl was to remain in London while the Countess spent her Hallowmas at Lewes. He offered, bless the man, to help me frame my argument. But I had spent too much time on my own up in his attic, not to have practiced it a hundred times, and have it word for word!

My Lady kept me waiting for the best part of an hour, before she sent down to the castle gate-house, to say that she'd receive me. A page escorted me across two baileys – to a modest third floor chamber in the keep, where the Countess had a chimney-hearth all to herself.

'You say he raped you?' She turned my statement back into a question. 'How many times?

'Once was enough, My Lady, for I'm with child and pray he may be punished for the injury he's done me.' It was the first phrase I'd rehearsed and caused a murmur of excitement amongst her waiting ladies.

'He did it only once and you're with child?'

Seated by the hearth with one dog on a cushion in her lap and two more in a basket at her feet, My Lady's face when she examined me was frigid. 'And when exactly do you claim that this occurred?'

'At harvest time, My Lady, Saint Augustine's week.'

'And how long is it since his wife, the Lady Constance, died?'

318

'She died soon after Christmas ten months ago.'

'Ten months, as long ago as that? Well we all know what stallions are when they're denied a mare.' The Countess glanced around her women, who obliged her with a titter.

'Does that excuse them rape?'

I hadn't meant to sound so angry. It wasn't how I planned to speak. The words came by themselves. 'You call him a stallion, and the law demands he should be gelded if it's proven.'

The Countess turned back to consider me and ask my age. For once without its wimple, her neck was circled with a string of yellow topaz the size of pigeons' eggs – the skin beneath them positively scrotal!

I told her I'd be twenty-three next month.

'Your husband?'

'Twenty-six.'

'And was he able to perform as a man should to validate the marriage?'

'He was, My Lady.'

'And for how long did you share a bed before he left for the croisade?'

'For a little more than five months, My Lady'. Another question I'd expected.

'You lay for five months with a young and lusty man, and conceived no child?' The passionless, poached eyes regarded me attentively. 'Yet from a single tumble with Sir Hugh you have contrived to quicken.'

I said I couldn't help how it appeared. 'It is the truth,' I blurted, stung into incivility again by the suspicion in her voice. 'Believe me I would not deceive you, Lady. I swear it on my mother's life.'

'What I choose to believe is neither here nor there – and whether the man forced you once, or fifty times, is immaterial,' she told me stonily. 'As is your claim to have resisted.'

'But I DID! I tried to fight him off. He hit me and he raped me!'

'And who was there as witness?'

'No one.'

'Your word against the man's?'

She knows I speak the truth but doesn't care, I thought – and recklessly plunged on.

319

'He raped me, and will go on to rape the Haddertun demesne. I know he will if you allow it.'

She didn't answer that at once. The whole place held its breath. Then – 'If you wish to continue with this interview, I would advise you to compose yourself,' My Lady snapped, 'and listen carefully to what I am about to tell you. In all appeals of rape, the practice in Crown Court is to establish at the outset if the plaintiff was a virgin at the time of ravishment. In your case, after five months in your husband's bed, I see no likelihood of that being true. It follows therefore that you have no legal claim against his Sir Hugh.'

I begged her pardon for my ignorance, knowing I'd said too much already. 'But are you saying that in law, My Lady, a married woman cannot in any circumstance be raped?'

'Naturally.'

She looked at me with something like surprise. 'We seal a letter to prevent it being read by those who have no right to do so. But once the seal is broken, there can be no way of knowing who has read it. Or how many times.'

Between her thumb and fingernail the Countess cracked a flea she'd found behind her lapdog's ear. 'I'm willing to believe that in this instance you were forced,' she acceded. 'But that will not excuse you in the eyes of other men. We are all women here, and may say frankly that the act itself contains an element of force, as all wives are aware. Men seldom make distinctions between a willing and unwilling woman.' She sniffed. 'It comes naturally to men to treat us badly. And since it's men who make the laws, you may be sure they make them for their own advantage. Which is to tell you once again, you have no case.'

She didn't soften it or say 'my dear', would never stoop to anything so frivolous. I felt like some poor beast bred only to be chased, caught in the meshes of men's laws and men's desires, speared for their sport.

'But what of the Haddertun domain?' I said in a defeated voice. 'So is Sir Hugh to have the manor too?'

'The land's another matter altogether.'

My Lady's stern expression and brisk change of manner made it clear that we were talking now of far more serious concerns. 'Our canon law seeks to protect the land of absent crucesignati. But judgements out of Rome are *easier to make than to enforce – and we must face the fact that all our territory across the River Ouse is at risk of incursion by Earl John, who's brother to the King. My Lord of Warenne is in London at this present to uphold the government of the Queen's Justiciar against the Earl.*

'So it may be as well for the defence of Haddertun,' the Countess considered, 'to keep Sir Hugh in place there to defend it.'

'But you'd not send me back there to him?'

My faith in justice and fair dealing faltered in the face of that unfeeling woman. 'My Lady, you would not abandon me to one who seeks my ruin?'

The Countess frowned. 'What I will send to Hugh de Bernay is an instruction to hold the Hadderton domain against incursion through these unsettled times,' she said. 'I will assure him we have every confidence in his intention to uphold the rights of his departed lady's son, against the day that he returns to claim them. For if he fails to do so, the land will naturally escheat to My Lord of Warenne. I will inform Sir Hugh that I've removed my kinswoman, his step-daughter by marriage, into my household for her better safety.' *Again the yellow stare.* 'I trust that satisfies?'

I curtsied gratitude.

'In the meanwhile you may be interested to hear that King Richard has now taken Acre, and expects to be in Jerusalem by Christmas.

'So by the time your child is born, in April or in May?' *My lady's probing eyes moved from my breasts down to my belly.* 'Well, shall we say by spring – the croisade will most like be over, and our soldiers of the cross returned. With a fair wind we'll have a king again in England by Eastertide, and I dare swear you'll know by then if you're a widow or a wife.'

The Countess stooped to settle her dog into the basket with the others, and rose to indicate the interview was drawing to a close.

'I think it might be best if I were to find a decent woman, to raise this child of yours for you somewhere away from England. Always supposing it survives the birth,' *she added, brushing dog hairs from her gown.*

'But what if I should wish to keep it?'

And what on God's earth made me say that, when the offer plainly made good sense? Was it old Sara and the blessings she attached to babies? Or something more to do with the strange stirrings I'd begun to feel each time the little creature moved?

321

'It is your right to keep it, naturally. But I'd advise against it. As we've agreed, men see things differently to women,' My Lady pointed out. 'When he returns from the croisade, IF he returns – your husband may insist you're parted from the child. Which will be all the harder for you when it's grown.'

CHAPTER EIGHT

The Pisan Harbour, Acre: October 1192

CROISADE; THE BITTER END

More than a year has passed since the pyrrhic victory of Arsuf. King Richard finally leaves Palestine on the Feast Day of Saint Denys early in October, having sent ahead of him his wife and sister and pubescent mistress to make their own way home as best they may. Jerusalem was never sieged, let alone recaptured; and the Kings' Croisade which began at Vézelay with stirring cries of *Sanctum Sepulchrum adjuva!* – ends on the royal galley in near silence.

The Sultan Salahuddin's strategy of harassing and demoralising the Christian armies to the point where they're too weak to mount another siege, has been successful. At Arsuf he reduced King Richard's cavalry to less than half its strength. At Joppa and at Ascalon he blocked the harbours and destroyed the towns' defences to deny them to the Christians. But he left intact the orchards about Joppa as a distraction for their troops. A ploy which proved remarkably effective.

'There were so many grapes and figs, pomegranates, almonds growing in plenty round about, large fruits wherewith the trees were laden, that the host took them without price and were greatly refreshed,' one Christian annalist recorded. *'The army remained there long, enjoying indolence and pleasure. Their sins grew daily upon them; whores came to them from Acre to stir up their passions and multiply misdeeds.'*

Hearing from the prostitutes that in Acre the taverns had re-opened, and that ships were leaving daily from its harbours, a steady trickle of defectors began to make their way back up the coast – while outside Joppa, even Richard found time to relax. He went off hawking in the ilex woods behind the coastal plain. He sent to Acre for his wife and sister and the (no-longer-maidenly) Princess of Cyprus, to join him in his orchard camp – and there, to everyone's surprise, arranged to meet the Sultan's brother, Sayfuddin al-Adil ibn Ayyub, beneath a flag of truce.

At a banquet in the royal pavilion, gifts were exchanged and fantastic promises extended. Al-Adil presented the English King with a copy of the Qur'an bound in emerald kidskin, a matched set of seven near-white camels and a damascened campaign tent. In return, King Richard offered his own sister, the Queen of Sicily. If Sayfuddin would but renounce his faith, Jehanne was his to wed and bed, her brother promised with a warm and friendly smile. Then together (and what could possibly be neater?) the pair of them could rule Jerusalem as its new King and Queen!

But if Sayfuddin, who's brief was to delay al-Malik Rik as long as possible at Joppa, appeared to see the sense of the proposal, Jehanne most definitely did not. Her fury when she heard of it was said to equal anything their carpet-chewing father could produce. She shrieked that she'd as soon cut off her hand, as give it in marriage to a Moslem. Without in any way intending to be funny, she added that she'd rather take to bed a loathsome, yellow-spotted cacodemon with horns and hooves and a spiked tail worn front-to-back, than a black infidel with a platoon of other wives – concluding with some pertinent remarks about her brother's character and carnal preferences, that ended turning Richard's face the same royal purple shade as hers. Meantime, while Sayfuddin pretended to consider the English King's outrageous plan in Joppa, his brother, Salahuddin, was treating with Conrad in Tyre, for an alternative and smaller Latin Kingdom linked to France.

By late October, faced with the failure of his own negotiations, King Richard ordered his depleted army to advance on

Jerusalem without a realistic hope of taking it. By then the Sultan had destroyed all habitations with their crops and orchards all along the route, polluting wells and watercourses to deny the Christians anything that might sustain them. It took them two months to re-establish a defensible supply line from their base in Joppa, creeping forward to arrive at Christmas at the ruined town of Bayt Nuba in the Judaean hills, just four leagues from the Holy City. But by that time the Christian army were not only blocked by a large force of Muslim reinforcements recently arrived from Egypt, but afflicted by appalling weather.

'Their misery of mind and body was so great that no pen can write nor tongue describe it,' King Richard's annalist recorded, before demonstrating that if anyone could do it, he was the man. *'Their earlier sufferings were nothing to those they now endured from fatigue, rain, hail and floods.'* (Outraged, as men have always been, when adverse weather spoils their plans.) *'It seemed that heaven itself intended to destroy them. The ground beneath them was so treacherous and muddy that men and horses were hard put to keep their footing, and some sank never more to rise. Who can report the calamities they suffered! The bravest soldiers shed tears like rain and wearied of their very lives! When their sumpter beasts fell in the mud, the provisions that they carried were either spoiled or saturated. And in this manner, cursing the day they had been born, beating their mules with their bare hands, they retreated like roaches from the lamplight to the Port of Ascalon, which they found so dismantled by the Saracens that they could scarcely enter through its gates for heaps of stones.'*

King Richard and his army spent the early spring rebuilding Ashkelon to consolidate their southerly advance, with Jerusalem as unattainable as ever.

In February, Conrad de Monferrat made an abortive move to annex Acre, assisted by the Genoese and what remained of the French army. In April, things came to a head with news from Normandy that its French neighbours were threatening King Richard's borders abetted by his brother John. The time for his adventuring in Palestine was running out. The Latin Kingdom was without a king to take his place. The feud between Conrad de Montferrat and Guy de Lusignan was unresolved – and if Richard was to have a chance of reaching Normandy before winter closed the sea lanes and the mountain passes, he had to find a swift solution. So he called a council of the Christian leaders, and simply put it to a vote: Guy or Conrad? Which for king?

It was a big mistake from Richard's point of view; tactically huge. For, as before and to a man, they voted for the stronger leader – King Philippe's cousin Conrad.

Historians have consistently fudged what happened next, to divert blame from King Richard and *his* cousin Isabella. So for the sake of argument, let us suppose that I'm a Justice and you're a knight-juror, sitting in one of the new Crown Courts set up in England by Richard's father, Henry.

These are the facts. So let's suppose that they await your verdict on King Richard and his part in Conrad's death.

APRIL 17th 1192. Two days after the leaders' council votes for Conrad, King Richard sends the Marquess a message that he's to be crowned King of Jerusalem. The messanger he sends by ship to Tyre is Count Henri of Toulouse – a son of his half-sister, Marie, a grandson of Eléonore and his own acknowledged favourite.

APRIL 20th. Henri and his embassy arrive in Tyre to give Conrad the good news (and Isabella the bad news that she's no longer to be sole Queen of the Kingdom, but must herself crown Conrad King in his own right). That April Isabella is just twenty. Count Henri, described as 'tall and handsome', is twenty-five. Conrad de Montferrat, who less than two years earlier was forced on Isabella as a husband, is grim-visaged and well past his prime. It's not recorded that Isabella and Count Henri speak privately. But he stays in Tyre at least two days and has the opportunity to do so.

APRIL 28th. Isabella leaves her palace for the hamman bath-house at an unusually late hour of the morning. Conrad receives an invitation to dine with the Bishop of Beauvais, but on arriving at his house in Tyre finds that he's dined already. Riding home, he is attacked by two young men, who stab him in the back and chest. One is killed by Conrad's escort, the other held for questioning. Conrad himself is taken to the Hospitaller's infirmary and dies there shortly afterwards. His attackers supposedly belong to a fanatical sect of religiously inspired killers known as *hashishiyun* (the prototype for all future 'assassins'). But the dead assassin is recognised as a servant of the young Queen's mother, while the other has been seen in Isabella's own household.

APRIL 29th. French troops camped outside Tyre demand admittance to the city. But Isabella locks the gates and sends a message to Count Henri, then in Acre, to the effect that she and the Latin Kingdom are at the disposal of his uncle, King Richard. At the same time it's rumoured that, under torture, the surviving assassin confesses he was hired by Richard – an accusation bitterly contested in the King's Itinerarium.

'Oh infamous and malicious envy that always carps at virtue, hates what is good and endeavours to blacken the splendour it cannot extinguish!' protests its loyal author.

APRIL 30th. Count Henri of Toulouse returns to Tyre, and is reported on arrival to have been admitted 'at night' by Isabella.

April 31st. A hasty betrothal is announced between Queen Isabella and Count Henri.

MAY 9th. Henri and Isabella are married a bare eleven days after Conrad's interment. Isabella is already pregnant with Conrad's child. But they still consummate the union – to the disgust of the Muslim, Muhammad ibn Hamed Isfahani, who's present at the wedding.

'You see the licentiousness of these foul unbelievers,' he later writes. 'I asked one of their courtiers to whom paternity would be awarded, and he said it will be the Queen's child.'

What's more, by prior agreement Henri has reinstated Isabella as sole Queen of the Latin Kingdom, modestly declining to have himself crowned king.

MAY 11th. Henri announces that he and the Queen, accompanied by the Duke of Burgundy and the remains of his army, will join King Richard in his proposed attack on the Muslim stronghold of Darum, ten leagues south of Ashkelon. Which in due course they do.

My case, as they say, rests.

At the very least, the murder of Conrad was fortunate for Isabella, for Count Henri – and most especially for King Richard, who was quoted as remarking afterwards that the Marquess's fate had been predictable; adding, to account for his own cheerful mood, that excessive mourning was of no help to a dead man.

Yet in the end, not even the removal of Conrad de Montferrat could save Richard from the humiliation of a negotiated peace, which achieved neither of the stated aims of his campaign.

The city of Jerusalem remained, as Sultan Salahuddin had always sworn it would, in Muslim hands. So did the holy relic of the Cross – although, in much the way of Conrad's timely death and of the emergence the magic sword Escalibor in time for the croisade – by some miraculous coincidence, two hitherto lost fragments of the One True Cross had come to light that very June. One surfaced from a bishop's reliquary. The other, if you will believe it (and I'm sorry but I don't) – from an inspired scrape in the sand. Two lucky (more than lucky) finds for Richard to present as evidence of his success as a redeemer. But Jerusalem was still too big a rabbit altogether for him to pull out of his pot helm. So when the other Christian leaders chose to demonstrate their loyalty to Henri and Queen Isabella by marching in a body on the Holy City, he told them wearily that they would never take it; and when they finally abandoned the assault, he left them for his palace up the coast in Acre.

King Richard's final months in Outremer were marked by bouts of sickness and ill-temper. In August he returned by sea to Joppa – to defend its Christian garrison against a Saracen attack, and provide his chroniclers with one last chance to praise him for his courage and heroic presence. Tricked out in silver armour on his fabulous Fauvel, he knew by then (and Sultan Salahuddin, whose reinforcements outnumbered his troops six to one, knew better still) that the *Bellum Sacrum* was already over bar the shouting.

Early in September, Richard agreed a three-year truce to salvage something from the wreck of his croisade, granting Isabella and the Latin Kingdom a hundred mile strip of sandy littoral from Tyre to Joppa that excluded Ashkelon and Darum – and naturally the Holy City. The deposed king, Guy de Lusignan, was offered Cyprus as a compensation. In all its main essentials it was the deal the Sultan and King Philippe had agreed in Tyre two years before – to render Richard's whole campaign unnecessary, his military failure absolute.

We are at war. The war is over. How often have we trotted out those phrases through Man's long and violent history – with always so much lost, so little gained between them?

One condition of the peace was that Christian pilgrims should be given leave to worship at the holy places of Jerusalem; a privilege the Sultan had never actually withdrawn. Amongst the first to take advantage of the extended offer was Bishop Hubert Walter – and having knelt before the shrine that all the wretched fuss was over, he was received by Salahuddin, for what can only be described as a debrief. Inevitably the two men discussed the absent king,

329

who had returned by then to Acre for his voyage home. But in the end they could agree on only one aspect of His Christian Majesty's personality. His courage.

The Bishop praised King Richard for his generosity. But God's Shadow on the Earth, who'd buried what was left of three thousand Muslim hostages at al-Ayadiyeh, called him 'precipitate and reckless' – a more than generous understatement in the circumstance!

'Thy King is far too careless of his own existence,' remarked the Sultan, who in the recent skirmish over Joppa had felt obliged to send replacement mounts for Richard when Fauvel was shot beneath him. 'I will go further and tell you for my own part that, however much I have achieved by conquest, I'd sooner rule my territories with wisdom and with moderation than indulge in arrogance and vain displays of valour.'

The Sultan Salahuddin's words to Bishop Hubert Walter, as recorded by his clerk, are likely to ring true. King Richard's declamation from the deck of his departing galley three weeks later, as detailed in the *Itinerarium*, sounds more like spin.

'O Holy Land, I commend thee to God, and if His heavenly grace shall grant me so long to live, that I may in His good pleasure afford thee assistance, I hope as I propose to be able some day to succour thee.'

His annalists claim great achievements for King Richard in the mere sixteen months of his campaign. But if the King himself says anything at all when his new flagship, *Franche-Nef*, puts out to sea, I'd think it likely that he's drawing on his extensive stock of oaths involving God's most personal anatomies, while he lies bathed in sweat with a return of his old fever. He is the only man in Palestine who doesn't welcome peace. Jerusalem has always been for him as much an idea as a real city built of stone and mortar – which is perhaps why he declined to visit it with Bishop Walter when he had the chance. In any case, he's not the hero of the moment.

I know the man I'd cast as hero of the Kings' Crusade, and I think you do as well.

It isn't Richard, is it?

In my book (which after all this is), the true hero of the conflict has to be al-Malik al-Nasir, Salahuddin al-Din Abu 'l-Muzaffar Yusuf ibn Ayyub ibn Shadi; Allah's Deputy, God's Shadow on the Earth, Defender of The One True Faith, Sultan of Egypt, Syria and Yemen, Ruler of Aleppo and Damascus, Prince of Believers, Commander of the Faithful, Giver of Unity and the True Word, Adorner of the Standard of Truth, Corrector of the World and of the Law. The man that we call Saladin.

'I'll march if you say *march*. But I'll not... not fight!'

I had already drunk too much to be sure if I spoke the words or shouted them. They just came out of me because they had to. And when they hauled me shambling, stinking of the tavern, to face our Bishop Walter in his tent, they came out backwards. 'Fight – not, not fight...'

'Suppose you tell me why then. You are a little young I think for full retirement.' The bishop seemed more amused than angry – a long-limbed man with a slight stoop and steady way of looking at you underneath his brows.

'Because I've come to see – you see, Your Grace,' I told him blearily, 'you see we only learn by lis'... by lis'-ening.'

'You are extremely drunk, young man.'

'I know. But doesn' matter, does it – 'cos I wouldn' fight if I was sober as a pope. 'Cos when you're fightin' you aren' lis'-en-ing...' I said it very slowly to be sure of being understood. 'And when you kill, you kill y'er chance of uner'stanning, d'ye see?'

For a moment he did not reply, perhaps to let me hear the slurring echo of my words – and even then, in my inebriated state, I saw myself as Bishop Walter must have seen me. Swaying gently. Trying to explain and sounding idiotic.

'Come, you must know that a soldier doesn't need to understand, needs only to obey,' he said at last. 'Is that not what you've trained for?' (My father's wretchedly demanding voice again: *'A knight who isn't skilled in arms can count for nothing in this world.'*)

'Right you are – you're right.' I nodded, a thick-headed a fool with salt tears running down my face. 'Trained to kill an' can't, an' won't. Haven' drawn my sword since Acre. Won' draw it now an' never will. Useless as a soldier – *useless!*'

I'd long since given up the struggle to stay sober, drinking steadily through the three weeks we spent in the green citrus groves which grew on three sides of the ruined port of Joppa – flagons of Burgundy from Acre, al-yazil spirit, fermented date wine, anything that I could lay my hands on. I knew as well as any man that alcohol was not the answer. But it helped to drown the questions – even for a time to smother memory. And when the Bishop's criers rode through the camp to summon us to join the force that was advancing on Jerusalem, it was the drink that helped me to deny them.

'You're standing on one foot, Sir Garon.'

It surprised me that a man as great as Bishop Walter should recall my name, and even in my drunken state I sensed a kindness in him. God knows, I felt as old as Moses, but see that in the Bishop's eyes I must have still seemed very young – and foolish, obviously.

'When you came in I noticed you were limping,' he told me as I slouched before him in his tent, one-legged like a stork.

'I broke my toes.'

'How so?'

'At Acre in the siege... My squire, my Jos and I, moving blocks under the Tower.' I brushed my hand across my swollen eyes. 'Killed him. The block that killed my squire crushed my own foot. But tha's not why...'

He gave me a measured look. 'So you believe that fighting is the only gift you have to offer? Yet you have worked with stone?'

'Yes in a way, but...'

The Bishop raised a hand for silence. 'Very well, I'll hazard that 'tis best for you to stay at Joppa,' he decided. 'The Count de Châlons needs more knights with some experience of masonry to oversee the labour of rebuilding.'

'But I know only how to pull down, not how to build...'

'Which means you'll find the process beneficial. Trust me, you will not feel worse when you have built a length of wall, far from it. The solace to be found in alcohol is false, my son, at best is temporary. But confidence to be gained from achievement – even from the simple task of rebuilding a stone wall – is real, and with God's Grace is lasting.'

Even in my parlous state, with dry mouth and splitting head, I could feel grateful for the understanding in Bishop Walter's smile.

They let me bring John Hideman with me. Which was as well because I couldn't have survived without him. Steadfast John, my rod and staff. I'd always taken him so much for granted, and barely noticed until that time how much he had matured. He found me after Arsuf on the seashore like something washed up on the tide, slumped against the body of the mare. All through the drunken days, the torpid nights and mind-numbing headaches which had followed, he never left my side. He listened to me when I ranted, rambled, wallowed in the misery of my condition and woke me weeping from my nightmares. With the help of Guillemette and Maud – who were still washing shirts and braies, and men for aught we knew, in a makeshift laundry set up against a standing section of the old town wall – John saw to it that I was fed and decently attired.

Without the drink, I was afraid to sleep. But John took the coin to buy it for me and held the bowl when I was sick. 'That's it, Sir Garry, take it steady now,' he said. 'That's the way – jus' let 'er come.'

I was as much his child those weeks in camp at Joppa, as his master. And it was John who woke me, washed me, sobered me with quiet deliberation and led me through the ruins of the town to the rows of shallow mortar pits they'd told us to report to. On that first day, a master mason from King Richard's stone-yards back in Caen showed us how pug was made. The mix was two parts sand to one part lime – watered, turned and watered twenty times between two shovels – to reach the masons in a pliant state no drier than well-kneaded dough, he told us, no wetter than a meat-fed turd.

My office was to ensure a constant stream of barrows loaded with the perfect mix, to supply the men who worked up on the scaffolds round the walls. But as I soon discovered, it was not the kind of work a drunkard could perform. There were loads of sifted sand and lime in

333

sacks to be ordered and unloaded from the wagons, reservoirs to be replenished, carriers and shovellers and gangs of captive Moslem barrow-men to supervise. If the pug we made verged either on the constipated or the dysenteric, it came back smartly from the masons with a range of rude suggestions. So in the end we found it best if I stayed by the pits to oversee the mixing, while John took orders to the wagoners and kept the masons happy.

We were already halfway to being experts in the business, John and I, when autumn rain swept in across the site to force us under canvas, and long before we saw the citadel completed, I knew the Bishop had been right. The hard days of labour, dawn to dusk, were not the worst I'd known. My muscles were in want of exercise, and day by day and course by mortar-course, and stone by stone, the rising walls had the effect on me that he'd predicted. I felt the knots inside me loosen, the lethargy retreat. I drank less in the evenings and for a while slept better.

Yet all it took was a chance word from a wagon driver to bring the nightmares back. He told us that the lime we used was brought by camel, every sack of it, from the quarries at al-Ayadiyeh – and that night I dreamt that they were burning hostages instead of lime in kilns beside the pits. Again I heard Khadija's shrieks. Again I could not save her – and when the sacks were emptied by the mixing troughs, her severed hand lay coated with grey powder in the lime All but the red-stained fingertips, which moved still as in life. It was John's living hand though, not Khadija's dead one, that finally shook me awake.

News came in January, that King Richard had abandoned his advance on Jerusalem in favour of re-fortifying the strategic port of Ashkelon a three-day journey to the south. The King was there already with his army – and on the eve of Candlemas, his criers summoned every man who could be spared from Joppa to help him in the undertaking.

The harbour of Ashkelon was blocked with rubble, we were told, the sea too rough for landings. So we marched overland to gain our first sight of the city from the coast road to the north. We'd heard in Joppa four months earlier that Saladin had burned and levelled it, to save Ashkelon from falling into Christian hands. But nothing could prepare us for the sight of it in ruins. Or the rebuilding task that lay ahead of us.

When we'd first come to work on Joppa citadel, the town was occupied by Christians, its streets part-cleared of debris. But here the scene was one of devastation. We'd heard that Ashkelon was famous for the fifty-three great towers which ringed its outer walls. But not a single one of them was standing. Their shattered battlements lay in the moat or in the harbour with the ruins of its piers. The houses, the bazaars, the mosques and hammans had been consumed in the great fire which had destroyed the city, and all that now remained of them were blackened fangs of masonry protruding here and there from deserts of grey ash.

Down on the beach and in the littered moat, King Richard's army – together with Hospitallers and Templars and the Duke of Burgundy's French force – were loading stones with their own hands into the wagons. Or making ramps for winching larger blocks back into place. The King decreed that all who could, must work without distinction to carry stones to the skilled masons who'd rebuild the city walls. The blocks for their construction passed from hand to hand, from King to subject, silk-clad grandee to ragged peasant – from conqueror to prisoner, from son of God to child of Allah. From man to man.

Not that King Richard had remained long in the workforce. For after two days of striding round the place, shouting encouragements and cursing failures, and lobbing the odd block himself into the transports, he'd departed with a company of Templars to reconnoitre further south. Before he left, we'd happened to catch sight of him down by the harbour wall, in the act of lecturing an engineer who doubtless knew already on how to gear a treadmill hoist.

We were surprised how stout he looked without his armour.

'Double-arsed and lardy as a flitch pig,' was John's comment. But I didn't smile.

I didn't smile because…

It must have been because it was right there and then. No, look this is important. It was there. Right there. Right then that I first understood what

335

made a villain of the king I'd worshipped for so long. What I had always seen in him was what I wished to be myself, a hero. But what I saw at Ashkelon was entirely the reverse. King Richard talked but wouldn't listen. King Richard looked, but couldn't see – had no idea of loyalties or commitments. Which meant he placed no value on the lives of others – took all we offered him. Gave nothing in return.

Yet in the end was I much better – I who'd killed in Lewes and at sea, and on the River Belus and at Acre – and felt nothing at those times beyond a thrill of self-congratulation? A careless mummer with a real sword rather than a wooden one? Could I claim to be better than King Richard?

It made me sick to realise that I couldn't.

And now? Am I much better now? (I'll think about all that when I am done with this.)

The King was next in Ashkelon for Easter, to find that we'd cleared most of the rubble from the moat, and deepened it to make the outward-battered glacis hard to climb. With so many expert masons there already, John and I worked with the common labourers who swarmed the site, and I for one was glad of work which exercised so little of my brain. The old city was constructed of a soft local sandstone known as *kukar*, which was easy to reshape. So by the time the King returned, its new walls had risen several courses, strengthened in places with the Roman columns we'd recovered from the ruins.

Delighted with the progress, King Richard sent his criers to announce a feast for Lady Day outside the city, with all welcome to attend and mounted knights invited to display their skill at jousting *à plaisance*.

John didn't need to ask if I'd compete. Without a word I handed him my purse – and he returned, not with a horse or lance, but with a hogshead of red wine, which with unflinching application through the festival, I drank down to the dregs.

On Easter Monday, the King came out as he had sworn to do, to labour with his own hands on the city wall. But he never could stay in one place for long, and three days later left for Gaza. In May, when they brought news of Marquess Conrad's death, the King was in Ramula. In July he was in Acre, then in Joppa to repel an Infidel attack. In September, while his engineers at Ashkelon were letting in the sea to flood the city moat, we heard he was at Caesarea nursing a fever.

By then we knew our King had signed a treaty with the Sultan. But what happened in the world beyond the walls of Ashkelon was of less matter to us at that time than the great walls themselves. We worked all day out in the sun, squint-eyed. We carried, rolled and levered building stones until our skin took on the colour of tanned hide, our hands its leathery texture. Worked anywhere that we were needed – even took our turn in treadmills lifting cranes. Then in the evenings while the sun sank back into the sea, we stood together in our filthy, sweat-soaked clothing, John and I, to admire the rising lines of dressed and interlocking blocks, dyed indigo in shadow, crimson where they caught the dying light…

But wait. I have forgotten something earlier, much earlier than that!

John found it growing in a crevice of the old foundations of the Moslem wall. A bird-borne seedling from some garden which had long since disappeared beneath the ash, he knew it from the blossom as the rose he'd watered by Khadija's pool – and took a deal of trouble to uproot it, tend it for me, plant it in an earthen crock.

And although he never voiced it in so many words, I understood the point that John was making: *If a rose can grow out of a ruin, so can you and so can I.*

The truce between the King and Sultan was set to last three years, three months and three days, on the sound principle that a thrice-ravelled rope is the most difficult to break; and long crocodiles of troops trekked north throughout that final summer, in the hope of taking ship from Joppa or from Acre before the autumn storms.

By the beginning of September, the outer walls of Ashkelon were near complete. Without their scaffolding, they rose sheer thirty foot from skirted glacis to crenellated parapet, reflected in the waters of the moat to seem still higher. Massively unyielding, voluptuously curved between stiff ranks of barrel towers retreating into distance, we saw them as our gift to Palestine. Something salvaged, something positive that we had made with our own hands to leave behind us.

So when they told us that by the terms of our King's treaty with the Sultan, the walls of Ashkelon were once again to be destroyed – and when we saw the first stone crash into the moat and sink from view – we knew that it was time to go.

BOOK FOUR

CHAPTER ONE

Mmm, yes. What a relief! It isn't until you squat to use the pot, that you know how much you needed to!

He's still asleep, my little lamb. You'd think he'd wake, the moonlight through the window is so bright – and surely will at any moment now to start bawling for his feed!

My son was born in the first hours of May, on Garland Day, while the monks of Reigate Priory were still on their knees for Matins. The birth was an ordeal of cramping pain, from which there'd seemed to me no possible escape – until the baby came, and I began to think I wouldn't die.

'A boy, no doubt of that lamb the way the nipper's tackled 'pon my soul!'

Hod's triumphant face appeared above the midwife's, somewhere down between my knees. To be followed in the shortest time by something even more surprising. And that's the first part of the wonder of becoming a new mother. It makes no sense when you have cursed and carried him for so long, then worked so hard with so much pain to push him out into the world, that you should be in any way surprised by his arrival. Yet I was totally astonished!

When Garda showed me her first baby, he was already tucked up in his cradle looking halfway civilized. But what I saw when I first beheld my own son in the dim light of the birthing chamber, was a pagan little creature with a bright puce face and lardy fluid smeared all over him. When Hoddie lifted him onto my pillow, he waved a pair of scrawny arms, pulled puny legs with strangely purple feet in tightly to his belly – then opened an enormous mouth to tell the world in no uncertain terms how furious he was with it!

So very small, so very cross – one moment something alien and agonising. An obstruction that had made me call for help from any saint who might be listening – the next an autocrat in miniature, shouting for his own attention!

I stared at him in utter disbelief.

I smiled at him. I almost laughed at his outrageous masculinity!

I'd planned to have a girl whose life and mine would be the easier if she were valueless to anyone but me. But when I saw my son, I fell in love with him completely. There was no question. He was mine and I was his, and would be for as long as we both lived. He was my reason for existence.

All through the winter months at Reigate, while other people's sons and husbands staggered home from the croisade with injuries that ranged from simple disillusionment to missing arms and legs, I spent my time parading possibilities for my own future (and quite a few impossibilities, besides!).

In the last month of my confinement, when I looked like a sow about to farrow and waddled like an eggbound duck, the Countess sent a guard in Warenne livery to Haddertun, to fetch my Hoddie to me for my lying in – a kindness I thought remarkable. The man was told to offer no more explanation to Sir Hugh than that the tirewoman, Hodierne, was needed by her lady. And when the poor thing finally arrived – to find me almost circular, round as a herring tub – it had been hard to tell from her exhausted face if Hod was glad or sorry.

'To say the truth I wasn't sure myself if I should be made up with you for showing ye could catch a swollen belly,' she told me afterwards with a wry smile. 'Or fearful for ye lamb for catching it the wrong side of the blanket, an' from a famous knave.'

Which hadn't stopped her telling me who he was like, when she had cleaned me up and they brought back the baby to be fed. 'See 'ere's the varmint's nose stuck on the child.'

She pointed with a bony finger. 'Pore kiddy only wants a suit of clothes an' something of a beard, to be 'is father's spit.'

'Nonsense, how dare you say so. He isn't!' I said sharply. 'He's nothing like him!'

But he was, however I denied it.

In those first hours it was incredible how a tiny, gummy scrap could so exactly replicate a grown man with a head of hair and a full set of teeth – although I'm glad to say that after that first shock of recognition, my son began at once to change into himself. However others see it, he's unlike his father in every way that counts – and ever will be, if I have aught to do with it!

342

Although he seemed so strong, they took him to the castle chapel for baptism while I was still confined – and most approved the Christian name I'd chosen, Hamelin, in honour of the Earl. My Lord of Warenne was abroad in Kent to help defend its seaports against a possible invasion by Earl John. But My Lady came with two of her own tirewomen to see me with the child.

'Well, in the scale of things, when we are presently unsure which prince will rule in England,' she declared, 'Another chance-born child is neither here nor there.' (Which came a little rich from her, I thought, considering she'd married one!) My Lady Isabel had looked so stern and cold, that I was taken by surprise again when she reached out a heavily-ringed hand to stroke my baby's head.

'Helpless creatures. I never cared for mine until they walked,' she told her ladies. But I'd swear I caught a momentary softening of her hard mouth as she looked down upon my son.

As for me, I couldn't get enough of little Hamel – loved nothing better than to feel his weight, the heat of his small body pressed against me. With every day that passed he seemed to me more perfect, from his minute, shell-pink toenails to the silky hair that fringed his crown. I loved him, loved him as much I believed it possible to love. Yet now I love the rascal even more!

What I loved then when I first had him, was the warm baby smell of his soft skin – the new sensation of him snuffling for the nipple whenever I unlaced my bodice, tugging like a piglet to draw out the milk. And when he cried, I couldn't wait to lift him from his cradle and unwind his swaddle bands, to hold him close where he belonged.

''Tis best to let him cry awhile before ye feed him, Lady,' the midwife advised. 'Belike he'll need a strong voice as a man, an' here's the way to breed it. And Lady, 'tisn't right to loose the bands so regular,' the stupid woman said. 'For one, he needs 'is legs kept straight to set the bones whiles they're still soft – an' for another, a child who's spent a ninemonth in the belly still wants a tidy bit o' swaddlin' round him. The last thing he needs, ye may believe, is freedom from his bonds.'

But I did not believe her. I was convinced that I knew better than she ever could exactly what my own child needed. And what I knew he needed was the feeling of his mother close against him, and not the hard wood of a cradle

– needed to feel my beating heart as he had felt it from the first. To know that he was safe and I was there, and always would be to protect him.

'An' who's to say that ye've not got the right sow by the ear,' Hod unexpectedly agreed.

'I loosed your bands an' all, whenever your Maman weren't looking – 'tis more'n likely why ye're such a blessed fidget now.'

Dear Hod, how I had missed her!

In his first weeks of life, my little Hamelin grew steadily in size and strength. His narrow slate-blue eyes began to open wider and to follow mine. Until one day while I was telling him how beautiful he looked, and cooing at him like a lovesick turtle, the blue eyes sparkled in a way they'd never done before and his pink mouth produced a gummy grin.

And it was then in the enchantment of my son's first smile, that I began to see what Mary Mother had wanted for me all along!

When Garon bedded me that second time, I'd thought that I was all grown up, a finished woman. Then, when I failed to keep him back from the croisade, and when the Blessed Virgin failed to save me from Sir Hugh, I felt that she'd abandoned me completely – when all the time it had been ME who'd failed to understand, or see that she'd planned all along for me to share the miracle of birth and all the joys of motherhood! I'd been a child myself – I saw that in my son's first smile – expecting to direct my own steps through life.

By early summer, the Reigate castle sewers gave notice in their usual noxious fashion that it was time for My Lady and her household to decamp to Lewes, and the fresh air of the Sussex downs.

We'd heard by then that King Richard had been captured by the German Emperor on his way home from Outremer. We'd heard My Lord of Warenne was in Saint Albans with Queen Eléonore, to uphold her government against the intrigues of Earl John, and help her to accumulate the ransom that the Germans were demanding for the King's release.

But what cared I for kings and queens and princes? Or for absent husbands bound on fruitless quests? The Countess told me that the Old Queen was demanding a quarter of the income from everyone's estates to go toward the ransom of her son. She told me that in Garon's absence, his stepfather must pay – not only for the Manor at Meresfeld, but for my Haddertun as well. And serve the bastard right, I thought!

Meanwhile my little piglet child grew fat and rosy. His cries when he was hungry shook the castle, and when he'd sucked me dry, he filled his padded napkins with a bright, egg-yellow cack that made him near as lethal as the sewers we were to leave behind us!

Hod called him 'Stinky-Hamkin'. But if the stink was easy to discard with his soiled linen, the changes to his name began to stick – and by the time we left for Lewes, he was most often known to Hod and me as 'Hammy', 'Ham' or 'Hamkin' – or some other nonsense of the kind.

Garda always said a baby was more fun and far less trouble than a husband, and she was right!

The long day's journey south to Lewes was the same we'd made almost four years before, when I had come to marry Garon. Except that this time we rode in style within a curtained litter – not near so splendid in appearance as My Lady Isabel's, but plenty fine enough for Ham and me. (And although they slow things down to walking pace, and lurch about when bearers change, I'll swear there's nothing to compare with litters as the best means on God's earth of getting babies off to sleep!)

We departed at an early hour to put a league or two between us and the castle drains before the sun gained too much heat. For the first stretch of the journey I lay propped on a pillow in abandoned fashion, with Hamkin latched to one breast or the other, and the curtains of the litter open to let in the light. The Countess could never understand why I must feed my own child instead of taking on a wet nurse. But once I had embarked on dairy work – and even after Hamkin gummed my nipples raw – I would not have another woman acting as his milch cow for all the treasures of the Indies!

We had already left the sandy heaths that lap the south side of the Surrey hills, before my little leech had filled himself to bursting (and pungently beyond it!) and fallen senseless from the breast. Birch trees by then had given place to oak and beechwood. Butterflies danced all along the wayside. Swallows swooped about our caravan, flashing their white bellies. Everywhere the peasantry were busy with their hay. (Until we gave them an excuse that is, to down their tools and run to see the Countess with her furnishings, her cage-birds and her little dogs.) The children were the worst for begging alms, hanging from cart sides and yelling like mussulmen until My Lady's Marshal judged his chance to fling them the loose coins she kept for her largesse. To leave the urchins scrabbling for pennies in the grass while we passed on our way.

They called a halt for dinner by the river, in the lee of Ashdowne Ridge – and set up a trestle with a canopy to shade the Countess from the sun. We sat with backs to trees, or perched on tussocks while we ate. But My Lady had a cushioned chair as if in her own hall – with linen and plate silver, and sweet malmsey wine, and slices of cold beef to feed her dogs.

With little Hamkin cleansed, topped-up with milk and sleeping off the effort – I walked beside the litter when we started off again, to stretch my legs and shake my dinner down. Hod plodded on behind on her safe riding mule, fanning her face with a green burdock leaf, and commenting on all she saw along the way – a flock of sheep, a donkey foal, a fallen oak, more sheep, the monks' drawers bleaching on the grass at Hatchgate, a charcoal burners' camp – and long after I'd crawled back into the litter for the climb up to the ridge, I could still hear her voice advising the poor litter men of every point of interest in the way ahead.

The main problem, the chief disadvantage of the journey, was that our road to Lewes had to cross the sandy stretch of Meresfeld Heath, a straight crow's flight from Ashdowne – and Meresfeld was the last, the very last place in the world I wished to see – with living in its bounds the very first man on this earth I wanted to avoid!

'Sancta Maria, Mater Dei, if in your wisdom you can find a means of keeping him away,' I prayed, 'I swear I'll light a candle at your altar in the fortress chapel each morning at the hour of Tierce.' And all the way from Nutley Cross to Cackle Street, I begged the Lady of All Goodness to lend an ear to my best thoughts on how we might avert a meeting.

'You might send Sir Hugh to Haddertun to see their hay brought in? Or confine him to his chamber with a summer fever?' I suggested.

'Or, Dear Mother of Christ, have you considered that if he heard the Countess and her retinue were crossing his domain, and rode in haste to meet us... well then, his horse might stumble on a hidden branch or something of the sort. It's likely in the circumstance, that kind of accident. And when a horse comes down it's not unknown for riders to sustain the fracture of an arm – or of a leg? Maybe even of the skull...?

'Dear Holy Mother – you know, who better, of the injury that man has done me. Is it too much to ask, for him to break his wretched neck?'

It was too much as it turned out, or else too unimportant as a detail for the Mater Dei to attend to. Because he came! And worse! He came exactly as I prayed he wouldn't – when Countess Isabel was seated at her supper in the shelter of a sandstone bluff on Meresfeld Heath – with me in plain view at her side!

'She says to say that ye're expected at 'er table,' Hod had whispered through the curtains of the litter to save waking little Hamkin. 'An' short of dropping dead, there en't no way for you to tell 'er nay.'

He brought his daughter with him mounted like a lady on a white Welsh pony – although still child enough to wave excitedly and call my name, before her father frowned her into silence. He had shaved off the beard I'd always so admired, and actually looked better for it. Dressed all in red, as he had been when I first saw him in the fortress bailey, he seemed as he always seemed, in confident control.

The Countess's guards drew round her, and her little dogs barked wildly as he leant forward to dismount. For months I'd dreaded seeing him. Now after the first glance I made a point of smiling past the father to the child – with both my hands clenched underneath the cloth to stop them shaking.

Sir Hugh uncovered to make some kind of an extravagant salute. 'My Lady Isabel, I see you are in health.'

(That voice, that mocking voice! 'Please what? Please spare me your uncouth attention? Or please to use me like a bitch on heat, knowing I've been begging for it this twelvemonth?')

'Sir Hugh?' In the act of rinsing her long fingers while a page held back her sleeve, My Lady Isabel acknowledged his obeisance.

'I bid you welcome Lady to your lands of Sussex.'

'I hear you Sir, but misdoubt your welcome will be quite so heartfelt when you've understood my errand.'

She raised her voice so all should hear what I already knew. 'I come at the behest of My Lord the Earl of Warenne, as overseer for collection of the ransom for the King's release. I am in Sussex to demand from all our vassals a fourth part of the income from their holdings – in your case, Sir Hugh, from the land hereabouts which you hold in the right of Lady Constance, and from that within our ward at Haddertun which you uphold still for her son.'

'Who is invisible, My Lady, and likely to remain so.'

'Not certainly from what we hear. The roads of Europe throng with returning soldiers, and Sir Garon may very well be of their number.' The Countess selected a small wooden pick from its receptacle and prepared to use it on her teeth.

'Meantime his little wife, who should be managing the manor in his absence, sits idle at your side.'

I felt rather than saw My Lady stiffen.

'As we have ordered for her own protection, Sir,' she told him coldly. 'The lady is my ward. A fact I would advise you not to question.'

An awkward pause. But not for long. For in that moment, Hamkin woke to find that he was hungry, and announce the fact – if not in quite the loudest wail that he was capable of voicing – then in something not far off it!

Oh God! I mustn't move, I thought – or show concern in any way. (He couldn't know in any case. He might count up the months, as any man might do. He might suspect, but couldn't know!)

'Whose is the child?' The question quietly spoken and precise. (But still he couldn't know. He surely couldn't know? Unless someone had told him? Unless he had a spy at Reigate? Unless he'd met with someone at the fortress who had come ahead of us to make it ready?)

'He's no concern of yours Sir,' the Countess snapped.

'I wonder if that's true?'

And so he knew! He knew then after all! (And Lady Isabel said HE – had told him that the baby was a boy!)

If I had been a mallard or a lapwing, I would have flapped in front of him to show my broken wing and draw him from the nest. But I was not a bird. My best defence was not to move – to stay exactly where I was between My Lady and her apothecary, Bonfil. All I could do was to keep my head down *and my hands clenched in the cloth – my eyes fixed on My Lady's silver salt dish...*

But where was Hod? She'd have the sense, she'd surely have the sense to see what I was doing (wasn't doing), and just let the baby cry? Hamkin by then had worked himself into a strident state of desperation I knew that it would take me hours to calm.

And then I saw Hugh make his move before the Countess could recall him.

'Attend to me Sir. Attend I say! You have not been excused.' Through Hamkin's cries I heard her jewelled knuckles rap the board.

But I was on my feet by then – and there before him, with Hod appearing out of nowhere at my side.

I stood between them, placed the body he'd abused between the father and the child.

And when my eyes met his, I had to hold them, dared not show him weakness. Could not look away.

I'd known, had always known that he was dangerous – God help me, was excited by the thought, believing that I could control him. Now I knew otherwise, and as I faced Sir Hugh, my thoughts diminished, narrowed to the point of absolute defiance!

With lips clamped shut, his nostrils flared at every breath he took – all the intelligence in his black eyes directed on my face. To search my eyes, as if to gauge my will – to weigh my youth and inexperience against my instinct as a mother.

Every muscle in my body tensed, unflinching. Hard as iron!
I was a tigress with her cub between her paws -
knowing that I must oppose the man
with all of the strength I had.

'No,' I thought, 'this isn't
going to happen!'
No. NO.
NO!

349

CHAPTER TWO

Now I've come so far with this, I won't waste time on the voyage from Joppa to Brindisi, except to recall the pilgrim ship on which we made it – a trim two-master laden to the rails with monks and nuns and friars and priors and priests, who'd made the journey to Jerusalem and now were bound for home. Oh, and maybe to record that when we hit the squall off Crete, the uproar of the pilgrims' prayers to God the Father, Son and Holy Ghost fair bid to drown the howling of the storm.

'Which makes ye wonder how they'd fare,' John said, 'without so firm a faith?'

Soon after we came into port, the pilgrims extracted their heads from storm-basins to find a guide to lead them through the mountains to Salerno, and from thence to Rome to seek the blessings of the Pope. Which came as a relief to us. For having lost all trust in Christian charity, we felt our coin would be the safer if we travelled on our own. Before we sailed, the Paymaster had changed our bezants into silver shillings, two for one, and advised us on our best route north by way of Apulia and the Italian duchies. In Joppa we had sold our armour, all of it – kept only daggers and my sword (which I could not quite bear to part with, although it never left its scabbard). Finding there was nowhere in the port where ponies could be had, I parted with three shillings for a pair of draught mules, which would take a rider but refused to trot.

'They like to sulk 'tis but the jackass in 'em,' John Hideman thought. 'The trick's to tell 'em that they're horses, an' not neddies, every day until they come to see it for theirselves.

'Works with the ladies too, so's I've heard tell,' he added with a fair counterfeit of Jos's famous grin.

We planned to take the awkward beasts as far as possible before the winter overtook us. Then in the spring to cross the alps with them to journey north for home. The land of Apulia, which owed allegiance to the King of Sicily, was broad and flat with stubbled cornfields ready for the plough – and for the first few leagues we rode the mules along its sandy beaches, splashing through the salty shallows.

In every red-tiled fishing village on that coast, the peasants recognised us as crucesignati despite our plain appearance. They swarmed round us, gabbling and smiling, and at another time their welcome might have touched me. But by then I was so wrapped in misery, that it was all that I could do to stop myself from shouting at them angrily to stand away and let us pass. In Ashkelon I'd felt of use so long as I could work. But with its destruction, and nothing to divert me since, I had been overtaken with a sense of my own failure.

As John and I rode north, we saw the coastal plains give way to wooded slopes and olive groves – saw castles perched on ragged hilltops, and passed clusters of round houses with strange shingled cones for roofs. But I stared through them all into a void of lost beliefs. My only loyalty now to John. My only purpose to get him safe home to Haddertun where he belonged.

Yet John himself, who'd faced the horrors I saw only in my nightmares, remained unchanged, as stalwart and dependable as ever. Somewhere about our third or fourth night on the road, when he had picketed the mules, unpacked the potted rose he'd brought from Ashkelon and spread our bed-rolls in the olive grove we'd chosen for our camp, I asked him gloomily how he contrived to be so strong. We spoke in French, and John as ever took his time, staring at a knotted olive trunk and whistling a passage from *The Gown of Green* to help him find the words.

'Rain falls, grass grows, cows crop it, an' men milk 'em,' he said at last. ''Tis what they're fashioned for, I reckon. An' all must take what's sent.'

He paused to work a piece of loose bark from the trunk and use it as a wedge to level up his pot-plant on the sloping soil. 'When all's said I am the same as they, Sir. My work's to serve ye, now ye've lost yer squire. But that comes to me as natural as doing nothin', mind. I wouldn't say it makes me strong.'

(What was it Jos said at the siege of Acre? *I'm your man, Sir Garry, that's the shape of it, and ever will be I daresay so long as God's above the Devil.*)

'An' there again, if the task ye've set yesself of takin' back Jerusalem turns out to be the best part of a tidy bit more'n what any man was made to do.' John looked up briefly as if to read my face. 'Why then I'd never think that makes ye weak Sir, no more'n you should neither. We none of us know what we're doin' mostly – as the man said, when he put his wife out in the dark an' fucked the bleddy cat!'

It was the first time I had laughed since Acre.

We awoke next morning to the sound of voices, sat up to rub our eyes and play for time – as sleep-hardened men are apt to, when woken suddenly by strangers – and found ourselves confronted by a crowd of smiling peasants. They carried rakes and ladders and led donkeys loaded with stacked baskets, stakes and rolls of hempen sheeting. And by the time that John and I were able to stand decently without our cloaks, they were already busy harvesting their olives – climbing ladders, tying baskets to their waists and spreading out their sheets beneath the trees.

So then what else was there for us to do, a pair who'd bedded in their orchard, but offer them our help?

If anyone had told me that first day, that weeks of picking small black fruit no sweeter than our bitter English sloes would have a good effect on my sour mood, I wouldn't have believed them. But life springs surprises where it may – and there were more of *those* to come.

For such as we, who'd laboured to destroy and then rebuild the ports of Outremer, the work itself was not demanding, and John especially was quick to master all its skills. The peasant women stripped the lower branches with long-handled combs. The men set up pine ladders to reach the higher limbs, leaning out with shorter combs to rake the olives down. The children climbed like squirrels high into the treetops, to send down showers of hard black fruit onto the waiting sheets – or foreign heads like mine. For although the folk accepted John as one of them, they treated me as something other – holding ladders for me, ducking shyly when I looked their way, admonishing their youngsters when they used me as a target. And as we dressed alike, and neither spoke their language, I can't say to this day how they could tell we were not of the same rank.

They were small, wiry people, dark-haired and narrow-framed. The scorching summers of Apulia browned their skin. But the faces of their girls and youths were round and comely, and the groves resounded to their cheerful chatter as they moved from tree to tree. In the main, I stuck to ladder-work to make the most of my long reach. But John was ever where he was most needed by the pickers, pegging out the sheets for them, or bearing their full baskets to the carts – and somehow managing to comprehend their rapid, arbalest-fire speech. At noon we shared their crusty bed and cheese. Then, when the light became too dim for us to find the fruit amongst the leaves, they took us down to stall our mules in an old farmstead built around a yard. To sup on toast soaked in olive oil, and sleep in comfort in a barn that stank of goats.

We stayed a week in that place, picking every day – and then moved on to other groves and other farms along the road they called the *strade dell'olio,* to earn our keep amongst the olives. Behind my misery, I think I'd always known that I would have to find the strength from somewhere to continue. And I believe it was the way those peasants lived and worked that finally began to lift the weight of guilt from my bowed shoulders. Whatever tithes or duties they might owe their lord, it had to be the cycle of the seasons – the soil, the sun, the rain, the crops and animals they raised – which gave these folk the sense of fitness I had lost.

Or was there more to it than that?

Did I respond to them because I missed the same thing back in Sussex? It's true that one young man who drove a donkey cart, reminded me so much of Martin Reeve, I half expected him to pull out a set of bagpipes and deafen everyone in earshot with their frightful pig-squeal music. In another place, a stocky little woman with a bright twinkle in her eye and muscles like a man's, might well have been Dame Martha – if she'd been two shades lighter and near twice the width. A pair of urchins we found catching frogs in a green pool behind a village press-mill, were like – so very like my John and I had been as boys in the old days of the mudsquelch. In happy days at Haddertun before I trained to be a soldier.

Me as a boy? Me as I could have been if I'd stayed home to live a simple, useful life? Could I have done that? Held the manor, without my time in Lewes Fortress – without my military training?

'A knight who isn't skilled in arms can count for nothing in the world.' But Father didn't tell me to abandon Haddertun, did he? What he said was that I must be ready every hour of every day to govern my estates. 'You have to be the strongest man, the bravest and the best. It is expected of you even by the peasants.'

Which didn't mean I was to ride away, or steal the peasants from their homes, to die in Outremer for someone else's idea of a holy quest. Well, did it?

I raised the subject with John Hideman, as we lay at ease beside the fire of an Apulian farmhouse at the end of a long day – stretched out on the warm beaten earth beneath a row of smoking hams.

'What made you leave your mother's cottage and come with me in the first place?' I asked him (and realised to my shame that it was the first time since we'd sailed from England that I'd done so).

'I think you said that you were ready for adventure?'

'We all were, make no doubt of that, Sir. Aye, an' found it too for certain sure. We'd never have rubbed shanks with kings an' bishops an' the like, without we came. Nor sailed the open sea to set our feet on God's own holy shore.'

'Nor died out there,' I said, 'like Jos and Bert. But wouldn't you say, John, that…'

'What I say, Sir Garry is that we all must die as surely as we live. Unless ye'r goin' to tell me that they've found some other way of fillin' graves?'

'But not out there so far away from everything they knew. They should have died in Haywards Heath or Haddertun where they were born. That's surely what they would have wanted?'

John disagreed. 'Who told ye so?' he asked the blazing logs. ''Tis how we die, not where, as matters. An' our old manor boys all died good deaths, as swift an' sure as any man could ask. Even Albie – swoopin' like a blessed swallow from that bridge 'afore the angels had the time to show him how to fly.'

John smiled at that, his brown face ruddy in the firelight. And at the thought of anyone as hairy and ungainly as poor Albie, growing wings and soaring like a bluebird, I had to smile as well.

'I'll get you back, John, at the least,' I promised him – the last of the men from Haddertun to put his trust in me as his Seigneur.

'It's all my purpose now; all that I want to see you safe at home where you belong.'

It's likely I'd have done it too, but for the broken moldboard.

Somewhere about the time of Martinmas in mid-November, the peasants held a festival to mark the ending of the harvest. Sounding horns and beating drums, they bore a festal statue of the Virgin, with a big brass cross and the sad relics of some local saint, all through the olive groves and down the hillside to their church. With John and me behind them on our mules. We watched them take the painted effigy inside, and while they crowded the church doorway, turned the mules' heads north. By then the weather had turned cooler. We rode in cloaks and woollen hose, and when it rained took shelter anywhere that we could find it. From the flat coast, the road wound inland through forests of dark pine, which seemed as much at home on rising slopes as in the deepest valleys. And if the mules made little of the climbs and sharp descents, their ill-fitted saddles gave some parts of us good reason to be grateful whenever the track found a level.

On the third day following the olive festival, we came on a small village hidden by the trees. Whether from war or pestilence, the place was dismally untended. Thistles choked its fields and gardens, seeding in its lanes. Doors gaped and shutters hung askew. Roofs here and there were stripped of shingles – and, in case some taint of sickness lingered, we slept that night in a nut coppice well beyond its ruins.

We were woken the next morning – not this time by human voices, but by the self-important crowing of a rooster over the next rise. We found him scratching in the stubble of a wheat strip – a big, red-feathered fellow, clucking in his hens to feed where he uncovered grain, and waiting only for the simple creatures to up-end before he hopped onto their backs to tread them. A group of grey stone buildings set apart were evidently occupied. Smoke hung about their roofs. A haystack had been breached. A cat sat in a doorway washing its black face, and in a field beside the barn a ploughman toiled to break the soil behind a single horse.

Our first surprise when we approached, was to discover that our ploughman was a *girl*! The second thing that struck us was that she'd cut her hair extremely ill. It stuck out in awkward tufts around her pinched brown face as if she'd hacked it off with shears – and having never seen a woman with short hair, I fear we must have stared. The third, most shocking thing, was that the girl was weeping. She'd brought her old horse to a halt before we reached her, and the reason wasn't hard to see. The wooden moldboard of her plough lay split in two beside the rock it must have struck when she looked up to see us coming. And now she stood and wept as if the accident was more than she could bear.

At which John Hideman did a thing that at the time astonished me. Dismounting, and without a word, he walked up to the girl and put his arms about her.

Well, to cut this part of a long story short, I stayed with them a fortnight. I say *with them* because, almost from that first day, I knew that he was not about to leave her.

The girl's name, she told us, was Michela. And although she showed us three graves in the plot behind the cattle byre – one old, and two much fresher – we couldn't tell if they contained her parents, with a brother or a sister. Or her husband? We only knew for sure she was on her own.

John found a piece of wood to make a new board for the plough. Together we dug out the rock, along with several others in her way.

Then John went on to yoke the mules. To plough, and then cross-plough the strip – to bring a whole lot more stones to the surface, for me to transfer to the boundaries.

There's more to language than mere words, and despite their different speech, it was soon obvious that John Hideman and Michela understood each other very well. She treated both of us with equal gratitude for helping her about the farm, and always served me first at our plain meals of eggs and winter-greens or coarse frumenty porridge. But it was John's solid form her dark eyes followed through the buildings and the yards – the more so when he shaved his beard to show her all his face. I noticed that, for any task needing a second pair of hands and regardless of the space around them, some part of John would always end up touching some part of Michela.

She wasn't beautiful, or even handsome, with her thin little face and hedgepig hair. But she was young and quite alone, with land that needed working. Which made her irresistible of course to someone like my John.

As I've recalled before, he'd somehow learned from Jos the knack of knowing what I thought and what I'd say almost before I knew myself. So when I admitted that, in spite of all I'd done since Acre to seem hopeless and pathetic, I was certain I could manage on my own... 'Aye, I know,' he said impassively.

'And if I told you that all I wanted was to see you safe at home in Haddertun,' I said, 'then I was wrong. It isn't.'

'I know,' he said.

'What I really want is to free you, John, to do whatever you think best.'

'Thing is I always have been free,' he told the pigsty roof that we were busy patching. 'An' done what I thought best an' all, Sir, all along.'

'So, John?'

'So's I would say we've both known for a middlin' while, that I am bound to stay.'

My turn to nod at the sty roof. 'Then it's agreed,' I said.

'Fact is, I reckon she needs me a deal more'n you do, Sir – an' I'll tell ye somethin' else for free,' John offered without looking up. 'Time's come for you to find yer own path home, an' to learn the reason why ye'r doin' it. 'T'isn' me, Sir Garry, an' never was.'

And that was all of our exchange until I came to leave.

I had already given John his mule and twenty silver shillings – a fourth part of all I had. Michela had packed food enough to last me several days, and did her best to hide her joy beneath a solemn face. She stood away for me to take my leave of him, with one hand on her beating heart – and all her thoughts, I have no doubt, bent on the question of how long he'd wait after I'd cleared the boundary of her land, before John followed her upsteps to the wide bed she'd sheeted fresh for them in her clean loft.

'You'll be wantin' this to take along with ye, Sir Garry.' He held up the plant he'd brought from Ashkelon. A twig with two small leaves attached, still in its earthen pot.

'I'll grant ye that she don't look too clever,' he confessed. 'But see, here's a bud and there's another – now then, give her some air each night, a splash o' water every second week. An' take my word she'll shoot for ye come spring, as sure as Sunday.'

'But you should plant the rose here, John,' I told him in a voice that sounded rougher-edged than I had meant. 'Beside the cottage door where you can see it flower.'

'See it eaten by the goats, more like.

'No Sir. She's for yer Lady's garden, always was.' John spoke, not to the barn wall or the mule, but for once directly face to face. 'She's all I have to give to ye now, Sir Garry, for a fact.'

His last gift of so many.

'Well then, I'll do my best,' I said unsteadily, with one foot in the stirrup. 'And thank you – thank you, John.'

He knew. I know he understood I wasn't talking of the rose.

'Make sure that she's well wrapped, Sir, if ye get to frost.' The plant was helpful in that way. It gave him something else to say.

John sent his duty to his dead father's wife. 'An' tell Rob an' Mat to be good boys for me. A' give 'em each a kiss,' he said.

And then before I mounted, he embraced me just as he had hugged

Michela. Except the tears this time were on his brown familiar face, not hers. Nor yet on mine.

He hadn't whistled for at least an hour. John looked as I felt when I cut Raoul's throat, when I stood at the edge of Jos's grave.

'You'll do, Sir Garry, on my life.' His final words.

I turned away. I blinked. I closed my eyes, which felt as if two bony fingertips were pressing on their inside corners – did everything that I could think of not to cry. Although I'm not sure why, because a show of feeling then could hardly have disgraced me. I only know I couldn't weep until I'd waved three times, and turned the mule that I called Jacomo out of Michela's yard. To force out of him the swiftest pace he could produce (some kind of a fast dawdle).

You do know why you couldn't weep in front of John. Why tell yourself you don't? If his gift was the rose, yours was to leave without a scene.

Well then, when we were out of sight – I'm not ashamed to own it now, in view of all John meant. The sluice gates opened. I was blinded.

So what exactly DID he mean to you?

Admit it, yours weren't just the feelings of a master losing a good servant. Well were they?

You wept because you lost a friend that day, one of the few. Perhaps the best friend you have ever had?

Later on my bed-roll – forlorn, damp-eyed still, quite alone beneath a clear night sky – I saw Elise's privy garden at the manor with the rose grown at its centre, smothered in pink blossoms. John behind me. Khadija. Jos. Both dead. Elise at Haddertun. Had she forgotten me? Or, thinking I was dead, already planned to take another husband? A gentle man to suit her taste? Although I found it hard to form a picture of her face, I could recall the colour of her hair and feel the warmth and texture of her skin. Could see myself where John was at that moment – doing with my wedded wife what John was doing with Michela, performing deftly as in all he did...

For the first time in so many months, I turned to another old friend for comfort. The need was there, the means to hand. But somehow when it came to it, I'd not the heart to dust off *Fisty Flora*. But lay cupping my balls instead. For reassurance, nothing more – and fell asleep.

But now awake beneath another sky, with views between the stars of soft cloud-portals opening? With curtains parting and pink passages unfolding to my view.

Not NOW! Not Fisty Flora! Christ Garon, what in heaven or on earth can you be thinking?!

So, moving on – and at a swifter pace than Jacomo could ever manage...

Well, there's no point in dwelling on the journey north. Not now. Enough for now to gallop through eight weeks of travel on the roads and waterways of the Italian Duchies. The Roman arch at Rimini. Bologna with its painted colonnades. Christmas in a rowdy tavern somewhere. The sale of Jacomo himself beside a causeway in Lombardia – a river barge, tall spires of poplars and the everlasting swamps... I'll think of all that when I have more time.

For now, move on – move on to where I am, and what I'm doing here – and, most importantly, why I am doing it.

Well no, all right – perhaps not quite that far. Enough for now perhaps to reach the alps. Or come at least within clear sight of their amazing peaks. Enough to think about the Biellese and meet with my companions for the next stage of the journey. Thirty thousand of them. Mostly sheep.

CHAPTER THREE

Down there in the world of men, beneath the clouds, beyond the waterways. That's where I spent the winter. In another life.

There was a carving back at Haddertun in the church of Saint Peter, which showed a sturdy shepherd with a lamb across his shoulders visiting the newborn baby Jesus in his stable.

'Wouldn' happen hereabouts,' I once heard the manor shepherd, Harald, telling Father Gerard. 'Ewes drop their lambs by Candlemas for certain-sure. They'd never keep the Chris'child in his straw so long to see a sock lamb, would they Father? Wouldn' make no kind o' sense, that wouldn't!'

But if Christ had first seen light of day in the shadow of the alpine range, he might have seen a newborn lamb at Christmas. For in the sheepfolds of the Biellese the ewes lambed through the autumn into winter. 'Though truly most were half the size of their own mothers when I first saw them at the start of Lent.

I came to work amongst the folds on the advice of a cloth merchant I met up with in a river tavern on the Lombard marshes in view of the high mountains I must cross – a man who'd taken something of an interest in me, when he heard the journey I was planning. Another episode among so many looking back in which I played the fool!

The merchant was a portly, self-important individual in an expensive fur-lined surcoat – so tall he had to stoop beneath the ceiling of the inn. A native of Biella, he spoke its local dialect until he saw I couldn't understand – then changed to French and ordered me a mug of German ale to go with my stale bread and stew. While he was bound for Venice with a bargeload of cloth for sale on the Rialto – my own best plan, he told me firmly, was to join the *transumanza* with the shepherds.

361

'You'd have to be a wealthy man to pay for guides and sleds to try a winter crossing. And then you'd likely lose to frost some part of you you'd rather keep,' he said. 'Much better wait until the spring, lad, and climb the mountains with the flocks.'

Which came to me as a surprise, because I'd hardly seen a single sheep north of Bologna, leave alone a flock.

'You will,' the merchant told me with a fat sort of chuckle. 'There's more wool this side of the Biella I dare say, than anywhere on God's good earth. We think sheep, eat sheep, fuck sheep in the Biellese. And if you'll listen to a man who knows, you'll go by water to Cossato where the river narrows.' He used both hands to demonstrate.

'Then join a fold somewhere between the landing and the old walled town. Stick to the wool, is what I'm saying, lad. Do everything the shepherds do. Tup ewes if you've a fancy for hot mutton!' He demonstrated that as well, obscenely – laughed again at my embarrassment, and ordered me a second draught of ale.

There would be work aplenty on the levels, the cloth merchant assured me. From Lent clear through to transumanza. 'Then when they drive the sheep up to their summer pastures, you'll go with 'em, do you see – and know that way for sure that the San Bernard pass is safe to cross.'

So that's just what I did (well, not the thing about the ewes).

Nor were the Biellese flocks hard to find. Before I'd even left the river at Cossato, the ceaseless bleating that would fill my hours awake and sleeping through the weeks that followed was carried to me on the breeze – and with it the piss-mutton stench of multitudes of sheep. Their folds were set in rows and patchwork patterns for as far as you could see across the plain. The woolly squares they occupied, the green they'd move to later, blocked out like a giant chessboard beneath the mountain wall.

The Comun of Biella was famous for its woollen trade from Amiens to Antioch, or so the merchant boasted. And when I confided to my beaker in the tavern that I'd never heard of it, and wouldn't know a *comun* from a bull's foot if I should stumble on one, he set himself at once to educate me.

362

'A comun is the best and fairest form of government there ever was or will be. Never doubt it, lad. You've heard, I take it, of Amalfi, Pisa, Venice, Genoa, Ancona and Ragusa,' he asked, 'to name but six of our great maritime republics?'

The alcohol was working fast on me. Well I was thirsty and it had been a while since I'd laid hands on quite so much of it. So 'though I'd heard of only three of the republics that he mentioned, I nodded at him with the utmost gravity. And although the tavern's beery atmosphere was pressing on my eyelids, I tried my best to concentrate on everything the merchant said, while staring at my own reflection in the ale.

'So if I tell you that our Biellese share with those states the freedom to conduct their own affairs without the interference of a king, a duke, a count or any overlord except their bishop. Then you will understand,' he said, 'that comuns are created for the benefit of all.'

It was a subject, I could tell, that was dear to the man's heart.

'But who is there... I mean, how can such places be defended?' I thought confusedly of Haddertun without its service to the Honour of Warenne – without the Earl's protection.

'How can that be expected to succeed?' I waved my tankard, splashing ale across the table. 'Who judges their disputes, Iwant'erknow?' I said, running the words together. 'Who caresfor'emwhentheycan'twork?'

'Aside from our own garrison, the Lombard League protects us from the German Empire,' the cloth merchant patiently explained.

'Each year at Martinmas four consuj are elected from the populace, tasked by our bishop to pass judgement in its courts, inspect its hospital and keep its soldiery in order. You may be interested to hear, lad, that I myself have held the bâton of a consuj, when...'

But that was all that penetrated. For it was then that I fell forward senseless in a puddle of spilled ale.

Luckily, the worst effects of my instruction had more or less worn off when I came to Cossato. To leave me with little more than a foul aftertaste, a beard that stank of ale, and a familiar ache behind the eyes.

363

At the third farm I reached on the road to Biella, I was taken on as a hireling under-shepherd, a *cavalin* – which in the dialect of *Piemontèis* means 'colt'. (I would have said I was a *dogsbody*, if that position was not already filled by working dogs, who knew more of the business than I'd ever learn.)

As a boy at Haddertun I'd watched the manor shepherds with their flock. But now I saw that there was more to what they did than I supposed. Within a week I had been shown a dozen ways to make a fold, and how to use a pitching iron and carry hurdles on a pole. I learned how long to leave the tegs on kale for the first folding, when to chase them out before they blew, and when to bring them back. If I'd but had a penny for each gate I opened and each hurdle I set down and shackled to its neighbour, I'd have needed something a great deal larger than the leather bag I carried in my tunic to contain my earnings. But even as things stood, I was still paid a silver *sold*, the local version of a shilling, for every second week that I worked in the pens.

The other shepherds shared their knowledge gladly, treating me much as the olive pickers of Apulia had, with a strange blend of courtesy and curiosity – watching all my movements, ready to correct me when I went astray, and calling me *Sgnor*, although I'd told no one I was a knight. Well used to solitude by then, I gave them little cause for friendship. But still they taught me how to use a crook to catch a ewe, a knife to trim a hoof, a dirt-knocker to loosen mud from wool, a drenching horn for medication. I learned their given names; Nicolo, Elijo, Fiorello and Stefano – all the o's. On my first visit to the town I bought myself a sheepskin coat like theirs, with felted leggings held in place by thongs – and in the evenings at the farmstead, rubbed the sore bones in my broken foot and tried to learn their language.

The husbandman who hired us was not a man to show an interest in anything about his shepherds but their work. So long as we did all he asked of us for six days out of seven, he was satisfied. On Sundays, when the sheep were safely folded on their turnip-tops or kale, he undertook to mind the pens himself, while we were free to lie at ease within our huts. Or else to walk the half league to the Comun of Biella

– perched on a hill set like a footstool before the great rock settle of the alps, and fortified with walls and gates against attack.

To say the comun rode to fortune on the broad backs of its sheep, is but another way to prove the merchant's boast. It seemed to me when I first saw it, that every yard and building in the place which wasn't occupied with carding, spinning, weaving, fulling wool or dyeing it, must be employed in making clothing out of sheepskin. Or jointing what remained of the sheep's carcase. There were three hundred looms, so I was told, within the town walls of Biella. Its inns were mostly patronised by men who worked with sheep. And as I found, the three or four times that I sought relief there – its brothels followed the old practice of dipping rams before a shearing. As a matter of routine the *putane* washed all their clients in hot water. Shepherds, fullers and sheep-butchers – soaped and scrubbed without distinction, to save bed linen from the greasy taint they all called 'mutton-sweat'.

The snow had fallen and had melted, before I ever came to work amongst the folds. It fell again before the end of Lent, to spread the whiteness of the mountains all across the plain. Then froze, to clothe the sheep in icy mailcoats, and keep us busy thatching shelters for them or carrying fresh hay. By Lady Day, when sheep were dipped to cleanse their wool of winter grime, the last of the snow had thawed. And by the first Wednesday in Holy Week, the time by long tradition for sheep-shearing to begin, the spring was well advanced.

The sky was blue. The cuckoo called, and butterflies emerged to dance in sunlit spaces. The dense coppices which fringed the plain were hung with saffron catkins. Wildflowers carpeted the earth between their trunks; anemones and aconites and clumps of the yellow *pampocét* – the flower the monks call *prima rosa* and we call 'primerose'... Which prompts me to recall that other rose, the plant from Ashkelon. Because that too survived. All through the winter frosts I'd kept it wrapped in sheepswool in the hut I shared with Fiorello – and in the spring, to my surprise, it sprouted two green shoots which opened in the sun to four, then eight small glossy leaves with jagged edges.

The seasons turned, is what I'm saying. And we turned with them, following the cycles of the sheep.

The cycles of the seasons and the sheep. The circles of our lives... Is that the way we live and think? In loops and circles meeting and repeating? Is it what I am doing now?

I'm such a clod, so thoroughly confused still. I scarce know what I'm thinking. The thoughts keep looping, spinning through my mind like the repeating verses of a chanson. Chains of recollections and results – all linked together, but in ways that I can't seem to grasp. I never have been good at finding words to fit ideas. And the harder I attempt to pin them down the quicker they fly off into the night!

It was something I heard from a French native of Orléans that started it, while he and I were being dipped. Had I not heard that my King Richard had been captured on his way home overland from Outremer? – the Frenchman asked, as we sat back-to-back in the whores' soapy bath. Now prisoner of the German Emperor, the King of England had been accused of ordering the death of the Emperor's own kinsman, Marquess Conrad, whose birthplace of Montferrato was – as I must know – less than a day's ride from Biella.

Except I didn't know. How could I? No one had told me that the man who'd starved us in the camp at Toron, had first seen light of day here under these same mountains. And that coincidence came somehow more as a surprise to me than news of our King's capture and disgrace. I can't explain it now, I couldn't then. But I could not believe that it was all by chance – the Marquess Conrad's birth in this strange land of sheep – his death at Richard's hands – the way I came to hear it...

Circles, loops and circles deliberately inscribed. As if someone is drawing them with a fine pen? Or someone else is rambling on without a clear thought in his head – someone by name of Garon, catching water in a sieve!

I knew I wouldn't be much good at this, am so confused, need something solid to rely on. Could it be Fisty Flora?

NO GARON! No, just stick to facts. Go back to what you know and can recall – the Shearing Fair outside Biella.

Take it from there – the Wednesday after Easter, the day that you first met the Bérgé...

The Shearing Fair the Wednesday after Easter marked the beginning of Biella's pastoral year. The shearing gangs of ten or a dozen brawny fellows – some local men and others from as far abroad as Novara or Vercelli – pursued their trade from farm to farm, overseen by officers appointed by the consuj, who claimed one fleece in every six for use or resale by the comun.

In the clear light of early April, the gangs toiled manfully in yards spread with clean canvas. Or else in barns with doors flung open to admit the sun. On our farm Nicolo and I were set to work as catchers, lugging ewes into the holding pens where they'd be handy for the shearers. Elijo and Stefano wound the fleeces. A boy stood by to stamp each shaven ewe with a bold 'B' for Biella in cold tar. Then Fiorello daubed the sheep with two sticks dipped in dye, to show the colours of our flock. Red on the rump – green on the neck, where the shearers had left woolly tufts to make the creatures easier to catch.

It was thirsty work for all. Back-breaking for shearers, who were tasked with stripping up to forty animals a day, with little time for rest. We toiled all day from dawn to dusk, until the Vesper bell of the Biella Baptistery signalled for the last sheep to be shorn and marked – and dusty gullets to be sluiced with ale in barns and sheds across the plain.

The drinking continued steadily throughout the day they called *final*, when gangs foregathered at the Shearing Fair outside the town – to spend their earnings exercising upright at archery and quarter-staves. Or prone on mattresses with the putane, who knew the best ways to ease aching spines.

The fair itself was much like those I'd known in Sussex, at Offham and Glynde Meadows – with at its heart long rows of pens, where cattle, goats, cull ewes, yearling lambs and breeding rams awaited buyers. A circular turnspit rotated joints of pork. Open tents sold lakes and mountains of refreshments, and closed ones peddled female flesh.

Booths and stalls set up wherever there was space, sold hurdles, shears, sheep bells and crooks. And local wool – twilled, felted, woven, fulled and knitted.

I saw him first on my way to the ale tent with Fiorello and Stefano. By then I understood a little more of their rough dialect. So when Fiorello, pointing at a fellow on a bench, identified him as *Bérgé dal becce*, as *flockmaster* – the man entrusted by the consuj of Biella, to lead the transumanza of the comun's flocks up to their summer pastures in the mountains – I knew he was the fellow I had come to find. And thought him old, before I came to know him better than to think of age in his regard.

A man of theescore years or more, he sat with knees apart – a bulky individual in a sheepskin coat and low felt hat. Long-faced, big-nosed with weather-reddened skin. He held a shepherd's crook in either hand. One old and dull, the other gleaming new.

'So which is it to be?' he asked, as we approached him. 'Time, would you say, to let the old hook go?'

I looked behind, to see who he was talking to. Looked back and found that it was me!

'Or am I being tempted by appearance?' the Flockmaster said in a softly-spoken French that was so close to mine, the difference was unimportant.

'What is your view, young man? Can you see any sense in seeking novelty, when what we have in hand still suits the purpose?'

His deepset eyes as they met mine were pale, sea-coloured – and so penetrating that I felt he might have read the very thoughts inside my head (if there'd been any in it worth the reading). And it was only later that I asked myself if he was talking less of crooks in that first conversation, than of my own confusion.

I muttered at the time that I'd no skill to help him choose. But when he pointed out that an untried sheep-hook might fail in use up on the mountain slopes, I saw my chance to introduce myself, and beg that I might travel with the flocks on my way to the pass of San Bernard.

'You must of course.' The Bérgé dal becce gave a little grunt as he rose stiffly from the bench. 'I have already saved you a position up in front beside me, where we set the pace, Sir Garon.'

'You have?' I stared at him in blank astonishment – and then accusingly at my companions, who shrugged in unison.

'But I don't understand. How did you know my name? Or that I'd come to find you?'

The Bérgé's mouth, which had a downward turn, stretched out and up into a wider smile than John's – a smile as wide as Jos's, maybe wider – tightening the loose skin of his neck and lifting his whole face. A network of deep wrinkles wreathed his eyes and fanned across his cheeks. And when that happened – when that happens, when the Bérgé smiles – you have no choice but to smile back.

'It is my business to know who you are and see you on your way,' was all he told me then. 'Yours, my young friend, is to convince me that you're worth the effort.' And even now I can't think how he came to know so much about me.

Unless he heard it from the cloth merchant, and I was even drunker than I thought?

Unless he has the second sight?

Sheep have been driven up to the high pastures since ancient times, according to the Bérgé – long centuries before the Church fixed on a mid-May festival to mark Christ's own ascent (in His case higher still). These days it is the cows and pigs that leave Biella for the mountains on Ascension Day. And by that time we had already reached the snowline with the sheep.

A deluge of shorn backs and coloured tufts, of drumming hooves, bells, bleats and barking dogs – the spectacle of close on thirty thousand sheep embarking on their transumanza, is not a thing that anyone who's been a part of it, is ever likely to forget. It made the daily journeys of our flocks at Haddertun seem paltry, less than nothing, as they moved about the chalkhills.

I walked in front with the Flockmaster, as he'd promised. A risky place to be – when you consider what a stampede of thirty thousand animals, with four times that number of small pointed hooves, might do to a prone man – had not the multitude been broken into smaller flocks of fifteen hundred. Or at most two thousand sheep, with groups of milking goats dispersed between them. Each flock was led by a horned billy goat and a castrated wether, with harsh-toned clucket bells around their necks. On either flank were shepherds with their horses and their dogs, and larger hounds on leashes to keep the wolves at bay. The laden donkeys with the baggage mules, the carts that carried tents and hurdles, fold-nets and cheese presses, moved as they must in the flat centre of the road surrounded on all sides by sheep.

But that was only part of what it meant to join the transumanza.

'There's riches for you if you like,' the Bérgé said when we looked back across the sea of bleating heads. 'There's wool, meat, gut and sinew, leather, horn, hoof, bone and marrow to be got from every sheep, leaving aside the dung they make to sweeten soil. You could say each of them's more valuable in any sense that counts, than a king's golden crown. And we have more of them back there than you could ever count.'

The day we left the plain, it seemed to me that the whole population of the Biellese were there to cheer us on our way – the townsfolk of Biella and Cossato with their consuj and the soldiers from the garrison. Their priests to bless the enterprise. Workers from the fulling mills in aprons soaked with urine. Weavers and wool dyers, with their arms stained red or green or blue – woodsmen, stockmen, dairymaids with flowers in their hair. Bargees from the waterways. Cowherds blowing horns and guardsmen beating drums – and someone up on stilts with raucous children running circles round them. The noise deafening.

'Sheep don't like it, nor do dogs,' the Bérgé shouted through the din – holding out his crook-stick level with his shoulders, to signal the flock leaders to keep back.

'Old Barbon here could tell you.' He nodded at the sheepdog trotting at his side. 'Dog 'ud tell you that he hates their blessed racket – wants to round 'em up and pen them somewhere out of trouble.'

He reached down with his free hand to fondle Barbon's ears. 'So do I old feller, so do I.'

I noticed that he walked as I did with a slight halt to his step. A thing that neither of us mentioned to the other. Just then a shout of laughter from behind drew our attention to a pair of ewes, who'd run out from the flock to prove his point by stamping fiercely at a screeching child.

'These lowland folk have never learned to gentle livestock, an' never will – can't be taught and can't be driven. Can't even manage to walk far. Which you may say is just as well, for otherwise the beggars might come with us!'

The Bérgé made a sound I couldn't hear distinctly, but might have been a chuckle. 'You'll see, young man. Before we pass Tollegno, half of them will fall into the river, and the other half will have recalled a score of things they'd rather do than climb a mountain greased with sheep-shit.'

Which was what happened, more or less.

Further up the valley, where the road narrowed to less than fifteen paces between the surging river and a solid village wall, the flocks themselves became a torrent – bell-clenking, jostling for footspace, until they could spread again across the bottom in a surge of cobbled rumps and bleating heads. It was there we turned them to the higher pathway, jogging ahead to lead the way, while shepherds clicked and whistled to their dogs. And those who'd followed from Biella – the few who still remained – dropped back at last to watch us make the climb.

The sloping track, an ancient *senté*, took us around the outskirts of the village. Past fenced-in plots defended by men waving hats and women flapping aprons. Then upwards through the ash woods, to a view of snow-capped mountains sparkling against the wide blue sky.

I can't find the words to say what that sight meant to me when I stepped from the trees – except to say it seemed a place without restrictions. It took away my breath. Or what was left of it after the long climb from the river. The Bérgé pointed with his chin to where the track unspooled across the sunlit slopes, rebounding from one rise to another.

'Come. This is where it all begins,' he said.

CHAPTER FOUR

*Which brings me back to where I started in the mountains looking down,
from heaven as I've called it, on the story of my life.*

Or does it, Garon? Isn't it too soon still to complete the circle?

*I would have cut the story shorter long ago if I'd believed that it would
work. Now I'm almost there, not far to go. But if I don't continue with the
climb, and think through everything the Bérgé had to say along the way, it's
likely I could miss the point of this and end by drawing all the wrong
conclusions.*

Well then... We spent the first night of the transumanza at the highest
point to which the mule carts could be dragged – in a broad, grassy
basin caught between two ridges, where a shallow lake provided
drinking water for the thirsty beasts. That other flocks had rested there
in years gone by, was obvious from the pattern of stone walls which
crossed the valley floor. A low barn and two shepherds' huts, with tidy
stacks of firewood underneath their eaves, provided some rough
shelter. And a number of small rings of blackened stones, showed
where the hearths were set.

It took an hour or so for all the flocks to reach the place, and the
remainder of that day for gaps in walls to be made good and divisions
to be made with netting in the larger folds. One of the mule carts with
our flock was driven by a woman in a hooded cloak. I'd first seen her
talking to the Bérgé at Biella, and noticed her again each time I turned
to look behind me – whipping her mule up the steeper sections of the
senté and calling to the crofters at their orchard gates. But when the
Bérgé introduced her as his wife, it came as a surprise. I'm not sure why.
He'd given me no reason to believe him solitary.

A pretty, round-faced woman with a direct unflinching look and thick grey hair pulled back into a plait, she asked my name over her shoulder as she descended backwards from the cart – and then while she unstrapped its breeching, if I was fond of mutton stew?

'You will be when you've tasted it the way I cook it, lad,' she told my nodding head – and I found then, as I have found repeatedly through all the days and nights between that time and this, that there are few things as reassuring to a man as the motherly attention of a woman.

That first night in the mountains, in air thick with the sound and smell of sheep, the Bérgé and his wife and I sat stirring the red embers of the fire she'd lit. And as they burned to ash, we traded stories from each other's lives. (This story in my own case. But not all of it. Not that night, anyway.) Encouraged by a bowl of stew, and more than one mouthful of harsh wine from a goatskin flask, I told them about Haddertun, my parents and my father's words – and then of Lewes Fortress – and then, because I'd seen the way the woman looked at me when I described the rigours of my training, I told her what I'd never told before.

'I tried to smile when I was hurt, to cover up my pain,' I said, 'and if I sometimes missed my old nurse and my mother, and wept upon my pallet, I made sure that I did it quietly in the dark.'

And then the Bérgé's wife, whose name she told me was Léonie, confessed with a wry smile that as a child she had been warned a hundred times never to unsheath her father's knife. But that one day she disobeyed, and fumbling with the blade had cut her finger to the bone. Like me she'd cried alone, and bound the wound and hidden it from both her parents rather than admit to weakness. Or to disobedience. But when her mother found her kerchief soaked in blood, she took Léonie up into her lap to clean the cut and kiss her pain away.

'Remember, little one, that God forgives his children everything,' she'd said. 'And so do we. We guide your steps, but will not punish you for straying. It is for you to find the way by trial to your salvation.'

'You should know that her parents were of the Albigensian persuasion,' Léonie's husband put in quietly. 'Some people call it *The Good Faith* in this part of the world. It came originally from Albi in the

Languedoc, where they were taught that God is gentle, all forgiving – that killing men or animals is wrong. That everything we have should be shared equally between us, and that salvation will be universal. Whereas the Catholic Church, which sent you off on your croisade, believes in a merciless Creator whose word, you have been told, is sharper than the sharpest sword – and who will grant a place in Paradise to anyone who slaughters unbelievers for His sake.'

He pulled off his black felt hat to scratch his head. But before I could tell him that there was no God and never had been, he was giving me the reasons why he thought the same.

'It seems to me that a belief in God enthroned in Heaven is very much about our own delusive quest for immortality, a basic fear of dying.'

The Bérgé smiled into the darkness. 'In our arrogance and self-obsession, we judge ourselves too precious to be snuffed out like candles – and in seeking meanings for the things in life that hurt and puzzle us, we come up with a set of answers that defy our own intelligence – turn from an open road into a winding labyrinth of superstition and restriction. You could say that the faithful use the idea of an all-seeing god to frighten themselves into obedience, and then attempt to force its contradictory terms on all who disagree.'

I'd never heard a man speak so. As if such heresies could be discussed as easily as a change in the weather.

'But naturally there's nothing new about dissention,' he continued calmly. 'Not every sheep will follow the flock blindly, and I've no doubt that in Babylon and Egypt there were men who questioned the idea of gods and of religion as earnestly as you and I do.'

He put it all so much more clearly than I could have done, that I was glad I hadn't interrupted.

'You may be sure that there were Greeks who questioned the idea of a Zeus, and Jews of a Jehovah who bestrides the world like a colossus, but doesn't seem to have the first idea of how to benefit mankind. Or cure him of his futile rituals and appallingly obsequious forms of prayer.' The mane of disordered hair the Bérgé ruffled as he spoke was a pale sandy colour, streaked with white. Unusual for a Piemontese.

374

Or would be if he was one?

I've heard it said that hill men and shepherds are a breed apart. But who is this one, really? Where was he born and when? And how was it that the consuj and the farmers and the shepherds of Biella came to choose him in the first place as their *Bérgé dal Becce*?

But that they'd chosen well was obvious. The next day from early dawn 'til sunset, the Bérgé could be seen consulting with the shepherds, loading baggage beasts with nets and hurdles, scratching maps on slabs of rock – as first one flock and then the next, and sometimes two or three at once, climbed out of the green basin to the higher pastures he'd assigned to each. I followed him from fold to fold, helping where I could. I stood beside him, shading eyes against the sun to watch the plodding lines of sheep creep up the slopes – until, by mid-afternoon, the shepherds mounted and on foot, the barking dogs, the last signs of movement on the hillsides, all had disappeared. To leave in the stone holding pens, only the flock that we ourselves had brought up from Biella.

On the third day we began our own ascent. In addition to the Bérgé and his wife, there were six more of us to move our flock of eighteen hundred sheep, our goats, our horses and our baggage beasts. A stooped, grey-bearded fellow called Bartholomeo was mounted on one of the shaggy little ponies I'd seen around the farmsteads of the Biellese. Three younger men with dogs followed on foot. A cavalin of twelve or thirteen summers, a cheerful imp who answered to the name of Aubri, brought on the goats. I led a pair of laden mules and two grey donkeys roped in line. Léonie rode a second pony in the rear – while the Bérgé strode lopsidedly ahead to show the way across a bed of broken shale into the beechwood hangers on the slopes above – where suddenly the patter of a multitude of hooves on shifting stone were silenced, as the flock surged onto leafmould in the aisles between the trunks.

He stood waiting for me, broad hands folded one upon another over the curved headpiece of his crook, as I persuaded the last donkey in the train to clear the far side of the trees, and panted up to join him.

'Men call the mountains 'alps',' he said. 'But if you were to use that word in front of these old baas,' he nodded at to the streams of woolly backs and munching heads that were already fanning out across the slopes, grabbing greedy mouthfuls as they ran. 'They wouldn't think of alps as windy slopes and barren rock, not they. They'd think of something sweet to taste and tender underfoot – fresh air, fresh water and warm sunshine on the high roof of the world. The *alp* are not the mountains, but their *pastures* – an' the reason why sheep like to climb.'

He straightened up to sweep his crook-stick out across the landscape. 'Take a good look at our *alp*, boy, and find me one good reason why they wouldn't be the nearest thing to heaven any man or beast could dream of.'

As if I could have found one!

The mules and donkeys in their efforts to reach new grass, by then had dragged me past the Bérgé to a bluff that offered a clear view across the treetops to the nearest mountain peaks. Huge blocks of naked rock jutted like pillars through the trees. The faded plain so far away below appeared like something from another life and time. And what was real – the only things that seemed entirely real – were the great quilted fields of colour and abundance that lay all about us. Bright sunshine. Teeming insects. Spring flowers blossoming far later at this altitude than on the plain. Violets and primeroses, bluebells, globe-flowers, scented white narcissus, unfurling fronds of fern. A miser's fortune in gold-besant dandelions, jostling for space amongst the grass stems.

The air was clearer, brighter, fresher than anything I'd known. I saw the dog, Barbon, lift his black nose to savour it – and for myself felt like the cowherd in the fable, who scaled the highest beanstalk anyone had seen, to find himself above the clouds in an enchanted world where hens laid golden eggs, and vines grew silver leaves.

'Al-Jannah, same word for paradise and garden.' 'Alp, the nearest thing to heaven any man or beast could dream of.'

It was then I think, when I first found myself in paradise, that I decided not to press the Bérgé for directions to the mountain pass.

That evening and every evening since then, the shepherds have sent out the dogs to fetch the grazing sheep back to the temporary *cort* we make for them from netting, hurdles, deadwood from the forests –

anything that we can find to keep them safe from wolves. Those creatures hunt in darkness. So we and all the other flocks who've made the climb, light fires and keep them burning through the night.

I see them all about me winking in the darkness, hear the wolf packs howling their frustrations to the moon. We reinforce the cort each night, until the melting snow uncovers fresh green swathes of grass still higher on the slopes.

'This way of life is older than nations, older than their fields and furrows,' according to the Flockmaster. 'I sometimes think that mankind makes his greatest error,' I have heard him say, 'when he abandons herds and flocks to work the land instead, and build his squalid cities from its profit.'

Every second day the Bérgé mounts a pony or a donkey to ride out round the other flocks within his care and see how they are faring. Each morning when the sheep have been released, Léonie and Aubri milk the goats and separate the curds from whey, and hang out bags of soft white cheese to drip from the wooden tripods they set up in the grass. Then every night we sit and talk beside the fire. Léonie cooks. Bartholomeo plays a flute made from the hollow shinbone of a ram, and afterwards we roll ourselves in our warm sheepskin coats – the Bérgé and his wife apart from us yet very much together – to sleep the light sleep of the watchful shepherd.

With natural springs fed by the melting snow, we're never far from water. Where two streams meet or under falls, pools here and there have been contrived as drinking wallows for the sheep. It's not unusual to find shrines there to the Virgin Mary and the infant Jesus, crudely painted, with round peasant cheeks and haloes that look like yellow sunhats pushed back from their faces. And at one such place I happened to be kneeling with cupped hands to drink the icy water, when the Bérgé stooped to do the same.

'The image makes you angry, Garon?' he observed. 'Now why is that?'

'Why? Because I've seen what Christian soldiers do to mothers with small children, and watched vultures tearing at the flesh of someone who's still living!'

377

I had to raise my voice for him to hear above the tumbling of the water. 'Because I don't believe in any sort of god, that's why!' I shouted, snatching up a fern frond from the rocks that fringed the pool and stripping it of leaflets one by one. 'You don't believe in him either,' I added sullenly. 'You told me so yourself.'

'I think I said that I could see no sense in a belief in the overbearing grandfather-god that Jews and Christians call Jehovah and the Moslems know as Allah, and suggested their belief in him was mostly about a fear of death and personal obliteration.'

He sat down heavily beside me on a rock, stretched out one leg and rubbed the bent knee of the other as if to ease some pain. 'Although why death should concern them quite so much, I've never understood. We have no memory of life before our births when our minds were unformed. So why should anyone expect his brain with all its thoughts and images intact to go on functioning after his body dies? It makes no sense to wish for it, or fear to end as we began in darkness.'

He looked up from massaging his knee. 'In spite of which I do revere a force, a power, a kind of deity,' he said. 'And so do you, my friend.'

'Not me!' I tossed the naked fern stem back into the pool and watched it slowly turning in the current. 'No loving god could have allowed what I have seen, what I have done – and I'm no better than the rest. You've said yourself that there's no sense in believing in a god who's violent and uncaring.'

'Look here then at this painting, and tell me what you see.' He pointed at the figures in the shrine.

'I see a mother, with a son sent down to her by a cruel father who plans to have him whipped and crowned with thorns, and watch him die in agony nailed to a wooden cross.'

I noticed that the Bérgé's lips moved slightly as I spoke, as if my words were known to him already.

'You see a mother and a manchild. Forget the rest, it isn't represented here,' he said. 'This mother in this place stands for Creation, all of it. The child she holds is *you*, the human creature.'

He waited for the sense of it to sink into my brain. 'As a goddess she's been known as *Gaia* by the Greeks, *Uni* by the Tyrrhenians, *Dea*

Matrona by the Celts and Romans, *Mare* by the Piemontese. She's been worshipped in all those guises in this region, likely at this very shrine. She is *Natura*, the Eternal Mother, the womb that bears all living things. She orders sun and rain and fills us with the need to reproduce our kind. She is the force of life itself, within whose governance we all must live from the moment we draw in our first breath to the day that we breathe our last.'

He flung out a broad, short-fingered hand in an expansive gesture which embraced the moss and fern around the wallow, the flowering alp, the distant landscape of the valley.

'She is the earth and everything that it supports. In death we all return to her and from her comes new growth. She pre-dates cities, armies, kings, and yet survives them all. And who's to say (except a Christian or a Muslim or a Jew) that other creatures are not as deserving as we humans of all *Natura* has to offer?

'Men seek wonders beyond existence. But ask yourself what is more wonderful than life itself. We're born to live on earth, not up in heaven. We see the sky. We feel the warmth of sunlight on our skin – and it's ironical you must agree, that those who turn their eyes from it to contemplate a better world may miss the best of this one. We grow, we love, we wither and we die as flowers do, as every other living creature must, we simply cease. What's wrong with that?' he asked.

'Rain falls, grass grows, cows crop it an' men milk 'em.' John said. *"Tis what they're fashioned for I reckon, an' all must take what's sent.'*

The Bérgé dal becce rose to take a closer look at the flaking figures in their gabled shrine.

'Simple people need someone to represent all that, a mother they can speak to face to face. But how surprised you'd be, my anything-but-immaculate little Mary-Miriam, to see yourself enthroned and aureoled and venerated as *Mare-Madonna*,' he told the painted image in her halo-hat. 'A dusky little peasant girl, fifteen or sixteen at the most, much less concerned with mothering the world than how you're going to cope with your first baby!'

The Bérgé has a greater gift with words than any man I've met. Perhaps because he spends so many months of every year high in the mountains looking down, he sees the world of men long-sightedly and likes to speculate on all the whys and wherefores of their being.

'Abraham and Moses, King David and Muhammad, all minded sheep at some time in their lives,' he said another day at noontime, as we sat with Aubri and Léonie, eating salted mutton from the woman's store. 'We shepherds have a history as thinkers and as guides. It's why the Kings of Egypt and the bishops of the church hold shepherd's crooks, to show the people they've a true head on their shoulders.'

'Or else to warn them that flockmasters love nothing better than the sound of their own voices,' Léonie put in with a wink at Aubri, who gave a snort of laughter.

'Why wouldn't we, my dear?' her husband asked, 'when it's the instrument we have been given for the purpose? Although I think you do know there is something that I love more?'

He leant across to brush a cheese crumb from Léonie's smiling lips.

But if he likes to talk, the Bérgé's also a good listener. Through all the weeks I've spent with him, he's constantly encouraged me to tell him what I think and how I feel about the places I have seen, the people that I've met, and everything about my former life. In his company and in his mountain world I felt – I feel, as I once felt at Acre in the siege. Apart and separate from all that's gone before.

The rams we'd brought up with us from Biella were constantly at work through spring and early summer, tupping ewes for autumn lambing on the plain, and challenging their rivals for the right to do it. With hardly time for them between the fucking and the fighting, poor beasts, to snatch a living from the grass. They normally began by circling each other at close quarters.

'And will fight unless the challenger decides the other is too big or heavy for him,' the Bérgé explained when we came on a pair of them about the business. *Silly as a sheep*, the saying goes. But sheep know what they are about as well as you or I.'

'When Bishop Walter wanted me to fight at Joppa, I refused, and told him no one on this earth could make me do it.'

I spoke before I thought, which isn't too unusual, just as the rams completed their third circle of inspection, head to tail. 'I suppose it might have helped a bit that I was drunk,' I thought it fair to add, as the rams backed away from one another for a charge.

'And how did he react, His Grace the Bishop?'

'He said that as a soldier I'd no choice but to obey.'

CHOK! The bony skulls met with a sound like an axe chopping wood, which echoed through the mountains.

'But I wouldn't listen to him. Said I knew that I was trained to kill, but couldn't. Never would again.'

The rams backed off and charged again. And then again. With shorter runs each time but almost equal force. By then the heads of both were slippery with blood, which when they next met, deflected one beast down onto his knees and slid the other over him to land across his haunch.

But that was not the end of it. Like duellists who fought by *plaisance* rules, they gave each other space to rise. Then charged again.

CHOK! CHOK! CHOK! They butted heads, and fell and rose another dozen times or more. Before one of them showed simply that he'd had enough, and ambled off to leave the victor in possession of his ewes.

I realised while I watched them that the Bérgé was still speaking. '... wounds seldom serious, despite the blood,' I heard him say '...skulls hard as rock. They only fight each other long enough to show who's fittest to father the next crop of new lambs.'

He turned to look me in the face. 'D'ye see it's not the fighting that's important.'

'What then?'

'It is the reason *why* they fight. These fellows battle to create lives rather than destroy them. And if you think about it, the creation of our own kind is what we're all of us about.'

As we looked on, the winning ram lifted his bloody head and wrinkled his white nose to snuffle at the ewe whose scent had launched him into combat in the first place. But when he mounted her, she simply went on chewing calmly, staring absent-mindedly into the distance, as if the frantic pounding motion at her rear had nothing much to do with anything that mattered.

The sight was comical and made us laugh.

'Are we so different in the end? I think not.' The Bérgé answered his own question. 'If you'd lived with sheep as long as I have, and with dogs, and watched the marmoté sporting every summer since you were a boy, then you would see yourself as I do, Garon – not as a lord of creation, but as a child of nature with no greater claim than any other creature to the gift of life.'

'If you are spared to see more summers, will you eventually acquire a few more grains of sense do we suppose?' A cool voice intruding from another time. Sir Hugh's.

We came upon the *marmoté* four weeks later up near the melting snowline – fat little brindled people near the size of coneys. Once they'd recalled that sheep and shepherds posed no kind of threat, the creatures totally ignored us, biting off the mountain herbs beneath the very noses of the ewes and sitting up to nibble them with plump backs confidently turned. Their little dark-furred pups played heedlessly amongst the crocus flowers of the high alp – rolling, squeaking, chasing one another round the grazing sheep. Until a high-pitched whistle from an adult perched up on a cairn of stones, warned of a circling eagle. To send them scuttling for the safety of their burrows in the rocks.

'See to him, Barbon!' the Bérgé called out sharply to his dog, who stood with hackles raised and sent a volley of short barks into the sky. The sheep lifted their heads. The eagle gave his own thin cry, flapped languidly, rose higher, disappeared. The dog glanced at his master with his ginger eyebrows cocked. Then, seeing nothing more was needed, gave a silent yawn and padded back to roll onto his side against the Bérgé's rawhide boot.

'Takes dogs a longish time to learn what patience is. But not so long as men.'

The Flockmaster waited for his sheep to return to grazing and the marmoté to reappear, before continuing. 'So here's the recipe for alpine life,' he offered with a smile. 'A pinch or two of tolerance, a dash of danger for excitement, and a big measure of cooperation to bind the thing together. How different would you say their taste is to our own?'

'The difference is that they're unthinking creatures, and we are *men* with laws and understanding!'

I shocked the sheep with that. Shocked the marmoté, who shot back into their burrows. Shocked myself, to hear my own voice echo through the peaks – and even shocked old Barbon, who studied me from where he lay for signs of lunacy. Only the Bérgé seemed unconcerned.

'Ah yes, the curse and the dilemma of mankind, our *understanding*. I see you think of us as some kind of a hybrid – half beast and half immortal – man as a piece of work incapable of simple living, famed for his intellect and yet more restless and dissatisfied than any other creature. You think men have to understand life's deeper meanings to find their own way to achievement and success?'

'I thought I knew the way to find success. But I was wrong,' I said pathetically. 'You say that sheep and other animals know how to live as well as you or I. My problem is that I know only what I'm not, and what I haven't done – not what I am, or what I ought to do.'

The Bérgé exchanged a look with his old dog, which if I'd not known better, I would have have sworn was one of mutual pity. 'What you are is a young man with a deal of life ahead, who is no different to so many others in his need to question what he has been taught.'

'So do you think a man can change?'

'Not in his essential nature, but in the way he sees himself perhaps?'

'So tell me what I ought to do.'

'You've climbed these mountains for a reason. And since you ask, I'd recommend you make another climb through your own memories, your history if you like. Climb that long path, and *then* look back to see if you can't learn from your mistakes.'

'As a kind of test? Is that what you're suggesting?'

'Yes, if you will. But for your benefit, not mine.'

'You're telling me to think back through my life – rake through the ashes of my past mistakes?'

He smiled. 'The image is too sterile. What I'm inviting you to do is

383

to see your life another way. If you can, to hold your actions to the light, see how they have changed the way you feel – the way you are – the way you wish to be. See through them to your future.'

'*Every day muhibb, a page of story.*' That's how Khadija put it in her moonlit garden. '*Yesterday is flown, tomorrow Allah's is to order.*'

Uncannily the Bérgé's next words answered the unspoken thought. (*How could he do that? See inside me, read my thoughts?*)
     'No, *your* tomorrow, not Allah's, Garon,' he said quietly. 'This is *your* time, no one else's.'
     I felt his eyes on mine. 'Then in the morning you can tell us all that you've discovered,' he suggested.

So that night – last night. Was it really only last night? I did as I was bidden.
     After we had driven the last ewe into the cort we'd made two nights before. When all the fires were lit. When I had filled my belly with roast kid, and then made room for its digestion in a smelly squat behind a boulder on the fringes of the camp. When that was done, I left the Bérgé and Léonie and the others to their rest, and climbed up to the place I've chosen – this place on the higher slope. To sit in comfort with my back against a rock. My head above the clouds, the world beneath my feet – to watch the sunset stain the snow that clothes the highest peaks.
     I saw it only hours ago. That's how I can recall it so exactly. The breeze was cool and smelled of ice. The valley had become a sea of mist with pine trees spiking through it like the masts of ships, inviting me to walk where I could not. A single glowing cloud clung to the slope like a lost sheep. Until that too was lost in shadow.

The soft bell-music from the fold sings to the moon, brings out the stars. The sound of the sheep bells, the distant view of moon and stars. They lifted me from my high perch still higher to the heavens, attached to earth by nothing but a handspan. Out of time. Adrift from the world of men to which I must eventually return.

Sitting with my back against the rock, hands clasping knees. Imagining the shadowed plain beneath its pall of mist – imagining a chequerboard of fields and waterways – and wattle pens, filled in the place of sheep with the mistakes and triumphs of my life; the ghosts of everyone I've known who's lived and died.

Memories of past experience like saint's bones in a reliquary – seen looking back and looking down.

CHAPTER FIVE

Some things stand out as clear as day. Others fade completely, or possibly were never very vivid in the first place? I wish I could remember everything about my first meeting with Elise. But oddly it's the hardest thing to call to mind when I look back. Since then I've taxed my brain until it aches to find a memory that I can trust, and failed completely. The more I try the more it seems to slip away. Which isn't a good start for all of this.

As I look down from heaven on the story of my life and try to work out where it all went wrong, I think perhaps that I should start with what my father said when I was seven. Or come to it as quickly as I can.

Or should I start with guilt? Because when I look down on the world I used to share with her, to see myself as I was when I first met Elise – I am ashamed, no other word for it. I was so set on doing what I thought right. But where was judgement? Was it my fault I was such a self-regarding fool?

It takes an effort to remember what was in your mind when you have changed it since. But when I try to make some sense of what I was and how I acted, I see that I was fated from the cradle to become a soldier.

'You have to be the strongest man. D'ye hear me, Garon? The bravest and the best. It is expected of you even by the peasants.'

'But how?' my childish treble, 'How must I do it, Father?'

'We'll send you to the sergeantry at Lewes to be trained, my boy, that's how. A knight who isn't skilled in arms can count for nothing in this world, remember that. It is your destiny to fight.'

My father died soon afterwards, before he'd time to teach me any of his skills, before I'd time to know him. I only know that from that day his words rang in my memory like verses from a chanson: '*A knight who isn't skilled in arms can count for nothing in this world, remember that. It is your destiny to fight. You have to be the strongest man. Do you hear me, Garon. The bravest and the best. It is expected of you, even by the peasants.'*

Was I more real then in the body of that child than I am here and now? It hardly seems so from this distance and this height above the world, and yet I have to try to understand the difference... And yes, I see it now, the things that came to count with me when I'd put Haddertun behind me were the approval of my peers and my dead father.

Haddertun. Why wasn't it enough? Why couldn't I have understood that men do best in every way when they are left to work and bring some order to a limited existence? To make a gift to life of all they have to offer? I knew it later in Khadija's house and in the olive groves, have found it with the Bérgé. But back then at Haddertun contentment on so small a scale was not a thing I valued. Back then I was a fool!

Up here beyond the toils of man, I shake my head but cannot change my foolish past. Though what if I could change the tongue-tied bridegroom of that night to what I have become in this place here and now? Given all that's happened since and given one more chance, could I do better with Elise?

At no time is a man more totally a man, I truly now believe, than when he feels compelled to be joined to a woman.

All right, I mustn't wallow in all this. Not here. How can it help? It can't be what the Bérgé can have meant by learning from my past mistakes.

Where am I in their catalogue? I need to have it clear.

She said it took more courage to stand out against men's expectations than to prove myself a hero. But did I ever understand Elise, know her at all?

When I try to think of how I felt to see her, set-faced standing in the gateway, all I can feel is what I'm feeling now.

It's not as if her hands had been bound like Khadija's. She could have waved, *she* wasn't bound.

Why did they have to bind their hands?

We thought to be a part of that great enterprise, to make a gift to it of everything we had to offer, was all we wanted in the world. Our former lives all purposeless and petty.

Up here in Heaven I've become a god, poking at an anthill with a stick. Khadija told me once that she believed each mortal had their own star, which shone the moment they were born and darkened with their final breath. Maybe I saw her star one breathless night from the poop deck of the tarida? But if I did, it isn't in this sky.

Considering where this is taking me, I'm loathe to turn the page and see the next illumination. That's what I do. I dodge unpleasant truths. It's what I've always done but can no longer get away with.

Yet when I entered her and saw Khadija's eyes beneath me blacker than the blackest pool, and heard her moan, and felt the hunger of her mermaid's clasp. And when I dived and dived again with her into the tropic fathoms, then I remembered how Elise had been with me and how I'd been with her the second time we bedded, and understood the need in all of us to give as well as take.

'Muhibb, accept. There is a saying of my people: *If we could find a merchant for regrets, we must be wealthy all.* Death waits for us as Allah wills. We are as roses, we bloom then blow and fall in dust.'

It was another kind of way – another journey I suppose which from its start in Acre would lead me down into the very pit of hell, and out of it to take the steep path that's brought me to this place. I discovered beauty – in Acre, in myself and in Khadija. Discovered it and lost it.

Have I? Have I lost it?

When you come to love a place you take possession of it in a way, and it possesses you, becomes a part of who you are. Who lives there now, I wonder, in Khadija's house? Who tends her garden?

And what is love? Do joy and true affection have to reach a certain pitch before you call them by that name?

She said, 'Al-Qalb al'Ashiq Yawa,' and told me what it meant, 'A loving heart will find love where it may.' Was that too from her Qur'an? When I recall Khadija talking of incha-Allah with her hand upon my sleeve, I see three versions of myself – the Garon of the moment, gripping her and feeling fear. Another Garon, staring past her to a future that will hold the memory forever in his mind. And now a third – this Garon of the present high above the earth, groping through his memory to view the scene, and feel the fear, and live it all again.

I so much wanted to protect them, should have managed to protect them.

Why did they have to bind their hands?

I can't, I can't go on with this......

I've had a rest to set my thoughts in order. The Bérgé says that I must face it. He thinks I can, and I've agreed to try.

Oh God, if I could only lose my memory, halt time, or else jump clear from that day into this. Oh God, oh God, oh God! I'm sweating, panting – beseeching her God, my God, anyone's idea of God, to intervene and save them! But I must look the devil in the face and enter hell. I must remember how it feels to be among the damned!

They held us back until the tumbrels were unloaded...

It's said that when God seeks to punish you He grants you what you've prayed for. I prayed in the port of Tyre for victory and death to infidels, and I was punished. How I was punished! But not by God. Because it was as if a curtain had been wrenched aside to reveal an empty void. My faith was gone and with it everything that I believed in – and in its place a thought that terrified me. Because I knew that as a soldier primed to hate and trained to kill – knew then and know it now – I might myself have waded through the blood of men and women, even children. Because somewhere inside me, as I lay there with my knees beneath my chin, there crouched the monster that is man!

How long is it since then? Weeks pass these days without the nightmares. But they haven't left me even here amongst the stars. Their spirits haunt me and perhaps they always will...

I had drunk steadily through the three weeks we spent in the green groves which grew on three sides of the ruined port of Joppa. I knew as well as any man that alcohol was not the answer. But it helped to drown the questions. And when the Bishop's criers rode through the camp to summon us to join the force that was advancing on Jerusalem, it was the drink that helped me to deny them.

It was there that I first understood what made a villain of the king I'd worshipped for so long. What I had always seen in him was what I wished to be myself, a hero. But what I saw at Ashkelon was entirely the reverse. King Richard talked but wouldn't listen. King Richard looked, but couldn't see – had no idea of loyalties or commitments. Which meant he placed no value on the lives of others. Took all we offered him. Gave nothing in return.

Yet in the end was I much better? I who'd killed in Lewes and at sea, and on the River Belus and at Acre – and felt nothing at those times beyond a thrill of self-congratulation? A careless mummer with a real sword rather than a wooden one? Could I claim to be better than King Richard? It made me sick to realise I couldn't...

Behind my misery, I think I'd always known that I would have to find the strength from somewhere to continue, and I believe it was the way those peasants lived and worked that finally began to lift the weight of guilt from my bowed shoulders. Whatever tithes or duties they might owe their lord, it had to be the cycle of the seasons – the soil, the sun, the rain, the crops and animals they raised – which gave these folk the sense of fitness I had lost. Or was there more to it than that? Did I respond to them because I missed the same thing back in Sussex?

A pair of urchins we found catching frogs in a green pool behind a village press-mill, were like – so very like my John and I had been as boys in the old days of the mudsquelch; in happy days at Haddertun before I trained to be a soldier.

Me as a boy? Me as I could have been if I'd stayed home to live a simple, useful life? Could I have done that? Held the manor, without my time in Lewes Fortress. Without my military training?

You do know why you couldn't weep in front of John. Why tell yourself you don't? If his gift was the rose, yours was to leave without a scene.

John behind me. Khadija. Jos. Both dead. Elise at Haddertun. Had she forgotten me? Or, thinking I was dead, already planned to take another husband? A gentle man to suit her taste? Although I found it hard to form a picture of her face, I could recall the colour of her hair and feel the warmth and texture of her skin...

The cycles of the seasons and the sheep. The circles of our lives. Is that the way we live and think? In loops and circles meeting and repeating?

Is it what I am doing now?

I'm such a clod, so thoroughly confused still. I scarce know what I'm thinking. The thoughts keep looping, spinning through my mind like the repeating verses of a chanson. Chains of recollections and results – all linked together, but in ways that I can't seem to grasp. I never have been good at finding words to fit ideas. The harder I attempt to pin them down the quicker they fly off into the night.

Which brings me back to where I started in the mountains looking down, from heaven as I've called it, on the story of my life. Or does it, Garon? Isn't it too soon still to complete the circle?

'It is for you to find the way by trial,' Léonie said, 'to your salvation.'

'It seems to me that a belief in God enthroned in Heaven is very much about our own delusive quest for immortality, a basic fear of dying.' The Bérgé smiled into the darkness. 'In our arrogance and self-obsession, we judge ourselves too precious to be snuffed out like candles – and in seeking meanings for the things in life that hurt and puzzle us, we come up with a set of answers that defy our own intelligence.

'D'ye see it's not the fighting that's important but the reason for it. These fellows battle to create lives rather than destroy them, and the creation of our own kind is what we're all about. If you'd lived with sheep as long as I have, and with dogs, and watched the marmoté sporting every summer since you were a boy – then you would see yourself as I do, Garon. Not as a lord of creation, but as a child of nature with no greater claim than any other creature to the gift of life.'

'So do you think a man can change?'

'Not in his essential nature, but in the way he sees himself perhaps?'

Memories like saint's bones in a reliquary. Seen looking back and looking down...

'Every day muhibb, a page of story.' That's how Khadija put it in her moonlit garden, her words alive in me when so much else has died.

'Yesterday is flown,' she said.

'Tomorrow is, tomorrow is... TO-MORR-OW IS...'

Hullo, I must have dozed off. Christ, it's cold!

Ouch, bloody foot... (How long for hob's sake have I been asleep?) Light, it's getting light – sun's coming through...

Uh-ooh, a yawn – and another – and again... Oo-haa!

And... S-T-R-E-T-C-H!

That's better! Christ in heaven, so much better – like letting out a fart. Before the stink arrives.

And here it comes – the sun!

So beautiful. So round and red – a rising cock, a breaching child, reborn like me. Oh God... (Stop calling on a god you don't believe in, Garon!)

Well anyway, it's going to be a *wonderful new day!*

The sheep trotting up already from the open cort – grass drenched with dew...

In my mind's eye I can see Elise's face – I really can! The way she lifts her chin when she's about to smile.

'So tell us what you think you've learned up there between the airs from heaven and the blasts from hell?' He sounds almost impatient.

392

'But no need to tell us if you'd rather not.' Léonie hands me up the bowl. Warm goats' milk, smelling of warm goats.

'He may think that he has all the answers. But he hasn't, no one has.' She strokes my cold unshaven cheek. 'You have to find your own way through, as do we all.'

'So what d'ye think you've learned?' the Bérgé prompts a second time, as if she hadn't interrupted.

'I see the truth is simpler than I thought. I've learned that life's a gift we mustn't squander – that men and women need each other, and children need protection.'

I've hardly slept. I should be tired, exhausted by the hours of silent memories and raw emotions. But I'm speaking fast, collectedly, and with a kind of freedom I have never known – ideas, beliefs are founting through my mind and out of my wide-open mouth into the mountain air!

'I've learned that war's inglorious, that men construct religion out of fear. I learned in Acre that there is no sin in carnal love when it is granted freely – that there's as much to be gained from the giving as the taking – that virtue lies much less in winning than in tolerance and kindness.' (All that in one long panting breath!) 'I've come to understand that we are made to fight, but not for a white cross or an uncaring god. We should be striving rather to protect our own.'

'Indeed we should.' The Bérgé's sitting by his wife with one arm round her shoulders – but pats me with the other hand as if to slow me down.

'Which doesn't mean that you can't tolerate the beliefs of others without relinquishing your own. Or understand them when they're frightened and confused, as you have been yourself. The problems of the world derive, as we've agreed, much less from people claiming to be right, than from believing others to be wrong, and venturing to change their minds for them by force.'

'I know. I know that we are at our best when we are living simple, useful lives – and at our worst when acting blindly to impress false heroes. I see that I've been led too easily, have always been too eager

393

for other men's approval. I see I have been eager all my life to make a gift of what I am to anyone who'll take it. My father said it was my destiny to fight, to be the strongest and the best. He didn't say, but maybe... Maybe he meant to – that I should strive to be the best *I can be*, as a husband and Seigneur.'

'Bravo! Your father would be proud of you. I am.'

The Bérgé smiles. 'So would you say that in a night spent leafing through the pages of your past, you've seen the consequence of what you've done, and can begin to think of building something from the wreckage?'

Léonie, free of his embrace and on her feet now busy with her cheese curd, looks down to search my eyes, but doesn't speak.

'I know I have no one to blame for my misfortunes but myself, if that is what you mean? And no one to rely on but myself to set things right.'

'I only asked to hear you frame it in the words I knew you'd choose.' (Which is good as admitting he can read my mind.)

'You couldn't know what I would say, not word for word!' If I can hear the bluster in my voice, he must as well. 'I mean how could you know?'

'In the way I always have – and if you don't believe me, I will tell you what you're thinking at this moment, and what you have decided. You're thinking you need peace, security and love. You feel a need to *make* something, to see things grow. You need another chance to understand your wife and show her how you've changed. In other words you're ready to go home.'

He's rising to his own feet, holding out a hand to pull me onto mine.

'And before you say it, Garon – you're about to ask me if I can find time to show you the shortest way to the San Bernard pass – and I am about to tell you that I'm at your service. Unless Léonie has more food to cram into your belly, we'll leave this moment if you like.'

So now he's pointing down the valley to the road which rises through it to the the Hospice on the mountain pass. The tracks we've ridden have been steep and difficult in places, even for the asses' little hooves.

But now I am dismounting, to leave my donkey in his care – telling him I never could have found my way alone (and of course I don't just mean the way up to the pass). My thanks are heartfelt, and for once I can express them. Because that is something else they've given me, the Bérgé and Khadija, the words to say what's in my heart.

'Can lost time ever be made up?' My final question.

'It doesn't need to be. We make time as we live it.'

He hands me cheese and mutton from his satchel for the journey, rests a paternal hand a moment on my shoulder.

Our eyes meet and we smile.

I set my foot with care upon the narrow path, to climb back into the world I'd left behind me – knowing that the figure on the donkey will watch me until I'm out of sight.

I feel his pale sea-coloured gaze and turn to wave.

SORTILEGUS

'We make time as we live it.'

He treads the narrow path with care to climb back into the world he's left behind him. He won't make a slip, not now, and knows I'll watch until he's out of sight. He feels my eyes on him. I let him turn to wave – as once he waved at poor Elise, before I made him ride away from Haddertun and everything he knew.

The colour's fading from the mountains. From Garon's viewpoint my mounted figure gradually grows smaller, sinks into shadow.

Alone, I stare, no longer at the alpine landscape or the Valle d'Aosta, but at the final sentence on this screen. My donkey creaks – becomes a donkey-coloured swivel chair. Which means I've lost it altogether, damn it!

Where's my coffee cup?

Oh WHAT?

Now surely somewhere in that last chapter, or in the one before, you started to see through my nameless Bérgé and his suspicious take on life? (Including more than one illicit misquote from Shakespeare, incidentally, who wasn't to be born for another 370 years).

Surely you suspected that the Bérgé has a name, and that it's printed underneath the title of this book?

If on the other hand you caught me cheating with my possibly-too-modern Flockmaster, but overlooked the fact to let yourself read on, you may be cross with me for breaking cover, playing games?

But do be fair. You know as well as I do that novels by their very nature involve pretence on both sides of their covers – and you play games as well, you know you do. Can you say honestly, with hand on heart, that you have never skipped or skimmed, or dipped, or jumped ahead in books to see what's happening a little further on? Or worse, sneaked in from the back cover for a quick peek at the ending? You've dog-eared me, or slipped in a marker when you have read enough. Or plonked me face-down on the bedside table. Or fallen fast asleep with me across your face (it happens)! You may have left me on the train? Or, if you've read me on some kind of ebook reader, tried to change my font size, make me bigger? Shown me to your friends?

So tell me, while I give my reading specs a wipe, why I shouldn't be allowed a little break myself after the hard slog of writing all those sheep and shepherds up into the alps? It's not as though you haven't heard me speak directly to you elsewhere in the novel. I've used my own voice from the start – in the PROLOGUS and the Coronation chapter, and in every other passage representing 'history' as I see it. I've even asked you for a judgement on King Richard in the matter of Marquess Conrad's assassination.

Nor am I by any means the first author to engage his readers in this kind of dialogue. John Fowles did it in *The French Lieutenant's Woman* – and so of course did an earlier Victorian generation of 'dear reader' novelists. Jane Eyre steps from the pages (or if you must, from the screen of an e-reader) hand in hand with Charlotte Brontë. And not just once, but continually until the final famous: '*READER, I married him,*' with *READER* in capitals.

In any case, who sets the rules? The reader or the writer? And who's to say what's real or isn't once you have begun to read?

But why at this point, *SORTILEGUS?*

Well, a *sortilegus* in the Latin is a seer, a kind of clairvoyant who can, as Garon has discovered, read others' minds and tell their fortunes. In which capacity (if you'll bear with me for just a little longer?) I have a point to make about my characters before we put them through their final paces. Which is that they've the same capacity as we have, you and I, for learning from experience – that I'm convinced twelfth century people acted and reacted much as we do; could be as cynical as you and me, as cheerful or as pessimistic. Don't ask me to agree with academics versed in the writings of cloistered monks, who use such phrases as *'the medieval mind'* to describe unfeeling patterns of behaviour. Because in saying that, they sweep aside the gentle and forgiving beliefs of the Albigensian pacifists of medieval Aragon and Catalonia, Gascony, the Languedoc and Piemonte (as did the Catholics in their inquisitions), and they ignore the freedoms exercised within the medieval city states and communes of maritime and subalpine Italy, Dalmatia, Flanders and the Rhineland.

It's frankly sickening to hear military historians describe atrocities in terms of 'medieval mind-set'. As if that phrase provides some kind of an excuse. As if all medieval Christians were programmed to forget the things their Founder had to say of tolerance and forgiveness.

Put it another way. Would you call Hitler *'medieval'*? Or Stalin? Or Amin, Pol Pot, Saddam, Mugabe or Gaddafi – or any other modern tyrant? Or our own obtusely genocidal British High Command in the Armageddon of the First World War, who counted casualties like cricket scores with three or four noughts added – who sent nine hundred thousand young men to their deaths in Flanders and the Middle East, rather than negotiate for peace when opportunities presented? Were they all *'medieval'*?

I'm sorry but I don't believe you need a modern education to understand what kindness is, or love, or loyalty, or forgiveness. I see those as inherent qualities – not necessarily Christian, or even human ones – which can survive all periods and faiths. Just as, unfortunately, those other natural traits of thoughtless imitation, greed, intolerance, blind fear and the reactive violence it can lead to, are resistant to all efforts to expunge them.

In many things we're individual, in much else the same. Ask

anyone who's made a study of wolf packs, bonobos (or alpine marmots, for that matter), and I think they'll tell you that without the benefits of education or religion, those animals have all developed disciplines, moralities to help them to survive. Have meerkats changed essentially in their behaviour since the twelfth century? Has *Homo sapiens*? I don't think so.

'We can never fully understand the medieval mind. We would do well to hesitate before we blame the men of a different and in so many ways a better age.'

That is a quote *verbatim* from King Richard's admiring biographer of 1933 in defence of that medieval king's decision to slaughter three thousand bound and utterly defenceless men, women and small children on the Plain of Acre. Another more recent writer uses Latin, *in tempore gwerrae: in time of war* to excuse the inexcusable. A third attempts to let King Richard off the hook by pointing out that in his time the concept of *war criminals* had yet to be invented (and what a cop-out that is!).

So much for modern writers. His own contemporary, the French Bishop of Beauvais who laid the death of Conrad at King Richard's door, described him as: *'a man of singular ferocity, of harsh and repulsive manners, subtle in treachery and most cunning in dissimulation.'*

But I digress – and more about my *bête noire*, Richard, in the EPILOGUS at the end. Let's just say here that his chief role so far as this book is concerned, has been to help define its actual hero, Garon. So what I'm saying by extension, and why I've interrupted both of us to say it, is that, even as a *'medieval'* character, my Garon is as capable of reformation as any modern man – although I will agree it might have taken him a little longer without the Bérgé's intervention. And if you think of him as nothing more than a figment of my imagination, I have to tell you that from where I'm sitting at my desk, his character is actually more real to me than yours, the readers'.

Poor Garon, cast from the beginning as a follower, an imitator, too little a free-thinker. Poor faulted hero, induced by me to look back on his life through one long summer night high in the alps (which – sorry, yes I tried to trick you into seeing as some kind of a celestial perch beyond the grave). Poor pilgrim, forced through every physical and mental trial I could devise for him – including what we might now term post-traumatic stress, and a disquieting sense that he was being scripted – to arrive at last back in the present in a more hopeful state of mind.

Which rather begs the question of whether I have left enough time – in what? Three chapters? Four at most, to bring things for my hero to a reasonable conclusion.

And what would you call reasonable? Should I let Garon triumph in the end, like David Copperfield, Jane Eyre or Lucky Jim? Does real life ever work that way? Is *'happy ever after'* no more than a traditional convention? Or do I owe it after all to you, dear reader, considering the time you've put into this book, to do my best at very least to tie up the loose ends?

And then, what of Elise? It's been a while, too long perhaps, since she reported on her latest brush with that archetypal, almost mandatory, black villain of romantic fiction – Sir Hugh de Bernay. Where would Elise be now? In bed at Haddertun? (I think I've made it clear that she's in bed there at some point of her narrative.) But where will we find our heroine if we fast-forward six months, to the spring following her husband's shepherding adventure in the high alps? At Lewes still? Is that where Garon will discover her at the end of his long journey home? (IF he gets home?) She can't be under the protection of Earl Hamelin, because the records tell us he was in Canterbury that March, assisting with the celebrations for King Richard's long delayed return to England.

But maybe Countess Isabel is still in Lewes? If she is, it's more than it likely that we'll find Elise, with little Hamkin and her faithful

Hodierne, somewhere in My Lady's household where they'll be safe from Hugh.

Elise has changed as well of course, a great deal since the early chapters...

But look, I'm sure you've had enough of all this introspection. So if you're with me still, and haven't thrown the book or ebook reader at a wall – shall we get on?

It's a little tricky, this next bit. But if the brain's in gear, I think that I might manage half a page before it's time for lunch.

So... a last swig of tepid coffee from my favourite mug (it's chipped, but I still like its sturdy shape), a last look through the window of my office, across our own fields to the blue line of the Sussex downs (with somewhere underneath them, incidentally, the prototype for Haddertun, a little less than four miles distant as the swallow flies from where I'm sitting now).

Then back to my old steam-driven Dell Computer, and to Elise.

And okay let's say she *is* in Lewes, in a shared bedchamber somewhere in the fortress.

Let's say she's just received a summons to attend the Countess in her solar...

THE WHITE CROSS, **BOOK FOUR**

The chapter heading font is Trajan Pro Bold – until we get down to the text in *Chaparral Pro Italic*.

Centre for the chapter, arrow down ▾

Left click on Century Gothic 11, then up to Trajan Pro Bold size 14...

and on to CHAPTER SIX

'My Lady, you are bidden to attend the Countess Isabel, and if you please to bring the child.'

It was the message I'd awaited, delivered by the page-boy, Thomas, from the door of our women's chamber in the fortress.

That day, I'm thinking of THAT day! How long ago? Six weeks or seven – it doesn't seem that long – and, Holy Mary, how can so much happen in a single day!

He hasn't woken, isn't ready for his feed, may even hold out long enough for me to think through everything that happened on that day, and all that followed.

My feather bed's so comfortable, so warm beneath the covers…

'It's getting cold outside,' young Thomas offered on his own account. 'I think Ham better wear his woollen gown.'

A child himself of seven summers at the most, he'd shown an interest in my little Hamkin from the first. On Sundays and on evenings when the Countess freed him, he was ever in our chamber, to see how we fed and dressed our little boy. To play with him, and try to make him laugh.

'Tommie!' As soon as he clapped eyes on Thomas, Hamkin dropped his leather skittle ball and wriggled round to face his friend – his soft cheeks creasing into dimples, his fat little arms held out for an embrace.

'Good morning!' he shouted happily (the two words that Ham loved best and used at any time of day) – struggling to pull himself upright on Thomas's silk tabard and hug him round his spindly knees.

'Now Master Tommie, don't ye try to lift 'im now 'e's grown so big.' Hod flapped about them like an old grey goose. 'Jest bring 'im 'ere then, there's the boy, for 'im to 'ave 'is breeks changed.'

'There won't be time, you'll have to come!' The little page was bursting with excitement. 'Sir Hugh of Bernay's with My Lady, and you know she can't be made to wait.'

I carried him myself down to the inner bailey, across the empty court and past the kitchens to the banquet hall – with Thomas trotting at my heels and Hod, who had refused to be excluded, bringing up the rear. The sun lit the white blossoms of a thorn tree growing hard against the bailey wall. But I felt nothing of the hope it should have brought me, knowing what I had to face.

'Donkey!' Hamkin pointed to the stags' heads high above him in the empty hall, when I halted to shift his weight. But although Hod offered to relieve me of it, nothing would persuade me to hand him over. Not then or on the stairway to My Lady's solar – nor ever in the future!

I hadn't seen the villain since we passed through Meresfeld back in June. But the Countess had informed me of his visit to the fortress three weeks later, to pay his dues on both the manors – and to petition for her judgement in a case against me. My claim of rape, he said, must prove our carnal knowledge of each other – and then (the brazen-faced presumption of the man!), he'd put it to My Lady that since all could see I was uninjured, my right to redress for a physical assault could be no stronger than his right to claim the boy as his own son. He even had the face to offer marriage, for pity's sake, as soon as Garon's death could be established. As if he would be doing me a favour by raping me as often as he chose! And as if that wasn't bad enough, instead of dismissing the black devil out of hand, the Countess told him it was not for her but for My Lord of Warenne to judge the case. She held that while the Earl was off abroad collecting funds to free the King, Sir Hugh would have to bide his time.

'But My Lady, don't you see that you've encouraged him to think he has a case?' I blurted when she told me what had passed – and earned myself a sharp rebuke for speaking out of turn.

'The man is doing all we could expect of him.' My Lady's tone was cutting. 'He oversees your husband's manor in his absence, and has moreover paid the quarter ransom dues on both demesnes. Sir Hugh *informs us that he's willing in addition to repay Sir Garon's croisade loan when it falls due at Michaelmas, and in the meantime offers you a home and status as his wife.'*

'But he raped me and abused me, and now intends to steal my child!' I wailed.

'Are you disputing that the boy is his?'

What could I do but shake my head. 'Well then. I've told Sir Hugh that until My Lord's at liberty to pass his judgement, he is forbidden to attempt to see you or the boy. For which security I would expect you to be grateful?'

My cue to curtsy. To thank My Lady humbly for her favour, and then remove my person and my problem from her presence.

But if we had been free of Hugh's attentions for the eight months that passed since then, I knew why he'd come now. The Earl had not returned to Lewes in the autumn or in winter, but had travelled with the old Queen into Germany instead, to pay the Emperor the ransom he demanded for the King's release. In Lent the Countess came south again to Lewes – only to hear that Eléonore and Richard, with the Earl in train, were already on their way back home to England.

I heard the rest on a visit to the Jews' house with my little boy, to demonstrate to his admirers Hamkin's newfound skill of walking, holding hands.

'On Saturday your King and Queen made landfall, Lady, at the port of Sandwich,' I was told by Jacob, who always had the latest news. 'Next week they come to London, where My Lady of Warenne will join them for the King's crown-wearing at Westminster.'

As soon as Jacob said it, I was as sure as if he'd written it for me on parchment that Sir Hugh would seize his chance before My Lady left the fortress to state his claim a second time.

But this time I was ready for him!

A pleasant scent of woodsmoke came to meet us through the solar door. The Countess in her chair, ringed by the usual group of ladies and attendants sat but a few feet from the brazier. A shaft of sunlight from an upper casement glittered on the pikes and hauberks of her standing guards. More people, vassals, members of the household, sat in the shadows of the shuttered window seat, where... How long ago now was it? Four years? Five – when I'd sat up in the window to see Sir Hugh ride in across the bailey . Dressed like Satan, all in red!

I took a breath and held it as I curtsied to the chair, a little awkwardly, with Hamkin kicking at my knees. The torch-flames wavered when they closed the door behind us, throwing light onto the man who stood before the Countess, cap in hand. Again he was dressed in a single colour. A wolf in fox's clothing, tawny brown this time from head to foot.

All faces turned towards us as we entered.

'So here we have the girl and child in question.' My Lady of Warenne surveyed us with composure.

'My son,' Sir Hugh said levelly, devouring Hamkin with his eyes.

'Which is the first point that we need to clarify. Lady Elise, will you state clearly before this company whether the child you hold was sired by Sir Hugh de Bernay here, as he asserts? Or by another?' Countess Isabel commanded.

'The child is mine, not his. He forced me to the act illegally and therefore has no claim.' I was holding Ham too tightly and he began to whimper, struggling to be free.

'By claiming that he forced you, you are in other words confirming his paternity.'

'Which prompts the offer I've already made to make my amends by offering the child protection,' Sir Hugh concluded.

I turned to hand the wriggling Hamkin back to Hod, while Thomas slipped away to join the servitors behind My Lady's chair. The two boys grinned at one another. From where he stood between the guards, the pageboy moved the fingers of one hand in a tight little wave.

'Tommie!' Hamkin cried out through the silence, gurgling with laughter. Hod tutted at him and the Countess frowned. But I was ready, only waiting for the moment.

'Now that we can assume the lady to be widowed, I will repeat my offer to legitimise our union with a bond of marriage.' A bright edge of impatience to Hugh's voice that he could not conceal.

'Without clear proof of Sir Garon's death, there could be no question of a marriage. Nor would I willingly allow the child to leave our care without a judgement from My Lord.'

The Countess shifted to rest her elbows on the arms of her carved chair. 'But Sir Hugh, I have to tell you that this visit is most opportune.' A strange expression crossed her face which it was hard to read. 'There is a reason why I have allowed you to repeat your claim, Sir, at this time, which is...'

'I wish to speak and I have a right to do so!' I simply couldn't wait for her to finish, not another moment!

'I call on heaven and all here to witness that this man's impugned my honour, slighted and abused me.' My voice shook but I had to get it out, the idea I had fixed in mind since Lady Isabel herself convinced me that there was no other way. 'In sight of all, I challenge Sir Hugh de Bernay to combat with my champion, to prove the justice of my claim for reparation!'

My Lady's eyebrows disappeared into her wimple.

'And who have you in mind, ma chère, to champion your cause?' Sir Hugh was quick to fill the silence. 'Some young contender in the garrison who's pining for your favour? A youthful wizard with a sword and lance who's spoiling for a fight?'

I had my mouth already open to reply. But he'd described Sir Berenger, the young brute I'd picked to challenge him, so pretty well entirely to the life – that just to answer, 'Yes' seemed far too lame.

'If the lady seeks a champion, I am that man!'

I knew the voice – but not, in that first moment of surprise, the face. The beard had gone. His jaw looked narrower with loss of weight, the big-boned frame more angular. Something in the almost casual way he stepped out from the shadows by the window made him seem older, more assured.

Then he was turning back to face me, and
with a sudden, shocking jolt...

Oh dear God in heaven!
I KNEW HIM!

406

We stand like players in a mummers' pantomime, each with our role to play. I step out into the silence to speak my lines.

'If the lady seeks a champion, I am that man.'

She stands stock still, mouth open, fists pressed into her skirts. If she had heard the Last Trump sound, she couldn't have looked more surprised.

But she's smaller than I thought, and plumper in her plain grey gown, has netted her long hair into a caul low on her neck, which suits her well. The sight of her is almost more than I can bear. And how could I have ever failed to understand Elise, with everything about her so obviously expressed? From the moment she came through the door, the stubborn lift of chin, the way she grasped the squirming child, the pitiful expression in her eyes – all spoke to me directly of her pain, her fear, the strength of her determination.

Another thing Khadija said: *'Be sure then when you meet that thou wilt bring her joy.'*

But not this time at this first meeting, at another.

My part is written for this meeting and I must perform it. 'Who better to restore her honour, than the man who risked it in the first place – the man who left her undefended?'

I jab a finger at my own hard chest. 'I am the man who was her husband before the Kings' Croisade; and would be again if she will have me.'

She's closed her mouth. Her eyes are sparkling with tears. Behind her Hodierne's smiling broadly – the child's face the very image of his father's, but for blond curls in place of Hugh's dark pelt.

'Behold the warrior returns and with his head attached.'

He almost manages to seem amused, his right hand resting on his left as if relaxed. Yet rigid – everything about him rigid, with two bright spots of colour on his cheekbones.

'With peace broken out in Outremer, it would appear our prancing knight's in want of a new quest,' he's saying. 'The poor boy evidently needs someone else to kill.

'We've missed you, Garon,' he adds cynically, 'if only for the entertainment.'

'Enough!' The Countess turns to face my wife. 'You might ask, Lady, and with justice, why you were not informed of Sir Garon's presence earlier. But I fear we had no time.'

For one so stately she sounds almost apologetic. 'The one man had hardly crossed our threshold before the other was admitted at the gate.'

She drops something a page has brought her, into the mouth of the small creature on her lap. 'I thought it only fair before his presence was revealed, to let your husband hear all that Sir Hugh had to relate, and witness your reaction.'

'I understand, My Lady.'

She makes a second curtsey to the chair. But the question in her eyes is not for Countess Isabel, it is for me.

'Now having heard us both, it would appear my husband's willing to defend my cause in person?'

With all ears in the chamber flapping, all that is needed from me is a single word.

'YES.' I have agreed.

'Sir Garon's loyalty does him credit, but hardly solves the problem. These days judicial combats are outmoded and discouraged both by Church and State, and rightly so,' the Lady Isabel continues smoothly. 'We settle our disputes by means of evidence and judgement, not by brute force; and even if My Lord might be persuaded to consider combat as a remedy, he could not apply it to the forcing of a married woman, which is not held to be a criminal offence.'

'Then can I ask, My Lady, what offences to a married woman may be decided by trial of arms, if such an action were to be allowed?'

'Arson, theft or murder,' the Countess of Warenne recites.

'A man is a criminal, in other words, if he should steal a married woman's necklace. But not when he throws her on her back and rapes her? In such a case she is no more entitled to redress than if she were a common whore?'

The dialogue is public, and all await My Lady's next pronouncement. Elise and Hodierne, the tirewomen, the maids and nursemaids who attend the Countess every day – all the women have an interest.

'I did not make the law, and I do not apply it. What's more, in Lent I make a practice of avoiding any violent sport that sets a dog against a bull or bear, much less a man against a man.'

My Lady leaves a pause. But when she speaks again it's in a musing tone of voice while she adjusts a ribbon round a lapdog's scrawny neck. 'On the other hand, what happens down there in the tiltyard can hardly be of my concern. If men decide to tilt against each other, or make a trial of skill and stamina on foot with quarterstaves and shields, as they do daily in their practice, I see no reason why I'd have to be involved.'

'Not even if they fought in earnest,' Elise enquires, 'with short-swords for example?'

'The soldiers in the outer ward choose their own weapons, make their own rules for encounters,' the Countess tells her little dog.

'In a judicial combat, it is the offended knight who makes the choice – and that calls to mind the choice you have yourself to make, Lady.' She's speaking now directly to Elise.

'I leave for Rochester as soon as we have broken fast tomorrow, to join My Lord the Earl for the King's progress into London. Which gives you until nightfall to decide whether you and your child will travel with my household in the morning, or leave the fortress under the protection of one or other of the gentlemen who stand before us.

'It is your choice,' My Lady Isabel concludes. 'By my calculation you have approximately seven hours in which to make it.'

The Countess stonily forbade him to escort us to our chamber. But Garon came within the hour – and after I'd endured a suffocating embrace which all but crushed my bones, and he'd saluted Hod and tried to tempt out Hamkin from behind her skirts – we stood apart like wary strangers. To talk at first of everything except what mattered most.

Or rather he talked and I listened.

He didn't fidget as he used to, or avoid my gaze, but told me frankly that the Croisade had proved a huge mistake for him and everyone who'd gone. He said that Saracens are far less savages than we are – that we'd dealt monstrously with them in ways he'd not repeat. He told me how poor Joscelin had died, and Alberic and Bertram, and where he'd left John Hideman on the journey home. He claimed the years we'd been apart, the time he'd spent up in the mountains with the shepherds and their flocks, had made him question everything that he believed. He said that he'd been eager to convince me of the ways in which his life and mine could be improved, but was delayed from reaching me by sickness on his way through Burgundy – then by deep snow, and finally by storms in Normandie which hindered his sea crossing.

And he certainly HAD changed! That's what I thought while he talked on and on about himself and his ideas. Then, after I had offered up a silent prayer for God to sharpen them a bit, and steered the conversation back to what Sir Hugh had done, and told him how I'd fled from Haddertun to the old moneylender's house and later to the fortress – I was floored, totally, by Garon's calm reaction!

The hasty young man I had married would have railed and shouted at the insult, paced about and knocked things over, cursed Sir Hugh and searched and failed to find the words to say how much he hated and despised him. But what did this new Garon, do when I had finished with my tale of woe? He told me that he UNDERSTOOD (as if he, or any man, could ever understand what women have to go through!). He said he'd heard the story first at Haddertun from Kempe, and again that morning from the Countess – and then went on to tell me to my face, that he believed all men to be capable of carnal violence. Even he himself!

'You cannot have forgotten, Lady, that I forced you on the night before I left,' he said. 'And much as I'm ashamed to own it, would willingly have forced another woman when we captured Acre, if she'd not submitted first.'

I had decided while I waited for him in our chamber, to beg my husband's pardon for appearing to parade my shame by keeping Hamkin with me. But when he stood before me and confessed to understanding carnal violence, I stared at him in utter disbelief!

Of course I'd known that he was bound to lie with other women over there – absolutely bound to. That hadn't shocked me, not at all. What shocked me was that he could dare suggest – or even think – that there could ever be in any circumstance a possible excuse for rape!

410

'How can you stand there and defend a man who has abused us both?'

'I'm not defending him, that isn't what I said.'

'You should be in a stamping rage and grateful for the chance to fight!' She's suddenly ablaze herself.

'I'm pledged to fight, you heard me say so – have just now come from seeing that the tiltyard's cleared and sanded.' (She hasn't said how glad she is to have me back, hasn't kissed me, hasn't touched me since our first embrace.)

I reach out to unfist her hands and take them in my own. 'We've found a pair of bucklers that will suit. They're sharpening the swords, and in a while I'm going down to practice for the bout.' (It's what she wants to hear.)

'But you must know there is no anger in me. I have come home to give, not to destroy.' (It's what I need to tell her.)

'I am fighting Hugh, not for revenge and not because I think one act of violence has to be matched with another. I'm fighting him to prove the justice of your case, to show the world the child is yours, not his. And if I win, I'll win the means for us to live in peace.'

I seek her eyes and hold them steadily. 'If you are sure that's what you want?'

'How can you ask? Of course I'm sure!' She snatches back her hands.

'But are YOU sure, Sir? That's the question here. From all you've said, it's clear to me that you have no idea of how I've suffered, or of how fearful I've been of letting Hamelin fall into that man's power.'

She steps back impatiently with hands on hips to glare at me for all she's worth. 'You tell me that you have no anger in you. But HE has, he's full of it. If you can't match his anger you will lose, that's all there is to it. Sir Hugh will win!'

'Which sounds like something I'd have said four years ago.'

'Well if you listen carefully, you'll hear me say it twice. If you can't find the fire, the heat, whatever you men have to feel to work yourselves into a killing rage, then you are going to lose. And that won't do, because you may as well know that unless you finish it – unless you KILL that man – there'll be no peace for me, or you, or Hamelin or any of us ever! We never can feel safe again until he's dead!'

411

She steps toward me, holds her right hand up for me to see.

'I mean it, Garon – if this is going to be the only way that I can strike the spark to give you what you need to fight...

Her arm swings back, right back. I see what's coming and the force of it.

'*THERE THEN!*'' Elise's stinging palm lands square across my mouth.

CHAPTER SEVEN

The pain surprised me. A spark of indignation flares in me and dies. The ring she wears has left an angry mark, but nothing more. The blow expressed her anger, but it cannot kindle mine.

'I will not fight,' I told the Bishop.

Now I must, and to the death because Elise demands it. She is the plaintiff and the choice is hers, not mine. Sir Hugh has been informed the bout is to be *à la outrance*. He accepts. By nightfall one of us must die.

He's out there on the sand already, sparring with some fortress knight who is himself adept. All swordsmen worthy of the name must master early in their training the art of short-sword and buckler combat. I learned the steps, the many uses of a shield, the reflexes required. So did Hugh – and from the way he's moving, lunging and recoiling, stepping wide, it's clear that he's retained the skill. I can't tell yet if I have.

In a judicial bout, God is supposed to 'take the right'. To guide the victor's hand and prove the virtue of his cause. But without God, you are left with what? With skill, with strength and stamina – and with that *something other*, which can determine who wins or loses. If that's a sense of future, I may have the edge over Sir Hugh. But if it's anger, as Elise believes, I'm at a disadvantage.

'My lord, here is your sword.'

The tow-headed smith's boy holds it up – the fine Toledo blade I purchased in Marseille and carried with me all the way, and never used on the croisade except in exercise with Jos. The sword that fell with me at al-Ayadiyeh!

"'Tis very keen, Sir, if ye care to feel?' The lad's blackened fingers turn each edge for me to try. Both are sharp as razors.

'Would you believe, My Lord, that when I brought it to the stone an' drew it out, all this was over it, with more inside the sheath.' He holds out the buckler in his other hand, to show its hollow strewn with grey sand from the lime pits outside Acre. 'Is it from Oversea, my lord, where Our Lord Jesus lived?'

I cannot meet his shining eyes, or show the pain in mine. 'It was from Outremer, but now like me is come to Sussex.'

I make him tip it out to join the sea-sand of the tiltyard, and turn from the poor lad's disappointed face, to the smart fellow from the garrison, who is to help me try my paces. 'Now, Sir Osberne, if you're ready?'

Elise is watching from the window as we cross the yard. The solar is in shadow with the light behind it. But I can't mistake the flax-blue of her gown. Her hands, both hands, are on the mullions, which means the child is elsewhere. I'm glad. He is too young to see a death.

The Countess had the chamber cleared of ladies, servants, men-at-arms, Hod with Hamkin – everyone but me and little Thomas, who she kept beside her chair. She'd had the shutters taken from the window, and ordered me to watch…

Watch their shadows stripe the sand when they walked out across the yard. Behind them, high above the stable roofs, the hill I'd crossed in pouring rain glowed palely in the sun. He glanced up once. I think he must have seen me.

'You chose this course and you must see it through.'

For once without a dog upon her knee, My Lady held a holland shirt, which she was stitching with an expert hand. 'The bout's unsanctioned. It is not for me to judge the outcome.'

She pulled a silk thread taut, then used the needle as a pointer. 'But what I will do, is to see you witness every pass and cut and wound those men sustain until the very last. For this is your choice, girl. Not theirs, not God's, and certainly not mine.'

414

By then the rage I'd felt with him for being so damn calm, had given place to numbing guilt and every kind of fear. I'd wanted this to happen, but was now terrified it would go wrong in the worst way. Why couldn't I have waited for the Earl to judge the case when he returned? Instead of rushing in. Instead of always rushing in, Elise, to force the issue – force poor Garon to defend us with his life!

I didn't even have the sense My Lady had, to think of sending Hamkin back to spare the child the sight of blood.

He limped a little as he crossed the tiltyard with Sir Osberne, looking unprepared. I hadn't thought they'd be so lightly armoured. Should have made it long swords, with helms and shields and linkmail hauberks to offer him some kind of real protection – something more than boiled leather over a padded gambeson, a coif and gauntlets, with a buckler hardly larger than a capon salver.

Oh, Sancta Maria, Mater Dei, Queen of Heaven,
see it in your wisdom to protect him –

Sweet Mother, let him win!

This time no trembling excitement. Just a feeling like a cold, hard stone pushed up inside my ribs. Walk swiftly to conceal the limp – three, four more paces. Here I think.

The young man reminds me so much of myself before the tournament and the croisade. 'Sir Osberne, shall we show them how it's done?'

Swords vertical for the salute, buckler left-handed to the chest – and now *ligacio* position. I have not forgotten. Right foot forward, buckler in a straight line from the other shoulder to protect the sword-hand...

Something about a balanced blade to make it feel like an extension of your body, an extra limb that has no mission but to injure or to kill. Blades crossed at the erotic angle in a mutual bind, eyes on opponent.

The four best weapons in a soldier's armoury are bone an' sinew, strength of grip, sharpness of eye. Trust to your training, Garon – and begin!

The swish, the whisper of the steel as the blades disengage. The kind of sound Sir Hugh and his opponent are already making – a sound that triggers years of practice, something ingrained deep inside. Those who know nothing of the art of swordplay, imagine that its object is continually to crash one blade against the other with all the strength you have – a method which would soon make sawteeth of their edges. In truth the loudest sound comes from the clashing bucklers, not the swords – the greater skill that of *avoiding* one another's blades whilst probing for the weakness in a guard; the skill of dancers, jugglers, acrobats – not blacksmiths!

Thrust, block, block thrust. Level balance. Feet shoulder-width apart, soles to the ground... anticipate his second lunge and your return, even as you block the first.

And now. And now. And now. He's helping, but it's coming back, there still. I've not forgotten.

But Christ, I am unfit!

I held my breath while they saluted and began, then felt relief to see he knew the strokes, could hold his own against the fortress knight. But then I saw the others circling behind them, faster! So much faster! The clatter of their bucklers louder and more frequent, their blades a blur of flashing steel.

The difference between the pairs was clear to all – and I was horribly afraid!

Arrête! We both put up. I'm panting, sweating like a pig – must turn as if at ease to pat the lad, Sir Osberne, on the shoulder.

'You have my thanks, Sir, 'twas exactly what I needed.' We bow. He's breathless too, which I suppose is something?

I found that I'd lost bulk and muscle tone when they released me from the abbey hospital at Fontenay, but must have made some up on the long walk from Winchester along the downland ridges.

Breathe slowly, deeply. Accept the squire's towel as if you hardly need it. A quick wipe, an easy smile. Hugh mustn't see and mustn't guess what that first bout has cost you...

He's coming over. Strolling, looking (wouldn't he) as fresh as a field daisy!

'Well, Garon?' Wry smile, raised brows, the old familiar mocking tone.

'So here we have the answer to all our disagreements. We end the argument as knights and gentlemen, fighting one another to the death.'

The kind of thing he would say, wouldn't he, to cover what he really feels?

'Believe me, it is not my choice.'

'Ah quite. The lady snaps her fingers, and the faithful husband hastens to obey.'

'You warned me not to leave and told me what could happen if I did.'

'And you were not persuaded.'

'But you were right, and I was wrong. Is that what you wish to hear?'

'You have my full attention.'

'I was so desperate to serve a cause that I was blind to folly.'

'Well I confess, I'm gratified to hear you admit it. So are we to gather that you've exchanged a war for something, shall we say more *personal*?' Again the smile, the upraised brows. Yet, strange to say, no longer so provoking.

'And if you have, can you explain to me, as a matter of immediate interest, why the prospect of two cocks fighting in a pit is not an equal folly? Can you make sense of that, my friend? For I confess I can't.'

'It's not about sense is it? Or even which of us is stronger?' Breath steady, voice is good...

'What it's about is justice for a lady who has no other means of gaining it. It is about the threat she sees in you to everything that she holds dear – the child especially.'

'But *you*, my brave avenging angel? What is it that *you* see in me?'

'I see a smiling mask, and behind it someone who has already lost all chance of self-respect, or any kind of true contentment – even if he wins.'

'Which would suggest that I have something still to prove.' His mouth is straight, unsmiling now, with anger and resentment in the eyes.

'So now we are in earnest? And shall we tell them that the fighting cocks are ready – to give no quarter and receive none? Shall we ask them to relieve us of our hoods?'

I see us suddenly, and comically, with bright red combs unfolding on our heads. I see the folly.

They've brought old Guillaume out to marshal us. He's put on weight, but is in good shape still, considering his age.

I dip my leather coif at him. He'll not acknowledge me, but blinks instead into the sun. Or – did I imagine it? Was it but half a blink – a wink?

He leads us out bow-legged to the centre of the yard, the hard tutor of my youth. Stiffer now, but no whit gentler in his speech. 'Attend to me, boys, listen well.' He barks out his instructions as he's always done in the way of a pack-leader.

'For all this bout is unofficial, I say ye're to hold yerselves bound by the rules of a *duellum*. If you agree say *Aye*.'

We say it, both together as if we had rehearsed it.

'The duellum's *to excess*, which is to death or mortal wound. If either combatant takes a lesser wound, is maimed or is exhausted, he may cry "*Craven!*" an' be spared his life. Or else relinquish it by *coup de grâce*.'

Guillaume recites from memory. 'The victor who shirks the *coup* must be accounted loser. The loser who cries *craven* must be outlawed, excluded from his lord's protection. If at the time of sunset. neither combatant has triumphed – the defendant (in this case, Sir Hugh) must be judged innocent of charges. Got it? Understand it, both?'

He waits. We nod.

'Then I am here to offer ye the chance to think again, an' settle for *first blood* instead.' The stern blue stare on his worn face turns first on me, then Hugh.

'There's no sense, lads, in goin' further to decide the thing,' he growls, 'unless ye're silly in the head.'

418

'Or the lady in the case insists that one of us, and me for choice, should part with *all* our blood,' Hugh says, 'and we've agreed to set all sense aside to satisfy her on the point.'

Old Guillaume grunts, coughs twice, returns to his recital.

'Then knights of Sussex, hear the laws by which ye may compete. You are required to swear that ye've concealed about yer person no weapons other than those in yer hand. Nor herb, nor magic charm whereby the laws of Heaven may be abased, or those of Satan exalted.

'Do ye so swear? So help ye God?'

'I do so swear.'

'So help ye God?'

'I doubt that the Almighty has the time to spare on such sordid affairs. But if I must, "So help me God" by all means.'

Amusement in the words, contempt in the tone. But Hugh swears, nonetheless – and so do I.

'Spectators, ye may neither speak, nor cough, nor spit during *duellum*.' Guillaume addresses all the men and boys who stand in clusters by the cattle byres, the stables, stores and armouries, around the tiltyard walls and up the wooden stairway to the northern motte. 'Nor may ye divert the combatants by movement of the hand or foot, on pain of floggin' if discovered.'

Elise up in her window? Would they dare to flog a lady if she cried out?

But now to us in the same ringing tone: 'Perform salute and bind!' We back four paces, raise our naked blades.

I feel the warmth of my gloved fists gripped on the strap and pommel, the pulse of my own blood...

> 'We borrow time from life is all.'
> 'We make time as we live it.'

But which? If the author of my life has planned this day, will he consider its extension? Or is the loan already overdue? And in an hour perhaps, or less, will these gloved hands, these legs, this thinking brain, be nothing more to me or anyone than so much meat and bone?

419

Advance one pace to cross swords for *ligacio*. Shields tight on wrists, to measure one another's weight and strength just as the rams did in the alps. My reach is longer, I've the height. I would have had the weight once, but no longer. He's limber, supple, quicker on his feet.

Guillaume's long marshal's staff rests in the crutch of the steel cross we've made. Touch blades. Lock eyes. Black Hugh, black frown, black eyes like flints. No trace of laughter now.

You eat for pleasure, sing for pleasure, fuck for pleasure, lad. But ye don't FIGHT for love of it, you fight to win.

And in my hands, and in my brain, the future. Mine, Elise's and the child's.

It's not enough to fight to win. I have to *kill* the man!

Abruptly Guillaume's staff jerks upward, breaks the bind.

'Commence!' A gust of indrawn breath runs round the outer ward.

Passing step, back on the left. Tread through. Hold middle distance. *Block!* Thrust and block. Step through.

Trust to training. Skill in place of hatred. Bone and sinew, strength of grip. First blow can be decisive. But that's past and we're still...

SMASH! Use the bucker! Boss on boss. *CHOK! CHOK!* Rams butting heads.

Clumsy, that was clumsy – work it as a weapon...

Hugh's dark eyes, slit like visors, giving, missing nothing. No sign in them of anything but total confidence in his ability to kill me. Keep his sword higher. Out of reach. Away from legs, from thighs – from hamstrings.

He's moving round, offline. A chance? I see what he's about! The sun, a fiery ball, it's...

PAIN! Pain out of light! A searing slice of fire! Jesus Christ, he's...

'He's cut already! God, his face is cut!' I couldn't help but scream it.

'Whose face? What kind of wound?' The Countess's cool voice helped me to look, and tell her that it wasn't serious.

420

'It is Sir Garon, and there's blood. But not so much – he's fighting on, My Lady.'

First blood. Stinging, warm where it's run down into my collar. But not so bad. Good to be done with. Makes you less afraid and brings its own new burst of strength.

Push forward and tread though, and round – block…

SMASH!

Recoil and thrust. Give him a taste of sun himself. Too much control can hamper your reactions.

And here at last, the *surge*! The feeling I have waited, hoped for! Hands. Feet. Reflex, instinct, something I can't put a name to, flowing through my arms and fists into the steel.

My body knows its business now – frees me to listen to the slither, whine of steel. Our gasps and grunts. A pair of rutting beasts, one of them black-bearded, the other with a bloody face.

Step wide. Step through. In line. Offline. Changing ground to place the blows – to force the other round to face the sun. I'm free to see its sparkle on our bucklers. Lightning flashes on our blades. We know the steps, are better matched than anyone believed. My eye as quick as his. His reach as good as mine. We tease, we tempt, we dance, we circle. Now in shadow. Now in light, slicing silver patterns through the sunlight.

I watched a spider in the angle of the window, working to repair his web. I watched the shadow of the solar creeping out across the tiltyard, to catch the fighting men as they stepped through it – into shade, and out of it into the light.

The blood's drying. But sweat's dripping from my cap-band. Shirt soaked. Throat raw. Arm muscles corded, screaming for relief! The pace is punishing and every move hard-fought. Keep on. Keep on. Maintain the rhythm. Save energy. Move only as you have to. Sheer stamina – in a protracted bout that can be what decides the outcome.

'You're favouring your right, Garon.'

Where does he find the breath to speak?

'Is it the knee?' His blade darts at me hissing like a snake, turned flat to penetrate the ribs.

Block. Counter-strike. Keep on. Keep on. No need to answer him or break the flow.

'Or is your problem with the foot? *IS–IT-THE-FOOT?*' Hugh's words timed to the movements of his sword.

Step wide to lunge. He's close. Close range. Shields clash and interlock. Grapple. Twist and grapple, thigh to thigh.

The stench of him! His sweat, his...

AAAH! CHRIST, THE FOOT!

Break free! Back! Back, out of range. Block. Thrust, and block...

Don't let him see. He couldn't know that it was broken then – or now again.

Sweet Jesus! I thought his time had come. The pain in his poor bleeding face!

'What is it child, what can you see?' I couldn't leave the window, couldn't even turn my head.

'Somehow he managed to lock shields, My Lady. Wrenched him round and stamped on him. His foot.'

'Who did? Whose foot?'

'Sir Garon's injured foot. Sir Hugh is pressing in...'

> *I knew that she expected me to tell her everything.*
> *But all I really wanted was to hide from it -*
> *escape from WHAT I KNEW WAS*
> *GOING TO HAPPEN!*

Flat feet. That's all you need for sword and buckler fighting. Can do without the toes.

Keep on. Keep on. Push through the pain. Push through, *YOU CAN*. To falter even for an instant is to die!

Their shadows had already crossed the yard – giant shadows, elongated, rearing back and forth across the stable roof. From light to shade, from life to...

Breath rasping, burning in my throat. Block. Block.

SMASH. SMASH! Pressing his advantage.

The dazzle of the sun. Low-slanted now and level with the keep. Stripes him with light reflected from my blade. Across his arm. Across his neck. A white cross. *Could it... could I?*

Too bright. Can't take it. Have to turn. Left foot passing step. Now right. *AAH*, close – too close! His sword-point's knicked my coif...

Sun's image ringed with red. Imprinted on my brain. The sound of bells, the Priory ringing Vespers. But can't last to sunset – know I can't. And if I could, he'd win. How long? How many steps as we turn back? How many strokes before the sun is hidden by the solar roof? How many chances to...

He's in! God, in again and grappling! His favoured move. A wrestler's throw – *I'M DOWN!*

Black eyes triumphant. Venomous! The upraised blade – *SMASH!* Blocked by the buckler covering my fists. Rams jarring brains. Two fists together, gripping sword and shield...

A chance! – just one, the very last. My blade cross-angled to the sun. Last burst of light above the ridge, *becomes a weapon*. Band of brilliance stripes his face, his eyes – through to the brain behind them.

To blind him. Send him wide, expose his sword-arm at the wrist...

AND NOW! AND NOW! Now undercut. Slice up behind the buckler, through the gauntlet...

CRACK! The sharp, clear sound of snapping bone. The grate of steel. The single cry of pain. The useless falling blade.

THE BLOOD! He staggers, spent. Drops to his knees.

I stumble upright through the pain. My weight on the good foot. My sword still firm in hand.

'He'd won! Thanks be to God!'

I turned back from the window, to show My Lady Isabel a face already wet with tears. Beside her chair, young Tom was grinning like an ape.

'So God has spoken through his sword,' My Lady said complacently. 'And is he dead? Has he received the coup?'

Down in the tiltyard, neither of the men had moved. Sir Hugh still knelt with right wrist gripped in left, still gouting blood. Sir Garon stood above him with sword held ready for the mercy blow – the coup de grâce to finish it and clear me of dishonour.

'Now, Garon, NOW,' I whispered.

'JÉSU, DO IT NOW!'

His right hand's useless. Lifeblood spurting, pouring through the fingers of the left. There is a moment when a hare, gripped in the falcon's talons, accepts its fate and ceases to resist. It's in the eyes.

It's in *his* eyes, the willingness to die.

'Kill me then, be done.'

'Say *craven* and be spared.'

Bared teeth and a contraction of the lips to imitate a smile.

'What? Spare you the pain of doing it, and lose in any case?' He lifts his chin unflinchingly and braces for the blow.

I drop the buckler. Raise the blade to catch the last rays of the sun – and strike, *less with the point than to it.*

He plunged his sword, point-first into the sand.

I turned back from the window
with a crimson face!

CHAPTER EIGHT

Lewes Fortress: March 1194

EXPEDIENCE

In sixty-four eventful years the Countess of Warenne has only ever sought her bed in daylight to conceive a child or to produce one. In fact she has the constitution of a draught-ox, but attributes her good health to daily doses of cranesbill and orris root in Bordeaux wine, and to the expert team of herbalists, astrologers, apothecaries, barber surgeons and personal physicians she employs.

Six of them are to travel with her to North Kent, and are already mounted in the outer bailey with their charts and cures and tonics packed behind them in a covered cart; only waiting for the signal to depart. A seventh has remained with his assistant in a basement chamber of the fortress, with instructions from My Lady to attend the wounded knight.

The physician, Bonfil, stands at the table they have cleared for him to mix his potions. He wears an apron stained with blood, a linen bonnet to confine his hair.

'Hogbile, hemlock, henbell, three spoons of each.' It helps in his experience to tell over the ingredients first before selecting them.

'Three more of neep and lactula and pape, a dash of vinegar. Let's see, that's six jars, with a bottle and a pan – you'll need a tray,' he tells his young assistant.

This is the part Bonfil enjoys the most, the measuring and mixing. With the containers, tightly corked and neatly labelled, set in an ordered row before him, he takes a silver spoon, the smallest of three sizes, and advises his apprentice to 'Observe and learn from observation.'

Bonfil has attended lectures and dissections at the universities of Oxford and Montpelier. He's read the *Hippocratic Corpus*, the *Canon of Medicine* and Galen's *Natural Faculties*. He practices the principles of humorism, to balance the four elemental fluids of the body with reference to the horoscope. So the preparation of an opiate, a dwale to keep the patient out of pain while his heart sucks vital blood from the nutritive fluid in his veins, makes perfect sense to Bonfil.

He measures out three spoonfuls of the dark green liquid labelled 'hogbile', is in the act of reaching for the hemlock jar, when the door opens quietly and a woman stoops to enter.

Physician and assistant both bow low. The Countess is alone, which is to say the least unusual, for she seldom takes two steps without a guard, a brace of pages or a maid hard on her heels.

She wears her dignity like an unyielding robe. 'The boy may go,' she says – and waiting only for the door to close behind him, comes directly to the point.

'Your patient, Bonfil. What is his condition?'

'My Lady, he's unconscious; and for the present I judge it best to keep him so.'

'But like to live? Or die?'

'We could not save the hand. The damage to the bone and tendon was too extensive; and when I cauterised the artery, there was no time to dull the pain of amputation. Many would have died of shock.'

'But not this man?' She purses her thin lips.

'His nature is predominantly sanguine, My Lady. Such people can surprise us if they're given time to make new blood,' the physician offers cautiously. 'We've set a pallet for Sir Hugh where it is warm beside the hog-spit in the kitchens, and in a day or two may move him to the Priory hospital. If he survives.'

'I doubt he'll manage that.' The Countess picks up a small steel knife and sets it down again. She sniffs the pan of hogbile with distaste. 'This potion is for him?'

'Indeed, My Lady; a fresh mixture of the soporific dwale he has already taken.'

'And these are its components?' She lifts a jar. '*Pape?* What is this?'

'An abbreviation for *papaver somniferum*; an opiate, My Lady, extracted from the poppy.'

'Henbell?' She points. 'Is that the same as henbane?'

'It is, My Lady, a decoction from the juice of Stinking Nightshade.'

'A poison then?'

'It may be, if given in too large a dose. I advocate but three salt spoons in a volume of exactly seven times that measure; then after boiling no more than two spoons of the mixture stirred into a potel of good red wine.'

'If more than that is taken?'

''T'would certainly prove fatal.'

'I see.' The Countess of Warenne looks thoughtful.

'I wonder, Bonfil, what a man of your experience would make of the belief the people have in Sussex, that if a stone's turned over outside a physician's door and a living creature's found beneath, it is a sign his patient will survive. If not, that he will die.'

''Tis but a local supersition, Lady, nothing more.'

Bonfil is unexpectedly reminded of a caged wildcat he once saw at a fair at Woodstock, with narrow golden eyes like Countess Isabel's as she regards him.

'Nonetheless. There is a fallen flint outside your door, and when I thought to turn it, I found nought beneath but a small worm – which took me but a moment to obliterate.'

My Lady lifts her skirt, to show her physician the destructive possibilities of a large velvet slipper. 'I think we must agree,' she says emphatically, 'it is unlikely, even undesirable, that your patient should survive to see another dawn.'

Her words are for Bonfil alone. No one beyond the closed door hears, or could repeat them in the future. She nods. Bonfil who is her man and owes his living to her, bows in acquiescence.

The Countess leaves the chamber. With the aplomb of a seasoned traveller she approaches her waiting litter, lowers her silk upholstered rear-end into a flurry of excited dogs, and gives the order to depart.

In Reigate the next morning she repeats the exercise. To meet the Earl her husband at the port of Rochester two days later on the feast day of Saint Ethelwald. To join him for King Richard's royal progress into London, and leave the pages of this story.

Which means in retrospect that three days earlier, at much the time My Lady left from Reigate castle, Sir Hugh's unhanded body was jolted down from Lewes Fortress to the Cluniac brothers of the Priory – not in a hot and feverish condition for bedding in their hospital. But cold and stiff for its interment in the cemetery behind their cloister.

Before I woke just now, I dreamt I was in Palestine, striding down the causeway into Tyre. The sun was shining on the white gates of the city with crushed shells sparkling in the lime-wash. And Raoul, my handsome Raoul – not as he was after three weeks at sea, but polished in the brilliant light. His coat like silk. His muscles bulging, gleaming in the sunlight.

No, not sunlight – it's the moon. It's *moon*light whitening the wall and floor. I've thrown the covers off. The square shape of the window's rimmed with light, stars winking in the vapours round the moon.

And where in Hades am I?

No colours in the room – pale stripes of beams. Grey patterns on the door... *the door!*

I know that door and where I am, outside it. (Elise on one side of the door, with me the wrong side on the other.)

When you wake with moonlight on your face, you're either like to go stark, staring mad, my nurse Grazilda used to say. Or, if you are a woman, will conceive a child.

Or *make* one, if a man? She didn't say. But I am rigid as a plank!

It's no good, I can't sleep. Not in this state. Not in this light. First foot, worst foot out of bed – ow-ouch! – still hurts. Where did I drop the robe? Bolt's stiff as well, needs oil.

The moon's not white, or silver or pale gold, but something of all three, its colour painted on the sky and every step of the stone stair. Outside, the scents of earth and straw and spring-growth fill the air. Where was I when the air was *warm as blood*? Where was I when I thought that?

Night guard's asleep and shouldn't be. But here's Elise's little garden, its winged statue. Gaskin blossom floating in the darkness. The sweet perfume of gillyflowers… And here's my Bruno, whimpering with excitement. A dog so desperate for adventure, so thoughtless and so foolish he should have been out there in Outremer, a Moslem or a Christian!

Gate's shut. But I can lift the bar. 'Quiet, Bruno, or I'll shut you in.'

When I walked home in March, I found it hard to see the cart track through the trees from Beacon Hill. Since then we've chalked it from the manor, all the way to the church glebe. A white strip in the moonlight – narrowing to where the village houses cluster.

And how could I forget the welcome that I had there? Dame Martha with both hands wedged tight betwixt her arms and breasts to stop her hugging me to death – with Bruno nearly wagging off his tail! Even Ida when I told her what had befallen Albie – even John's young brothers when I bent to kiss them as he'd asked, and told them why they'd never see his face again. They shamed me by their charity, who should have hated me for coming back alone. And yet they told me nothing of Elise. Left it to Kempe and old Dame Agnès to recount their versions of the story.

I ordered masses to be sung for those who'd died abroad, the least that I could offer to their kin. And took a horse when it was done, and galloped off to Lewes.

He rode beside my litter all the way from Lewes. I lay with Hamkin, held him tightly, kept the curtains closed.

'See how attentive he is now,' I told my little boy. 'Now that he's made his noble gesture at the cost of my good name!'

And when he came to me that night, I let him kiss me but did not return the kiss. I told him coldly that I knew my duty, was his prize and chattel for his use at any time he chose. Like all else that he owned. Like his horses, like his dogs!

'There's nothing new to me in being forced against my will,' I said. 'You had the chance to end it, but chose not to – and will never win from me a woman's love while I remain dishonoured.' (Which sounded rather too like something from a chanson, even to my own ears!)

'I fought him for your honour, but could not have killed him, any more than I could force you now,' he said. 'And I can wait.'

There was a strength and purpose in his voice which was not there before. He hobbled off on his ridiculous sore foot, to leave us on our own; Hamkin in his cradle, with me in sole possession of the curtained bed. Then when I heard him later, snoring peacefully beyond the beam, I asked myself with something like a new sense of affront, if I was not still young enough to be appealing to a man? Or if the Sarasine had been so blindingly attractive, that by comparison an English woman must seem dull?

I waited for him the next night – just for a while
before I locked the chamber door.

After the duel was over and Guillaume called for the physician. When they had bound Hugh's wrist and taken him away, I looked up to the solar window. To find it empty. She had gone.

The frogs are croaking in the mudsquelch. The nightingales are singing in the forest. Dozens of them, chirruping and chuckling to the moon – their notes like whip-cracks. Clear as silver. Sweet as syrup bubbled through a flute – I haven't words to do them justice. On the quays at Marseille and in Acre, they sold the little birds in wicker cages – as if the magic of a night-song in the darkness of a wood could be captured in a cage hung from a beam. Or touch your heart in the same way. The moon's reflected in the surface of the duckpond. Bruno is trying to drink it, making silver ripples with his snout...

Moonlight in Khadija's garden. A petal floating in the pool – and *air warm as blood*! That's where it was – in Acre in the garden. Air as warm as blood.

I told Elise about Khadija and her house and garden and her little girl, and how they died. I schooled myself to tell her calmly. But the tears still came.

As we turn up towards the barn, Bruno and I, our moon-shadows sweep round us like black-feathered birds.

Shadows, moving shadows. Hugh's and mine. He died in any case. We heard the news the day I told Elise about Khadija. Two women and two worlds, with only me between them. But when I tried the door that night, she had it locked and bolted.

The day we saw the first swallows return to Haddertun, I rode up through the forest to take stock of the Meresfeld Manor. My sister Edmay hardly knew how she should greet me – as a brother or her father's killer?

But now we've sent her Hodierne, to mother her and state my case. We trust she'll come to Haddertun in course of time – and when she does (she's twelve now, near a woman), we should talk of marriage plans. When all is done we have to look ahead.

Hod spoke of him before she left. She'd have to wouldn't she, to tell me my own business!

'Ye won't thank me for saying it, my lamb. But 'e's a proper straw-yard bull, an' no mistake.'

'All right, I know you're simply dying to explain,' I answered wearily. 'Go on then, tell me what you mean.'

'Starved of company an' full of spunk. There then!' She nudged me with a bony shoulder. 'What ye going to do about 'im now ye're safe an' that black

432

varmint's dead, is what I want to know? Lord save us! Set 'im loose? Is that yer plan? To find another cow to serve?'

We've spent the best part of our marriage separated. But now our paths run in the same direction. Or they should do.

If it is still too soon, it's not too late to do some good, and spread some joy, and make the best of what we have to give? It's not too late.

It wants an hour at least to sunrise. The downs look pearly, ghostly through the branches of the orchard. Nothing to them – nothing to compare with the great mountains I have crossed to reach them. Except that I was born here in their shadow – first heard the sound of sheep bells on their slopes. Clucket bells and upland grazing for the sheep, for thousands from Biella. So why not here at Haddertun and on the downs?

Oh god, I have to pee. Come on old faithful, here will do…

We'll breed more sheep, that's what we'll do – produce as much wool as the Sussex looms can take…

What would she think if she could see what I was doing now? I shake the drips, can see the urine glitter in the grass. Bruno inspects, sniffs where I've peed and lifts his leg to add his signature to mine – a manuscript for creatures of the night to read.

What would she think if, like the Bérgé, she could look into my mind, to see a simple function of the flesh transform my fine ideas of weal and plenty into something far more basic? My robe's still open to the air. I stand with cock in hand, face tilted to the moon. Feel younger than I've ever been – now horny as a unicorn. As ready and alive!

What drives the body of a man? What drives the moon across the sky?

> Come in the stillness of the night;
> Come soon, come soon and bring delight…
> Come now! Oh, come tonight!

That's what my nurse, Grazilda used to sing, a charm to bring the faeries out.

433

And Bruno's certain that I'm mad! Is it the moon? An old moon for a new beginning? Is it the spring, the month of May, that brings this rising feeling?

Is this the night I'll tell her all that happened in the house at Acre? How it was, and how it changed me? Is this the night that every day I've lived has brought me to?

I must not, cannot break my word.

I've heard the story of the monk at Glastonbury who scrambled down into the open tomb of Arthur and his Queen and snatched a lock of Gwenevere's fair hair where it lay on her stained brown skull. But snatched too greedily, to feel it crumble in his grasp.

If she still needs more time, then time is in my gift. I've borne it this long and can bear it longer, the waiting part of it, the ache, the yearning. A kind of breathless *gaping* deep inside. *IMSAK!* Impossible to separate the pleasure from the pain! The waiting as important as the having.

Maybe more important?

On that hot day a week ago... I hadn't bargained for it. Saw him from the window helping to load barley for the mill, stripped to his hose and breeches with his hair grown long and tied back in a horse-tail. Saw him – and saw the way the village women looked – and shared their judgement of my husband as a proper man, despite his injured foot.

I longed to hear his tales of Outremer, but was too proud to ask. He worked outside. I worked within. We worked together but apart.

Another day I caught him watching me with an expectant, eager look, before he masked it with a smile.

Gates closed behind. Bar back in place. The white spectre of an owl across the yard. Soft-feathered wings that make no sound. The thin wail of a crying child.

'No, Bruno, stay!' Inside the cries are louder. Surely she can hear them from the bed?

So shall I try the door? Will it be locked?

When I first met Sir Garon, I so wanted him to be the hero of a chanson, courteous and gentle. But when Hugh raped me, proved to me that men were animals – I needed one of them, one of the beasts, to kill the other and restore my honour!

(What hour is it? How long have I been lying wide awake?)

Yet when I saw the eager look in Garon's face before
he smiled, I felt a sudden stab of – was it hope?
Is that why I left the door unbolted?
Because he'd shown me he was
neither a finished hero nor
a senseless beast -
that if I...

CLACK!

THE LATCH,
the creaking board.
His shadow by the cradle.
Hamkin's surprised, stops agitating,
offers to be lifted and then carried over to the bed
where I've been waiting for them both behind the curtains.

(There's violet muscadin to sweaten breath, if I can only find it?)

And past time to reward the poor man, as I should have have done a month ago – if I had been less of a pigheaded prune!

Impossible that she could sleep through all that lusty howling. And she hasn't – sitting up against the pillows with her hair about her. Smiling.

The boy's so small and helpless. So trusting in the way his little hands cling to my robe. When he is older, if he lives, I'll take him on my horse about the manor to show him all it offers. Wherever he has come from, he's a child to guide towards a better future – as my father might have guided me. If he had lived.

'He's hungry, let me have him.'

A pair of white hands reach into the moonlight, take the child.

'You'll find a rush light on the sill, and flints if you can work them.'

Her voice is soft without the jagged edge. But for the moment I can't
see her face.

I manage at the fourth attempt to make a flame. The silver of the
moonlight turns to gold; to pink and gold. And I'm rewarded with
another smile. She's naked with one marbled breast already suckling
the child, the other swollen, carmine-nippled – doing likewise for my
eyes. Woman about her natural business as a mother.

I watch her, fascinated.

The small boy works with the determination of the man to come,
another Hugh.

He's finished. Flushed. Fluffy-haired – already dropping off to sleep.

'Well then?'

'Then what?'

'Then are you going to take him back, and then return yourself? Do you want
to, Garon?'

A question in no need of a reply. A scent of violets in the air. And I'm
the ram who wrinkles his white nose to savour what he's fought for.
She sees it otherwise.

'You're panting like a hound.'

'I'm not.' (Not yet.)

'Then I suppose it must be me.'

Seven words, to smash the lock and fling the door, and fling her arms wide open. But still too soon, too soon to take, with so much first to give...

How could he know? Where has he learned to use his hands this way?

IMSAK, the joy of waiting... My love is lark song, heart song, Lark flight, soaring, mounting, panting and proclaiming. Waiting for the surge to lift us and engulf us.

'Aaah – careful of my foot!'

Which surely is the moment to let them get on with it, now they're together in the here and now, and poised for a new future – time to turn the page.

Too soon to go? I don't agree. They have their own new time to make, and so do you.

No really, I insist. If I can turn my back on what they're doing (please don't use that word, it's inappropriate), then so can you.

So *go on*, turn the page >

Oh, I'm as bad as Garon. I forgot the rose!

It didn't die in the frosts of Biella, or in the alps, or anywhere on his long journey home.

He planted it – a rooted stem with six or seven slender branches, in Elise's palisaded garden by the manor stairway. It put out more shoots that spring, to flower two years later in June of 1196 (the month in which construction was begun on Haddertun's first fulling mill, down on the mudsquelch). After that it bloomed unfailingly each summer, forming scarlet rosehips in the autumn in bold defiance of the English climate.

My Lady Isabel was given cuttings; and in due course of time, the rose's progeny spread clear across the south of England.

Would you believe it if I told you we've a number of them here in our own garden at the farm?

EPILOGUS

1196 -1867

Bullies. We hate them. Don't we?

Then what of Alexander, called *The Great*? What of Napoleon, called *Le Grand*? Doesn't history tend to back the winners, bullies who succeed; admire celebrity, however selfishly impelled? We talk of confident, aggressive men, even of women with those qualities, as having 'balls'. Which would suggest that it's testosterone, virility, that makes a hero of a bully – a tendency to find the clash of arms, the sound of detonations, the sight of blood, envigorating?

And our King Richard, as a case in point? We call him *Lionheart* for his courage (as no one is recorded to have done in his own lifetime, incidentally). Great-hearted hero? Or a heartless bully? It shouldn't be too difficult to spot the difference.

King Richard returned from the Holy Land a finished hero, to bring to heel his traitorous brother, John; pausing only in a leafy glade of Sherwood Forest, to bestow an Earldom on the outlawed Robin Hood, before riding off into the sunset of English history as our nation's best-loved medieval king.

Come on, you know as well as I do that is nonsense!

King Richard sailed from Acre in the autumn of 1192, to make landfall eventually on the Adriatic coast near Venice, and travel overland (as bad luck, or lack of sense would have it) through the territory of his slighted ally from the siege of Acre, King Philippe's cousin, Duke Leopold of Babenberg; the very man whose banner Richard's followers had cast into the city moat.

The King and his small group of followers were dressed as common pilgrims. But it's likely one of them was not all that he seemed. The records show that Leopold was told by an informant exactly where to find him, and even how the King of England was disguised; and speaking for myself, I wouldn't be at all surprised to hear that Sultan Salahuddin learned of his enemy's arrest outside the city of Vienna in the bare time it took his pigeons to fly down through Asia Minor to Damascus.

The reason given by Duke Leopold for the King's imprisonment was his belief that he'd betrayed his Christian allies by ordering the murder of Conrad de Montferrat. But it's untrue that Richard spent long years in German dungeons. Because, in less than fifteen months, we find him kneeling at the shrine of Thomas Becket in Canterbury Cathedral – to thank the God that he so often cursed for his return to England. During his detention by the Duke of Austria and his liege, the Emperor of Germany, he'd been escorted westward from one comfortably appointed castle to another, growing ever fatter on German pastries and Rhenish wine: *'Drinking and sporting,'* his annalist recorded, *'with the young men they set to guard him'.*

Meanwhile, the Emperor proposed to sell the King of England to the highest bidder. A ransom of one hundred thousand marks was first agreed with Eléonore his mother and her agent, Bishop Hubert Walter. But the King of France, in league with Richard's brother John, promptly offered half as much again for his custody or further detention in the German Empire; and in the end, Queen Eléonore was forced to raise one hundred and fifty thousand marks to pay for his release. (A a jaw-dropping sum, amounting to nearly thirty-four tons' weight in silver; the highest value placed on any man in our recorded history, and one which virtually bankrupted England.)

Worse still, in further payment for his freedom, the King of England blithely pledged allegiance to the Emperor, Heinrich. In

440

other words he made a gift of something neither the Kaiser nor the Führer were able to beat out of Britain in two world wars – to make this kingdom part of Heinrich's German Empire.

But then Richard never did care much for England – had never heard of Robin Hood (who wasn't to emerge out of the greenwood, if he emerged at all, for at least another century), and wouldn't have approved of funding outlawed peasants in any case. When it came down to it, he spent a bare eight weeks in England after his release. Just long enough to add a British *leopardé guardant* to his lion escutcheon, and to frustrate his brother's hopes to wear a crown – before he crossed back to the Continent to pursue a new war with King Philippe for control of Normandy and the dower lands he held illicitly for Philippe's jilted sister.

It was in this last phase of his life that Richard built, for his defence of Norman Rouen, the Château Gaillard; a fortress famous for its strength and beauty – to satisfy, perhaps the one and only constructive aspect of his character, and illustrate the paradox (as he had done when he rebuilt the Palestinian towns of Acre, Joppa and Ashkelon) that even the most destructive men can be creative.

To manage England in his absence, he left behind him Hubert Walter – who had by then assumed poor Baldwin's role of Primate; and was never to set foot again on English soil. The previous year, while he was still a prisoner in Germany, Richard's old adversary, Salahuddin, died quietly of pneumonia.

The Sultan passed into the peace and mercy of Allah in Damascus, surrounded by the weeping women of his harem. He was buried in a simple wooden coffin in a kiosk in the palace gardens; and the emir, Baha-uddin Karakush, who had been spared at al-Ayadiyeh, put into words what all his mourners felt.

'*The world is filled with so much grief,*' he said, '*that God alone can measure its true depth.*' And after the passage of eight centuries, the man whom we call Saladin is still admired, as much for his nobility of character, as the brief glory of his Arabian empire.

King Richard's own death six years later was consistent with so much of his career, in that it was vainglorious and violent. In the year 1199, during a truce in his territorial war with France, he was addressed directly from the pulpit of the church of Neuilly-sur-Marne, by a courageous curé who ordered Richard in the name of Christ to set aside his *three corrupt and shameless daughters*.

'By God's throat priest, you know I have no daughters!' the lion king's reputed to have roared out from the nave.

'You have My Lord,' the curé told him with the moral courage of a Becket or a Baldwin. 'Their names are *Pride* and *Avarice* and *Lust!*'

It was not the first time since his return from the crusade that a cleric had reminded Richard of the weight he'd laid upon his soul by sinning in the style of Soddom and Gommorah, or had rebuked him for sexual preferences which by comparison with patricide, infanticide and, genocide might seem to modern eyes the very least of his infringements. But I have to tell you it was *Avarice*, not *Lust*, that killed him.

In March of that same year 1199, a peasant ploughing in the Limousin near Châlus turned up an impressive Roman treasure trove of golden artifacts and coins. Half of it was offered by established custom to the King. But half was not enough for Richard. Ignoring Lent with its unhelpful traditions of penance and humility, as ever spoiling for a fight, he rode at once with a full company of horse and foot and a platoon of sappers, to siege the castle of Châlus-Chabrol and take the treasure's other half by force. A forge-hammer to crack a nut? Well what would you expect?

The little garrison consisted of no more than two or three armed knights, and forty peasant bondmen with their families and livestock, who'd taken shelter in the castle when they heard an angry king was on the warpath. For protection they had nothing more than cloth or leather, and were so ill-equipped, we're told that one man had to use a frying pan as a rough shield.

442

Predictably, at the end of three days of intense bombardment, the castle's pathetic garrison offered to surrender for their lives. But Richard had already sworn to hang the lot of them. And in just the way that a real hero wouldn't, he killed them without mercy – men, women and small children.

All but one.

In the final hours of siege, a young arbalester on the battlements contrived to wound the King whilst he was making one of his theatrical appearances before the literally captive audience in the castle. The biographers who still insist on seeing Richard as some sort of medieval cricket captain would have us believe that he applauded ('*Oh, good shot!*') before summoning the surgeons to attend his wound. The quarrel had missed his vital organs. But the King by then was more or less rectangular. So by the time they'd cut down though his body-fat to extract the missile, the outcome was inevitable.

We're told the arbalester shot again at Richard after he was dragged into his presence. This time with words.

'You have already killed my father and two brothers,' he's reported to have said. 'So take your revenge on me in any way you like. Now that I've seen you on your deathbed I am ready to endure it.'

Legend credits the royal hero with a chivalrous decision, not only to forgive the boy for shooting and defying him, but to reward him for it with a fortune; a hundred silver shillings. But all we know for sure is that the arbalester was saved – not actually from hanging, but only from the privilege of hanging in his skin. Because they tied the poor boy to a cart's tail and subjected him to the agonising death of having the skin flayed from his still-living body, before hoisting what was left of it to hang beside his father and his brothers on the gallows.

Do I believe from what I know of him, that wasn't on the orders of the dying king, who'd learned the art of flaying prisoners in Palestine? Do you? In any case, the crossbow quarrel carried shreds of dirty fabric deep into the wound – to start the gangrenous infection which was to take eleven days to kill the King.

He died in early April, before the Easter festival – coincidentally on the very Tuesday Garon and Elise of Haddertun's fourth child was brought into the world.

After his death, King Richard's bearded chin and all his servants' heads were shaved in preparation for his funeral. His horses' ears were sliced, their tails were docked. His mother came, flint-faced with grief, to see him on his deathbed. Queen Bérangère preferred to stay away. By usual custom, a wax impression was taken of the royal features. The remainder of the Body Royal was first eviscerated and then divided – and you may be sure that there was plenty of it to go round!

King Richard's blood was sent to Aquitaine, his brain and liver to Poitou, his heart to Normandy, his bowels to stay within the Limousin where he was killed. The rest of him was soaked in frankincense, wrapped in a white-crossed cloak, stitched into a bull's hide, placed in a coffin sealed with lead and buried at his father's feet in Fontevraud. For England, which had paid so handsomely for his release and bound itself to Germany for his return, there wasn't so much as a pared toenail.

So King dead, end of story? If only!

Dissection first, then *distribution*; and finally in course of time for Richard – *resurrection!* (Not as he'd been in life, you understand, but as something considerably finer.)

In London's Hyde Park, at the western entrance of Prince Albert's Crystal Palace Exhibition of 1851, a huge three-times-life-sized plaster statue of the Lionheart on a prancing Fauvel was erected – to prove that you should never underestimate the power of glamour. It showed the King in his (imaginary) prime, muscled like a wrestler in lycra-tight linkmail with sword upraised in triumph. All who passed beneath it understood the sculpture to stand for everything that was aggressively colonial, patriotic and

444

indestructibly heroic in Victoria's great empire; King Richard in the image of Saint George.

Nine years later, cast by then in bronze and largely paid for by public subscription, King Richard's statue was re-erected in Old Palace Yard outside the Houses of Parliament, to become the most unlikely champion of democratic principle that you could possibly imagine. And there he still sits, flourishing his sword; a crusading warrior whose bloodthirsty idea of justice is even now associated with our kingdom in the Middle East. On one side of his statue's plinth, a bas relief shows Richard on his deathbed forgiving his assailant. On the other he is mounted and in battle, at Joppa or Arsuf. (The bodies of eviscerated women and beheaded children have been tactfully omitted.)

And why, one has to ask, is Richard still there in his monumental pride of place outside Westminster Hall? Apathy? Because it's easier to ignore a thing than change it? Or ignorance?

'We still think of him, you know, as one of our great heroes.'

Either would be bad enough as motives. Worse would be to think that we are honouring a bully, sanctioning negotiation with a naked sword. I'd hate to think he's there to justify our willingness to go to war in countries where the word *'crusade'* has once again become a byword for violent Western intervention. I like to think, like Garon, that we're capable of learning from our past mistakes.

But back to the Victorians and Richard's legend.

Fuelled by Sir Walter Scott's romances (and that heroic statue), by 1867 the Lionheart's mythic power was such, that the Empress Queen herself petitioned the French government to send to England from Anjou King Richard's chalkstone funerary effigy, which she'd been told the French were not maintaining as they should. The French response was to decline, while surreptitiously touching up the paint on the old image. So to this day, the likeness, which Queen Eléonore commissioned, can still be seen in the Abbey Church of Fontevraud. It shows her son as she intended, as staggeringly handsome – tall and slim with the heroic visage of a god and all deformities of physique and character removed.

Her own effigy lies close beside him with an open prayer book, and a smug expression on its face.

A third likeness of King Richard, evidently modelled from a death mask, may be seen in Rouen Cathedral on the tomb which covers Normandy's share of his body; Richard's heart. It wears what seems to be an oriental crown, and shows a short-necked and balefully unpleasant-looking man with beetling brows and a pugnacious downturned mouth. The heart itself – the legendary 'coeur de lion', described as twice the size of any normal man's – still lies beneath; and when in 1838 an inquisitive historian was licensed to exhume it, he found the famous organ wrapped in linen in a crystal box within a leaden casket and holding still to a material form.

But then the truth wrapped in clean linen, as my Elise maintained, is still the truth; and time by then had shrivelled Richard's heart to something black and leathery, and really RATHER SMALL.

ACKNOWLEDGEMENTS

I am grateful to Clare Christian of Red Door Publishing and Elaine Sharples of typesetter.org.uk for invaluable help with this novel. I am indebted to Dr David Abulafia, to Dr Paul Brand, and to Christopher Whittick of the East Sussex Records Office for the many useful clues they supplied to help me find my fictional path through the medieval labyrinth; also to Mr Whittick for his original translations of Archbishop Baldwin's Latin tracts and sermons, to Enid Nixon for access to contemporary details of King Richard's coronation, to David Skinner and Mr A. North of the Victoria and Albert Museum for help with my researches on *Greek Fire*, to Mebrak Ghebrewelhdi and Simon McLaren of Vandu Language Services in Lewes for access to translators, to Abdel Rahim, John Kinory and Marcella Marzona, respectively, for editing my Arabic, Hebrew and Piemontèis quotes and depictions, to Mohammad Talib Ali for his insights into Islamic culture, to Stephen Bamber for helping me to live with my curiously temperamental computer – and as ever to my wife, Lee, for her unfailing support, her perceptive comments, her skill at spotting literal errors and for her general forbearance. I asked her repeatedly if she had the patience to see me through the horrendously selfish process of writing another novel, and amazingly she had.

For additional, helpful assistance my thanks are due to Dale Anderson, Jane Atkinson, Kate Burt, Julia Forrest, David Garst, Annie Garwood, Professor Brian Hill, Julie Hodder, Sir David and Lady Hunt, Maggie Justice, Jane and Richard D. Lewis, Robert, Georgina and Luke Masefield, Will and Stephanie Masefield, Ivan and Lara Rudd, Vivienne Schuster, The British Museum, The Science Museum, The Barbican House Museum at Lewes, the

Jordanian National Museum of Archaeology and to the staff of the London, Westminster Abbey and Lewes Libraries.

RICHARD MASEFIELD

CHALKHILL BLUE is an epic story of war and peacetime, a descriptive novel of tremendous scope and a must read for anyone with a taste for the authentic and the unusual.

From the parched landscapes of Queensland and the Andes to the chalky scarps of the Sussex downs; from the Victorian heyday through the cataclysm of the First War to the uncertain new world of the 1920s, the novel follows the lives of two very different women who have dared to flout the rules of their society, and those of the men they choose – the double strands of a remarkable love story with a heart-stopping double-twist in the tail that makes it unforgettable.

'Beautifully and lovingly brought to life, with a warmth that makes it linger kindly in the mind long after the book is closed.'
THE LITERARY REVIEW

BRIMSTONE is a story of ambition and temptation in the Georgian world of Sussex contrabanding and convict transports to New South Wales. The novel's two heroes are brothers bound by love, but separated by opposing characters which come to represent the two faces of eighteenth century England – its brutality and its enlightenment. Ellin Rimmer, daughter of a 'fire and brimstone' preacher, marries one brother to escape the loneliness of life in a parsonage, only to find herself hopelessly attracted to the other – and to be compelled through him to an impetuous decision that will have drastic consequences for all three.

'A brilliant evocation of the eighteenth century world.'
MELBOURNE ADVERTISER

PAINTED LADY is a delightful, romping adventure that introduces an unforgettable new heroine to historical fiction. As a prostitute in Regency Brighton, Sary Snudden has no faith in love between a man and woman, until she meets Lord David Stanville. Caught up in a passionate affair with the heir to a great Sussex estate, she and her lover cross the Alps in a perilous journey by coach and sled to the excitement of a popular revolution in Turin and an erotically charged idyll in the Italian lakes. But the question of how she'll bridge the greater gulf between her humble origin and the noble status David seeks for her, remains for Sarah the central problem of her life.

'Jane Austen below the waist!'
CAMPAIGN MAGAZINE